The Library

of

Indiana Classics

"Soon she was close enough to prove that she was
young and very lovely"

The
Harvester
Gene Stratton-Porter

INTRODUCTION BY Mary E. Gaither

ILLUSTRATED BY W. L. Jacobs

Indiana University Press

Bloomington and Indianapolis

First Midland Book Edition 1987

The Library of Indiana Classics is available in a special
clothbound library-quality edition and in a paperback edition.

Introduction
© 1987 by Mary Gaither

Manufactured in the United States of America

Library of Congress Cataloging-in-Publication Data

Stratton-Porter, Gene, 1863-1924.
The harvester.

(The library of Indiana classics)
I. Title. II. Series.
PS3531.07345H3   1987   813'.52   87-3685
ISBN 0-253-32746-6
ISBN 0-253-20457-7 (pbk.)

4 5 6 7 99 98 97 96

THIS PORTION OF THE LIFE OF A MAN OF TO-DAY
IS OFFERED IN THE HOPE THAT IN CLEAN-
LINESS, POETIC TEMPERAMENT,
AND MENTAL FORCE, A
LIKENESS WILL
BE SEEN

TO

HENRY DAVID THOREAU

CONTENTS

CHARACTERS

DAVID LANGSTON, A Harvester of the Woods.
RUTH JAMESON, A Girl of the City.
GRANNY MORELAND, An Interested Neighbour.
DR. CAREY, Chief Surgeon of the Onabasha Hospital.
MRS. CAREY, Wife of the Doctor
DR. HARMON, Who Concludes to Leave the City.
MOLLY BARNET, A Hospital Nurse with a Heart.
HENRY JAMESON, A Trader Without a Heart.
ALEXANDER HERRON, Who Made a Concession.
MRS. HERRON, A Gentle Woman.
THE KENNEDYS, Philadelphia Lawyers.

INTRODUCTION

Known as the Bird Woman and the Lady of the Limberlost to her friends and host of readers worldwide, Gene Stratton-Porter started her career first as a photographer of nature and then as a writer about nature before she wrote the popular novels that brought her fame and, not incidentally, fortune. Her lifelong study of birds, flowers, trees, land, and water resulted in a dedicated conservancy that is central to almost everything she wrote. To the general public she is known for the three novels that tell fanciful stories against the background of the great northern Indiana swamp, the Limberlost, a rich and vast expanse of water, trees, verdant land, full of wild animals, birds, and flora of great variety. From the time of her marriage, she knew this natural laboratory firsthand, until its seemingly wanton destruction by loggers and industrialists early in the twentieth century.

Born in 1863 in Wabash County in Indiana, the youngest of twelve children, Geneva Stratton was tutored and lovingly guided by her earnest farmer father to love the land. Through him she early learned lessons in ecology and conservation that were to lie at the heart of her naturalist activity. In 1886 she married Charles Dorwin Porter, a successful druggist. When they moved from Decatur, Indiana to Geneva, both in Adams County, Gene Stratton-Porter began her love affair with the great Limberlost swamp, daily tramping its trails, observing its variety of wild life, especially the birds, and recording her findings. In 1895, the now prosperous Porters built a large, fourteen-room log "cabin" near the swamp, naming it Limberlost Cabin. It was to be the model for the Harvester's log cabin in his beloved Medicine Woods. They remained here until 1913—until the destruction of the swamp—when with the profits from her writing, Gene Stratton-Porter bought land on Sylvan Lake near Rome City in Noble County, and built an even larger cabin. Here she established a wildflower conservancy program. Today Wildflower Woods is a memorial to Gene Stratton-Porter. Beginning in 1919, she started making visits to California and in 1923 made her home permanently in the Los Angeles area. Embarking upon nature studies in California and founding a movie company to film her novels as she felt they should be interpreted, she was beginning a new phase of a writing career that was cut short when she was killed in a car accident in 1924, only a year after her new residency.

Porter's first published writings were magazine articles on birds illustrated with her own photographs in *Recreation* (1900-1901) and *Outing* (1901-1902). Her first work of fiction was *The Song of the Cardinal* (1908), an anthropomorphic account of the life of a pair of cardinals, again illustrated with her own photographs. These writings and other published titles, including *What I Have Done with Birds* (1907), *Birds of the Bible* (1909), and *Friends in Feathers* (1917), are responsible for her Bird Woman epithet, taken from a character in *Freckles*. Yet despite her widely published nature articles and popular "Gene Stratton-Porter's Page" in *McCall's Magazine*, gathered and published posthumously as *Let Us Highly Resolve* (1927), she is best known for the novels of the Limberlost: *Freckles* (1904), *A Girl of the Limberlost* (1909), and *The Harvester* (1911). The first two sold well over two million copies each. With only a million and a half copies sold, *The Harvester* was listed as a best-seller. It is an impressive sales record and amply proves her popularity. Later novels, particularly *The Keeper of the Bees* (1921) and *The White Flag* (1923), were well received but not as popular as the earlier nature novels, including also *Laddie* (1913), an autobiographical novel of farm life in Indiana after the Civil War.

The reasons for Porter's popularity are not hard to discover. In addition to the dedicated love for nature, her novels consistently present the themes of courage, strength of purpose, idealistic vision, successful battle against odds, and emphasis upon spiritual as opposed to material values. And to demonstrate these themes the stories are well-plotted, with easily identifiable characters, although at times the reader's sympathy for them may rest upon illness, obscure origins, unjust treatment, or privation rather than upon the intrinsic nature of the characters.

The Harvester can be seen as the epitome of these characteristics. Foremost, it is a fiction in which the natural setting truly assumes a significance in its making of character, in molding the qualities and determining the career that spell success for the naturalist hero, David Langston, the Harvester. Lest we miss this relationship between nature and man, Porter in a dedication writes: "This portion of a life of a man of to-day is offered in the hope that in cleanliness, poetic temperament and mental force, a likeness will be seen to Henry David Thoreau." While David Langston practices no philosophy of civil disobedience and pursues a vocation of collecting and selling medicinal herbs that nets him more than ample funds for all his needs and wants, he is indeed a model of cleanliness both physically and mentally, keeps to an exceptionally productive schedule of work, and is propelled by the highest and most visionary of ideals— humanitarian and personal. His whole life is based upon the harvesting and conservation of some 600 acres of lush woods, swamp, field and stream. In his life there is no place for the commercialism of the city: "Instead of the senseless roar of commerce, manufacture, and life of a city [there were] sounds that varied and carried the Song of Life in unceasing measure and absorbing meaning" (Ch. XV, p. 310). Appreciation of and love for nature exert a healing power and, in this particular instance, are the source of Ruth's recovery and salvation as she rejects the shallow opulence of her grandparents for the simplicity and depth of life in the Medicine Woods with the Harvester.

David's driving search to find the girl of his literal dream is rewarded because he is humane, morally upright, independent, and capable. Virtue is not its own reward for him, but rather success, professional acclaim, and the winning of the love of the ideal woman he finds and rescues. Such an idealistic vision that he has for his woods seems impractical for one person and the idealistic vision he has for his dream girl hopeless. But perseverance, hard work, patience, and unselfishness bring fruition. At one point in his search, having at last located but not won the girl of his dreams, David tells Ruth about this dream. Her response is, "It sounds like the wildest romancing." But for David, "it is the veriest reality" (Ch. XI, p. 209). It is this conviction that sees David through. And it is Porter's conviction as well.

There is much in *The Harvester* that the seasoned reader may find a bit difficult to accept: the too easy resort to coincidence to resolve parts of the plot, the clearly assigned male and female roles, the anthropomorphic treatment of birds and animals in an otherwise realistic setting, and the sentimentality of the personal relationships. Yet with a strong willing suspension of disbelief this reader can enjoy, as did its first readers, *The*

Harvester for the well-narrated and colorful fiction it is, as well as for its recalling the glorious natural beauty of a part of Indiana that is no more.

Mary E. Gaither
Indiana University

THE HARVESTER

CHAPTER I

Beslhazzar's Decision

"BEL, come here!"

The Harvester sat in the hollow worn in the hewed log stoop by the feet of his father and mother and his own sturdier tread, resting his head against the casing of the cabin door when he gave the command. The tip of the dog's nose touched the gravel between his paws as he crouched flat on earth, with beautiful eyes steadily watching the master, but he did not move a muscle.

"Bel, come here!"

Twinkles danced in the eyes of the man when he repeated the order, while his voice grew more imperative as he stretched a lean, wiry hand toward the dog. The animal's eyes gleamed, his sensitive nose quivered, yet he lay quietly.

"Belshazzar, kommen Sie hier!"

The body of the dog arose on straightened legs and his muzzle dropped in the outstretched palm. A wind slightly perfumed with the odour of melting snow and unsheathing buds swept the lake beside them, lifting

3

a waving tangle of light hair on the brow of the man, while a level ray of the setting sun flashed across the water and illumined the graven, sensitive face, now alive with keen interest in the game being played.

"Bel, dost remember the day?" inquired the Harvester.

The eager attitude and anxious eyes of the dog betrayed that he did not, but was waiting with every sense alert for a familiar word that would tell him what was expected.

"Surely you heard the killdeers crying in the night," prompted the man. "I called your attention when the first bluebird waked the dawn. All day you have seen the gold-yellow and blood-red osiers, the sap-wet maples and spring tracing announcements of her arrival on the sunny side of the levee."

The dog found no clew, but he recognized tones he loved in the suave, easy voice; his tail beat his sides in vigorous approval. The man nodded gravely.

"Ah, so! Then you realize this day to be the most important of all the coming year to me; this hour a solemn one that influences my whole after life. It is time for your annual decision on my fate for a twelve-month. Are you sure you are fully alive to the gravity of the situation, Bel?"

The dog felt himself safe in answering a rising inflection ending in his name uttered in that tone, and wagged eager assent.

"Well then," said the man, "which shall it be? Do I leave home for the noise and grime of the city, open an office and enter the money-making scramble?"

Every word was strange to the dog, almost breath-lessly waiting for a familiar syllable. The man gazed steadily into the animal's eyes. After a long pause he continued: "Or do I remain at home to harvest the golden seal, mullein, and ginseng, not to mention an occasional hour with the black bass or tramps for partridge and cotton-tails?"

The dog knew each word of that. Before the voice ceased, his sleek sides were quivering, his nostrils twitch-ing, his tail lashing, while at the pause he leaped up to thrust his nose against the face of the man. The Har-vester leaned back laughing in deep, full-chested tones; then he patted the dog's head with one hand, renewing his grip with the other.

"Good old Bel!" he cried exultantly. "Six years you have decided for me, and right——every time! We are of the woods, Bel, born and reared here as our fathers before us. What would we of the camp fire, the long trail, the earthy search, we harvesters of herbs the famous chemists require, what would we do in a city? And when the sap is rising, the bass splashing, and the wild geese honking in the night! We never could endure it, Bel.

"When we delivered our hemlock at the hospital to-day, did you hear that young doctor talking about his 'lid?' Well up there is ours, old fellow! Just sky and clouds overhead for us, forest wind in our faces, wild perfume in our nostrils, muck on our feet, that's the life for us. Our blood was tainted to begin with, and we've lived here so long it is now a passion in our hearts. If ever you sen-tence us to life in the city, you'll finish both of us, that's

what you'll do! But you won't, will you? You realize
what God made us for and what He made for us, don't
you, Bel?"

As he lovingly patted the dog's head the man talked,
while the animal trembled with delight. Then the voice
of the Harvester changed, dropping to tones of gravest
import.

"Now how about that other matter, Bel? You decide
that also. The time has come again. Steady now! This
is far more important than the other. Just to be wiped
out, Bel, pouf! That isn't anything and it concerns
only ourselves. But to bring misery into our lives and
live with it daily, that would be a condition to rend the
soul. So careful, Bel! Cautious now!"

The voice of the man dropped to a whisper as he asked
the question: "What about the girl business?"

Trembling with eagerness to do the thing that would
bring more caressing, bewildered by unfamiliar words and
tones, the dog hesitated.

"Do I go on as I have ever since mother left me, rustling for grub, living in untrammelled freedom? Do I go
on as before, Bel?"

The Harvester paused and awaited the answer, with
anxiety in his eyes as he searched the beast face. He
had talked to that dog, as most men commune with their
souls, for so long and played the game in such intense
earnest that he felt the results final with him. The animal was immovable now, lost again, his eager eyes watching the face of the master, his twitching ears waiting for
words he recognized. After a long time the man con-

tinued slowly and hesitantly, as if fearing the outcome. He did not realize that there was sufficient anxiety in his voice to change its tones.

"Or do I go courting this year? Do I rig up in uncomfortable store-clothes, and parade before the country and city girls and try to persuade the one I can get, probably——not the one I would want——to marry me, and come here and spoil all our good times? Do we want a woman around scolding if we are away from home, whining because she is lonesome, fretting for luxuries we cannot afford to give her? Are you going to let us in for a scrape like that, Bel?"

The bewildered dog could bear the unusual scene no longer. Taking the rising inflection, that sounded more familiar, for a cue, and his name for a certainty, he sprang forward, his tail waving as his nose touched the face of the Harvester. Then he shot across the driveway and lay in the spice thicket, half the ribs of one side aching, as he howled from the lowest depths of dog misery.

"You ungrateful cur!" cried the Harvester. "What has come over you? Six years I have trusted you, and the answer has been right, every time! Confound your picture! Sentence me to tackle the girl proposition! I see myself! Do you know what it would mean? For the first thing you'd be chained, while I pranced over the country like a half-broken colt, trying to attract some girl. I'd have to waste time I need for my work and spend money that draws good interest while we sleep, to tempt her with presents. I'd have to rebuild the cabin and there's not a chance in ten she would not fret the life

out of me whining to go to the city to live, arrange for her
here the best I could.   Of all the fool, unreliable dogs that
ever trod a man's tracks, you are the limit!   And you
never before failed me!   You blame, degenerate pup,
you!''

The Harvester paused for breath while the dog subsided
to a pitiful whimper.   He was eager to return to the
man who had struck him the first blow his pampered
body ever had received; but he could not understand a
kick and harsh words for him, so he lay quivering with
anxiety and fear.

"You howling, whimpering idiot!" exclaimed the Harvester.   "Choose a day like this to spoil!   Air to intoxi-
cate a mummy!   Roots swelling!   Buds bursting!   Harvest close and you'd call me off to put me at work like
that, would you?   If I ever had supposed you'd lost all
your senses, I never would have asked you.   Six years
you have decided my fate, when the first bluebird came,
and you've been true blue every time.   If I ever trust
you again!   But the mischief is done now.

"Have you forgotten that your name means 'to protect?'   Don't you remember it is because of that, it is
your name?   Protect!   I'd have trusted you with my
life, Bel!   You gave it to me the time you pointed that
rattler within six inches of my fingers in the blood-root
bed.   You saw the falling limb in time to warn me.   You
always know where the quicksands lie.   But you are
protecting me now, like sin, ain't you?   Bring a girl
here to spoil both our lives!   Not if I know myself!   Protect!''

The man arose and going inside the cabin closed the door. After that the dog lay in abject misery so deep that two big tears squeezed from his eyes and rolled down his face. To be shut out was worse than the blow. He did not take the trouble to arise from the wet leaves covering the cold earth, but closing his eyes went to sleep.

The man leaned against the door, running his fingers through his hair as he anathematized the dog. Slowly his eyes travelled around the room. He saw his tumbled bed by the open window facing the lake, the small table with his writing material, the crude rack on the wall loaded with medical works, botanies, drug encyclopædias, the books of the few authors who interested him, and the bare, muck-tracked floor. He went to the kitchen, where he built a fire in the cook stove, then to the smoke-house, from which he returned with a slice of ham and some eggs. He set some potatoes boiling and took bread, butter and milk from the pantry. Then he laid a small note-book on the table before him and studied the transactions of the day.

10 lbs.	wild cherry bark	6 cents	$ .60
5 "	wahoo root bark	25 "	1.25
20 "	witch hazel bark	5 "	1.00
5 "	blue flag root	12 "	.60
10 "	snake root	18 "	1.80
10 "	blood root	12 "	1.20
15 "	hoarhound	10 "	1.50
			$7.95

"Not so bad," he muttered, bending over the figures. "I wonder if any of my neighbours who harvest the fields

average as well at this season. I'll wager they don't.
That's pretty fair! Some days I don't make it, but
when a consignment of seeds go or ginseng is wanted the
cash comes in right properly. I could waste half of it on
a girl and yet save money. But where is the woman who
would be content with half? She'd want all and fret
because there wasn't more. Blame that dog!"

He put the book in his pocket, prepared and ate his
supper, heaped a plate generously, placed it on the floor
beneath the table, then set away the food that remained.

"Not that you deserve it," he said to space. "You get
this in honour of your distinguished name and the faith-
fulness with which you formerly have lived up to its import. If you hadn't been a dog with more sense than
some men, I wouldn't take your going back on me now so
hard. One would think an animal of your intelligence
might realize that you would get as much of a dose as I.
Would she permit you to eat from a plate on the kitchen
floor? Not on your life, Belshazzar! Frozen scraps
around the door for you! Would she allow you to sleep
across the foot of the bed? Ho, ho, ho! Would she have
you tracking on her floor? It would be the barn, and
growling you didn't do at that. If I'd serve you right,
I'd give you a dose and allow you to see how you like it.
But it's cutting off my nose to spite my face, as the old
adage goes, for whatever she did to a dog, she'd probably
do worse to a man. I think not!"

He entered the front room and stood before a long shelf
on which were arranged an array of partially completed
candlesticks carved from wood. There were black and

white walnut, red, white, and golden oak, cherry and curly maple, all in original designs. Some of them were oddities, others were failures, but most of them were unusually successful. He selected one of black walnut, carved until the outline of his pattern was barely distinguishable. He was imitating the trunk of a tree with the bark on, the spreading, fern-covered roots widening for the base, from which a vine sprang. Near the top was the crude outline of a big night moth climbing toward the light. He stood turning this stick with loving hands and holding it from him for inspection.

"I am going to master you!" he exulted. "Your lines are right. The design balances and it's graceful. If I have any trouble it will be with the moth, and I think I can manage. I've got to decide whether to use cecropia or polyphemus before long. Really, on a walnut, and in the woods, it should be a luna, according to the eternal fitness of things——but I'm afraid of the trailers. They turn over and half curl so I believe I had better not tackle them for a start. I'll use the easiest to begin on, then if I succeed I'll duplicate the pattern and try a luna."

The Harvester selected a knife from the box and began carving the stick slowly and carefully. His brain was busy, for presently he glanced at the floor.

"She'd object to that!" he said emphatically. "A man could no more sit and work where he pleased than he could fly. At least I know mother never would have it, and she was no nagger, either. What a mother she was! If one only could stop the lonely feeling that will creep in, and the aching hunger born with the body, for a mate; if a fellow only could stop it with a woman like mother! How she revelled in sunshine and beauty! How she loved earth and air! How she went straight to the marrow of the finest line in the best book I could bring from the library! How clean and true she was and how unyielding! I can hear her now, holding me with her last breath to my promise. If I could marry a girl like mother——great Cæsar! You'd see me buying an automobile to make the run to the county clerk. Wouldn't that be great! Think of coming in from a long, difficult day, to find a hot supper, and a girl such as she must have been, waiting for me! Bel, if I thought there was a woman similar to her in all the world, and I had even the ghost of a chance to win her, I'd call you in and forgive you. But I know the girls of to-day. I pass them on the roads, on the streets, see them in the cafés, stores, and at the library. Why even the nurses at the hospital, for all the gravity of their positions, are a giggling, silly lot; and they never know that the only time they look and act presentably to me is when they stop their chatter, put on their uniforms, and go to work. Some of them are pretty, then. There's a little blue-eyed one, but all she needs is feathers to make her a 'ha! ha! bird.' Drat that dog!"

The Harvester took the candlestick and the box of knives, opened the door, and returned to the stoop. Belshazzar arose, pleading in his eyes, and cautiously advanced a few steps. The man bent over his work and paid not the slightest heed, so the discouraged dog sank to earth, fixedly watching the unresponsive master. The carving of the candlestick continued steadily. Occasionally the Harvester lifted his head and repeatedly drew his lungs full of air. Sometimes for an instant he scanned the surface of the lake for signs of breaking fish or splash of migrant water bird. Again his gaze wandered up the steep hill, crowned with giant trees, whose swelling buds he could see and smell. Straight before him lay a low marsh, through which the little creek that gurgled and tumbled down hill curved, crossed the drive some distance below, and entered the lake of Lost Loons.

While the trees were bare, and when the air was clear as now, he could see the spires of Onabasha, five miles away, intervening cultivated fields, stretches of wood, the long black line of the railway, and the swampy bottom lands gradually rising to the culmination of the tree-crowned summit above him. His cocks were crowing warlike challenges to rivals on neighbouring farms. His hens were carolling their spring eggsong. In the barnyard ganders were screaming stridently. Over the lake and the cabin, with clapping snowy wings, his white doves circled in a last joy-flight before seeking their cotes in the stable loft. As the light grew fainter, the Harvester worked slower. Often he leaned against the casing, closing his eyes to rest them. Sometimes he whistled snatches of old songs to which his mother had cradled him, and again bits of opera or popular music he had heard on the streets of Onabasha. As he worked, the sun went down, then a half moon appeared above the wood across the lake. Once it seemed as if it were a silver bowl set on the branch of a giant oak; higher, it rested a tilted crescent on the rim of a cloud.

The dog waited until he could endure it no longer, then straightening from his crouching position, he took a few velvet steps forward, making faint, whining sounds in his throat. When the man neither turned his head nor gave him a glance, Belshazzar sank to earth again, satisfied for the moment with being closer. Across Loon Lake came the wavering voice of a night love song. The Harvester remembered that as a boy he had shrunk from those notes until his mother explained that they were made by a little brown owl asking for a mate to come and live in his hollow tree. Now he rather liked the sound. It was eloquent of earnest pleading. With the lonely bird on one side, and the reproachful dog eyes on the other, the man grinned foolishly.

Between two fires, he thought. If that dog ever catches my eye he will come tearing as a cyclone. I would not kick him again for a hundred dollars. First time I ever struck him, and didn't intend to then. So blame mad and disappointed my foot just shot out before I knew it. There he lies half dead to make up, but I'm blest if I forgive him in a hurry. And there is that insane little owl screeching for a mate. If I'd start out making sounds like that, all the girls would line up in competition for possession of my happy home.

The Harvester laughed. At the sound Belshazzar took courage to advance five steps before he sank belly to earth again. The owl continued its song. The Harvester imitated the cry and at once it responded. He called again, then leaned back waiting. The notes came closer. The Harvester cried once more, peering across the lake, watching for the shadow of silent wings. The moon was high above the trees now, the knife dropped in the box, the long fingers closed around the stick, the head rested against the casing, while the man intoned the cry with all his skill; then watched and waited. He had been straining his eyes over the carving until they were tired, and when he watched for the bird the moonlight tried them; for it touched the lightly rippling waves of the lake in a line of yellow light that stretched straight across the water from the opposite bank, directly to the gravel bed below, where lay the bathing pool. It made a path of gold that wavered and shimmered as the water moved gently, but it appeared sufficiently material to resemble a bridge spanning the lake.

"Seems as if I could walk it," muttered the Harvester.

The owl cried again while the man watched the opposite bank. He could not see the bird, but in the deep wood where he thought it might be he began to discern a misty, moving shimmer of white. Marvelling, he watched closer. So slowly he could not detect motion it advanced, rising in height and taking shape.

"Do I end this day by seeing a ghost?" he queried.

He gazed intently, then saw that a white figure really moved in the woods of the opposite bank.

"Must be some boys playing fool pranks!" exclaimed the Harvester.

He watched fixedly with interested face; then amazement wiped out all other expression while he sat motionless, breathless, looking, intently looking. For the white object came straight toward the water and at the very edge unhesitatingly stepped upon the bridge of gold and lightly, easily advanced in his direction.   The man waited. On came the figure, and as it drew closer he could see that it was a very tall, extremely slender woman, wrapped in soft robes of white.   She stepped along the slender line of the gold bridge with grace unequalled.

From the water arose a shining mist, and behind the advancing figure a wall of light outlined and rimmed her in a setting of gold.   As she neared the shore the Harvester's blood began to race in his veins while his lips parted in wonder.   First she was like a slender birch trunk, then she resembled a wild lily, and soon she was close enough to prove that she was young and very lovely. Heavy braids of dark hair rested on her head as a coronet. Her forehead was low and white.   Her eyes were wide-open wells of darkness, her rounded cheeks faintly pink, her red lips smiling invitation.   Her throat was long, very white, and the hands that caught up the fleecy robe around her were rose-coloured and slender.   In a panic the Harvester saw that the trailing robe swept the undulant gold water, but was not wet; the feet that alternately showed as she advanced were not purple with cold, but warm with a pink glow.

She was coming straight toward him, wonderful, alluring, lovely beyond any woman the Harvester ever had seen.   Straightway the fountains of twenty-six years' repression overflowed in the breast of the man and all his being ran toward her in a wave of desire.   On she came, until her feet were on the white gravel.   When he could see clearly she was even more beautiful than she had appeared at a distance. He opened his lips, but no sound came. He struggled to rise, but his legs would not bear his weight. Helpless, he sank against the casing. The girl walked to his feet, bent, placed a hand on each of his shoulders, smiling into his eyes. He could scent the flower-like odour of her body and wrapping, even her hair. He struggled frantically to speak to her as she leaned closer, yet closer, and softly but firmly laid lips of pulsing sweetness on his in a deliberate kiss.

The Harvester was on his feet now. Belshazzar shrank into the shadows.

"Come back!" cried the man. "Come back! For the love of mercy, where are you?"

He ran stumblingly toward the lake. The bridge of gold was there, the little owl cried lonesomely. Did he see or did he only dream he saw a mist of white vanishing in the opposite wood?

His breath came between dry lips. He circled the cabin searching eagerly, but he could find nothing, hear nothing, save the dog at his heels. He hurried to the stoop and stood gazing at the molten path of moonlight. One minute he was half frozen, the next a rosy glow enfolded him. Slowly he lifted a hand to touch his lips. Then he raised his eyes from the water and swept the sky in a penetrant gaze.

"My gracious Heavenly Father," said the Harvester reverently. "Would it be like that?"

CHAPTER II

The Effect of a Dream

FULLY convinced that he had been dreaming, the Harvester picked up his knives and candlestick and entered the cabin. He placed them on a shelf and turned away, but after a second's hesitation he closed the box and arranged the sticks neatly. Then he set the room in order, carefully sweeping the floor. As he replaced the broom he thought for an instant, then opened the door and whistled softly. Belshazzar came at a rush. The Harvester pushed the plate of food toward the hungry dog, which ate greedily. The man returned to the front room, closing the door.

He stood a long time before his shelf of books; at last he selected a volume of "Medicinal Plants" and settled to study. His supper finished, Belshazzar came scratching and whining at the door. Several times the man lifted his head and glanced in that direction, but he only returned to his book. Tired and sleepy, he placed the volume on the shelf, undressed, opened the door, and ran to the lake. He plunged with a splash and swam vigorously for a few minutes, his white body growing pink under the sting of the chilled water. He rubbed to a glow and turned back the covers of his bed. The door and window stood wide. Before he lay down, the Harvester paused in arrested motion a second, then stepped to the kitchen door, lifting the latch.

As the man drew the covers over him, the dog's nose began making an opening: a little later he quietly walked into the room. The Harvester rested, facing the lake. The dog sniffed at his shoulder, but the man was rigid. Then the click of nails could be heard on the floor as Belshazzar went to the opposite side. At his accustomed place he paused to set one foot on the bed. There was not a sound, so he lifted the other. Then one at a time he drew up his hind feet, crouching as he had on the gravel. The man lay watching the bright bridge. The moonlight entered the window, flooding the room. The strong lines on the weather-beaten face of the Harvester were mellowed in the light, so that he appeared young and good to see. His lithe figure stretched the length of the bed, his hair appeared almost white, while his face, touched by the glorifying light of the moon, was a study.

One instant his countenance was swept with ultimate scorn; then gradually that would fade, the lines would soften, until his lips curved in child-like appeal while his eyes were filled with pleading. Several times he lifted a hand to gently touch his lips, as if a kiss were a material thing that might leave tangible evidence of having been given. After a long time his eyes closed. He scarcely was unconscious before Belshazzar's cold nose met the outstretched hand. The Harvester lifted and laid it on the dog's head.

"Forgive me, Bel," he muttered. " I never did that.

I wouldn't have hurt you for anything. It happened before I had time to think."

They both fell asleep. The clear-cut lines of manly strength on the face of the Harvester were touched to tender beauty. He lay smiling gently. Far in the night he realized the frost-chill so he divided the coverlet with the happy Belshazzar.

The golden dream never came again. There was no need. It had done its perfect work. The Harvester awoke the next morning a different man. His face was youthful and alive with alert anticipation. He began his work with eager impetuosity, whistling or singing the while. He found time to play with and talk to Belshazzar, until that glad beast almost wagged off his tail in delight. They breakfasted together and arranged the rooms with unusual care.

"You see," explained the Harvester to the dog, "we must walk neatly after this. Maybe there is such a thing as fate. Possibly your answer was right. There might be a girl in the world for me. I don't expect it, but there is a possibility that she may find us before we locate her. Anyway, we should work so as to be ready. All the old stock in the storehouse goes out as soon as we can cart it. A new cabin shall rise as fast as we can build it. There must be a basement and furnace, too. Dream women do not have cold feet, but if there is a girl living like that, and she is coming to us or waiting for us to come to her, we must have a comfortable home to offer. There should be a bathroom, too. She couldn't dip in the lake as we do. And until we build the new house we must keep the old one clean, on the chance of her happening on us. She might be visiting some of the neighbours or come from town with some one or I might see her on the street, or at the library or hospital or in some of the stores. For the love of mercy, help me watch for her, Bel! The half of my kingdom if you will point her for me!"

The Harvester worked as he talked. He set the rooms in order, put away the remains of breakfast, and started to the stable. He turned back, standing for a long time scanning the face in the kitchen mirror. Once he went to the door, then he hesitated; finally took out his shaving set, using it carefully and washing vigorously. He pulled his shirt together at the throat, then hunting among his clothing, found an old red tie that he knotted around his neck. This so changed his every-day appearance that he felt wonderfully dressed and whistled gaily on his way to the barn. There he confided in the old gray mare as he curried and harnessed her to the spring wagon.

"Hardly know me, do you, Betsy?" he inquired. "Well I'll explain. Our friend Bel, here, has doomed me to go courting this year. Wouldn't that dumfound you? I was mad as hornets at first, but since I've slept on the idea, I rather like it. Maybe we are too lonely and dull. Perhaps the right woman would make life a very different matter. Last night I saw her, Betsy, and between us, I can't tell even you. She was the loveliest, sweetest girl on earth; that is all I can say. We are going to watch for her to-day, and every trip we make, until we find her, if it requires a hundred years. Then some glad time we are going to locate her, and when we do, well, you just keep your eye on us, Betsy, then you'll see how courting straight from the heart is done, even if we lack experience."

Intoxicated with new and delightful sensations his tongue worked faster than his hands.

"I don't mind telling you, old faithful, that I am in love this morning," he said. "In love heels over, Betsy, for the first time in all my life. If any man ever was a bigger fool than I am to-day, it would comfort me to know about it. I am acting like an idiot, Betsy. I know that, but I wish you could understand how I feel. Power! I am the head-waters of Niagara! I could pluck down the stars and set them in different places! I could twist the tail from the comet! I could twirl the globe on my palm, topple mountains and wipe lakes from the surface! I am a live man, Betsy. Existence is over. So don't you go at any tricks or I might pull off your head. Betsy, if you see the tallest girl you ever saw, one who wears a dark diadem, has big black eyes and a face so lovely it blinds you, why you have seen Her; then you balk, right on the spot, and stand like the rock of Gibraltar, until you make me see her, too. As if I wouldn't know she was coming a mile away! There's more I could tell you, but that is my secret, and it's too precious to talk about, even to my best friends. Bel, bring Betsy to the storeroom."

The Harvester tossed the hitching strap to the dog and walked down the driveway to a low structure built on the embankment beside the lake. One end of it was a dry-house of his own construction. Here, by an arrangement of hot water pipes, he evaporated many of the barks, roots, seeds, and leaves he grew to supply large concerns engaged in the manufacture of drugs. By his process crude stock was thoroughly cured, yet did not lose in weight and colour as when dried in the sun or outdoor shade.

So the Harvester was enabled to send his customers big packages of brightly coloured raw material, while the few cents per pound he asked in advance of the catalogued prices were paid eagerly. He lived alone, never talking of his work; so none of the harvesters of the fields adjoining dreamed of the extent of his reaping. The idea had been his own. He had been born in the cabin in which he now lived. His father and grandfather were old-time hunters and trappers. They had added to their earnings by gathering in spring and fall the few medicinal seeds, leaves, and barks they knew. His mother had been of different type. She had loved and married the picturesque young hunter, and gone to live with him on the section of land taken by his father. She found life, real life, vastly different from her girlhood dreams, but she was one of those changeless, unyielding women who suffer silently, but never rue a bargain, no matter how badly they are cheated. Her only joy in life had been her son. For him she had worked and saved unceasingly. When he was old enough she sent him to the city to school, then kept pace with him in the lessons he brought home at night.

Using what she knew of her husband's work as a guide, and profiting by pamphlets published by the government, every hour of the time outside school and in summer vacations she worked in the woods with the boy, gathering herbs and roots to pay for his education and clothing. So the son passed the full high-school course, then selecting such branches as interested him, continued his studies alone.

From books and drug pamphlets he had learned every medicinal plant, shrub, and tree of his vicinity, and for years roamed far afield and through the woods collecting. After his father's death expenses grew heavier, so the boy saw that he must earn more money. His mother frantically opposed his going to the city, so he thought out the plan of transplanting the stuff he gathered, to the land they owned and cultivating it there. This work was well developed when he was twenty, but that year he lost his mother.

From that time he continued steadily enlarging his species, transplanting trees, shrubs, vines, and medicinal herbs from such locations as he found them, to similar conditions on his land. Six years he had worked cultivating these beds, and hunting through the woods on the river banks, government land, the great Limberlost Swamp, and neglected corners of earth for barks and roots. He occasionally made long trips across the country for rapidly diminishing plants he found in the woodland of men who did not care to bother with a few specimens. Many big beds of profitable herbs, extinct for miles around, now flourished on the banks of Loon Lake, in the marsh, and through the forest rising above. To what extent and value his venture had grown, no one save the Harvester knew. When his neighbours twitted him with being too lazy to plow and sow, of "mooning" over books, or derisively sneered when they spoke of him as the Harvester of the Woods or the Medicine Man, David Langston smiled and went his way.

How lonely he had been since the death of his mother he never realized until that morning when a new idea really had taken possession of him. From the storehouse he heaped packages of seeds, dried leaves, barks, and roots into the wagon. But he kept a generous supply of each, for he prided himself on being able to fill all orders that reached him. Yet the load he took to the city was much larger than usual. As he drove down the hill and passed the cabin he studied the location.

"The drainage is perfect," he said to Belshazzar beside him on the seat. "So is the site. We have the cool breezes from the lake in summer and the hillside warmth in winter. View down the valley can't be surpassed. We will grub out that thicket in front, move over the driveway, build a couple of two-story rooms, with basement for cellar and furnace, and a bathroom in front of the cabin, then use it with some fixing over for a dining-room and kitchen. Then we will deepen and widen Singing Water, stick a bushel of bulbs and roots and sow a peck of flower seeds in the marsh, plant a hedge along the drive, and straighten the lake shore a little. I can make a beautiful wild-flower garden and arrange so that with one season's work this will appear very well.

We will express this stuff and then select and fell some trees to-night.   Soon as the frost is out of the ground we will dig our basement and lay the foundations.   The neighbours will help me raise the logs; after that I can finish the inside work.   I've got some dried maple, cherry, and walnut logs that would work into beautiful furniture. I haven't forgot the prices McLean offered me.   I can use it as well as he.   Plain way the best things are built now, I believe I could make tables and couches myself.   I can see plans in the magazines at the library.   I'll take a look when I get this off.   I feel strong enough to do all of it in a few days and I am crazy to commence.   But I scarcely know where to begin.   There are about fifty things I'd like to do.   But to fell and dry the trees and raise the walls come first, I believe.   What do you think, old unreliable?"

Belshazzar thought the world was a place of beauty that morning.   He sniffed the icy, odorous air while with tilted head he watched the birds.   A wearied band of ducks had settled on Loon Lake to feed and rest, for there was nothing to disturb them.   Signs were numerous everywhere prohibiting hunters from firing over the Harvester's land.   Beside the lake, down the valley, crossing the railroad, and in the farther lowlands, the dog was a nervous quiver, as he constantly scented game or saw birds he wanted to point.   When they neared the city, he sat silently watching everything with alert eyes.   As they reached the outer fringe of residences the Harvester spoke to him.

"Now remember, Bel," he said.   "Point me the tallest

girl you ever saw, with a big braid of dark hair, shining black eyes, and red velvet lips, sweeter than wild crab apple blossoms. Make a dead set! Don't allow her to pass us. Heaven is going to begin in Medicine Woods when we find her and prove to her that there lies her happy home.

"When we find her," repeated the Harvester softly and exultantly. "When we find her!"

He said it again and again, pronouncing the words with tender modulations. Because he was chanting it in his soul, in his heart, in his brain, with his lips, he had a hasty glance for every woman he passed. Light hair, blue eyes, and short figures got only casual inspection: but any tall girl with dark hair and eyes endured rather close scrutiny that morning. He drove to the express office to deliver his packages and then to the hospital. In the hall the blue-eyed nurse met him and cried gaily: "Good morning, Medicine Man!"

"Ugh! I scalp pale-faces!" threatened the Harvester, but the girl was not afraid for she stood before him laughing. She might have gone her way quite as well. She could not have differed more from the girl of the newly begun quest. The man merely touched his wide-brimmed hat as he walked around her to enter the office of the chief surgeon.

A slender, gray-eyed man with white hair turned from his desk, smiled warmly, pushed a chair, and reached a welcoming hand: "Ah, good morning, David," he cried. "You bring the very breath of spring with you. Are you at the maples yet?"

"Begin to-morrow," was the answer. "I want to work all my old stock off hands. Sugar water comes next, then the giddy sassafras and spring roots rush me, and after that, harvest begins full force, with all my land teeming. This is going to be a big year. I have decided to enlarge the buildings."

"Storeroom too small?"

"Everything!" said the Harvester comprehensively.

"Ho, ho!" laughed the doctor. "'Crowded everywhere.' I had not heard of cramped living quarters before. When did you meet her?"

"Last night," replied the Harvester. "Her home is already in construction. I chose seven trees as I drove here that are going to fall before night."

So casual was the tone the doctor was disarmed.

"I am trying your nerve remedy," he said.

Instantly the Harvester tingled with interest. "How does it work?"

"Finely! Had a case that presented exactly the symptoms you mentioned. High-school girl broken down from trying to lead her classes, lead her fraternity, lead her parents, lead society——the Lord only knows what else. Gone all to pieces! Pretty a case of nervous prostration as you ever saw in a person of fifty. I began on fractional doses with it, and at last got her where she can rest. It did precisely what you claimed it would, David."

"Good!" cried the Harvester. "Good! I hoped it would be effective. Thank you for the test. It will give me confidence when I go before the chemists with it.

I've got several more compounds I wish you would try when you have safe cases where you can do no harm."

"You are cautious for a young man, son!"

"The woods do that. You not only discover miracles and marvels in them, you not only trace evolution and the origin of species, but you learn the greatest lessons taught in all the world, early and alone——courage, caution, and patience."

"Those are the rocks on which men are stranded as a rule. You think you can breast them, David?"

The Harvester laughed.

"Aside from breaking a certain promise mother rooted in the blood and bones of me, if I am afraid of anything, I don't know it. You don't often see me going headlong, do you? As to patience! Ten years ago I began removing every tree, bush, vine, and plant of medicinal value from the woods around to my land; I set and sowed acres in ginseng, knowing I must nurse, tend, and cultivate seven years. If my neighbours had understood what I was attempting, what do you think they would have said? Cranky and lazy would have become adjectives too mild. Lunatic would have expressed it better. That's close the general opinion, anyway. Because I will not fell my trees, and the woods hide the work I do, it is generally conceded that I spend my time in the sun reading a book. I do, as often as I have an opportunity. But the point is that this fall, when I harvest my ginseng bed, I will clear more money than my stiffest detractor ever saw at one time. I'll wager my bank account won't compare so unfavourably with the best of them now.

I did well this morning. Yes, I'll admit this much: I am reasonably cautious, I'm a pattern for patience, and my courage never has failed me yet, anyway. But I must rap on wood; for that boast is a sign that I probably will meet my Jonah soon."

"David, you are a man after my own heart," said the doctor. "I love you more than any other friend I have. Now I must hurry to my operation. Remain as long as you please if there is anything that interests you; but don't let the giggling little nurse who always haunts the hall when you come make any impression. She is not up to your standard."

"Don't!" said the Harvester. "I've learned one of the big lessons of life since last I saw you, Doc. I have no standard. There is only one woman in the world for me. When I find her I shall know her, and be happy for even a glance; as for that talk of standards, I shall be only too glad to take her as she is."

"David! I supposed what you said about enlarged buildings was nonsense or applied to storerooms."

"Go to your operation!"

"David, if you send me in suspense, I may operate on the wrong man. What has happened?"

"Nothing!" said the Harvester. "Nothing!"

"David, it is not like you to evade. What happened?"

"Nothing! On my word! I merely saw a vision and dreamed a dream."

"You! A rank materialist! 'Saw a vision and dreamed a dream!' And you call it nothing. Worst thing that could happen! Whenever a man of common

sense goes to seeing things that don't exist, and dreaming
dreams, why look out! What did you see? What did
you dream?"

"You woman!" laughed the Harvester. "Talk about
curiosity! I'd have to be a poet to describe my vision,
and the dream was strictly private. I couldn't tell it,
not for any price you could mention. Go to your operation."

The doctor paused on the threshold. "You can't fool
me," he said. "I can diagnose you all right. You are
poet enough, but the vision was sacred; and when a man
won't tell, it's always and forever a woman. I know all
now I ever shall, because I know you, David. A man with
a loose mouth and a low mind drags the women of his
acquaintance through whatever mire he sinks in; but you
couldn't tell, David, not even about a dream woman.
Come again soon! You are my elixir of life, lad! I revel
in the atmosphere you bring. Wish me success now, I
am going to a difficult, delicate operation."

"I do!" cried the Harvester heartily. "I do! But
you can't fail. You never have and that proves you
cannot! Good-bye!"

Down the street went the Harvester, passing over city
pave with his free, swinging stride, his head high, his
face flushed with vivid outdoor tints, going somewhere
to do something worth while, the impression always left
behind him. Men envied his robust appearance and
women looked twice, always twice, and sometimes oftener
if there were an opportunity; but twice at least was the
rule. He left a little roll of bills at the bank then started

toward the library. When he entered the reading room an attendant with an eager smile hastily came toward him.

"What will you have this morning, Mr. Langston?" she asked in the voice of one who would render willing service.

"Not the big books to-day," laughed the Harvester. "I've only a short time. I'll glance through the magazines."

He selected several from a table, then going to a corner settled with them and for two hours was deeply engrossed. He took an envelope from his pocket, traced lines, and read intently. He studied the placing of rooms, the construction of furniture, and all attractive ideas were noted. When at last he arose the Harvester slowly went down the street. Before every furniture store he paused to study the designs displayed in the windows. Then he untied Betsy, drove to a lumber mill on the outskirts of the city and made arrangements to have some freshly felled logs of black walnut and curly maple sawed into different sizes and put through a course in drying.

He drove back to Medicine Woods whistling, singing, and talking to Belshazzar beside him. He ate a hasty lunch and at three o'clock was in the forest, blazing and felling slender, straight-trunked oak and ash of the desired proportions.

CHAPTER III

HARVESTING THE FOREST

THE forest is never so wonderful as when spring wrestles with winter for supremacy. While the earth is yet ice bound, while snows occasionally fly, spring breathes her warmer breath of approach, then all nature responds. Sunny knolls, embankments, and cleared spaces become bare, while shadow spots and sheltered nooks remain white. This perfumes the icy air with melting snow. The sap rises in the trees and bushes, sets buds swelling, and they distil a faint, intangible odour. Deep layers of dead leaves cover the frozen earth, while the sun shining on them raises a steamy vapour unlike anything else in nature. A different scent arises from earth where the sun strikes it. Lichen faces take on the brightest colours they ever wear, and rough, coarse mosses emerge in rank growth from their cover of snow and add another perfume to mellowing air. This combination has breathed a strange intoxication into the breast of mankind in all ages, and bird and animal life prove by their actions that it makes the same appeal to them.

Crows caw supremacy from tall trees; flickers, drunk on the wine of nature, flash their yellow-lined wings and red crowns among trees in a search for suitable building places; nut-hatches run head foremost down rough trunks spying out larvæ and early emerging insects; titmice chatter; the bold, clear whistle of the cardinal sounds never so gaily; while song sparrows pipe from every wayside shrub and fence post. Coons and opossums stir in their dens, musk-rat and ground-hog inspect the weather, the squirrels race along branches and bound from tree to tree like winged folk.

All of them could have outlined the holdings of the Harvester almost as well as any surveyor. They understood where the bang of guns and the snap of traps menaced life. Best of all, they knew where cracked nuts, handfuls of wheat, oats, and crumbs were scattered on the ground, and where suet bones dangled from bushes. Here, too, the last sheaf from the small wheat field at the foot of the hill was stoutly fixed on a high pole, so that it was free to all feathered visitors.

When the Harvester hitched Betsy, loaded his spiles and sap buckets into the wagon, and started to the woods to gather the offering the wet maples were pouring down their swelling sides, almost his entire family came to see him. They knew who fed and every day protected them and so were unafraid.

After the familiarity of a long, cold winter, when it had been easier to pick up scattered food than to search for it, they became so friendly with the man, the dog, and the gray horse that they hastily ate the food offered at the barn and then followed through the woods. The Harvester always was particular to wear large pockets, for it was good company to have living creatures flocking after him, trusting to his bounty. Ajax, a shimmering wonder of gorgeous feathers, sunned on the ridge pole of the old log stable, preened, spread his train, and uttered the peacock cry of defiance, to exercise his voice or to express his emotions at all times. But at feeding hour he descended to the park and snatched bites from the biggest turkey cocks and ganders and reigned in power absolute over ducks, guineas, and chickens. Then he followed to the barn and tried to frighten crows and jays, and the gentle white doves under the eaves.

The Harvester walked through deep leaves and snow covering the road that only a forester could have distinguished. Over his shoulder he carried a mattock, and in the wagon were his clippers and an ax. Behind him came Betsy drawing the sap buckets and big evaporating kettles. Through the wood ranged Belshazzar, the craziest dog in all creation.

At camp the man unhitched Betsy and tied her to the wagon and for several hours distributed buckets. Then he hung the kettles and gathered wood for the fire. At noon he returned to the cabin for lunch, bringing back a load of empty syrup cans, and barrels in which to collect the sap. While the buckets filled at the dripping trees, he dug roots in the sassafras thicket to fill orders and supply the demand of Onabasha for tea. Several times he stopped to cut an especially fine tree.

"You know I hate to kill you," he apologized to the first one he felled. "But it certainly must be legitimate for a man to take enough of his trees to build a home. And no other house is possible for a creature of the woods but a cabin, is there? The birds use of the material they find here; surely I have the right to do the same."

He swung the ax and the chips flew as he worked on a straight half-grown oak. After a time he paused an instant and rested, and as he did so he looked speculatively at his work. "I wonder where she is to-day," he said. "I wonder what she is going to think of a log cabin in the woods. Maybe she has been reared in the city and is afraid of a forest. She may not like houses made of logs. Possibly she won't want to marry a Medicine Man. She may dislike the man, not to mention his occupation. She may think it coarse and common to work out of doors with your hands, although I'd have to argue there is a little brain in the combination. I must figure out all these things. But there is one on the lady: she should have settled these points before she became quite so familiar. I have that for a foundation anyway, so I'll go on cutting wood, and the remainder will be up to her when I find her. When I find her," repeated the Harvester slowly. "But I am not going to locate her very soon monkeying around in these woods. I should be out where people are, looking for her right now."

He chopped steadily until the tree crashed over, then, noticing an overflowing bucket, he stuck the ax in the wood and began gathering sap. When he had made the round, he drove to camp, filled the kettles, and lighted the fire. While it started he cut and scraped sassafras roots, made clippings of tag alder, spice brush and white willow into big bundles that were ready to have the bark removed during the night watch, and then cured in the dry-house.

He went home at evening to feed the poultry and re-plenish the ever-burning fire of the engine and to keep the cabin warm enough that food would not freeze. With an oilcloth and blankets he returned to camp and throughout the night tended the buckets and boiling sap, and worked or dozed beside the fire between times. Toward the end of boiling, when the sap was becoming thick, it had to be watched with especial care so it would not scorch. But when the kettles were freshly filled the Harvester sat be-side them and carefully split tender twigs of willow and slipped off the bark ready to be spread on the trays.

"You are a good tonic," he mused as he worked, "and you go into some of the medicine for rheumatism. Strange that I should be preparing medicinal bark by the sugar camp fire, but I have to make this hay, not while the sun shines, but when the bark is loose, while the sap is rising. I hope it will take the pain out of some poor body. Prices so low now, not worth gathering unless I can kill time on it while waiting for something else. That's all of you——— about twenty-five cents' worth. But even that is better than doing nothing while I wait, and some one has to keep the doctors supplied with salicin and tannin, so, if I do, others needn't bother."

He arose and poured more sap into the kettles as it boiled away and replenished the fire. He nibbled a twig when he began on the spice brush. As he sat on the piled wood, and bent over his work he was an attractive figure. His face shone with health and was bright with anticipa-tion. While he split the tender bark to slip out the wood he spoke his thoughts slowly: "The five cents a pound

I'll get for you is even less, but I love the fragrance and taste. You don't peel so easy as the willow, but I like to prepare you better, because you will make some miserable little sick child well or you may cool some one's fevered blood. If ever she has a fever, I hope she will take medicine made from my bark, because it will be strong and pure. I've half a notion to set some one else gathering the stuff and tending the plants and spend my time in the laboratory compounding different combinations. I don't see what bigger thing a man can do than to combine pure, clean, unadulterated roots and barks into medicines that will cool fevers, stop chills, and purify bad blood. The doctors may be all right, but what are they going to do if we men behind the prescription cases don't supply them with unadulterated drugs. Answer me that, Mr. Sapsucker. Doc says I've done mighty well so far as I have gone. I can't think of a thing on earth I'd rather do, and there's money no end in it. I could grow too rich for comfort in short order. I wouldn't be too wealthy to live the way I do for any consideration. I don't know about her, though. She is lovely, and handsome women usually want beautiful clothing, and a quantity of things that are expensive. I may need all I can get, for her. One never can tell."

He arose to stir the sap and pour more from the barrels to the kettles before he began on the tag alder he had gathered.

"If it is all the same to you, I'll just keep on chewing spice brush while I work," he muttered. "You are entirely too much of an astringent to suit my taste and you bring a cent less a pound. But you are thicker and dry heavier, and you grow in any quantity around the lake and on the marshy places, so I'll make the size of the bundle atone for the price. If I peel you while I wait on the sap I'm that much ahead. I can spread you on drying trays in a few seconds and there you are. Howl your head off, Bel, I don't care what you have found. I wouldn't shoot anything to-day, unless the cupboard was bare and I was starvation hungry. In that case I think a man comes first, and I'd kill a squirrel or quail in season, but blest if I'd butcher a lot or do it often. Vegetables and bread are better anyway. You peel easier than even the willow. What jolly whistles father used to make!

"There was about twenty cents' worth of spice, and I'll easy raise it to a dollar on this. I'll get a hundred gallons of syrup in the coming two weeks and it will bring one fifty if I boil and strain it carefully and can guarantee it contains no hickory bark and brown sugar. And it won't! Straight for me or not at all. Pure is the word at Medicine Woods; syrup or drugs it's the same thing. Between times I can fell every tree I'll need for the new cabin, and average a dollar a day besides on spice, alder, and willow, and twice that for sassafras for the Onabasha markets; not to mention the quantities I can dry this year. Aside from spring tea, they seem to use it for everything. I never yet have had enough. It goes into half the tonics, anodyne, and stimulants; also soap and candy. I see where I grow rich in spite of myself, and also where my harvest is going to spoil before I can garner it, if I don't step lively and double even more than I am now.

Where the cabin is to come in——well it must come if everything else goes.

"The roots can wait and I'll dig them next year and have more and larger pieces. I won't really lose anything, and if she should come before I am ready to start to find her, why then I'll have her home prepared. How long before you begin your house, old fire-fly?" he inquired of a flaming cardinal tilting on a twig.

He arose to make the round of the sap buckets again, then resumed his work peeling bark; so the time passed. In the following ten days he collected and boiled enough sap to make more syrup than he had expected. His earliest spring store of medicinal twigs, that were peeled to dry in quills, were all collected and on the trays; he had digged several wagon loads of sassafras and felled all the logs of stout, slender oak he would require for his walls. Choice timber he had been curing for candlestick material he hauled to the saw-mills to have cut properly, for the thought of making tables and chairs had taken possession of him. He was sure he could build furniture that would appear quite as well as the mission pieces he admired on display in the store windows of the city. To him, chairs and tables made from trees that grew on land that had belonged for three generations to his ancestors, trees among which he had grown, played, and worked, trees that were so much his friends that he carefully explained the situation to them before using an ax or saw, trees that he had cut, cured, and fashioned into designs of his own, would make vastly more valuable furnishings in his home than anything that could be purchased in the city.

As he drove back and forth he watched constantly for her.   He was working so desperately, planning far ahead, doubling and trebling tasks, trying to do everything his profession demanded in season, and to prepare timber and make plans for the new cabin, as well as to start a pair of candlesticks of marvellous design for her, that night was one long, unbroken sleep of the thoroughly tired man, but day had become a delightful dream.

He fed the chickens to produce eggs for her.   He gathered barks and sluiced roots on the raft in the lake, for her.   He grubbed the spice thicket before the door and moved it into the woods to make space for a lawn, for her. His eyes were wide open for every woven case and dangling cocoon of the big night moths that propagated around him, for her.   Every night when he left the woods from one to a dozen cocoons, that he had detected with remarkable ease while the trees were bare, were stuck in his hat band.   As he arranged them in a cool, dry place he talked to them.

"Of course I know you are valuable and there are collectors who would pay well for you, but I think not.   You are the prettiest thing God made that I ever saw, and those of you that home with me have no price on your wings.   You are much safer here than among the crows and jays of the woods.   I am gathering you to protect you, and to show to her.   If I don't find her by June, you may go free.   All I want is the best pattern I can get from some of you for candlestick designs.   Of everything in the whole world a candlestick should be made of wood. It should be carved by hand, and of all ornamentations on earth the moth that flies to the night light is the most appropriate. Owls are not so bad. They are of the night, and they fly to light, too, but they are so old. Nobody I ever have known used a moth. They missed the best when they neglected them. I'll make her sticks over an original pattern; I'll twine nightshade vines, with flowers and berries around them, and put a trailed luna on one, and what is the next prettiest for the other? Maybe she'll come before I reach carving and tell me what she likes. That would surpass my taste or guessing a mile."

Every trip he made to the city he stopped at the library to examine plans of buildings and furniture and to make notes. The oak he had hauled was being hewed into shape by a neighbour who knew how, and every wagon that carried a log to the city to be dressed at the mill brought back timber for side walls, joists, and rafters. Night after night he sat late poring over his plans for the new rooms, above all for her chamber. With poised pencil he wavered over where to put the closet and entrance to her bath. He figured on how wide to make her bed and where it should stand. He remembered her dressing table in placing windows and a space for a chest of drawers. In fact there was nothing the active mind of the Harvester did not busy itself with in those days that might make a woman a comfortable home. Every thought emanated from impulses evolved in his life in the woods, and each was executed with mighty tenderness.

A killdeer sweeping the lake close two o'clock one

morning awakened him. He had planned to close the sugar camp for the season that day, but when he heard the notes of the loved bird he wondered if that would not be a good time to stake out the foundations and begin digging. There was yet ice in the ground, but the hillside was rapidly thawing, and although the work would be easier later, so eager was the Harvester to have walls up and a roof over that he decided to commence.

He went after an ax and a board that he split into pegs. Then he took a ball of twine, a measuring line, and began laying out his foundation, when the hard earth would scarcely hold the stakes he drove into it. That afternoon the first robin of the season hailed him in passing.

"Hello!" cried the Harvester. "You don't mean to tell me that you have beaten the larks! You really have! Well since I see it, I must believe, but you are early. Come around to the back door if crumbs or wheat will do or if you can make out on suet and meat bones! We are good and ready for you. Where is your mate? Don't tell me you don't know. One case of that kind at Medicine Woods is enough. Say you came ahead to see if it is too cold or to select a home and get ready for her. Say anything on earth except that you love her, and want her until your body is one quivering ache, and you don't know where she is."

CHAPTER IV

A Commission for the South Wind

THE following morning the larks trailed ecstasy all over the valley, the cuckoos were calling in the thickets, a warm wind swept from the south and set swollen buds bursting, while the sun shone, causing the Harvester to rejoice. Betsy's white coat was splashed with the mud of the valley road; the feet of Belshazzar left tracks over lumber piles; the Harvester removed his muck-covered shoes at the door and wore slippers inside. The skunk cabbage appeared around the edge of the forest, rank mullein and thistles lay over the fields in big circles of green, and even plants of delicate growth were thrusting their heads through mellowing earth and dead leaves, to reach light and air.

Then the Harvester took his mattock and began to dig. His level best fell so far short of what he felt capable of doing and desired to accomplish that the following day he put two more men on the job. Then the earth did fly, and as soon as the required space was excavated the walls were lined with stone and a smooth basement floor was made of cement. The night the new home stood, a skeleton of joists and rafters, gleaming whitely on the banks of Loon Lake, the Harvester went to the bridge crossing Singing Water and slowly came up the driveway

to see how the work appeared. He caught his breath as
he advanced. He had intended to stake out spacious rooms,
but this, compared with the cabin, seemed like a hotel.

"I hope I haven't made it so large it will be a burden,"
he soliloquized. "It's huge! But while I am at it I
want to build big enough, and I think I have."

He stood on the driveway, his arms folded, looking
at the structure as he occasionally voiced his thoughts.

"The next thing is to lay up the side walls and get
the roof over. Must have plenty of help, for those logs
are hewed to fourteen inches square and some of them are
forty feet long. That's timber! Grew with me, too.
Personally acquainted with almost every tree of it. We
will bed them in cement, use care with the roof, and if
that doesn't make a cool house in the summer, and a warm
one in winter, I'll be disappointed. We must have a wide
porch, plenty of flowers, vines, ferns, and mosses, and when
I finish everything and she sees it——perhaps it will
please her."

A great horned owl swept down the hill, crossed the
lake, and hooted from the forest of the opposite bank.
The Harvester thought of his dream and turned.

"Any women walking the water to-night? Come if
you like," he bantered, "I don't mind in the least. In
fact, I'd rather enjoy it. I'd be so happy if you would
come now and tell me how this appears to you, for it's
all yours. I'd have enlarged the storeroom, dry-houses
and laboratory for myself, but this cabin, never! The
old one suited me as it was; but for you——I should have
a better home."

The Harvester glanced from the shining skeleton to the bridge of gold and back again.

"Where are you to-night?" he questioned. "What are you doing? Can't you give me a hint of where to search for you when this is ready? I don't know but I am beginning wrong. My little brothers of the wood do differently. They announce their intentions the first thing, flaunt their attractions, and display their strength. They say aloud, for all the listening world to hear, what is in their hearts. They chip, chirp, and sing, warble, whistle, thrill, scream, and hoot it. They are strong on self-expression, and appreciative of their appearance. They meet, court, mate, and *then* build their home together after a mutual plan. It's a good way, too! Lots surer of getting things satisfactory."

The Harvester sat on a lumber pile and gazed questioningly at the framework.

"I wish I knew if I am going at things right," he said. "There are two sides to consider: if she is in a good home, and lovingly cared for, it would be proper to court her and get her promise, if I could——no, I'm blest if I'll be so modest——get her promise, as I said, and let her wait while I build the cabin. But if she should be poor, tired, and neglected, then I ought to have this ready when I find her, so I could pick her up and bring her to it, with no more ceremony than the birds."

He went to the work room and began polishing a table top. He had bought a chest of tools and was spending every spare minute on tables, chair seats, and legs. He had decided to make these first and carve candlesticks

later when he had more time. Two hours he worked
at the furniture; then went to bed. The following morning he put eggs under several hens that wanted to set,
trimmed his grape-vines, examined the precious ginseng
beds, attended his stock, prepared breakfast for Belshazzar and himself, and was ready for work when the
first carpenter arrived. Laying hewed logs went speedily;
before the Harvester believed it possible the big shingles
he had ordered were being nailed on the roof. Then
came the plumber to arrange for the bathroom, while
the furnace man placed the heating pipes. The Harvester had intended the cabin to be mostly the work of
his own hands, but when he saw how rapidly skilled carpenters proceeded, he changed his mind and had them
finish the living-room, his room, and the upstairs, and
make over the dining-room and kitchen.

Her room he worked on alone, with a little help if he
did not know how to join the different parts. Everything was plain and simple, after plans of his own, but
the Harvester laid floors and made window casings, seats,
and doors of wood that the big factories of Grand Rapids
used in veneering their finest furniture. When one of
his carpenters pointed out this to him, and suggested
that he sell his lumber to McLean and use pine flooring
from the mills the Harvester laughed at him.

"I don't say that I could afford to buy burl maple,
walnut, and cherry for wood-work," said the Harvester.
"I could not, but since I have it, you can stake your life
I won't sell it and build my home of cheap, rapidly de-
caying wood. The best I have goes into this cabin and

what remains will do to sell. I have an idea that when this is done it is going to appear first rate. Anyway, it will be solid enough to last a thousand years, and with every day of use natural wood grows more beautiful. When we make some tables, couches, and chairs from the same timber as the casings and the floors, I think it will be fine. I want money, but I don't want it badly enough to part with the *best* of anything I have for it. Go carefully and neatly there; it will have to be changed if you don't."

So the work progressed rapidly. When the carpenters had finished the last stroke on the big veranda they remained a day more to make flower boxes, and a swinging couch; then the greedy Harvester kept the best man with him a week longer to help with the furniture.

"Ain't you going to say a word about her, Langston?" asked this man as they put a mirror-like surface on a curly maple dressing table top.

"Her!" ejaculated the Harvester. "What do you mean?"

"I haven't seen you bathe anywhere except in the lake since I have been here," said the carpenter. "Do you want me to think that a porcelain tub, this big closet, and chest of drawers are for you?"

A wave of crimson swept over the Harvester.

"No, they are not for me," he said simply. "I don't want to be any more different from other men than I can help, although I know that life in the woods, the rigid training of my mother, and the reading of only the books that would aid in my work have made me individual in many of my thoughts and ways. I suppose most men would tell you anything you want to know. There is only one thing I can say: the best of my soul and brain, the best of my woods and storehouse, the best I can buy with money is not good enough for her. That's all. For myself, I am getting ready to marry, of course. I think all normal men do and that it is a matter of plain common-sense that they should. Life with the right woman must be infinitely broader and better than alone. As soon as I get this house far enough along that I feel I can proceed by myself I am going to rush the marrying business as fast as I can, and let her finish the remainder to her liking."

"Well this ought to please her."

"That's because you find your own work good," laughed the Harvester.

"Not altogether!" The carpenter polished the board and stood it on end to examine the surface as he talked. "Not altogether! Nothing but good work would suit you. I was thinking of the little creek splashing down the hill to the lake; and that old log hewer said that in a few more days things here would be a blaze of colour until fall."

"Almost all the drug plants and bushes leaf beautifully and flower brilliantly," explained the Harvester. "I studied the location suitable to each variety before I set the beds and planned how to grow plants for continuity of bloom, and as much harmony of colour as possible. Of course a landscape gardener would tear up some of it, but seen as a whole it isn't so bad. Did you ever notice that in the open, with God's blue overhead and His green for a background, He can place purple and yellow, pink, magenta, red, and blue in masses or any combination you can mention and the brighter the colour the more you like it? You don't seem to see or feel that any grouping clashes; you revel in each wonderful growth, and luxuriate in the brilliancy of the whole. Anyway, this suits me."

"I guess it will please her, too," said the carpenter. "After all the pains you've taken, she is a good one if it doesn't."

"I'll always have the consolation of having done my best," replied the Harvester. "One can't do more! Whether she likes it or not depends greatly on the way she has been reared."

"You talk as if you didn't know," commented the carpenter.

"You go on with this now," said the Harvester hastily. "I must uncover some beds and dig my year's supply of skunk cabbage, else folk with asthma and dropsy who depend on me will be short on relief. I ought to take my sweet flag, too, but I'm so hurried now I think I'll leave it until fall; I do when I can, because the bloom is so pretty around the lake and the bees simply go wild over the pollen. Sometimes I think I can almost detect it in their honey. Do you know I've wondered often if the honey my bees make has medicinal properties and should be kept separate in different seasons. In early spring when the plants and bushes that furnish the roots and barks of most of the tonics are in bloom, and the bees gather the pollen, that honey should partake in a degree of the same properties and be good medicine. In the summer it should aid digestion, then in the fall cure rheumatism and blood disorders."

"Say you try it!" urged the carpenter. "I want a lot of the fall kind. I'm always full of rheumatism by October. Exposure, no doubt."

"Over eating of too much rich food, you mean," laughed the Harvester. "I'd like to see any man expose his body to more differing extremes of weather than I do, yet I'm never sick. It's because I am my own cook so I live mostly on fruits, vegetables, bread, milk, and eggs, a few fish from the lake, a little game once in a great while or a chicken, and no hot drinks; plenty of fresh water, air, and continuous work out of doors. That's the prescription! I'd be ashamed to have rheumatism at your age. There's food in the cupboard if you grow hungry. I am going past one of the neighbours on my way to see about some work I want her to do."

The Harvester stopped for lunch, carried food to Belshazzar, then started straight across country, his mattock, with a bag rolled around the handle, on his shoulder. His feet sank in the damp earth at the foot of the hill. He laughed as he leaped across Singing Water.

"You noisy chatterbox!" cried the man. "The impetus of coming down the curves of the hill keeps you talking all the way across this muck bed to the lake. With small work I can make you a thing of beauty. A few bushes grubbed, deepening where you spread too much, and some more mallows along the banks will do the trick. I must attend to you soon."

"Now what does the boy want?" laughed a white-haired old woman, as the Harvester entered her door. "Mebby you think I don't know what you're up to! I even can hear the hammering and the voices of the men when the wind is in the south. I've been wondering how soon you'd need me. Out with it!"

"I want you to bring a woman and come over to spend a day with me. I would like you to go through mother's bedding and have what needs it washed. All I want you to do is to superintend, and tell me now what I will want from town for your work."

"I put away all your mother's bedding that you were not using, clean as a ribbon."

"But it has been packed in moth preventives ever since and out only four times a year to air, as you told me. It must smell musty and be yellow. I want it fresh and clean."

"So what I been hearing is true, David?"

"Very true!" said the Harvester.

"Whose girl is she, and when are you going to jine hands?"

The Harvester lifted his clear eyes, then hesitated.

"Doc Carey laid you in my arms when you was born, David. I tended you 'fore ever your ma did. All your life you've been my boy, and I love you same as my own blood; it won't go farther if you say so. But I'm old and 'til better weather comes, house bound; so I get mighty lonely. I'd like to think about you and her, to plan for you, and love her as I always did you folks. Who is she, David? Do I know the family?"

"No. She is a stranger to these parts," said the unhappy Harvester.

"David, is she a nice girl 'at your ma would have liked?"

"She's the only girl in the world that I'd marry," said the Harvester promptly, glad of a question he could answer heartily. "Yes. She is gentle, very tender and ——and affectionate," he went on so rapidly that Granny Moreland could not say a word, "and as soon as I bring her home you shall come to spend a day and get acquainted. I know you will love her! I'll come in the morning, then. I must hurry now. I am working double this spring. I'm off for the skunk cabbage bed to-day."

"You are working fit to kill, the neighbours say. Slavin' like a horse all day, and half the night I see your lights burning."

"Do I appear killed?" laughingly inquired the Harvester.

"You look peart as a struttin' turkey gobbler," said the old woman. "Go on with your work! Work don't hurt a-body. Eat a-plenty, sleep all you ort, and you *can't* work enough to hurt you."

"So the neighbours say I'm working now? New story, isn't it? Usually I'm too lazy to make a living, if I remember."

"Only to those who don't sense your proceedings, David. I always knowed how you grubbed and slaved an' set over them fearful books o' yours."

"More interesting than the wildest fiction," said the man. "I'm making some medicine for your rheumatism, Granny. It is not fully tested yet, but you get ready for it by cutting out all the salt you can. I haven't time to explain this morning, but you remember what I say, leave out the salt, and when Doc thinks it's safe I'll bring you something that will make a new woman of you."

He went swinging down the road, and Granny Moreland looked after him.

"While he was talkin'," she muttered, "I felt full of information as a flock o' almanacs, but now since he's gone, 'pears to me I don't know a thing more 'an I did to start on."

"Close call," the Harvester was thinking. "Why the nation did I admit anything to her? People may talk as they please, so long as I don't sanction it, but I have two or three times. That's a fool trick. Suppose I can't find her? Maybe she won't look at me if I can. Then I'd have started something I couldn't finish. And if anybody thinks I'll end this by taking any girl I can get, if I can't find Her, why they think wrongly. Only the girl of my golden dream or no woman at all for me. I've lived alone long enough to know how to do it in comfort. If I can't find and win her I have no intention of starting a boarding house.

"'I'd rather keep bachelor's hall in Hell than go to board in Heaven!'" he quoted gaily. "That's my sentiment too. I haven't begun to hunt her yet. Until I do, I might as well believe that she will walk across the bridge and take possession as soon as I have the last chair leg polished. She might! She came in the dream; to come actually couldn't be any more real."

Across the lake, in the swampy woods, close where the

screech owl sang and the girl of the golden dream walked in the moonlight the Harvester began operations. He unrolled the sack, went to one end of the bed and systematically started a swath across it, lifting every other plant by the roots. Flowering time was nearly past, but the bees knew where pollen ripened, so they hummed incessantly over and inside the queer cone-shaped growths with their hooked beaks. It almost appeared as if the sound made inside might be to give outsiders warning not to poach on occupied territory, for the Harvester noticed that no bee entered a pre-empted plant.

With skilful hand each stroke brought up a root and he tossed it to one side. The plants were vastly peculiar things. First they seemed to be a curled leaf with no flower. In colour they shaded from yellow to almost black mahogany, and appeared as if they were a flower with no leaf. Closer examination proved there was a stout leaf with a heavy outside mid-rib, the tip of which curled over in a beak effect, that wrapped around a peculiar flower of very disagreeable odour. The handling of these plants by the hundred so intensified this smell the Harvester shook his head.

"I presume you are mostly mine," he said to the busy little workers around him. "If there is anything in my theory of honey having varying medicinal properties at different seasons, right now mine should be good for Granny's rheumatism and for nervous and dropsical people. I shouldn't think honey flavoured with skunk cabbage would be fit to eat. But, of course, it isn't all this. There is catkin pollen on the wind, hazel and sassafras are both in bloom now, and so are several of the earliest flowers of the woods. You can gather enough of them combined to temper the disagreeable odour into a racy sweetness, so all the shrub blooms are good tonics, too, and some of the earthy ones. I'm going to try giving some of you empty cases next spring and analyzing the honey to learn if it isn't good medicine."

The Harvester straightened, leaning on the mattock to fill his lungs with fresh air and as he delightedly sniffed it he commented: "Nothing else has much of a chance since I've stirred up the cabbage bed. I can scent the catkins plainly, being so close, while as I came here I could detect the hazel and sassafras all right."

Above him a peculiar, raucous chattering for an instant hushed other wood voices. The Harvester looked up, laughing gaily.

"So you've decided to announce it to your tribe at last, have you?" he inquired. "You are waking the sleepers in their dens to-day? Well, there's nothing like waiting until you have a sure thing. The bluebirds broke the trail for the feathered folk the twenty-fourth of February. The sap oozed from the maples about the same time for the trees. The very first skunk cabbage was up quite a month ago to signal other plants to come on; now you are rousing the furred folk. I'll write this down in my records——'When the earliest bluebird sings, when the sap wets the maples, when the skunk cabbage flowers, and the first striped squirrel barks, why then, it is spring!'"

He bent to his task. When he worked closer the water

he noticed sweet-flag leaves waving two inches tall beneath the surface.

"Great day!" he cried. "There you are making signs, too! And right! Of course! Nature is always right. Just two inches high and it's harvest for you. I can use a rake, and dried in the evaporator you bring me ten cents a pound; to the folks needing a tonic you are worth a small fortune. No doubt you cost that by the time you reach them; but I fear I can't gather you just now. My head is a little preoccupied these days. What with the cabbage, and now you, and many of the bushes and trees making signs, with a new cabin to build and furnish, with a girl to find and win, I'm what you might call busy. I've covered my book shelf. I positively don't dare look Emerson or Maeterlinck in the face. One consolation! I've got the best of Thoreau in my head; if I read Stickeen a few times more I'll be able to recite that. There's a man for you, not to mention the dog! Bel, where are you? Would you stick to me like that? I think you would. But you are a big, strong fellow. Stickeen was only such a mite of a dog. But what a man he followed! I feel as if I should put on high-heeled slippers and carry a fan and a lace handkerchief when I think of him. And yet, most men wouldn't consider my job so easy!"

The Harvester rapidly pitched the evil-smelling plants into big heaps while as he worked he imitated the sounds around him as closely as he could. The song sparrow laughed at him and flew away in disgust when he tried its notes. The jay took time to consider, but was not deceived. The nut-hatch ran head first down trees, larvæ hunting, but was never a mite deceived. The kill-deer on invisible legs, circling the lake shore, replied instantly; so did the lark soaring above, also the dove of the elm thicket close beside. The glittering black-birds flashing over every tree top answered the "T'check, t'chee!" of the Harvester quite as readily as their mates.

"'Now I see the full meaning and beauty of that word sound!'" quoted the Harvester. "'I thank God for sound. It always mounts and makes me mount!'"

He breathed deeply, then stood listening, a superb figure of a man, his lean face glowing with emotion.

"If she could see and hear this, she would come," he said softly. "She would come and she would love it as I do. Any one who understands, and knows how to translate, cares for this above all else earth has to offer. They who do not, fail to read as they run!"

He shifted feet mired in swamp muck, and stood as if loath to bend again to his task. He lifted a weighted mattock to scrape the earth from it, sniffing it delight-edly the while. A soft south wind freighted with aro-matic odours swept his warm face. The Harvester re-moved his hat and shook his head that the breeze might thread his thick hair.

"I've a commission for you, South Wind," he said whimsically. "Go find my Dream Girl. Go carry her this message from me. Freight your breath with spicy pollen, sun warmth, and flower nectar. Fill all her senses with delight, and then, close to her ear, whisper it softly. 'Your lover is coming!' Tell her that, O South Wind! Carry Araby to her nostrils, Heaven to her ears; then whisper and whisper it over and over until you arouse the passion of earth in her blood. Tell her what is rioting in my heart, and brain, and soul this morning. Repeat it until she must awake to its meaning: 'Your lover is coming.'"

CHAPTER V

WHEN THE HARVESTER MADE GOOD

THE sassafras and skunk cabbage were harvested. The last workman was gone. There was not a sound at Medicine Woods save the babel of bird and animal notes and the never-ending accompaniment of Singing Waters. The geese had gone over, some flocks pausing to rest and feed on Loon Lake, while ducks that homed there were busy among the reeds and rushes. In deep woods the struggle to maintain and reproduce life was at its height. The courting songs of gaily coloured birds were drowned by hawk screams and crow calls of defiance.

Every night before he plunged into the lake and went to sleep the Harvester made out a list of the most pressing work that he would undertake on the coming day. By systematizing and planning ahead he was able to accomplish an unbelievable amount. The earliest rush of spring drug gathering was over. He could be more deliberate in collecting the barks he wanted. Flowers that were to be gathered at bloom time and leaves were not yet ready. The heavy leaf coverings he had helped the winds to heap on his beds of lily of the valley, bloodroot, and sarsaparilla were removed carefully.

Inside the cabin the Harvester cleaned the glass, swept

the floors with a soft cloth pinned over the broom; then hung pale yellow blinds at the windows. Every spare minute he worked on making furniture, while with each piece he grew in experience and ventured on more difficult undertakings. He had progressed so far that he now allowed himself an hour each day on the candlesticks for her. Every evening he opened her door and with soft cloths polished the furniture he had made. When her room was completed and the dining-room partially finished, the Harvester stained the cabin and porch roofs the shade of the willow leaves, while on the logs and pillars he used oil that served to intensify the light yellow of the natural wood. With that much accomplished he felt better. If she came now, in a few hours he would be able to offer a comfortable room, enough conveniences to live until more could be provided, and of food there was always plenty.

His daily programme was to feed and water his animals and poultry, prepare breakfast for himself and Belshazzar, then go to the woods, dry-house or storeroom to do the work most needful in his harvesting. In the afternoon he laboured over furniture, putting finishing touches on the new cabin. After supper he carved and found time to read again, as before his dream.

He was so happy he whistled and sang at the beginning of his work; but later there came days when doubts crept in until all his will power was required to proceed steadily. As the cabin grew in better shape for occupancy each day, more pressing became the thought of how he was going to find and meet the girl of his dream. He would think of locking the cabin, leaving the drugs to grow undisturbed by collecting, hiring a neighbour to care for his living creatures, and starting a search over the world to find her. There came times when the impulse to go was so strong that only the desire to take a day more to decide where, kept him. Every time his mind was made up to start the following day came the counter thought, what if I should go and she should come in my absence? In the dream she came. That alone held him, even in the face of the fact that if he left home some one might know of and rifle the precious ginseng bed, carefully tended these seven years for the culmination the coming fall would bring. That ginseng was worth many thousands and he had laboured over it, fighting worms and parasites, covering and uncovering it with the changing seasons: a siege of loving labour.

Sometimes a few hours of misgiving tortured him, but as a rule he was cheerful and happy in his preparations. Without intending to do it he was gradually furnishing the cabin. Every few days saw a new piece finished in the workshop. Each trip to Onabasha ended in the purchase of some article he could see would harmonize with his colour plans for one of the rooms. He had filled the flower boxes for the veranda with delicate plants that were growing rapidly.

Then he designed and began setting a wild-flower garden outside her door and started climbing vines over the logs and porches, but whatever he planted he found in the woods or took from beds he cultivated. Many of the medicinal vines had leaves, flowers, twining tendrils, and berries or fruits of wonderful beauty. Every trip to the forest he brought back half a dozen vines, plants, or bushes to set for her. All of them either bore lovely flowers, berries, quaint seed pods, or nuts. Beside the drive and before the cabin he used especial care to plant a hedge of bittersweet vines, burning bush, and trees of mountain ash, so that the glory of their colour would enliven the winter when days might be gloomy.

He planted wild yam under her windows that its queer rattles might amuse her, and hop trees where their cas-tanets would play gay music with every passing wind of fall. He started a thicket on the opposite bank of Sing-ing Water where it bubbled past her window, in which he placed in graduated rows every shrub and small tree bearing bright flower, berry, or fruit. Those remaining he used as a border for the driveway from the lake, so that from earliest spring her eyes would fall on a procession of colour beginning with catkins and papaw lilies, and run-ning through alders, haws, wild crabs, dogwood, plums, and cherry intermingled with forest saplings and vines bearing scarlet berries in fall and winter. In the damp soil of the same character from which they were removed, in the shade and under the skilful hand of the Harvester, few of these knew they had been transplanted. When May brought the catbirds and orioles much of this growth was flowering quite as luxuriantly as the same species in the woods.

The Harvester was in the storehouse packing boxes for shipment. His room was so small and orders so numerous that he could not keep large quantities on hand. All crude stuff that he sent straight from the drying-house was fresh and brightly coloured. His stock always was marked prime A-No 1. On hearing a step behind him the Harvester turned. A boy held out a telegram. The man opened it to find an order for some stuff to be shipped that day to a large laboratory in Toledo.

His hands deftly tied packages, then he hastily packed bottles and nailed boxes. He ran to harness Betsy and load. As he drove down the hill to the bridge he looked at his watch.

"What are you good for at a pinch, Betsy?" he asked as he flecked the surprised mare's flank with a switch. Belshazzar cocked his ears, gazing at the Harvester in astonishment.

"That wasn't enough to hurt her," explained the man. "She must speed up. This is important business. The amount involved is not so much, but I do love to make good. It's a part of my religion, Bel. And my religion has so precious few parts that if I fail in the observance of any of them it makes a big hole in my performances. So we must deliver this stuff, not because it's worth the exertion in dollars and cents, but because these men patronize us steadily and expect us to fill orders, even by telegraph. Hustle, Betsy!"

The whip fell again, then Belshazzar entered indignant protest.

"It isn't going to hurt her," said the Harvester impatiently. "She may walk all the way back. She shall rest while I bill these boxes if she can be persuaded to get them to the express office on time. The trouble with

Betsy is that she wants to meander along the road with a loaded wagon as her mother and grandmother before her wandered through the woods wearing a bell to attract the deer. Father used to say that her mother was the smartest bell mare that ever entered the forest. She'd not only find the deer, but she'd make friends with them and lead them straight as a bee-line to where he was hiding. Betsy, you must travel!"

The Harvester drew the lines taut, then the whip fell smartly. The astonished Betsy snorted and pranced down the valley as fast as she could, but every step indicated that she felt outraged and abused. This was the loveliest day of the season. The sun was shining, the air was heavy with the perfume of flowering shrubs and trees, the orchards of the valley were white with bloom. Farmers were hurrying back and forth across fields, leaving upturned lines of black, swampy mould behind them, while one progressive individual rode a wheeled plow, drove three horses and enjoyed the shelter of a canopy.

"Saints preserve us, Belshazzar!" cried the Harvester. "Do you see that? He is one of the men who makes a business of calling me shiftless. Now he thinks he is working. Working! For a full-grown man, did you ever see the equal? If I were going that far I'd wear a tucked shirt, panama hat, have a pianola attachment, and an automatic fan."

The Harvester laughed as he again touched Betsy and hurried to Onabasha. He scarcely saw the delights offered on either hand; where his eyes customarily took in every sight, and his ears were tuned for the faintest note of earth or tree top, to-day he saw only Betsy and listened for a whistle he dreaded to hear at the water tank   He climbed the embankment of the railway at a slower pace, but made up time going down hill to the city.

"I am not getting a blame thing out of this," he complained to Belshazzar.   "There are riches to stagger any scientist wasting to-day, yet all I've got to show is one oriole.   I did hear his first note and see his flash, so unless we can take time to make up for this on the home road we will have to christen it oriole day.   It's a perfumed golden day, too; I catch that in passing, but how I loathe hurrying.   I don't mind planning things and working steadily, but it's not consistent with the dignity of a sane man to go rushing across country with as much appreciation of the delights offered right now as a chicken with its head off would have.   We will loaf going back to pay for this! And won't we invite our souls?   We will stop and gather a big bouquet of crab apple blossoms to fill the green pitcher for her.   Maybe some of their wonderful perfume will linger in her room.   When the petals fall we will scatter them in the drawers of her dresser, so they may distil a faint flower odour there.   We could do that to all her furniture, but perhaps she doesn't like perfume.   She'll be compelled to after she reaches Medicine Woods.   Betsy, you must travel faster!"

The Harvester stopped at the depot with a few minutes to spare.   He threw the hitching strap to Belshazzar, then ran into the express office with an armload of boxes.

"Bill them!" he cried. "It's a rush order. I want it on the next express. Almost due I think. I'll help you. We can book them afterward."

The expressman ran to bring a truck, then they hastily weighed and piled on boxes. When the last one was loaded from the wagon, a heap more lying in the office were added, pitched on indiscriminately as the train pulled under the sheds of the Union Station.

"I'll push," cried the Harvester, "and help you get them on."

Hurrying as fast as he could the expressman drew the heavy truck through the iron gates and started toward the train slowing to a stop, while the Harvester pushed. As they came down the platform they passed the dining and sleeping cars of the long train. They were several times delayed by descending passengers. Opposite the day coach the expressman narrowly missed running into several women leading small children and stopped abruptly. A toppling box threatened the head of the Harvester. He peered around the truck and saw they must wait a few seconds. He put in the time watching the people. A gray-haired old man, travelling in a silk hat, wavered on the top step then went his way. A fat woman loaded with bundles puffed as she clung trembling a second in fear she would miss the step she could not see. A tall, slender girl with a face coldly white came next. From the broken shoe she advanced, the bewildered fright of big, dark eyes glancing helplessly, the Harvester saw that she was poor, alone, ill, and in trouble. Pityingly he turned to watch her. As he gauged her height, saw her figure, and a dark coronet of hair came into view, a ghastly pallor swept his face.

"Merciful God!" he breathed, "that's my Dream Girl!"

The truck started with a jerk. The toppling box fell, struck a passing boy, and knocked him down. The mother screamed so the Harvester sprang to pick up the child and see that he was not dangerously hurt. Then he ran after the truck, pitched on the box, and whirling sped beside the train toward the gates of exit. There was the usual crush, but he could see the tall figure passing up the steps to the depot. He tried to force his way and was called a brute by a crowded woman. He ran down the platform to the gates he had entered with the truck. They were automatic and had locked. Then he became a primal creature being cheated of a lawful mate so he climbed the high iron fence and ran to the waiting-room. He gave it a glance, not forgetting the women's apartment and the side entrance. Then he hurried to the front exit. Up the street leading from the city there were few people. He could see no sign of the slight, white-faced girl. He crossed the sidewalk, ran down the gutter for a block and breathlessly waited for the passing crowd on the corner. She was not among it. He tried one more square. Still he could not see her. Then he ran back to the depot. He thought surely he must have missed her. He again searched the woman's and general waiting-room; then he thought of the conductor. From him it could be learned where she entered the car. He ran for the station, bolted the gate while the official called to him, reaching the track in time to see the train pull out within a few yards of him.

"You blooming idiot!" cried the angry expressman as the Harvester ran against him, "where did you go? Why didn't you help me? Have you lost your senses?"

"Worse!" groaned the Harvester. "Worse! I've lost what I prize most on earth. How could I reach the conductor of that train?"

"Telegraph him at the next station. You can have an answer in half an hour."

The Harvester ran to the office, and with shaking hand wrote this message:

"Where did a tall girl with big black eyes and wearing a gray dress take your train? Important."

Then he went out to minutely search the depot and streets. He hired an automobile to drive him over the business part of Onabasha for three-quarters of an hour. Up one street and down another he went slowly where there were crowds, faster as he could, but never a sight of her. Then he returned to the depot and found his message. It read: "Transferred to me at Fort Wayne from Chicago."

"Chicago baggage!" he cried, hurrying to the check room. He had lost almost an hour. When he reached the room he found the officials busy and unwilling to be interrupted. Finally he learned there had been half a dozen trunks from Chicago. All were taken save two, and one glance at them told the Harvester that they did not belong to the girl in gray. The others had been claimed by men having checks for them. If she had been there, the officials had not noticed a tall girl having a white face and dark eyes. When he could think of no further effort to make he drove to the hospital.

Doctor Carey was not in his office. The Harvester sat in the revolving chair before the desk and gripped his head between his hands as he tried to think. He could not remember anything more he could have done, but since what he had done only ended in failure, he was reproaching himself wildly that he had taken his eyes from the Girl an instant after recognizing her. Yet it was in his blood to be decent; he could not have run away leaving a frightened woman with a hurt child. Trusting to his fleet feet and strength he had taken time to replace the box also; then he had met the crowd and delay. For the instant it appeared to him as if he had done all a man could, yet he had not found her. If he allowed her to return to Chicago, probably he never would. He leaned his head on his hands, groaning in discouragement.

Doctor Carey whirled the chair so that it faced him before the Harvester realized that he was not alone.

"What's the trouble, David?" he asked tersely.

The Harvester lifted a strained face. "I want help," he said.

"Well, you will get it! What do you want?"

That seemed simplicity itself to the doctor. When it came to putting the case into words, it was not easy for the Harvester.

"Go on!" said the doctor.

"You'll think me a fool."

"No doubt!" he said soothingly. "No doubt, David! Probably you are; so why shouldn't I think so. But remember this, when we make the biggest fools of ourselves that is precisely the time when we need friends, and when they stick to us the tightest, if they are worth while. I've been waiting since latter February for you to tell me. We can fix it, of course; there's always a way. Go on!"

"Well I wasn't fooling about the dream and the vision I told you of then, Doc. I did have a dream—and it was a dream of love. I did see a vision—and it was a beautiful woman."

"I hope you are not nursing that experience as something exclusive and peculiar to you," said the doctor. "There is not a normal, sane man living who has not dreamed of love and the most exquisite woman who came from the clouds or anywhere and was gracious to him. That's a part of a man's experience in this world, and it happens to most of us, not once, but repeatedly. It's a case where the wish fathers the dream."

"Well it hasn't happened to me 'on repeated occasions' but it did one night, so by dawn I was converted. How *can* a dream be so real, Doc? How could I see as clearly as I ever saw in the daytime in my most alert moment, hear every step and garment rustle, scent the perfume of hair, and feel warm breath strike my face? I don't understand it!"

"Neither does any one else! All you need say is that your dream was real as life. Go on!"

"I built a new cabin and overturned the place. I've been making furniture I thought a woman would like, and carrying things from town ever since."

"Gee! It was reality to you, lad!"

"Nothing ever more so," said the Harvester.

"And of course, you have been looking for her?"

"And this morning I saw her!"

"David!"

"Not the ghost of a chance for a mistake. Her height, her eyes, her hair, her walk, her face; only something terrible has happened since she came to me. It was the same girl, but she is ill and in trouble now."

"Where is she?"

"Do you suppose I'd be here if I knew?"

"David, are you dreaming in daytime?"

"She left the Chicago train this morning while I was helping Daniels load a big truck of express matter. Some of it was mine, and it was important. At the wrong instant a box fell, knocking down a child, so I got in a jam——"

"As it was you, of course you stopped to pick up the child and do everything decent for other folks, before you thought of yourself, so you lost her. You needn't tell me anything more. David, if I find her, and prove to you that she has been married ten years and has an interesting family, will you thank me?"

"Can't be done!" said the Harvester calmly. "She has been married only since she gave herself to me in February. She is not a mother. You needn't bank on that."

"You are mighty sure!"

"Why not? I told you the dream was real, now that I have seen her, and she is in this very town, why shouldn't I be sure?"

"What have you done?"

The Harvester told him.

"What are you going to do next?"

"Talk it over with you and decide."

The doctor laughed.

"Here are a few things that occur to me without time for thought. Talk to the ticket agents, and leave her description with them. Make it worth their while to be on the lookout, and if she goes anywhere to find out all they can. They could make an excuse of putting her address on her ticket envelope, and get it that way. See the baggagemen. Post the day police on Main Street. There is no chance for her to escape you. A full-grown woman doesn't vanish. How did she act when she left the car? Did she appear familiar?"

"No. She was a stranger. For an instant she looked around as if she expected some one, then she followed the crowd. There must have been an automobile waiting or she took a street car. Something whirled her out of sight in a few seconds."

"Then we will get her in range again. Now for the most minute description you can give."

The Harvester hesitated. He did not care to describe the Dream Girl to any one, much less the living, suffering face and poorly clad form of the reality.

"Cut out your scruples," laughed the doctor. "You have asked me to help you; how can I if I don't know what kind of a woman to look for?"

"Very tall and slender," said the Harvester. "Almost as tall as I am."

"Unusually tall you think?"

"I know!"

"That's a good point for identification. How about her complexion, hair, and eyes?"

"Very large, dark eyes, and a great mass of black hair." The doctor roared.

"The eyes may help," he said. "All women have masses of hair these days. I hope——"

"Her hair is fast to her head," said the Harvester indignantly. "I saw it at close range, and I know. It went around like a crown."

The doctor choked down a laugh. He wanted to say that every woman's hair was like a crown at present, but there were things no man ventured with David Langston; those who knew him best, least of any. So he suggested: "And her colouring?"

"She was white and rosy, a lovely thing in the dream," said the Harvester, "but something dreadful has happened. That's all wiped out now. She was very pale when she left the car."

"Car sick, maybe."

"Soul sick!" was the grim reply.

Then Doctor Carey appeared so disturbed the Harvester noticed it.

"You needn't think I'd be here prating about her if I were not *forced*. If she had been rosy and well as she was in the dream, I'd have made my hunt alone and found her, too. But when I saw she was sick and in trouble, it took all the courage out of me, so I broke for help. She must be found at once. When she is you are probably the first man I'll want. I am going to put up a stiff search myself. If I find her I'll send or get her to you if I can. Put her in the best ward you have and anything money will do——"

The face of the doctor was growing troubled.

"Day coach or Pullman?" he asked.

"Day."

"How was she dressed?"

"Small black hat, very plain. Gray jacket and skirt, neat as a flower."

"What you'd call expensively dressed?"

The Harvester hesitated.

"What I'd call carefully dressed, but——but poverty poor, if you will have it, Doc."

Doctor Carey's lips closed, then opened in sudden resolution.

"David, I don't like it," he said tersely.

The Harvester met his eye, then purposely misunderstood him.

"Neither do I!" he exclaimed. "I hate it! There is something wrong with the whole world when a woman having a face full of purity, intellect, and refinement of extreme type glances around her like a hunted thing; when her appearance seems to indicate that she has starved her body to clothe it. I know what is in your mind, Doc, but if I were you I wouldn't put it into words, and I wouldn't even *think* it. Has it been your experience in this world that women not fit to know skimp their bodies to cover them? Does a girl of light character and little brain have the hardihood to advance a foot covered with a broken shoe? If I could tell you that she rode in a Pullman, and wore exquisite clothing, you would be doing something. The other side of the picture shocks you. Let me tell you this: no other woman I ever saw anywhere on God's footstool had a face of more delicate refinement, eyes of purer intelligence. I am of the woods. While they don't teach me how to shine in society, they do instil always and forever the fineness of nature and her ways. I have her lessons so well learned they help me more than anything else to discern the qualities of human nature. If you are my friend, and have any faith at all in my common sense, get up and do something!"

The doctor arose promptly.

"David, I'm an ass," he said. "Unusually lop-eared, and blind in the bargain. But before I ask you to forgive me, I want you to remember two things: first, she did not visit me in my dreams; and, second, I did not see her in reality. I had nothing to judge from except what you said: you seemed reluctant to tell me, and what you did say was——was——disturbing to a friend of yours. I have not the slightest doubt if I had seen her I would agree with you. We seldom disagree, David. Now, will you forgive me?"

The Harvester suddenly faced a window. When at last he turned, "The offence lies with me," he said. "I was hasty. Are you going to help me?"

"With all my heart! Go home and work until your head clears, then come back in the morning. She did not come from Chicago for a day. You've done all I know to do at present."

"Thank you," said the Harvester.

He went to Betsy and Belshazzar, slowly driving up and down the streets until Betsy protested and calmly turned homeward. The Harvester smiled ruefully as he allowed her to proceed.

"Go slow and take it easy," he said as they reached the country. "I want to think."

Betsy stopped at the barn, the white doves took wing, and Ajax screamed shrilly before the Harvester aroused in the slightest to anything around him. Then he looked at Belshazzar and said emphatically: "Now, partner, don't ever again interfere when I am complying with the observances of my religion. Just look what I'd have missed if I hadn't made good with that order!"

CHAPTER VI

To Labour and to Wait

"WE HAVE reached the 'beginning of the end,' Ajax!" said the Harvester, when the peacock ceased screaming to search for food from his hand. "We have seen the Girl. Now we must locate her and convince her that Medicine Woods is her happy home. I feel quite equal to the latter proposition, Ajax, but how the nation to find her sticks me. I can't make a search so open that she will know and resent it. She must have all the consideration ever paid the most refined woman, but she has got to be found also, and that speedily. When I remember that look on her face, as if horrors were snatching at her skirts, it takes the grit out of me. I feel weak as a sapling. And she needs all my strength. I've simply got to brace up. I'll work a while, then perhaps I can think."

So the Harvester began the evening routine. He thought he did not want anything to eat, but when he opened the cupboard and smelled the food he learned that he was a hungry man so he cooked and ate a good supper. He put away everything carefully, for even the kitchen was dainty and fresh and he wanted to keep it so for her. When he finished he took a key from his pocket to unlock her door. Every day he had been going there to improve upon his work for her. He loved the room, the outlook from its windows; he was very proud of the furniture he had made. There was no paper-thin covering on her chairs, bed, and dressing table. The tops, seats, and posts were solid wood, worth hundreds of dollars for veneer.

To-night he folded his arms, standing on the sill hesitating. While she was a dream, he had loved to linger in her room. Now that she was reality, he paused. In one golden May day the place had become sacred. Since he had seen the Girl the room was so hers that he was hesitating about entering because of this fact. It was as if the tall, slender form stood before the chest of drawers or sat at the dressing table and he did not dare enter unless he were welcome. Softly he closed the door, turning away. He wandered to the dry-house to see the bark and roots on the trays, but the air stifled him so he hurried out.

He espied a bundle of osier-bound, moss-covered ferns that he had found in the woods. He brought the shovel to transplant them; but the work worried him, so he hurried through with it. Then in looking for something else to do he saw an ax. He caught it up and with lusty strokes began swinging it. When he had chopped wood until he was very tired he went to bed. Sleep came to the strong, young frame. He awoke in the morning refreshed and hopeful.

He wondered why he had bothered Doctor Carey. The Harvester felt able that morning to find his Dream Girl without assistance before the day was over. It was merely a matter of going to the city and locating a woman.

Yesterday, it had been a question of whether she really existed. To-day, he knew. Yesterday, it had meant a search possibly as wide as earth to find her. To-day, it was narrowed to only one location so small, compared with Chicago, that the Harvester felt he could sift its population with his fingers, separating her from others at his first attempt. If she were visiting there probably she would be on the streets to-day.

When he remembered her face he doubted it. He decided to spend part of the time on the business streets, the remainder in the residence portions of the city. Because it was uncertain when he would return, everything was fed a double portion, while Betsy was left at a livery stable with instructions to care for her until he came. He did not know where the search would lead him. For several hours he slowly walked the business district and then ranged farther, but not a sight of her. He never had known that Onabasha was so large. On its crowded streets he did not feel that he could sift the population through his fingers, nor could he open doors and search houses without an excuse. He went to the hospital.

"I expected you early this morning," was the greeting of Doctor Carey. "Where have you been and what have you done?"

"Nothing," said the Harvester. "I was so sure she would be on the streets I watched, but I didn't see her."

"We will go to the depot," said the doctor. "The first thing is to keep her from leaving town."

They arranged with the ticket agents, expressmen, telegraphers, and as they left, the Harvester stopped and tipped the train caller, offering further reward worth while if he would find the Girl.

"Now we will go to the police station," said the doctor. "I'll see the chief and have him issue a general order to his men to watch for her, but if I were you I'd select half a dozen in the downtown district, giving them a little tip with a big promise!"

"Good Lord! How I hate this," groaned the Harvester.

"Want to find her by yourself?" questioned his friend.

"Yes," said the Harvester, "I do! And I would, if it hadn't been for her ghastly face. That drives me to resort to any measures. The probabilities are that she is lying sick somewhere; if her comfort depends on the purse that dressed her, she will suffer. Doc, do you know how awful this is?"

"I know that you've a great imagination. If the woods make all men as sensitive as you are, those who have business to transact should stay out of them. Take a common-sense view. Look at this as I do. If she were strong enough to travel in a day coach from Chicago, she can't be so very ill to-day. Leaving life by the inch isn't that easy. She will be alive this time next year, whether you find her or not. The chances are that her stress was mental anyway, and trouble almost never overcomes any one."

"You, a doctor and say that!"

"Oh, I mean instantaneously——in a day! Of course if it grinds away for years! But youth doesn't allow it to do that. It throws it off, and grows hopeful and happy again. She won't die; put that out of your mind. If I were you I would go home now and go straight on with my work, trusting to the machinery you have set in motion. I know most of the men with whom we have talked. They will locate her in a week or less. It's their business. It isn't yours. It's your job to be ready for her, when they find her. Try to realize that there are now a dozen men on hunt for her, and trust them. Go back to your work. I will come full speed in the motor when the first man sights her. That should satisfy you. I've told all of them to call me at the hospital. I will tell my assistant what to do in case a call comes while I am away. Straighten your face! Go back to Medicine Woods and harvest your crops. Before you know it she will be located. Then you can put on your Sunday clothes, show yourself, and see if you can make her take notice."

"Idiot!" exclaimed the Harvester, but he started home. When he arrived he attended to his work, then sat down to think.

"Doc is right," was his ultimate conclusion. "She can't leave the city, she can't move around in it, she can't go anywhere, without being seen. There's one more point: I must tell Carey to post all the doctors to report if they have such a call. That's all I can think of. I'll go to-night, then I'll look over the ginseng for parasites, and to-morrow I'll dive into the late spring growth and work until I haven't time to think. I've let cranesbill go a week too long now, and it can't be dispensed with."

So the following morning, when the Harvester had completed his work at the barn and breakfasted, he took a mattock, and a big hempen bag, and followed the path to the top of the hill. Where it ran along the lake bank he descended on the other side to several acres of cleared land; here he raised corn for his stock, potatoes, and coarser garden truck, for which there was not space in the smaller enclosure close the cabin. Around the edges of these fields, and where one of them sloped toward the lake, he began grubbing a variety of grass having tall stems already over a foot in height at half growth. From each stem waved four or five leaves of six or eight inches length, and the top showed forming clusters of tiny spikelets.

"I am none too early for you," he muttered to himself as he ran the mattock through the rich earth, lifting the long, tough, jointed root stalks of pale yellow, from every section of which broke sprays of fine rootlets. "None too early for you, and as you are worth only seven cents a pound, you couldn't be considered a 'get-rich-quick' expedient, so I'll only stop long enough with you to gather what I think my customers will order, and amass a fortune a little later picking mullein flowers at seventy-five cents a pound. What a crop I've got coming!"

The Harvester glanced ahead, where in the cleared soil of the bank grew large plants with leaves like yellow-green felt and tall bloom stems arising. Close them flourished other species requiring dry sandy soil, that gradually changed as it approached the water until it became covered with rank abundance of short, wiry grass, half the blades of which appeared red. Numerous everywhere he could see the grayish-white leaves of Parnassus grass. As the season advanced it would lift heart-shaped velvet higher, and before fall the stretch of emerald would be starred with white-faced, green-striped flowers.

"Not a prettier sight on earth," commented the Harvester, "than just swale wire grass in September making a fine, thick background to set off those delicate starry flowers on their slender stems. I must remember to bring her to see that."

His eyes followed the growth to the water. As the grass drew closer moisture it changed to the rank, sweet, swamp variety, then came bulrushes, cat-tails, water smartweed, docks, and in the water, blue flag lifted folded buds; at its feet arose yellow lily leaves and farther out spread the white. As the light struck the surface the Harvester imagined he could see the little green buds several inches below. Above all swayed wild rice he had planted for the birds. The red wings swayed on the willows and tilted on every stem that would bear their weight, singing their melodious half-chanted notes: "O-ka-lee!"

Beneath them the ducks gobbled, splashed, and chattered; grebe and coot voices could be distinguished; king rails at times flashed into sight then out again; marsh wrens scolded and chattered; occasionally a kingfisher darted around the lake shore, rolling his rattling cry as he flashed his azure coat and gleaming white collar. On a hollow tree in the woods a yellow hammer proved why he was named, because he carpentered industriously to enlarge the entrance to the home he was excavating in a dead tree. Sailing over the lake and above the woods in grace scarcely surpassed by any, a lonesome turkey buzzard awaited his mate's decision as to which hollow log was most suitable for their home.

The Harvester stuffed the grass roots in the bag until it would hold no more and stood erect to wipe his face, for the sun was growing warm. As he drew his handkerchief across his brow, the south wind struck him with enough intensity to attract attention. Instantly the Harvester removed his hat, rolled it up, and put it into his pocket. He stood an instant delighting in the wind, then spoke: "Allow me to express my most fervent thanks for your kindness," he said. "I thought probably you would take that message, since it couldn't mean much to you, and it meant all the world to me. I thought you would carry it, but, I confess, I scarcely expected the answer so soon. The only thing that could make me more grateful to you would be to know exactly where she is; but you must understand that it's like a peep into Heaven to have her existence narrowed to one place. I'm bound to be able to say inside a few days, she lives at number——I don't know yet, on strcct   I'll find out soon, in the closest city, Onabasha. And I know why you brought her, South Wind. If ever a girl's cheeks need fanning with your breezes, and painting with sun kisses, I wouldn't mind, since this is strictly private, adding a few of mine; if ever any one needed flowers, birds, fresh air, water, and rest! Good Lord, South Wind, did you ever reach her before you carried that message? I think not! But Onabasha isn't so large. You and the sun should get your innings there. I do hope she is not trying to work! I can attend to that; and so there will be more time when she is found, I'd better hustle now."

As he passed down the road to the cabin his face was a study of conflicting emotions; his eyes had a far-away appearance of deep thought. Every tree of his stretch of forest was rustling fresh leaves to shelter him; dogwood, wild crab, and hawthorn offered their flowers; earth held up her tribute in painted trillium faces, spring beauties, and violets, blue, white, and yellow. Mosses, ferns, and lichens decorated the path; all the birds greeted him in friendship, singing their purest melodies. The sky was blue, the sun bright, the air perfumed for him; Belshazzar, always true to his name, protected every footstep; Ajax, the shimmering green and gold wonder, came up the hill to meet him; the white doves circled above his head. Stumbling half blindly, the Harvester passed unheeding among them, and went into the cabin. When he came out he stood a long time in deep thought, but at last he returned to the woods.

"Perhaps they will have found her before night," he said. "I'll harvest the cranesbill yet, because it's grow-ing late for it, and then I'll see how they are coming on. Maybe they'd know her if they met her, and maybe they wouldn't. She may wear different clothing, and freshen up after her trip. She might have been car sick, as Doc suggested, and appear very different when she feels better."

He skirted the woods around the northeast end, stop-ping at a big bed of exquisite growth. Tall, wiry stems sprang upward almost two feet in height; leaves six inches across were cut in ragged lobes nearly to the base, while here and there, enough to colour the entire bed, a delicate rose or sometimes a violet purple, the first flowers were unfolding. The Harvester lifted a root and tasted it.

"No doubt about you being astringent," he muttered. "You have enough tannin in you to pucker a mushroom. By the way, those big, corn-cobby fellows should spring up with the next warm rain. The hotels and restaurants always pay high prices. I must gather a few bushels."

He looked over the bed of beautiful wild alum and hesitated. "I vow I hate to touch you," he said. "You are a picture right now, and in a week you will be a miracle. It seems a shame to tear up a plant for its roots, just at flowering time, and I can't avoid breaking down half I don't take, getting the ones I do. I wish you were not so pretty! You are one of the colours I love most. You remind me of red-bud, blazing star, and all those exquisite magenta shades that poets, painters, and the Almighty who made them, love so much they hesitate about using them lavishly. You are so delicate and graceful and so modest. I wish she could see you! I got to stop this or I won't be able to lift a root. I never would if the ten cents a pound I'll get out of it were the only consideration."

The Harvester gripped the mattock and advanced to the bed. "What I must be thinking is that you are indispensable to the sick folks. The steady demand for you proves your value, and of course, humanity comes first, after all. If I remain in the woods alone much longer I'll reach the place where I'm not so sure that it does. Seems as if animals, birds, flowers, trees, and insects as well, have their right to life also. But it's my job to remember the sick folks! If I thought the Girl would get some of it now, I could overturn the bed with a stout heart. If any one ever needed a tonic, I think she does. Maybe some of this will reach her. If so, I hope it will make her cheeks the lovely pink of the bloom. Oh Lord! If only she hadn't appeared so sick and frightened! What is there in all this world of sunshine to make a girl glance around her like that? I wish I knew! Perhaps they will have found her by night."

The Harvester began work on the bed, but he knelt and among the damp leaves from the spongy black earth he lifted the roots with his fingers, carefully straightening and pressing down the plants he did not take. This required more time than usual, but his heart was so sore, he could not be rough with anything, most of all a flower. So he harvested the wild alum by hand, heaping large stacks of roots around the edges of the bed. Often he paused as he worked to stare through the forest as if he hoped perhaps she would realize his longing for her, and come to him in the wood as she had across the water. Over and over he repeated, "Perhaps they will find her by night!" and that so intensified the meaning that once he said it aloud. His face clouded, growing dark.

"Dealish nice business!" he said. "I am here in the woods digging flower roots, while a gang of men in the city are searching for the girl I love. If ever a job seemed peculiarly a man's own, it appears this would be. What business has any other man spying after my woman? Why am I not down there doing my own work, as I al-

ways have done it? Who's more likely to find her than
I am? It seems as if there would be an instinct that
would lead me straight to her, if I'd go. And you can
wager I'll go fast enough."

The Harvester appeared as if he would start that instant, but with lips closely shut he finally forced himself to go on with his work. When he had rifled the bed,
uprooting all he cared to take during one season, he
carried the roots to the lake shore below the curing house,
spreading them on a platform he had built. He stepped
into his boat and began dashing pails of water over them,
then using a brush. As he worked he washed away the
woody scars of last year's growth, also the tiny buds appearing for the coming season.

Belshazzar sat on the opposite bank to watch the operation; Ajax came down, and flying to a dead stump,
erected and slowly waved his train to attract the sober-
faced man who paid no heed. He left the roots to drain
while he prepared supper, then placed them on the trays,
now filled to overflowing. He was glad to finish. He
could not cure anything else at present if he wanted to.
He was as far advanced as he had been at the same time
the previous year. Then he dressed neatly, locked the
Girl's room, and leaving Belshazzar to protect it, he went
to Onabasha.

"Bravo!" cried Doctor Carey as the Harvester entered his office. "You are heroic to wait all day for
news. How much stuff have you gathered?"

"Three crops. How many missing women have you
located?"

The doctor laughed. There was no sign of a smile on the face of the Harvester.

"You didn't really expect her to come to light the first day? That would be too easy! We can't find her in a minute."

"It will be no surprise to me if you can't find her at all. I am not expecting another man to do what I don't myself."

"You are not hunting her. You are harvesting the woods. The men you employ are to find her."

"Maybe I am; maybe I am not," said the Harvester slowly. "To me it appears to be a poor stick of a man who coolly proceeds with money making, trusting to men who haven't even seen her to search for the girl he loves. I think a few hours of this is about all my patience will endure."

"What are you going to do?"

"I don't know," said the Harvester. "But you can bank on one thing sure——I'm going to do something! I've had my fill of this. Thank you for all you've done, and all you are going to do. My head is not clear enough yet to decide anything with any sense, but maybe I'll hit on something soon. I'm for the streets for a while."

"Better go home and go to bed. You seem very tired."

"I am," said the Harvester. "The only way to endure this is to work myself down. I'm all right; I'll be careful, but I rather think I'll find her myself."

"Better go on with your work as we planned."

"I'll think about it," said the Harvester.

Until he was too tired to walk farther he slowly paced the streets of the city; then followed the home road through the valley and up the hill to Medicine Woods. When he came to Singing Water, Belshazzar heard his steps on the bridge, and came bounding to meet him. The Harvester stretched himself on a seat, turning his face to the sky. Insects were humming lazily in the perfumed night air; across the lake a courting whip-poor-will was explaining to his sweetheart how much and why he loved her. A few bats were wavering in air, hunting insects, and occasionally an owl or a nighthawk crossed the lake. Killdeer were glorying in the moonlight and night flight, crying in pure, clear notes as they sailed over the water. The Harvester was tired and filled with unrest as he stretched on the bridge, but the longer he lay the more the enfolding voices comforted him. All of them were waiting, working out their lives to the legitimate end; there was nothing else for him to do. He need not follow instinct or profit by chance. He was a man; he could plan and reason.

The air grew balmy, then some big, soft clouds swept across the moon. The Harvester felt the dampness of rising dew, so he went to the cabin. He looked at it long in the moonlight and told himself that he could see how much the plants, vines, and ferns had grown since the previous night. Without making a light, he threw himself on the bed in the outdoor room, then lay looking through the screening at the lake and sky. He was working his brain to think of some manner in which to start a search for the Dream Girl that would have some probability of success to recommend it, but he could settle on no feasible plan. At last he fell asleep. In the night soft rain wet his face. He pulled an oilcloth sheet over the bed, then lay breathing deeply of the damp, perfumed air as he again slept. In the morning brilliant sunshine awoke him. He arose to find the earth steaming.

"If ever there was a perfect mushroom day!" he said to Belshazzar. "We must hurry our work and gather some. They mean real money."

CHAPTER VII

THE QUEST OF THE DREAM GIRL

THE Harvester breakfasted, fed the stock, hitched Betsy to the spring wagon, then went into the dripping, steamy woods. If any one had asked him that morning concerning his idea of Heaven, he never would have dreamed of describing a place of gold-paved streets, crystal pillars, jewelled gates, or thrones of ivory. These things were beyond the man's comprehension. He would not have admired or felt at home in such magnificence if it had been materialized for him. He would have told you that a floor of last year's brown leaves, studded with myriad flower faces, big, bark-encased pillars of a thousand years, jewels on every bush, shrub, and tree, tilting thrones on which gaudy birds almost burst themselves to voice the joy of life, while their bright-eyed little mates peered questioningly at him over nest rims——he would have told you that Medicine Woods on a damp, sunny May morning was Heaven. He would have added that only one angel, tall and slender, with the pink of health on her cheeks and the dew of happiness in her dark eyes, was necessary to enter and establish glory. Everything spoke to him that morning, but the Harvester was silent. It had been his habit to talk constantly to Belshazzar, Ajax, his work, even

93

the winds and perfumes; in this manner he dissipated
solitude, but to-day he had no words for these dear friends.
He only opened his soul to beauty, as he steadily climbed
the hill to the crest, then down the other side to the rich,
half-shaded, half-open spaces, where big, rough mushrooms
sprang during such a night.

He could see them from afar. He began work with
rapid fingers, being careful to break off the heads, but not
to pull up the roots. When four heaping baskets were
filled he cut heavily leaved branches to spread over them,
then started to Onabasha. As usual, Belshazzar rode beside him and questioned the Harvester when he politely
suggested to Betsy that she make haste.

"Have you forgotten that mushrooms are perishable?"
he asked. "If we don't get these to the city all woodsy
and fresh we can't sell them. Wonder where we can do
the best? The hotels pay well. Really, the biggest prices
could be had by——"

Then the Harvester threw back his head and began to
laugh; he laughed, how he laughed! A crow on the fence
joined him, while a kingfisher, heading for Loon Lake, and
then Belshazzar, caught the infection.

"Begorry! The very idea!" cried the Harvester.
"'Heaven helps them that help themselves.' Now you
just watch us manœuvre for assistance, Belshazzar, old
boy! Here we go!"

Then the laugh began again. It continued all the way
to Onabasha, even into the city. The Harvester drove
through the most prosperous street until he reached the
residence district. At the first home he stopped, gave the

lines to Belshazzar, and taking a basket of mushrooms, went up the walk and rang the bell.

"All groceries should be delivered at the back door," snapped a pert maid, before he had time to say a word.

The Harvester lifted his hat.

"Will you kindly tell the lady of the house that I wish to speak with her?"

"What name, please?"

"I want to show her some fine mushrooms, freshly gathered," he answered.

How she did it the Harvester never knew. The first thing he realized was that the door had closed, while the basket had been picked deftly from his fingers and was on the other side. After a short time the maid returned.

"What do you want for them, please?"

The last thing on earth the Harvester wanted to do was to part with those mushrooms, so he took one long, speculative look down the hall then named a price he thought would be prohibitive.

"One dollar a dozen."

"How many are there?"

"I count them as I sell them. I do not know."

The door closed again. Presently it opened; the maid knelt on the floor before him and counted the mushrooms one by one into a dish pan and in a few minutes brought him seven dollars and fifty cents. The chagrined Harvester, feeling like a thief, put the money in his pocket, and turned away.

"I was to tell you," said she, "that you are to bring all

you have to sell here, but the next time please go to the kitchen door."

"Must be fond of mushrooms," said the disgruntled Harvester.

"They are a great delicacy, and we have visitors." The Harvester ached to set the girl to one side and walk through the house, but he did not dare; so he returned to the street, whistled to Betsy to come, and went to the next gate. Here he hesitated. Should he risk further snubbing at the front door or go back at once. If he did, he would see only a maid. As he stood an instant debating, the door of the house he just had left opened and the girl ran after him. "If you have more, we will take them," she called.

The Harvester gasped for breath.

"They have to be used at once," he suggested.

"She knows that. She wants to treat her friends."

"Well she has got enough for a banquet," he said. "I— I don't usually sell more than a dozen or two in one place."

"I don't see why you can't let her have them if you have more."

"Perhaps I have orders to fill for regular customers," suggested the Harvester.

"And perhaps you haven't," said the maid. "You ought to be ashamed not to let people who are willing to pay your outrageous prices have them. It's regular highway robbery."

"Possibly that's the reason I decline to hold up one party twice," said the Harvester as he entered the gate and went up the walk to the front door.

"You should be taught your place," called the maid after him.

The Harvester rang the bell. Another maid opened the door, once more he asked to speak with the lady of the house. As the girl turned, a handsome old woman in cap and morning gown came down the stairs.

"What have you there?" she asked.

The Harvester lifted the leaves to expose the musky crumpled, big mushrooms.

"Oh!" she cried in delight. "Indeed, yes! We are very fond of them. I will take the basket, and divide with my sons. You are sure you have no poisonous ones among them?"

"Very sure," said the Harvester faintly.

"How much do you want for the basket?"

"They are a dollar a dozen; I haven't counted them."

"Dear me! Isn't that rather expensive?"

"It is. Very!" said the Harvester. "So expensive that most people don't think of taking over a dozen. They are large and very rich, so they go a long way."

"I suppose you have to spend a great deal of time hunting them? It does seem expensive, but they are fresh, and the boys are so fond of them. I'm not often extravagant, I'll just take the lot. Sarah, bring a pan."

Again the Harvester stood and watched an entire basket counted over and carried away, while he felt the robber he had been called as he took the money.

At the next house he had learned a lesson. He carpeted a basket with leaves, counted out a dozen and a half into it, leaving the remainder in the wagon. Three blocks on one side of the street exhausted his store while he was showered with orders. He had not seen any one that even resembled a dark-eyed girl. As he came from the last house a big, red motor sped past, then suddenly slowed and backed beside his wagon.

"What in the name of sense are you doing?" demanded Doctor Carey.

"Invading the residence district of Onabasha," said the Harvester. "Madam, would you like some nice, fresh, country mushrooms? I guarantee that there are no poisonous ones among them, and they were gathered this morning. Considering their rarity and the difficult work of collecting, they are exceedingly low at my price. I am offering these for five dollars a dozen, madam, and for mercy sake don't take them or I'll have no excuse for going to the next house."

The doctor stared, then understood, and began to laugh. When at last he could speak he said: "David, I'll bet you started with three bushels, began at the head of this street, and they are all gone."

"Put up a good one!" said the Harvester. "You win. The first house I tried they ordered me to the back door, took a market basket full away from me by force, tried to buy the load, and I didn't see any one save a maid."

The doctor lay on the steering gear and faintly groaned. The Harvester regarded him sympathetically. "Isn't it a crime?" he questioned. "Mushrooms are no go. I can see that!——or rather they are entirely too much of a go. I never saw anything in such demand. I must seek a less popular article for my purpose. To-morrow look out for me. I shall begin where I left off to-day, but I will have changed my product."

"David, for pity sake," gasped the doctor.

"What do I care how I do it, so I locate her?"

"But you won't find her!"

"I've come as close it as you so far, anyway," said the Harvester. "Your mushrooms are on the desk in your office."

He drove slowly up and down the streets until Betsy wabbled on her legs. Then he left her to rest and walked until he wabbled; by that time it was dark, so he went home.

At the first hint of dawn he was at work the following morning. With loaded baskets closely covered, he started to Onabasha, beginning where he had quit the day before. This time he carried a small, crudely fashioned bark basket, leaf-covered, while he rang at front doors with confidence.

Every one seemed to have a maid in that part of the city, for a freshly capped and aproned girl answered.

"Are there any young women living here?" blandly inquired the Harvester.

"What's that of your business?" she demanded.

The Harvester flushed, but continued: "I am offering something especially intended for young women. If there are none, I will not trouble you."

"There are several."

"Will you please ask them if they would care for bouquets of violets, fresh from the woods?"

"How much are they, and how large are the bunches?"

"Prices differ, and they are the right size to appear well. They had better see for themselves."

The maid reached for the basket, but the Harvester drew back.

"I keep them in my possession," he said. "You may take a sample."

He lifted the leaves, drawing forth a medium-sized bunch of long-stemmed blue violets with their leaves. The flowers were fresh, crisp, and strong odours of the woods arose from them.

"Oh!" cried the maid. "Oh, how lovely!"

She hurried away with them and returned, carrying a purse. "I want two more bunches," she said. "How much are they?"

"Are the girls who want them dark or fair?"

"What difference does that make?"

"I have blue violets for blondes, yellow for brunettes, and white for the others."

"Well I never! One is fair, and two have brown hair and blue eyes."

"One blue and two whites," said the Harvester calmly, as if matching women's hair and eyes with flowers were an inherited vocation. "They are twenty cents a bunch."

"Aha!" he chortled to himself as he whistled to Betsy. "At last we have it. There are no dark-eyed girls here. Now we are making headway."

Down the street he went, with varying fortune, but with patience and persistence at every house he at last managed to learn whether there were a dark-eyed girl. There did not seem to be many. Long before his store of yellow violets was gone the last blue and white had disappeared. He calmly went on asking for dark-eyed girls, and explaining that all the blue and white were taken, because fair women were most numerous.

At one house the owner, who reminded the Harvester of his mother, came to the door. He uncovered and in his suavest tones inquired if a brunette young woman lived there and if she would like a nosegay of yellow violets.

"Well bless my soul!" cried she. "What is this world coming to? Do you mean to tell me that there are now able-bodied men offering at our doors, flowers to match our girls' complexions?"

"Yes madam," said the Harvester gravely, "and also selling them as fast as he can show them, at prices that make a profit very well worth while. I had an equal number of blue and white, but dark girls are very much in the minority. The others were gone long ago, so I now have flowers to offer brunettes only."

"Well forever more! And you don't call that fiddlin' business for a big, healthy, young man?"

The Harvester's gay laugh was infectious. "I do not," he said. "I have to start as soon as I can see, tramp long distances in wet woods and gather the violets on my knees, make them into bunches, and bring them here in water to keep them fresh. I have another occupation. I only kill time on these, but I would be ashamed to tell you what I have got from them this morning."

"Humph! I'm glad to hear it!" said the woman. "Shame in some form is a sign of grace. I have no use for a human being without a generous supply of it. There is a very beautiful dark-eyed girl in the house; I will take two bunches for her. How much are they?"

"I have only three remaining," said the Harvester. "Would you like to allow her to make her own selection?"

"When I'm giving things I usually take my choice. I want that, and that one."

"As my stock is so nearly out, I'll make the two for twenty," said the Harvester. "Won't you accept the last one from me, because you remind me of my mother?"

"I will indeed," said she. "Thank you very much! I shall love to have them as dearly as any of the girls. I used to gather them when I was a child, but I almost never see the blue ones any more, while I don't know as I ever expected to see a yellow violet again so long as I live. Where did you get them?"

"In my woods," said the Harvester. "You see I grow several members of the *Viola pedata* family, bird's foot, snake, and wood violet, and three of the *odorata*, English, marsh, and sweet, for our big drug houses. They use the flowers in making delicate tests for acids and alkalies. The entire plant, flower, seed, leaf, and root, goes into different remedies. The beds seed themselves and spread, so when I have more than I need for the chemists, I sell a few. I don't use the white and yellow in my business; I grow them for their beauty. I also sell my surplus lilies of the valley. Would you like to order some of them for your house or more violets for to-morrow?"

"Well bless my soul! Do you mean to tell me that lilies of the valley are medicine?"

The Harvester laughed. "I grow immense beds of

them in the woods on the banks of Loon Lake," he said. "They are the *convallaris majallis* of the drug houses. I scarcely know what the weak-hearted people would do without them. I use large quantities in trade, and this season I am selling a few because people so love them."

"Lilies in medicine; well dear me! Are roses good for our innards too?"

Then the Harvester did laugh.

"I imagine the roses you know go into perfumes mostly," he answered. "They do make medicine of Canadian rock rose and rose bay, laurel, and willow. I grow the bushes, but they are not what you would consider roses."

"I wonder now," said the woman, studying the Harvester closely, "if you are not that queer genius I've heard of, who spends his time hunting and growing stuff in the woods so people call him the Medicine Man."

"I strongly suspect madam, I am that man," said the Harvester.

"Well bless me!" cried she. "I've always wanted to see you and here when I do, you look just like anybody else. I thought you'd have long hair, and be wild-eyed and ferocious. And your talk sounds like out of a book. Well that beats me!"

"Me too!" said the Harvester, lifting his hat. "You don't want any lilies to-morrow, then?"

"Yes I do. Medicine or no medicine, I've always liked 'em, so I'm going to keep on liking them. If you can bring me a good-sized bunch after the weak-kneed——"

"Weak-hearted," corrected the Harvester.

"Well 'weak-hearted,' then; it's all the same thing. If you've got any left, as I was saying, you can fetch them to me for the smell."

The Harvester laughed all the way down town. There he went to Doctor Carey's office, examined a directory, and took the names of all the numbers where he had sold yellow violets. A few questions when the doctor came in settled all of them, but the flower scheme was better. Because the yellow was not so plentiful as the white and blue, next day he added buttercups and cowslips to his store for the dark girls. When he had rifled his beds for the last time, after three weeks of almost daily trips to town, and had paid high prices to small boys he set searching the adjoining woods until no more flowers could be found, he drove from the outskirts of the city one day toward the hospital. As he stopped, down the street came Doctor Carey frantically waving to him. As the big car slackened, "Come on David, quick! I've seen her!" cried the doctor.

The Harvester jumped from the wagon, threw the lines to Belshazzar, and landed in the panting car.

"For Heaven's sake where? Are you sure?"

The car went speeding down the street. A policeman beckoned and cried after it.

"It won't do any good to get arrested, Doc," cautioned the Harvester.

"Now right along here," said Doctor Carey. "Watch both sides sharply. If I stop you jump out, and tell the blame policemen to get at their job. The party they are hired to find is right under their noses."

The Harvester began to perspire. "Doc, don't you think you should tell me? Maybe she is in some store. Maybe I could do better on foot."

"Shut up!" growled the doctor. "I am doing the best I know."

He hurried up the street for blocks then back again, and at last stopped before a large store and went in. When he returned he drove to the hospital and together they entered the office. There he turned to the Harvester.

"It isn't so hard to understand you now, my boy," he said. "Shades of Diana, but she'll be a beauty when she has a little more flesh and colour. She came out of Whitlaw's and walked right to the crossing. I almost could have touched her, but I didn't notice. Two girls passed before me, and in hurrying, a tall, dark one knocked off one of your bunches of yellow violets. She glanced at it and laughed, but let it lay. Then your girl hesitated, stooped and picked it up. The crazy policeman yelled at me to clear the crossing so it didn't hit me for half a block how tall and white she was and how dark her eyes were. I was just thinking about her picking up the flowers, and that it was queer for her to do it, when like a brick it hit me, *that's David's girl!* I tried to turn around, but you know what Main Street is in the middle of the day. And those idiots of policemen! They ordered me on, I couldn't turn for a street car coming, so I called to one of them that the girl we wanted was down the street. He looked at me like an addlepate and said: 'What girl? Move on or you'll get in a jam here.' You can use me for a football if I

don't go back and smash him.   Paid him five dollars myself less than two weeks ago to keep his eyes open.   '*To
keep his eyes open!*'" panted the doctor, shaking his fist at
David.   "Yes sir!   'To keep his eyes open!'   And he
motioned for things to come along; so I lost her too."

"I think we had better go back to the street," said the
Harvester.

"Oh, I'd been back and forth along that street for nearly
an hour before I gave up and came here to see if I could
find you, and we've hunted it an hour more!   What's the
use?   She's gone for this time, but by gum, I saw her!
And she was worth seeing!"

"Did she appear ill to you?"

The doctor dropped on a chair and threw out his hands
hopelessly.

"This was awful sudden, David," he said.   "I was
going along as I told you, and I noticed her stop and
thought she had a good head to wait a second instead of
running in before me, then there came those two girls right
under the car from the other side.   I only had a glimpse of
her as she stooped for the flowers.   I saw a big braid of
hair, but I was half a block away before I got it all con-
nected, and then came the crush in the street, so I was
blocked."

The doctor broke down, wiped his face and expressed his
feelings unrestrainedly.

"Don't!" said the Harvester patiently.   "It's no use to
feel so badly, Doc.   I know what you would give to have
found her for me.   I know you did all you could.   I let her
escape me.   We will find her yet.   It's glorious news that

she's in the city.   It gives me heart to hear that.   Can't you just remember if she seemed ill?"

The doctor meditated.

"She wasn't the tallest girl I ever saw," he said slowly, "but she was the tallest girl to be pretty.   She had on a white waist, a gray skirt and black hat.   Her eyes and hair were like you said, and she was plain, white faced, with a hue that might possibly be natural, and it might be confinement in bad light and air and poor food.   She didn't seem sick, but she isn't well.   There is something the matter with her, but it's not immediate or dangerous. She appeared like a flower that had got a little moisture and sprouted in a cellar."

"You saw her all right!" said the Harvester, "and I think your diagnosis is correct too.   That's the way she seemed to me.   I've thought she needed sun and air.   I told the South Wind so the other day."

"Why you blame fool!" cried the doctor.   "Is this thing going to your head?   Say, I forgot!   There is something else.   I traced her in the store.   She was at the embroidery counter and she bought some silk.   If she ever comes again the clerk is going to hold her and telephone me or get her address if she has to steal it.   Oh, we are getting there!   We will have her pretty soon now. You ought to feel better just to know that she is in town and that I've seen her."

"I do!" said the Harvester.   "Indeed I do!"

"It can't be much longer," said the doctor.   "She's got to be located soon.   But those policemen!   I wouldn't give a nickel for the lot!   I'll bet she's walked over them

for two weeks. If I were you I'd discharge the bunch.
They'd be peacefully asleep if she passed them. If they'd
let me alone, I'd have had her. I could have turned
around easily. I've been in dozens of closer places."

"Don't worry! This can't last much longer. She's of
and in the city or she wouldn't have picked up the flowers.
Doc, are you sure they were mine?"

"Yes. Half the girls have been tricked out in yours the
past two weeks. I can spot them as far as I can see."

"Dear Lord, that's getting close!" said the Harvester
intensely. "Seems as if the violets would tell her."

"Now cut out flowers talking and the South Wind!"
ordered the doctor. "This is business. The violets
prove something all right, though. If she were in the
country, she could gather plenty herself. She is working
at sewing in some room in town, either over a store or in a
house. If she hadn't been starved for flowers she never
would have stopped for them on the street. I could see
just a flash of hesitation, but she wanted them too much.
David, one bouquet will go in water and be cared for a
week. Man, it's getting close! This does seem like a
link."

"Since you say it, possibly I dare agree with you," said
the Harvester.

"How near are you through with that canvass of yours?"

"About three-fourths."

"Well I'd go on with it. After all we have got to find
her ourselves. Those senile policemen!"

"I am going on with it; you needn't worry about that.
But I've got to change to other flowers. I've stripped the

violet beds. There's quite a crop of berries coming, but they are not ripe yet, and a tragedy to pick. The pond lilies are just beginning to open by the thousand. The lake border is blue with sweet-flag that is lovely and the marsh pale gold with cowslips. The ferns are prime and the woods solid sheets of every colour of bloom. I believe I'll go ahead with the wild flowers."

"I would too! David, you do feel better, don't you?"

"I certainly do. Surely it won't be long now!"

The Harvester was so hopeful that he whistled and sang on the return to Medicine Woods, and that night for the first time in many days he sat long over a candlestick, and took a farewell peep into her room before he went to bed.

The next day he worked with all his might harvesting the last remnants of early spring herbs, in the dry-room and storehouse, and on furniture and candlesticks.

Then he went back to flower gathering and every day offered bunches of exquisite wood and field flowers and white and gold water lilies from door to door.

Three weeks later the Harvester, perceptibly thin, pale, and worried entered the office. He sank into a chair and groaned wearily.

"Isn't this the bitterest luck!" he cried. "I've finished the town. I've almost walked off my legs. I've sold flowers by the million, but I've not had a sight of her."

"It's been almost a tragedy with me," said the doctor gloomily. "I've killed two dogs and grazed a baby, because I was watching the sidewalks instead of the street. What are you going to do now?"

"I am going home and bring up the work to the July

mark. I am going to take it easy and rest a few days so I can think more clearly. I don't know what I'll try next. I've punched up the depot and the policemen again. When I get something new thought out I'll let you know."

Then he began emptying his pockets of money and heaping it on the table, small coins, bills, big and little.

"What on earth is that?"

"That," said the Harvester, giving the heap a shove of contempt, "that is the price of my pride and humiliation. That is what it cost people who allowed me to cheek my way into their homes and rob them, as one maid said, for my own purposes. Doc, where on earth does all the money come from? In almost every house I entered, women had it to waste, in many cases to throw away. I never saw so much paid for nothing in all my life. That whole heap is from mushrooms and flowers."

"What are you piling it there for?"

"For your free ward. I don't want a penny of it. I wouldn't keep it, not if I were starving."

"Why David! You couldn't compel any one to buy. You offered something they wanted, and they paid you what you asked."

"Yes, and to keep them from buying, and to make the stuff go farther, I named prices to shame a shark. When I think of that mushroom deal I can feel my face burn. I've made the search I wanted to, and I am satisfied that I can't find her that way. I have kept up my work at home between times. I am not out anything but my time, and it isn't fair to plunder the city to pay that. Take the cussed money and put it where I'll never see or hear of it. When I wash my hands after touching it for the last time maybe I'll feel better."

"You are a fanatic!"

"If getting rid of that is being a fanatic, I am proud of the title. You can't imagine what I've been through!"

"Can't I though?" laughed the doctor. "In work of that kind you get into every variety of place; and some of it is new to you. Never mind! No one can contaminate you. It is the law that only a man can degrade himself. Knowing things will not harm you. Doing them is a different matter. What you know will be a protection. What you do ruins——if it is wrong. You are not harmed, you are only disgusted. Think it over, and in a few days come back and get your money."

"If you ever speak of it again or force it on me I'll take it home and throw it into the lake."

He went after Betsy, then slowly drove to Medicine Woods. Belshazzar, on the seat beside him, recognized a silent, disappointed master and whimpered as he rubbed the Harvester's shoulder to attract his attention.

"This is tough luck, old boy," said the Harvester. "I had such hopes and I worked so hard. I suffered in the flesh for every hour of it, and I failed. Oh but I hate the word! If I knew where she is right now, Bel, I'd give anything I've got. But there's no use to wail and get sorry for myself. That's against the law of common decency. I'll take a swim, sleep it off, straighten up the herbs a little, then go at it again, old fellow; that's a man's way. She's somewhere, so she's got to be found, no matter what it costs."

CHAPTER VIII

BELSHAZZAR'S RECORD POINT

THE Harvester set the neglected cabin in order; then he carefully and deftly packed all his dried herbs, barks, and roots. Next came carrying the couch grass, wild alum, and soapwort into the storeroom. Then followed July herbs. He first went to his beds of foxglove, because the tender leaves of the second year should be stripped from them at flowering time, which usually began two weeks earlier; but his bed lay in a shaded, damp location so the tall bloom stalks were only in half flower, their pale lavender making an exquisite picture. It paid to collect those leaves, so the Harvester hastily stripped the amount he wanted.

Yarrow was beginning to bloom. He gathered as much as he required, taking the whole plant. Catnip tops and leaves were also ready. As it grew in the open in dry soil in beds which had been weeded that spring, he could gather armloads of it with a sickle, but he had to watch the swarming bees. He left the male fern and mullein until the last for different reasons.

On the damp, cool, rocky hillside, beneath deep shade of big forest trees, grew the ferns, their long, graceful fronds waving softly. Tree toads sang on the cool rocks beneath them, chewinks nested under gnarled roots among them, rose-breasted grosbeaks sang in grape-vines clambering over the thickets, and Singing Water ran close beside. So the Harvester left digging these roots until nearly the last, because he so disliked to disturb the bed. He could not have done it if he had not been forced. All of the demand for his fern never could be supplied. Of his products none was more important to the Harvester because this formed the basis of one of the oldest and most reliable remedies for little children. The fern had to be gathered with especial care, deteriorated quickly, and no staple was more subject to adulteration.

So he kept his bed intact, lifted the roots at the proper time, carefully cleaned without washing, rapidly dried in currents of hot air, and shipped them in bottles to the trade. He charged and received fifteen cents a pound, where careless and indifferent workers were paid ten.

On the banks of Singing Water, at the head of the fern bed, the Harvester stood under a gray beech tree and looked down the swaying length of delicate green. He was lean and rapidly bronzing, for he seldom remembered a head covering because he loved the sweep of the wind through his hair.

"I hate to touch you," he said. "How I wish she could see you before I begin. If she did, probably she would say it was a sin, and then I never could muster courage to do it at all. I'd give a small farm to know if those violets revived for her. I was crazy to ask Doc if they were wilted, but I hated to. If they were from the ones I gathered that morning they should have been all right."

A tree toad dared him to come on; a chipmunk grew

saucy as the Harvester bent to an unloved task. If he stripped the bed as closely as he dared not to injure it, he could not fill half his orders; so, deftly and with swift, skilful fingers and an earnest face, he worked. Belshazzar came down the hill on a rush, nose to earth, and began hunting among the plants. He never could understand why his loved master was so careless as to go to work before he had pronounced it safe. When the fern bed was finished, the Harvester took time to make a trip to town, but there was no word waiting him; so he went to the mullein. It lay on a sunny hillside beyond the couch grass and joined a few small fields, the only cleared land of the six hundred acres of Medicine Woods. Over rocks and little hills and hollows spread the pale, grayish-yellow of the green leaves, while from five to seven feet arose the flower stems, the entire earth between being covered with rosettes of young plants. Belshazzar went before to give warning if any big rattlers curled in the sun on the hillside, and after him followed the Harvester cutting leaves in heaps. That was warm work, so he covered his head with a floppy old straw hat, with wet grass in the crown; stopping occasionally to rest.

He loved that yellow-faced hillside. Because so much of his reaping lay in the shade and usually his feet sank in dead leaves and damp earth, the change was a rest. He cheerfully stubbed his toes on rocks, and endured the heat without a complaint. It appeared to him as if a member of every species of butterfly he knew wavered down the hillside. There were golden-brown danais, with their black-striped wings, jetty troilus with an attempt at trailers, big asterias, velvety black with longer trails and wide bands of yellow dots. *Coenia* were most numerous of all and to the Harvester wonderfully attractive in rich, subdued colours with a wealth of markings and eye spots. Many small moths, with transparent wings and noses red as blood, flashed past him hunting pollen. Goldfinches, intent on thistle bloom, wavered through the air trailing mellow, happy notes behind them, while often a humming-bird visited the mullein. On the lake wild life splashed and chattered incessantly; sometimes the Harvester paused, standing with arms heaped with leaves, to interpret some unusually appealing note of pain or anger or some very attractive melody. The red-wings were swarming, the killdeers busy. He thought of the Dream Girl and smiled. "I wonder if she would like this," he mused.

When the mullein leaves were deep on the trays of the dry-house he began on the bloom, but that was a task he loved: to lay off the beds in swaths and follow them, deftly picking the stamens and yellow petals from the blooms. These he would dry speedily in hot air, bottle, and send at once to big laboratories. The listed price was seventy-five cents a pound, but the beautiful golden bottles of the Harvester always brought more. The work was worth while; he liked the location and gathering of this particular crop: for these reasons he always left it until the last, then revelled in the gold of sunshine, bird, butterfly, and flower. Several days were required to harvest the mullein, during the time the man worked with nimble fingers, while his brain was intensely occupied with the question of what to do next in his search for the Girl.

When the work was finished, he went to the deep wood to examine acres of thrifty ginseng. He was satisfied as he surveyed the big bed. Long years he had laboured diligently; soon came the reward. He had not realized it before, but as he studied the situation he saw that he either must begin this harvest at once or employ help. If he waited until September he could not gather one-third of the crop alone.

"But the roots will weigh less if I take them now," he argued, "and I can work at nothing in comfort until I have located her. I will go on with my search and allow the ginseng to grow that much heavier. What a picture! It is folly to disturb this now, for I will lose the seed of every plant I dig, and that is worth almost as much as the root. It is a question whether I want to furnish the market with seed, and so raise competition for my bed. I think, be jabbers, that I'll wait for this harvest until the seed is ripe, and then bury part of a head where I dig a root, as the Indians did. That's the idea! The more I grow, the more money; and I may need considerable for her. One thing I'd like to know: Are these plants cultivated? All the books quote the wild at highest rates and all I've ever sold was wild. The start grew here naturally. What I added from the surrounding country was wild, but through and among it I've sown seed I bought, and I've tended it with every care. But this is deep wood and wild conditions. I think I have a perfect right to so label it. I'll ask Doc. And another thing——I'll go through the woods west of Onabasha where I used to find ginseng, and see if I can get a little and then take the same amount of

plants grown here, and make a test.   That way I can discover any difference before I go to market.   This is my
gold mine, and that point is mighty important to me, so I'll
go this very day.   I used to find it in the woods northeast
of town on the land Jameson bought, west.   Wonder if he
lives there yet.   He should have died of pure meanness
long ago.   I'll drive to the river and hunt along the bank."

Early the following morning the Harvester went to
Onabasha, stopping at the hospital for news.   Finding
none, he went through town and several miles into the
country on the other side, to a piece of lowland lying
along the river bank, where he once had found ginseng
and carried home enough to reset a big bed.   If he could
get only half a pound of roots from there now, they would
serve his purpose.   He went down the bank, Belshazzar
at his heels, and at last found the place.   Many trees had
been cut, but there remained enough for shade; the
fields bore the ragged, unattractive appearance of old.
The Harvester smiled grimly as he remembered that the
man who lived there once had charged him for damage he
might do to trees in driving across his woods, then boasted
to his neighbours that a young fool was paying for the
privilege of doing his grubbing.   If Jameson had known
what the roots he was so anxious to dispose of brought a
pound on the market at that time, he would have been insane with anger.   So the Harvester's eyes were dancing
with fun, a wry grin twisted his lips as he clambered over
the banks of the recently dredged river, standing an instant to look at its pitiful condition and straight, muddy
flow.

"Appears to match the remainder of the Jameson property," he said. "I don't know who he is or where he came from, but he's no farmer. Perhaps he uses this land to corral the stock he buys until he can sell it again."

He went down the embankment, beginning to search for the location where he formerly had found the ginseng. When he came to the place he stood amazed, for from seed, roots, and plants he had missed, the growth had sprung up and spread, so that at a rapid estimate the Harvester thought it contained at least five pounds, allowing for shrinkage on account of being gathered early. He hesitated, thinking of coming later; but the drive was long and the loss would not amount to enough to pay for a second trip. About taking it, he never thought at all. He once had permission from the owner to dig the shrubs, bushes, and weeds he desired from that stretch of woods; he had paid for possible damages that might occur. As he bent to the task there did come a fleeting thought that the patch was weedless and in unusual shape for wild stuff. Then, with swift strokes of his light mattock, he lifted the roots, crammed them into his sack, whistled to Belshazzar, and going back to the wagon, drove away. Reaching home he washed the ginseng, and spread it on a tray to dry. The first time he wanted the mattock he realized that he had left it lying where he had worked. It was an implement that he had directed a blacksmith to fashion to meet his requirements. No store contained anything half so useful to him. He had worked with it for years and it suited him, so there was nothing to do but go back. Betsy was too tired to return that day, so he planned to dig his ginseng with something else, finish his work the following morning, and get the mattock in the afternoon.

"It's like a knife you've carried for years, or a gun," muttered the Harvester. "I actually don't know how to work without it. What made me so careless I can't imagine. I never before in my life did a trick like that. Now Betsy and half a day of wasted time must pay for my carelessness. Since I must go, I'll look a little farther. Maybe there is more. Those woods used to be full of it."

According to this programme, the following afternoon the Harvester again walked down the embankment of the mourning river, then through the ragged woods to the place where the ginseng had been. He went forward, stepping lightly, as men of his race had walked the forest for ages, swerving to avoid boughs; looking straight ahead. Contrary to his usual custom of coming to heel in a strange wood, Belshazzar suddenly darted around the man, taking the path they had followed the previous day. The animal was performing his office in life; he had heard or scented something unusual. The Harvester knew what that meant. He looked inquiringly at the dog, glanced around, then at the earth. Belshazzar proceeded noiselessly at a rapid pace over the leaves. Suddenly the master saw the dog stop in a stiff point. Lifting his feet lightly and straining his eyes before him, the Harvester passed a spice thicket, then came in line.

For one second he stood as rigid as Belshazzar. The next his right arm shot upward full length, beginning to describe circles, his open palm heavenward; while into his face leapt a glorified expression of exultation.   Face down in the rifled ginseng bed lay a sobbing girl.   Her frame was long and slender, a thick coil of dark hair bound her head. A second more the Harvester bent to gently pat Belshazzar's head.   The beast broke point, looking up.   The man caught the dog's chin in a caressing grip, again touched his head, moved soundless lips, then waved toward the prostrate figure.   The dog hesitated.   The Harvester made the same motions.   Belshazzar softly stepped over the leaves, passed around the feet of the girl, pausing beside her, nose to earth, softly sniffing.

In one moment she came swiftly to a sitting posture.

"Oh!" she cried in a spasm of fright.

Belshazzar reached an investigating nose, wagging an eager tail.

"Why you are a nice friendly dog!" said the trembling voice.

He immediately verified the assertion by offering his nose for a caress.   The girl timidly laid a hand on his head.

"Heaven knows I'm lonely enough to kiss a dog," she said, "but suppose you belong to the man who stole my ginseng, and then ran away so fast he forgot his——his piece he digged with."

Belshazzar pressed closer.

"I am just killed, so I don't care whose dog you are," sobbed the girl.

She threw her arms around Belshazzar's neck, laying her white face against his satiny shoulder.   The Harvester could endure no more.   He took a step forward, his face convulsed with pain.

"Please don't!" he begged. "I took your ginseng. I'll bring it back to-morrow. There wasn't more than twenty-five or thirty dollars' worth. It doesn't amount to one tear."

The girl arose so quickly, the Harvester could not see how she did it. With a startled fright on her face, her dark eyes swimming, she turned to him in one long look. Words rolled from the lips of the man in a jumble. Behind the tears there was a dull, expressionless blue in the girl's eyes while her face was so white that it appeared blank. He began talking before she could speak, in an effort to secure forgiveness without condemnation.

"You see, I grow it for a living on land I own, so I've always gathered all there was in the country and no one cared. There never was enough in one place to pay; no other man wanted to spend the time, and so I've always felt free to take it. Every one knew I did, no one ever objected before. Once I paid Henry Jameson for the privilege of cleaning it from these woods. That was six or seven years ago, but it didn't occur to me that I wasn't at liberty to dig what has grown since. I'll bring it back at once, and pay you for the shrinkage from gathering it too early. There won't be much over six pounds when it's dry. Please, please don't feel badly. Won't you trust me to return it, and make good the damage I've done?"

The face of the Harvester was eager, his tones appealing, as he leaned forward trying to make her understand.

"Certainly!" said the Girl as she bent to pat the dog, while she dried her eyes under cover of the movement. "Certainly! It can make no difference!"

But as the Harvester drew a deep breath of relief, she suddenly straightened to full height and looked at him.

"Oh, what is the use to tell a pitiful lie!" she cried. "It does make a difference! It makes all the difference in the world! I need that money! I need it unspeakably. I owe a debt I must pay. What——what did I understand you to say ginseng is worth?"

"If you will take a few steps," said the Harvester, "and make yourself comfortable on this log in the shade, I will tell you all I know about it."

The girl walked swiftly to the log indicated, seated herself, and waited. The Harvester followed to a respectful distance.

"I can't tell to an ounce what wet roots would weigh," he said as easily as he could command his voice to speak, with the heart in him beating wildly, "and of course they lose in drying; but I've handled enough that I know the weight I carried home will come to six pounds at the very least. Then you must figure on some loss, because I dug this before it really was ready. It does not reach full growth until September, so if it is taken too soon there is a decrease in weight. I will make that up to you when I return it."

The troubled eyes were gazing on his face intently, and the Harvester studied them as he talked.

"You would think, then, there would be all of six pounds?"

"Yes," said the Harvester, "closer eight. When I replace the shrinkage there is bound to be over seven."

"And how much did I understand you to say it brought a pound?"

"That all depends," answered he. "If you cure it yourself, and dry it too much, you lose in weight. If you carry it in a small lot to the druggists of Onabasha, probably you will not get over five dollars for it."

"Five?" It was a startled cry.

"How much did you expect?" asked the Harvester gently.

"Uncle Henry said he thought he could get fifty cents a pound for all I could find."

"If your Uncle Henry has learned at last that ginseng is a salable article he should know something about the price also. Will you tell me what he said, and how you came to think of gathering roots for the market?"

"There were men talking beneath the trees one Sunday afternoon about old times and hunting deer, then they spoke of people who made money long ago gathering roots and barks, and they mentioned one man who lived by it yet."

"Was his name Langston?"

"Yes, I remember because I liked the name. I was so eager to earn something, and I can't leave here just now because Aunt Molly is very ill, so the thought came that possibly I could gather stuff worth money, after my work was finished. I went out and asked questions. They said nothing brought enough to make it pay any one, except this ginseng plant, and the Langston man almost had stripped the country. Then uncle said he used to get stuff here, so he might have got some of that. I asked what it was like, so they told me and I hunted until I found that.   It seemed a quantity to me.   Of course I didn't know it had to be dried.   Uncle took a root I dug to a store, where they told him that it wasn't much used any more, but they would give him fifty cents a pound for it. What *makes* you think you can get five dollars?"

"With your permission," said the Harvester.

He seated himself on the log, drew from his pocket an old pamphlet, spread it before her, then ran a pencil along the line of a list of schedule prices for common drug roots and herbs.   Because he understood, his eyes were very bright; his voice a trifle crisp.   A latent anger springing in his breast was a good curb for his emotions.   He was closely acquainted with all of the druggists of Onabasha; he knew that not one of them had offered less than standard prices for ginseng.

"The reason I think so," he said gently, "is because growing it is the largest part of my occupation, while it was a staple with my father before me.   I am David Langston, of whom you heard those men speak.   Since I was a very small boy I have lived by collecting herbs and roots, and I realize more for ginseng than anything else.   Very early I tired of hunting other people's woods for herbs, so I began transplanting them to my own.   I moved that bed out here seven years ago.   What you found has grown since from roots I overlooked or seeds that fell at that time. Now do you think I am enough of an authority to trust my word on the subject?"

There was no change of expression on her white face.

"You surely should know," she said wearily, "and you

could have no possible object in deceiving me.   Please go on."

"Any country boy or girl can find ginseng, gather, wash, and dry it, and sell for five dollars a pound.   I can return yours to-morrow, you can cure and take it to a druggist I will name you, who will pay that.   But if you will allow me to make a suggestion, you can get more.   Your roots are now on the trays of an evaporating house.   They will dry to the proper degree desired by the trade, so that they will not lose an extra ounce in weight; while if I send them with my stuff to big wholesale houses I deal with, they will be graded with the finest wild ginseng.   It is worth more than the cultivated so you will be paid closer eight dollars a pound for it than five.   There is some speculation in it, and the market fluctuates: but as a rule, I sell for the highest price the drug brings, while at times when the season is very dry, I set my own prices.   Shall I return yours or may I cure and sell it, bringing you the money?"

"How much trouble would that make you?"

"None.   The work of digging and washing is already finished.   All that remains is to weigh it and make a memorandum of the amount when I sell.   I should very much like to do it.   It would be a comfort to see the money go into your hands.   If you are afraid to trust me, I will give you the names of several people you can ask concerning me the next time you go to the city."

She looked at him steadily.

"Never mind that," she said.   "But why do you offer to do it for a stranger?   It must be some trouble, no matter how small you represent it to be."

"Maybe I am going to pay you eight and sell for ten."

"I don't think you can. Five sounds fabulous to me. I can't believe that. If you wanted to make money you needn't have told me you took it. I never would have known. That isn't your reason!"

"Possibly I would like to atone for those tears I caused," said the Harvester.

"Don't think of that! They are of no consequence to any one."

"Don't search for a reason," said the Harvester, in his gentlest tones. "Forget that feature of the case. Say I'm peculiar, and allow me to do it because it would be a pleasure. In close two weeks I will bring you the money. Is it a bargain?"

"Yes, if you care to make it."

"I care very much. We will call that settled."

"I wish I could tell you what it will mean to me," said the Girl.

"If you only would," plead the Harvester.

"I must not burden a stranger with my troubles."

"But if it would make the stranger so happy!"

"That isn't possible. I must face life and bear what it brings me alone."

"Not unless you choose," said the Harvester. "That is, if you will pardon me, a narrow view of life. It cuts other people out of the joy of service. If you can't tell me, would you trust a very lovely and gentle woman I could bring to you?"

"No more than you. It is my affair; I must work it out myself."

"I am very sorry," said the Harvester.   "I believe you
err in that decision.   Think it over a day or so, and see if
two heads are not better than one.   You will realize when
this ginseng matter is settled that you profited by trusting
me.   The same will hold good along other lines, if you
only can bring yourself to think so.   At any rate, try.
Telling a trouble makes it lighter.   Sympathy should help,
if nothing can be done.   And as for money, I can show you
how to carn sums at least worth your time, if you have
nothing else you want to do."

The Girl bent toward him.

"Oh please do tell me!" she cried eagerly.   "I've tried
and tried to find some way ever since I have been here,
but every one else I have met says I can't; nothing seems
to be worth anything.   If you only would tell me something I could do!"

"If you will excuse my saying so," said the Harvester,
"it appeals to me that ease, not work, is the thing you require.   You appear extremely worn.   Won't you let me
help you find a way to a long rest first?"

"Impossible!" cried the Girl.   "I know I am white and
appear ill, but truly I never have been sick in all my life.   I
have been having trouble and working too much, but I'll be
better soon.   Believe me, there is no rest for me now.   I
must earn the money I owe first."

"There is a way, if you care to take it," said the Harvester.   "In my work I have become very well acquainted
with the chief surgeon of the city hospital.   Through him
I happen to know that he has a free bed in a beautiful
room, where you could rest until you are perfectly strong

again, and that room is empty just now. When you are well, I will tell you about the work."

As she arose the Harvester stood, then tall and straight she faced him.

"Impossible!" she said. "It would be brutal to leave my aunt. I cannot pay to rest in a hospital ward, and I will not accept charity. If you can put me in the way of earning, even a few cents a day, at anything I could do outside the work necessary to earn my board here, it would bring me closer to happiness than anything else on earth."

"What I suggest is not impossible," said the Harvester earnestly. "If you will go, inside an hour a sweet and gentle lady will come for you and take you to ease and perfect rest until you are strong again. I will see that your aunt is cared for scrupulously. I can't help urging you. It is a crime to talk of work to a woman so manifestly worn as you are."

"Then we shall not speak of it," said the Girl wearily. "It is time for me to go, anyway. I see you mean to be very kind, and while I don't in the least understand it, I do hope you feel I am grateful. If half you say about the ginseng comes true, I can make a payment worth while before I had hoped to. I have no words to tell you what that will mean to me."

"If this debt you speak of were paid, could you rest then?"

"I could lie down and give up in peace, and I think I would."

"I think you wouldn't," said the Harvester, "because you wouldn't be allowed. There are people in these days

who make a business of securing rest for the tired and over
weary.   They would come and prevent that if you tried it.
Please let me make another suggestion.   If you owe money
to some one you feel needs it and the debt is preying on
you, let's pay it."

He drew a small check-book from his pocket, slipping a
pen from a band.

"If you will name the amount and give me the address,
you shall be free to go to the rest I ask for you inside an
hour."

Then slowly from head to foot she looked at him.

"Why?"

"Because your face and attitude clearly indicate that
you are over tired.   Believe me, you do yourself wrong if
you refuse."

"In what way would changing creditors rest me?"

"I thought perhaps you were owing some one who
needed the money.   I am not a rich man, but I have no
one save myself to provide for and I have funds lying
idle that I would be glad to use for you.   If you make a
point of it, when you are rested, you can repay me."

"My creditor needs the money, but I should prefer owing him rather than a perfect stranger.   What you suggest would help me——not at all.   I must go now."

"Very well," said the Harvester.   "If you will tell me
whom to ask for and where you live, I will come to see you
to-morrow and bring you some pamphlets.   With these
and with a little help you soon can earn any amount a girl
is likely to owe.   It will require but a little while.   Where
can I find you?"

The Girl hesitated, for the first time a hint of colour flushed her cheek. But courage appeared to be her strong point.

"Do you live in this part of the country?" she asked.

"I live ten miles from here, east of Onabasha."

"Do you know Henry Jameson?"

"By sight and by reputation."

"Did you ever know anything kind or humane of him?"

"I never did."

"My name is Ruth Jameson. At present I am indebted to him for the only shelter I have. His wife is ill through overwork and worry. I am paying for my bed and what I don't eat, principally, by attempting her work. It scarcely would be fair to Uncle Henry to say that I do it. I stagger around as long as I can stand, then I sit through his abuse. He is a pleasant man. Please don't think I am telling you this to harrow your sympathy further. The reason I explain is because I am driven. If I do not, you will misjudge me when I say that I only can see you here. I understand what you meant when you said Uncle Henry should have known the price of ginseng if he knew it was for sale. He did. He knew what he could get for it, and what he meant to pay me. That is one of his original methods with a woman. If he thought I could earn anything worth while, he would allow me, if I killed myself doing it; and then he would take the money by force if necessary. So I can meet you here only. I can earn just what I may in secret. He buys cattle and horses so he is away from home much of the day; when Aunt Molly is comfortable I can have a few hours."

"I understand," said the Harvester. "But this is an added hardship. Why do you remain? Why subject yourself to force and work too heavy for you?"

"Because his is the only roof on earth where I feel I can pay for all I get. I don't care to discuss it, I only want you to say you understand, if I ask you to bring the pamphlets here and tell me how I can earn money."

"I do," said the Harvester earnestly, although his heart was hot in protest. "You may be very sure that I shall not misjudge you. May I come at two o'clock to-morrow, Miss Jameson?"

"If you will be so kind."

The Harvester stepped aside, she passed him and crossing the rifled ginseng patch went toward a low brown farmhouse lying in an unkept garden, beside a ragged highway. The man sat on the log she had vacated, held his head between his hands, trying to think, but he could not for big waves of joy that swept over him when he realized that at last he had found her, had spoken with her, had arranged a meeting for the morrow.

"Belshazzar," he said softly, "I wish I could leave you to protect her. Every day you prove to me that I need you, but Heaven knows her necessity is greater. Bel, she makes my heart ache until it feels like jelly. There seems to be only one thing to do. Get that fool debt paid like lightning, then lift her out of here quicker than that. Now, we will go see Doc, and call off the watch-dogs of the law. Ahead of them, aren't we, Belshazzar? There is a better day coming; we feel it in our bones, don't we, old partner?"

The Harvester started through the woods on a rush, and as the exercise warmed his heart, he grew wonderfully glad. He was so jubilant that he felt like crying aloud, shouting for joy, but by and by the years of sober repression made their weight felt, so he climbed into the wagon and politely requested Betsy to make her best time to Onabasha. Betsy had been asked to make haste so frequently of late that she at first almost doubted the sanity of her master, the law of whose life, until recently, had been to take his time. Now he appeared to be in haste every day. She had become so accustomed to being urged to hurry that she almost had developed a gait; so at the Harvester's suggestion she did her level best to Onabasha and the hospital, where she loved to rest near the watering tap under a big tree.

The Harvester went into the office on the run, while his face appeared like a materialized embodiment of living joy. Doctor Carey turned at his approach, then bounded halfway across the room, his hands outstretched.

"You've found her, David!"

The Harvester grabbed the hand of his friend. He stood pumping it up and down while he gulped at the lump in his throat, and big tears squeezed from his eyes, but he could only nod his proud head.

"Found her!" exulted Doctor Carey. "Really found her! Well that's great! Sit down and tell me, boy! Is she sick, as we feared? Did you only see her or did you get to talk with her?"

"Well sir," said the Harvester, choking back his emotions, "you remember that ginseng I told you about

getting on the old Jameson place last night. To-day, I
learned I'd lost that hand-made mattock I use most, so I
went back for it, and there she was."

"In the country?"

"Yes sir!"

"Well why didn't we think of it before?"

"I suppose first we would have had to satisfy ourselves
that she wasn't in town, anyway."

"Sure! That would be the logical way to go at it!
And so you found her?"

"Yes sir, I found her! Just Belshazzar and I! I was
going along on my way to the place, when he ran past me
and made a stiff point, and as I came up, there she was!"

"There she was?"

"Yes sir; there she was!"

They shook hands again.

"Then of course you spoke to her."

"Yes I spoke to her."

"Were you pleased?"

"With her speech and manner?——yes. But, Doc, if
ever a woman needed everything on earth!"

"Well did you get any kind of a start made?"

"I couldn't do so very much. I had to go a little slow
for fear of frightening her, but I tried to get her to come
here and she won't until a debt she owes is paid, and she's
in no condition to work."

"Got any idea how much it is?"

"No, but it can't be any large sum. I tried to offer to
pay it, but she had no hesitation in telling me she preferred
owing a man she knew to a stranger."

"Well if she is so particular, how did she come to tell you first thing that she was in debt?"

The Harvester explained.

"Oh I see!" said the doctor.   "Well you'll have to baby her along with the idea that she is earning money and pay her double until you get that off your mind, and while you are at it, put in your best licks, my boy; perk right up and court her like a house afire.   Women like it.   All of them do.   They glory in feeling that a man is crazy about them."

"Well I'm insane enough over her," said the Harvester, "but I'd hate like the nation for her to know it.   Seems as if a woman couldn't respect such an addlepate as I am lately."

"Don't you worry about that," advised the doctor. "Just you make love to her.   Go at it in the good old-fashioned way."

"But maybe the 'good old-fashioned way' isn't my way."

"What's the difference whose way it is, if it wins?"

"But Kipling says: 'Each man makes love his own way!'"

"I seem to have heard you mention that name before," said the doctor.   "Do you regard him as an authority?"

"I do!" said the Harvester.   "Especially when he advises me after my own heart and reason.   Miss Jameson is not a silly girl.   She's a woman, of twenty-four at least. I don't want her to care for a trick or a pretence.   I do want her to love me.   Not that I am worth her attention, but because she needs some strong man fearfully, while I am ready and more 'willing' than the original Barkis. But, like him, I have to let her know it in my way, and court her according to the promptings of my heart."

"You deceive yourself!" said the doctor flatly. "That's all bosh! Your tongue says it for the satisfaction of your ears, and it does sound well. You will court her according to your ideas of the conventions, as you understand them, and strictly in accordance with what you consider the respect due her. If you had followed the thing you call the 'promptings of your heart,' you would have picked her up by main force and brought her to my best ward, instead of merely suggesting it and giving up when she said no. If you had followed your heart, you would have choked the name and amount out of her and paid that devilish debt. You walk away in a case like that; then have the nerve to come here and prate to me about following your heart. I'll wager my last dollar your heart is sore because you were not allowed to help her; but on the proposition that you followed its promptings I wouldn't stake a penny. That's all tommy-rot!"

"It is," agreed the Harvester. "Utter! But what can a man do?"

"I don't know what you can do! I'd have paid that debt and brought her to the hospital."

"I'll go and ask Mrs. Carey about your courtship. I want her help on this, anyway. I can pick up Miss Jameson and bring her here if any man can, but she is nursing a sick woman who depends solely on her for care. She is above average size, and she has a very decided mind of her own. I don't think you would use force and do what you think best for her, if you were in my place. You would wait until you understood the situation better, and knew that what you did was for the best, ultimately."

"I don't know whether I would or not. One thing is sure: I'm mighty glad you have found her. May I tell my wife?"

"Please do! And ask her if I may depend on her if I need a woman's help. Now I'll call off the valiant police and go home and take a good, sound sleep. Haven't had much since I first saw her."

So Betsy trotted down the valley, up the embankment, crossed the railroad, over the levee, across Singing Water, and up the hill to the cabin. As they passed it, the Harvester jumped from the wagon, tossed the hitching strap to Belshazzar, and entered. He walked straight to her door, unlocked it, and uncovering, went inside. Slowly he passed from piece to piece of the furniture he had made for her, and then surveyed the walls and floor.

"It isn't half good enough," he said, "but it will have to answer until I can do better. Surely she will know I tried and care for that, anyway. I wonder how long it will take me to get her here. Oh, if I only could know she was comfortable and happy! Happy! She doesn't appear as if she ever heard that word. Well this will be a good place to teach her. I've always enjoyed myself here. I'm going to have faith that I can win her and make her happy also. When I go to the stable to do my work for the night if I could know she was in this cabin and glad of it, and if I could hear her down here singing like a happy care-free girl, I'd scarcely be able to endure the joy of it."

CHAPTER IX

THE HARVESTER GOES COURTING

S HE is on Henry Jameson's farm, four miles west of Onabasha," said the Harvester, as he opened his eyes the following morning, to lay a caressing hand on Belshazzar's head. "At two o'clock we are going to see her, and we are going to prolong the visit to the ultimate limit, so we should make things count here before we start."

He worked in a manner that accomplished much. There seemed no end to his energy that morning. Despatching the usual routine, he ate his lunch and hitched Betsy to the wagon. When it neared time to start he dressed carefully. He stood before his bookcase and selected several pamphlets published by the Department of Agriculture. He went to his beds and gathered a large armload of plants. Then he was ready to make his first trip to see the Dream Girl, but it never occurred to him that he was going courting.

He had decided fully that there would be no use to try to make love to a girl manifestly so ill and in trouble. The first thing, it appeared to him, was to dispel the depression, improve the health, and then do the love making. So, in the most business-like manner possible, without a shade of embarrassment, the Harvester took his herbs and books

and started for the Jameson woods.   At times as he drove
along he espied something that he used growing beside the
road and stopped to secure a specimen.

He reached the ginseng bed at half-past one.   He was
purposely early.   He laid down his books and plants,
rolling the log on which she sat the day before to a more
shaded location, where a big tree would serve for a back
rest.   He pulled away brush and windfalls, heaped dry
brown leaves, and tramped them down for her feet.   He
laid the books on the log, the armload of plants beside
them, then went to the river to wash his soiled hands.

Belshazzar's short bark told him the Girl was coming.
Between the trees he saw the dog race to meet her while she
bent to stroke his head.   She wore the same dress, appearing even paler and thinner.   The Harvester hurried up the
bank, wiping his hands on his handkerchief.

"Glad to see you!" he greeted her casually.   "I've
fixed you a seat with a back rest to-day.   Don't be
frightened at the stack of herbs.   You needn't gather all of
those.   They are only suggestions.   They are just common roadside plants that have some medicinal value and
are worth collecting.   Please try my davenport."

"Thank you!" she said as she dropped on the log, leaning
her head against the tree.   It seemed as if her eyes closed
a few seconds in spite of her; while they were shut the
Harv ster looked steadily and intently on a face of exquisite beauty, but so marred by pallor and lines of care
that search was required to recognize just how handsome
she was: if he had not seen her in perfection in the dream
the Harvester might have missed glorious possibilities.   To

bring back that vision would be a task worth while was his thought. With the first faint quiver of an eyelash the Harvester took a few steps, bending over a plant, while the Girl's eyes followed him.

He appeared so tall and strong, so bronzed by summer sun and wind, his face so keen and intense, that swift fear caught her heart. Why was he there? Why should he take so much trouble for her? With difficulty she restrained herself from springing up and running away. Turning with the plant in his hand, the Harvester saw the panic in her eyes, and it troubled his heart. For an instant he was bewildered, then he understood.

"I don't want you to work when you are not able," he said in his most matter-of-fact voice, "but if you still think that you are, I'll be very glad. I need help just now, more than I can tell you, for there seem to be so few people who can be trusted. Gathering stuff for drugs is very serious business. You see, I've a reputation to sustain with some of the biggest laboratories in the country, not to mention the fact that I sometimes try compounding a new remedy for some common complaint myself. I rather take pride in the fact that my stuff goes in so fresh and clean that I always get anywhere from three to ten cents a pound above the listed prices for it. I want that money, but I want an unbroken record for doing a job right and being square and careful, much more."

He thought the appearance of fright was fading, while a tinge of interest took its place. She was looking straight at him. As he talked he could see her summoning her tired forces to understand and follow him, so he continued:

"One would think that as medicines are required in cases of life and death, collectors would use extreme caution, but some of them are criminally careless. It's a common thing to gather almost any fern for male fern; to throw in anything that will increase weight, to wash imperfectly, and commit many other sins that lie with the collector; beyond that I don't like to think. I suppose there are men who deliberately adulterate pure stuff to make it go farther, but when it comes to drugs, I scarcely can speak of it calmly. I like to do a thing right. I raise most of my plants, bushes, and herbs. I gather exactly in season, wash carefully if water dare be used, clean them otherwise if not, and dry them by a hot air system in an evaporator I built purposely. Each package I put up is pure stuff, clean, properly dried, and fresh. If I caught any man in the act of adulterating any of it I'm afraid he would get hurt badly—and usually I am a peaceable man. I am explaining this to show how very careful you must be to keep things separate, to collect the right plants if you are going to sell stuff to me. I am extremely particular."

The Girl was leaning toward him, watching his face, while hers was slowly changing. She was deeply interested, much impressed, and more at ease. When the Harvester saw he had talked her into confidence he crossed the leaves, seated himself on the log beside her, picked up the books and opened one.

"Oh I will be careful," said the Girl. "If you will trust me to collect for you, I will undertake only what I am sure I know, and I'll do exactly as you tell me."

"There are a dozen things that bring a price ranging

from three to fifteen cents a pound, that are in season just now. I suppose you would like to begin on some common, easy things, that will bring the most money."

Without a breath of hesitation she answered, "I will commence on whatever you need most to have."

The heart of the Harvester gave a leap that almost choked him, for he was vividly conscious of a broken shoe she was hiding beneath her skirts. He wanted to say "thank you," but he was afraid to, so he turned the leaves of the book.

"I am working now on mullein," he said.

"Oh I know mullein," she cried, with almost a hint of animation in her voice. "The tall, yellow flower stem rising from a circle of green felt leaves!"

"Good!" said the Harvester. "What a pretty way to describe it! Do you know any more plants?"

"Only a few! I had a high-school course in botany, but it was all about flower and leaf formation, nothing at all of what anything was good for. I also learned a few, drawing them for leather embroidery designs."

"Look here!" cried the Harvester. "I came with an armload of herbs and expected to tell you all about foxglove, mullein, yarrow, jimson, purple thorn apple, blessed thistle, hemlock, hoarhound, lobelia, and everything in season now; but if you already have a profession, why do you attempt a new one? Why don't you go on drawing? I never saw anything so stupid as most of the designs from nature book covers and decorations, leather work and pottery. They are the same old subjects worked over and over. If you can draw enough to make original copies, I can furnish you with flowers, vines, birds, and insects, new, unused, and of exquisite beauty, for every month in the year. I've looked into the matter a little, because I am rather handy with a knife, so I carve candlesticks from suitable pieces of wood. I always have trouble getting my designs copied; securing something new and unusual, never! If you can draw only well enough to reproduce what you see, gathering drugs is too slow and tiresome. What you want to do is to reproduce the subjects I will bring, then I'll buy what I want in my work, and sell the remainder at the arts and crafts stores for you. Or I can find out what they pay for such designs at potteries and ceramic factories. You have no time to spend on herbs, when you are in the woods, if you can draw."

"I am surely in the woods," said the Girl, "and I know I can copy correctly. I often made designs for embroidery and leather for the shop mother and I worked for in Chicago."

"Won't they buy them of you now?"

"Undoubtedly."

"Do they pay anything worth while?"

"I don't know how their prices compare with others. One place was all I worked for. I think they pay what is fair."

"We will find out," said the Harvester promptly.

"I——I don't think you need waste the time," faltered the Girl. "I had better gather the plants for a while at least."

"Collecting crude drug material is not easy," said the Harvester. "Drawing may not be either, but at least you could sit while you work; while it would bring you more money. Besides, I very much want a moth copied for a candlestick I am carving. Won't you draw that for me? I have some pupæ cases and the moths will be out any day now. If I'd bring you one, wouldn't you make a copy?"

The Girl gripped her hands and stared straight ahead of her for a second, then she turned to him.

"I'd like to," she said, "but I have nothing to work with. In Chicago they furnished my material at the shop, I drew the design and was paid for the pattern. I didn't know there would be a chance for anything like that here. I haven't even proper pencils."

"Then the way for you to do this is to strip the first mullein plants you see of the petals. I will pay you seventy-five cents a pound for them. By the time you gather a few pounds I can have material you need for drawing here and you can go to work on whatever flowers, vines, and things you can find in the woods, with no thanks to any one."

"I can't see that," said the Girl. "It would appear to me that I would be under more obligations than I could repay, and to a stranger."

"I figure it this way," said the Harvester, watching nervously. "I can sell at good prices all the mullein flowers I can secure. You collect for me, I buy them. You can use drawing tools; I get them for you, and you pay me with the mullein or out of the ginseng money I owe you. You already have that coming, so it's just as much yours as it will be ten days from now. You needn't hesitate a second about drawing on it, because I am in a hurry for the moth pattern. I find time to carve only at night, you see. As for being under obligations to a stranger, in the first place all the debt would be on my side. I'd get the drugs and the pattern I want; in the second place, I positively and emphatically refuse to be a stranger. It would be so much better to be mutual helpers and friends of the kind worth having; so the sooner we begin, the sooner we can work together to good advantage. Get that stranger idea out of your head right now, and replace it with thoughts of a new friend, who is willing"—the Harvester detected panic in her eyes and ended casually—"to enter a partnership that will be of benefit to both of us. Partners can't be strangers, you know," he finished.

"I don't know what to think," said the Girl.

"Never bother your head with thinking," advised the Harvester with an air of large wisdom. "It is unprofitable and very tiring. Any one can see that you are too weary now. Don't dream of such a foolish thing as thinking. Don't worry over motives and obligations. Say to yourself: 'I'll enter this partnership and if it brings me anything good, I'm that much ahead. If it fails, I have lost nothing.' That's the way I look at it."

Then before she could answer he continued: "Now I want all the mullein bloom I can get. You'll see the yellow heads everywhere. Strip the petals and bring them here, and I'll come for them every day. They must go on the trays as fresh as possible. On your part, we will make out the order now."

He took a pencil and notebook from his pocket.

"You want drawing pencils and brushes; how many, what make and size?"

The Girl hesitated for a moment as if struggling to decide what to do; then she named the articles.

"And paper?"

He wrote that down, asking if there were more.

"I think," he said, "that I can fill this order in Onabasha. The art stores should keep these things. And shouldn't you have water-colour paper and some paint?"

Then there was a flash across the white face.

"Oh, if I only could!" she cried. "All my life I have been crazy for a box of colour, but I never could afford it, so of course, I can't now. But if this splendid plan works, and I can earn what I owe, then maybe I can."

"Well this 'splendid plan' is going to 'work,' don't you bother about that," said the Harvester. "It has begun working right now. Don't worry a minute. After things have gone wrong for a certain length of time, they always veer and go right a while as compensation. Don't think of anything save that you are at the turning. Since it is all settled that we are to be partners, would you name me the figures of the debt that is worrying you? Don't, if you mind. I merely thought perhaps we could get along better if I knew. Is it——say five hundred dollars?"

"Oh dear no!" cried the Girl in a panic. "I never could face that! It is not quite one hundred, and that seems big as a mountain to me."

"Forget it!" he cried. "The ginseng will pay more than half; that I know. I can bring you the cash in a little over a week."

She started to speak, hesitated, and at last turned to him.

"Would you mind," she said, "if I asked you to keep it until I can find a way to go to town? It's too far to walk and I don't know how to send it. Would I dare put it in a letter?"

"Never!" said the Harvester. "You want a draft. That money will be too precious to run any risks. I'll bring it to you and you can write a note and explain to whom you want it paid, then I'll take it to the bank for you and get your draft. Then you can write a letter, and half your worry will be over safely."

"It must be done in a sure way," said the Girl. "If I knew I had the money to pay that much on what I owe, and then lost it, I simply could not endure it. I would lie down and give up as Aunt Molly has."

"Forget that too!" said the Harvester. "Wipe out all the past that has pain in it. The future is going to be beautifully bright. That little bird on the bush there just told me so, and you are always safe when you trust the feathered folk. If you are going to live in the country any length of time, you must know them, for they will become a great comfort. Are you planning to be here long?"

"I have no plans. After what I saw Chicago do to my mother I would rather finish life in the open than return to the city. It is horrible here, but at least I'm not hungry, and not afraid——all the time."

"Gracious Heaven!" cried the Harvester. "Do you mean to say that you are afraid any part of the time? Would you kindly tell me of whom, and why?"

"You should know without being told that when a woman born and reared in a city, and all her life confined there, steps into the woods for the first time, she's bound to be afraid. The past few weeks constitute my entire experience with the country, and I'm in mortal fear that snakes will drop from trees and bushes or spring from the ground. Some places I think I'm sinking, and whenever a bush catches my skirts it seems as if something dreadful is reaching up for me; there is a possibility of horror lurking behind every tree and——"

"Stop!" cried the Harvester. "I can't endure it! Do you mean to tell me that you are afraid here and now?"

"Yes," she said. "It almost makes me ill to sit on this log without taking a stick and poking all around it first. Every minute I think something is going to strike me in the back or drop on my head."

"Am I one of the things you fear?"

"Why shouldn't you be?" she answered. "What do I know of you or your motives or why you are here?"

"I have had no experience with the atmosphere that breeds such an attitude in a girl."

"That is a thing for which to thank Heaven. Undoubtedly it has been gracious to you. My life has been different."

"Yet in mortal terror of the woods, and probably equal fear of me, you are here and asking for work that will keep you here."

"I would go through tortures for the money I owe. After that debt is paid——"

She threw out her hands in a hopeless gesture. The

Harvester drew forth a roll of bills and tossed them into her lap.

"For the love of mercy take what you need and pay it," he said. "Then get a floor under your feet, and try, I beg of you, try to force yourself to have confidence in me, until I do something that gives you the least reason for distrusting me."

She picked up the money, giving it a contemptuous whirl that landed it at his feet.

"What greater cause of distrust could I have by any possibility than just that?" she asked.

The Harvester arose hastily; taking several steps, he stood with folded arms, his back turned. The Girl sat watching him with wide eyes, the dull blue plain in their dusky depths. When he did not speak, she grew restless. At last she slowly arose and circling him looked into his face. It was convulsed with a struggle in which love and patience fought for supremacy over honest anger. As he saw her so close, his lips drew apart, while his breath came deeply, but he did not speak. He merely stood and looked at her, and looked; while she gazed at him as if fascinated, but uncomprehending.

"Ruth!"

The Girl shivered and became paler.

"Is that your uncle?" asked the Harvester.

She nodded.

"Will you come to-morrow for your drawing materials?"

"Yes."

"Will you try to believe that there is absolutely nothing, either underfoot or overhead, that will harm you?"

"Yes."

"Will you try to think that I am not a menace to public safety, and that I would do much to help you, merely because I would be glad to be of service?"

"Yes."

"Will you try to cultivate the idea that there is nothing in all this world that would hurt you purposely?"

"Ruth!" came a cry in gruff man-tones, keyed in deep anger.

"That *sounds* like it!" said the Girl, and catching up her skirts she ran through the woods, taking a different route toward the house.

The Harvester sat on the log and tried to think; but there are times when the numbed brain refuses to work, so he really sat and suffered. Belshazzar whimpered, licking his hands, so at last the man arose and went with the dog to the wagon. As they came through Onabasha, Betsy turned at the hospital corner, but the Harvester pulled her around and drove toward the country. "Not to-day, Betsy! I can't face my friends now. Someway I am making an awful fist of things. Everything I do is wrong. She no more trusts me than you would a rattlesnake, Belshazzar; while from all appearance she takes me to be almost as deadly. What must have been her experiences in life to ingrain fear and distrust in her soul at that rate? I always knew I was not handsome, but I never before regarded my appearance as alarming. And I 'fixed up,' too!"

The Harvester grinned a queer little twist of a grin that pulled and distorted his strained face. "Might as well have gone with a week's beard, a soiled shirt, and a leer! And I've always been as decent as I knew! What's the reward for clean living anyway, if the girl you love strikes you like that?"

Belshazzar reached across and kissed him. The Harvester put his arm around the dog. In the man's disappointment and heart hunger he leaned his head against the beast and said: "I've always got you to love and protect me, anyway, Belshazzar. Maybe the man who said a dog was a man's best friend was right. You always trusted me, didn't you, Bel? And you never regretted it but once, and that wasn't my fault. I never did it! If I did, I'm getting good and well paid for it. I'd rather be kicked until all the ribs of one side are broken, Bel, than to swallow the dose she just handed me. I tell you it was bitter, lad! What am I going to do? Can't you help me, Bel?"

Belshazzar quivered in anxiety to offer the comfort he could not speak.

"Of course you are right! You always are, Bel!" said the Harvester. "I know what you are trying to tell me. Sure enough, she didn't have any dream. I am afraid she had the bitterest reality. She hasn't been loving a vision of me, working and searching for me, and I don't mean to her what she does to me. Of course I see that I must be patient and bide my time. If there is anything in 'like begetting like' she is bound to care for me some day, for I love her past all expression, and for all she feels I might as well save my breath. But she has got to awake some day, Bel. She can make up her mind to that. She can't see 'why.' Over and over! I wonder what she would think if I'd up and tell her 'why' with no frills. She will drive me to it some day, then probably the shock will finish her. I wonder if Doc was only fooling or if he really would do what he said. It might wake her up, anyway, but I'm dubious as to the result. How Uncle Henry can roar! He sounded like a fog horn. I'd love to try my muscle on a man like that. No wonder she is afraid of him, if she is of me. Afraid! Well of all things I ever did expect, Belshazzar, that is the limit."

CHAPTER X

THE CHIME OF THE BLUE BELLS

THE Harvester finished his evening work, then went to examine the cocoons. Many of the moths had emerged and flown, but the luna cases remained in the bottom of the box. As he stood looking at them one moved. Smilingly he said:

"I'd give something if you would come out and be ready to work on by to-morrow afternoon. Possibly you would so interest her that she would forget her fear of me. I'd like to take you along, because she might care for you, and I do need the pattern for my candlestick. Believe I'll lay you in a warmer place."

The first thing the following morning the Harvester looked to find the open cocoon, while the wet moth clung by its feet to a twig he had placed for it.

"Luck is with me!" he exulted. "I'll carry you to her, being mighty careful what I say, then maybe she will forget about the fear."

All forenoon he cut and spread boneset, senna, and hemlock on the trays to dry. At noon he put on a fresh outfit, ate a hasty lunch, then drove to Onabasha. He carried the moth in a box, and when starting picked up a rake. He went to an art store, buying the pencils and paper she had ordered. He wanted to purchase everything he saw for her, but he was fast learning a lesson of deep caution. If he took more than she specified, she would worry over paying, then if he refused to accept money, she would put that everlasting "why" again. The water-colour paper and paint he could not forego. He could make a desire to have the moth coloured explain those, he thought.

Then he went to a furniture store and bought several articles, and forgetting his law against haste, he drove Betsy full speed to the river. He was rather heavily ladened as he went up the bank at one o'clock. There was an hour. He rolled away the log, raked together and removed the leaves to the ground. He tramped the earth level then spread a large cheap porch rug. On this he opened and placed a little folding table and chair. On the table he spread the pencils, paper, colour box and brushes, going to the river to fill the water cup. Then he sat on the log he had rolled to one side and waited. After two hours he arose and crept as close the house as he could through the woods, but he could not secure a glimpse of the Girl. He went back and waited an hour more, then undid his work and removed it. When he came to the moth his face was very grim as he lifted the twig and helped the beautiful creature to climb on a limb. "You'll be ready to fly in a few hours," he said. "If I keep you in a box you will ruin your wings and be no suitable subject, and put you in a cyanide jar I will not. I am hurt too badly myself. I wonder if what Doc said was the right way! It's certainly a temptation."

Then he drove away; again Betsy veered at the hospital;

once more the Harvester explained to her that he did not want to see the doctor. That evening and the following forenoon were difficult, but the Harvester lived through them, and in the afternoon went back to the woods, spread his rug, and set up the table. Only one streak of luck brightened the gloom in his heart. A yellow emperor had emerged in the night; now it occupied the place of yesterday's luna. She never need know this was not the one he wanted, and it would make an excuse for the colour box.

He was watching intently, so he saw her coming a long way off. He noticed that she looked neither right nor left, but came straight as if walking a bridge. As she reached the place she glanced hastily around, then at him. The Harvester forgave her everything as he saw the look of relief with which she stepped upon the carpet. Then she turned to him.

"I won't have to ask 'why' this time," she said. "I know that you did it because I was baby enough to tell what a coward I am. I'm sure you can't afford it; I know you shouldn't have done it, but oh, what a comfort! If you will promise never to do such an expensive, foolish, kind thing again, I'll say thank you this time. I couldn't come yesterday, because Aunt Molly was worse so Uncle Henry was at home all day."

"I supposed it was something like that," said the Harvester.

She advanced, handing him the roll of bills.

"I had a feeling you would be reckless," she said. "I saw it in your face, so I came back as soon as I could steal away, and sure enough, there lay your money, the books, and everything. I hid them in the thicket, so they will be all right. I've almost prayed it wouldn't rain. I didn't dare carry them to the house. Please take the money. I haven't time to argue about it or strength, but of course I can't possibly use it unless I earn it. I'm so anxious to see the pencils and paper."

The Harvester thrust the money into his pocket. The Girl went to the table, opened and spread the paper, then took out the pencils.

"Is my subject in here?" She touched the colour box.

"No, the other."

"Is it alive? May I open it?"

"We will be very careful at first," said the Harvester. "It only left its case in the night so it may fly. When the weather is warm the wings develop rapidly. Perhaps if I remove the lid——"

He took off the cover, exposing a moth, its lovely, pale yellow wings, flecked with heliotrope, outspread as it clung to a twig in the box. The Girl leaned forward.

"What is it?" she asked.

"One of the big night moths that emerge and fly a few hours in June."

"Is this what you want for your candlestick?"

"If I can't do better. There is one other I prefer, but it may not come at a time that you can get it right."

"What do you mean by 'right?'"

"So that you can copy it before it wants to fly."

"Why don't you chloroform and pin it until I am ready?"

"I am not in the business of killing and impaling exquisite creatures like that."

"Do you mean that if I can't draw it when it is just right you will let it go?"

"I do."

"Why?"

"I told you why."

"I know you said you were not in the business, but why wouldn't you take only one you really wanted to use?"

"I would be afraid," replied the Harvester.

"Afraid? You!"

"I must have a mighty good reason before I kill," said the man. "I cannot give life; I have no right to take it away. I will let my statement stand. I am afraid."

"Of what, please?"

"An indefinable something that follows me and makes me suffer if I am wantonly cruel."

"Is there any particular pose in which you want this bird placed?"

"Allow me to present you to the yellow emperor, known in the books as *eacles imperialis*," he said. "I want him as he clings naturally and life size."

She took up a pencil.

"If you don't mind," said the Harvester, "would you draw on this other paper? I very much want the colour, also, and you can use it on this. I brought a box along, I'll bring you water. I had it all ready yesterday."

"Did you have this same moth?"

"No, I had another."

"Did you have the one you wanted most?"

"Yes——but it's no difference."

"And you let it go because I was not here?"

"No. It went on account of exquisite beauty. If kept in confinement it would struggle and break its wings. You see, that one was a delicate green, where this is yellow, plain pale blue green, with a lavender rib here, and long curled trailers edged with pale yellow, and eye spots rimmed with red and black."

As the Harvester talked he indicated the points of difference with a pencil he had picked up; now he laid it down and retreated beyond the rug.

"I see," said the Girl. "And this is colour?"

"A few colours, rather," said the Harvester. "I ᵔelected enough to fill the box, with the help of the clerk ᴡho sold them to me. If they are not right, I have permission to exchange them for anything you want."

With eager fingers she opened the box, bending over it a face filled with interest.

"Oh how I've always wanted this! I scarcely can wait to try it. I do hope I can have it for my own. Was it expensive?"

"No. Very cheap!" said the Harvester. "The paper isn't worth mentioning. The little tin box was only a few cents, and the paints differ according to colour. I was surprised that the outfit was so inexpensive."

A skeptical smile wavered on the Girl's face as she drew her slender fingers across the trays of bright colour.

"If one dared accept your word, you really would be a comfort," she said, as she resolutely closed the box, pushed it away, and picked up a pencil.

"If you will take the trouble to inquire at the banks,

post office, express office, hospital or of any druggist in Onabasha, you will find that my word is exactly as good as my money, and taken quite as readily."

"I didn't say I doubted you. I have no right to do that until I feel you deceive me. What I said was 'dared accept,' which means I must not, because I have no right. But you make one wonder what you would do if you were coaxed for things and led by insinuations."

"I can tell you that," said the Harvester. "It would depend altogether on who wanted anything of me and what they asked. It would be unnecessary for you to coax or insinuate, because I'd see what you needed and have it at hand."

The Girl looked at him wonderingly.

"Now don't spring your recurrent 'why' on me," said the Harvester. "I'll tell you 'why' some of these days. Just now answer me this question: do you want me to remain here or leave until you finish? Which way would you be least afraid?"

"I am not at all afraid on the rug and with my work," she said. "If you want to hunt ginseng go by all means."

"I don't want to hunt anything," said the Harvester. "But if you are more comfortable with me away, I'll be glad to go. I'll leave the dog with you."

He gave a short whistle which brought Belshazzar bounding to him. The Harvester stepped to the Girl's side, and dropping on one knee, he drew his hand across the rug close to her skirts.

"Right here, Belshazzar," he said. "Watch! You are on guard, Bel."

"Well of all names for a dog!" exclaimed the Girl. "Why did you select that?"

"My mother named my first dog Belshazzar, and taught me why; so each of the three I've owned since have been christened the same. It means 'to protect' and that is the office all of them perform; this one especially has filled it admirably. Once I failed him, but he never has gone back on me. You see he is not a particle afraid of me. Every step I take, he is at my heels."

"So was Bill Sikes' dog, if I remember."

The Harvester laughed.

"Bel," he said, "if you could speak you'd say that was an ugly one, wouldn't you?"

The dog sprang up and kissed the face of the man, rubbing a loving head against his breast.

"Thank you!" said the Harvester. "Now lie down and protect this woman as carefully as you ever watched in your life. And incidentally, Bel, tell her that she can't exterminate me more than once a day, so the performance is accomplished for the present. I refuse to be a willing sacrifice. 'So was Bill Sikes' dog!' What do you think of that, Bel?"

The Harvester arose and turned to go.

"What if this thing attempts to fly?" she asked.

"Your pardon," said the Harvester. "If the emperor moves, slide the lid over the box a few seconds, until he settles and clings quietly again; then slowly draw it away. If you are careful not to jar the table heavily he will not go for hours yet."

Again he turned.

"If there is no danger, why do you leave the dog?"

"For company," said the Harvester. "I thought you would prefer an animal you are not afraid of to a man you are. But let me tell you there is no necessity for either. I know a woman who goes alone and unafraid through every foot of woods in this part of the country. She has climbed, crept, waded, and she tells me she never saw but two venomous snakes this side of Michigan. Nothing ever dropped on her or sprang at her. She feels as secure in the woods as she does at home."

"Isn't she afraid of snakes?"

"She dislikes snakes, but she is not afraid or she would not risk encountering them daily."

"Do you ever find any?"

"Harmless little ones, often. That is, Bel does. He is always nosing for them, because he understands that I work in the earth. I think I have encountered three dangerous ones in my life. I will guarantee you will not find one in these woods. They are too open and too much cleared."

"Then why leave the dog?"

"I thought," said the Harvester patiently, "that your uncle might have turned in some of his cattle, or if pigs came here the dog would chase them away."

She looked at him with utter panic in her face.

"I am far more afraid of a cow than a snake!" she cried. "It is so much bigger!"

"How did you ever come into these woods alone far enough to find the ginseng?" asked the Harvester. "Answer me that!"

"I wore Uncle Henry's top boots and carried a rake, and I suffered tortures," she replied.

"But you hunted until you found what you wanted, and came again to keep watch on it?"

"I was driven—simply forced. There's no use to discuss it!"

"Well thank the Lord for one thing," said the Harvester. "You didn't appear half so terrified at the sight of me as you did at the mere mention of a cow. I have risen inestimably in my own self-respect. Belshazzar, you may pursue the elusive chipmunk. I am going to guard this woman myself, and please, kind fates, send a ferocious cow this way, in order that I may prove my valour."

The Girl's face flushed slightly, but she could not restrain a laugh. That was more than the Harvester hoped for. He went beyond the edge of the rug, sitting on the leaves under a tree. She bent over her work while only bird or insect notes or occasionally Belshazzar's excited bark broke the silence. The Harvester stretched on the ground, his eyes on the Girl. Intently he watched every movement. If a squirrel barked she gave a nervous start, so precipitate it seemed as if it must hurt. If a windfall came rattling down she appeared ready to fly in headlong terror in any direction. At last she dropped her pencil, looking at him helplessly.

"What is it?" he asked.

"The silence and these awful crashes when one doesn't know what is coming," she said.

"Will it bother you if I talk? Perhaps the sound of my voice will help?"

"I am accustomed to working while people talk; it will be a comfort. I may be able to follow you, so that will prevent me from thinking. There are dreadful things in my mind when they are not driven out. Please talk! Tell me about the herbs you gathered this morning."

The Harvester gave the Girl one long look as she bent over her work. He was vividly conscious of the graceful curves of her lithe figure, the coil of dark, silky hair, softly waving around her temples and neck. When her eyes turned in his direction he knew that it was only the white, drawn face that restrained him. He was almost forced to tell her how he loved and longed for her; about the home he had prepared; of a thousand personal interests. Instead, he took a firm grip and said casually: "Foxglove harvest is over. This plant has to be taken when the leaves are in second year growth and at bloom time. I have stripped my mullein beds of both leaves and flowers. I finished a week ago. Beyond lies a stretch of Parnassus grass that made me think of you, it was so white and delicate. I want you to see it. It will be lovely in a few weeks more."

"You never had seen me a week ago."

"Oh hadn't I?" said the Harvester. "Well maybe I dreamed about you then. I am a great dreamer. Once I had a dream that may interest you some day, after you've overcome your fear of me. Now this bed of which I was speaking is a picture in September. You must arrange to drive home with me and see it then."

"For what do you sell foxglove and mullein?"

"Foxglove for heart trouble, and mullein for catarrh. I get ten cents a pound for foxglove leaves, five for mullein, and from seventy-five to a dollar for flowers of the latter, depending on how well I preserve the colour in drying them. They must be sealed in bottles and handled with extreme care."

"Then if I were not too childish to pick them, I could earn seventy-five cents a pound for mullein blooms?"

"Yes," said the Harvester. "But until you learned the trick of stripping them rapidly you scarcely could gather what would weigh two pounds a day, when dried. Not to mention the fact that you would have to stand and work mostly in hot sunshine, because mullein likes open roads and fields and sunny hills. Now you can sit securely in the shade, and in two hours you can make me a pattern of that moth, for which I would pay a designer of the arts and crafts shop five dollars, so of course you shall have the same."

"Oh no!" she cried in swift panic. "You were charged too much! It isn't worth a dollar, even!"

"On the contrary the candlestick on which I shall use it will be invaluable when I finish it, and five is very little for the cream of my design. I paid just right. You can earn the same for all you can do. If you can embroider linen, they pay good prices for that, too, and wood carving, metal work, or leather things. May I see how you are coming on?"

"Please do," she said.

The Harvester sprang up, looking over the Girl's shoulder. He could not suppress an exclamation of delight.

"Perfect!" he cried. "You can surpass their best drafting at the shop! Your fortune is made. Any time you want to go to Onabasha you can make enough to pay your board, dress you well, and save something every week. You must leave here as soon as you can manage it. When can you go?"

"I don't know," she said wearily. "I'd hate to tell you how full of aches I am. I could not work much just now, if I had the best opportunities in the world. I must grow stronger."

"You should not work at anything until you are well," he said. "It is a crime against nature to drive yourself. Why will you not allow——"

"Do you really think, with a little practice, I can draw designs that will sell?"

The Harvester picked up the sheet. The work was delicate and exact. He could see no way to improve it.

"You know it will sell," he said gently, "because you already have sold such work."

"But not for the prices you offer."

"The prices I name are going to be for *new, original designs.* I've got a thousand in my head, that old Mother Nature shows me in the woods and on the water every day."

"But those are yours; I can't take them."

"You must," said the Harvester. "I only see and recognize studies; I can't materialize them; so until they are drawn, no one can profit by them. In this partnership we revolutionize decorative art. There are actually birds besides fat robins and nondescript swallows. The crane and heron do not monopolize the water. Wild rose and golden-rod are not the only flowers. The other day I was gathering lobelia. The seeds are used in tonic preparations. It has an upright stem with flowers scattered along it. In itself it is not much, but close beside it always grows its cousin, tall bell-flower. As the name indicates, the flowers are bell shape, while I can't begin to describe their grace, beauty, and delicate blue colour. They ring my strongest call to worship. My work keeps me in the woods so much I remain there for my religion also. Whenever I find these flowers I always pause for a little service of my own that begins by reciting these lines:

> "'Neath cloistered boughs, each floral bell that swingeth
> And tolls its perfume on the passing air,
> Makes Sabbath in the fields, and ever ringeth
> A call to prayer."

"Beautiful!" said the Girl.

"It's mighty convenient," explained the Harvester. "By my method, you see, you don't have to wait for your day and hour of worship. Anywhere the blue bell rings its call it is Sunday in the woods and in your heart. After I recite that, I pray my prayer."

"Go on!" said the Girl. "This is no place to stop."

"It is always one and the same prayer," said the Harvester. "It runs this way——Let me take your pencil and I will write it for you." He bent over her shoulder, and traced these lines on a scrap of the wrapping paper:

> "Almighty Evolver of the Universe:
> Help me to keep my soul and body clean,
> And at all times to do unto others as I would be done by.
> Amen."

The Girl took the slip to study it; then she raised her eyes to his face curiously, but with a tinge of awe in them.

"I can see you standing over a blue, bell-shaped flower reciting those exquisite lines and praying this wonderful prayer," she said. "Yesterday you allowed the moth you were willing to pay five dollars for a drawing of, to go, because you wouldn't risk breaking its wings. Why you are more like a woman!"

A red stream crimsoned the Harvester's face.

"Well heretofore I have been considered strictly masculine," he said. "To appreciate beauty or to try to be commonly decent is not exclusively feminine. You must remember there are painters, poets, musicians, workers in art along almost any line you could mention, and no one calls them feminine, but there is one good thing I am. You need no longer fear me. If you should see me, muck covered, grubbing in the earth or on a raft washing roots in the lake, you would not consider me like a woman."

"Would it be any discredit if I did? I think not. I merely meant that most men would not see or hear the blue bell at all——while as for the poem and prayer! If the woods make a man with such fibre in his soul, I must learn them if they half kill me."

"You harp on death. Try to forget the word."

"I have faced it for months, then seen it do its grinding worst very recently to the only thing on earth I loved or that loved me. I have no desire to forget! Tell me more about the plants."

"Forgive me," said the Harvester gently. "Just now I am collecting catnip for the infant and nervous people, hoarhound for colds and dyspepsia, boneset heads and flowers for the same purpose. There is a heavy head of white bloom with wonderful lacy leaves, called yarrow. I take the entire plant for a tonic and blessed thistle leaves and flowers for the same purpose."

"That must be what I need," interrupted the Girl. "Half the time I believe I have a little fever, but I couldn't have dyspepsia, because I never want anything to eat; perhaps the tonic would make me hungry."

"Promise me you will tell that to the doctor who comes to see your aunt, and take what he gives you."

"No doctor comes to see my aunt. She is merely playing lazy to get out of work. There is nothing the matter with her."

"Then why——"

"My uncle says that. Really, she could not stand and walk across a room alone. She is simply worn out."

"I shall report the case," said the Harvester instantly.

"You better not!" said the Girl. "There must be a mistake about you knowing my uncle. Tell me more of the flowers."

The Harvester drew a deep breath and continued:

"These I just have named I take at bloom time; next month come purple thorn apple, jimson weed, and hemlock."

"Isn't that poison?"

"Half the stuff I handle is."

"Aren't you afraid?"

"Terribly," said the Harvester in laughing voice. "But I want the money, the sick folk need the medicine, and I drink water."

The Girl laughed also.

"Look here!" said the Harvester. "Why not tell me about your aunt, and let me fix something for her; or if you are afraid to trust me, let me have my friend of whom I spoke yesterday."

"Perhaps I am not so much afraid as I was," said the Girl. "I wish I could! How could I explain where I got it and I wonder if she would take it."

"Give it to her without any explanation," said the Harvester. "Tell her it will make her stronger and she must use it. Tell me exactly how she is, and I will fix up some harmless remedies that may help, and can do no harm."

"She simply has been neglected, overworked, and abused until she has lain down, turned her face to the wall and given up hope. I think it is too late. I think the end will come soon. But I wish you would try. I'll gladly pay——"

"Don't!" said the Harvester. "Not for things that grow in the woods and that I prepare. Don't think of money every minute."

"I must," she said with forced restraint. "It is the price of life. Without it one suffers——horribly——as I know. What other plants do you gather?"

"Senna," answered the Harvester. "A beautiful thing! You must see it. Tall, round stems, lacy, delicate leaves, big heads of bright yellow bloom, touched with colour so dark it appears black—one of the loveliest plants that grows. You should see my big bed of it in a week or two more. It makes a picture."

The words recalled him to the Girl.   He turned to study her.   He forgot his commission and chafed at conventions that prevented his doing what he saw was required so urgently.   Fearing she would notice, he gazed away through the forest, trying to think, to plan.

"You are not making noise enough," she said.

So absorbed was the Harvester he scarcely heard her. In an attempt to obey he began to whistle softly.   A tiny goldfinch in a nest of thistle down and plant fibre in the branching of a bush ten feet above him stuck her head over the brim and inquired: "P'tseet?"   "Pt'see!" answered the Harvester.   That began the duet.   Before the question had been asked and answered half a dozen times a catbird intruded its voice and hearing a reply came through the bushes to investigate.   A wren followed, becoming very saucy.   From——one could not see where, came a vireo, and almost at the same time a chewink had something to say.

Instantly the Harvester answered.   Then a blue jay came chattering to ascertain what all the fuss was about. The Harvester carried on a conversation that called up the remainder of the feathered tribe.   A brilliant cardinal came tearing through the thicket, his beady black eyes snapping, and demanded to know if any one were harming his mate, brooding under a wild grape leaf in a scrub elm on the river embankment.   A brown thrush silently slipped like a snake between shrubs and trees, then catching the universal excitement, began to flirt his tail and utter a weird, whistling cry.

With one eye on the bird, and the other on the Girl

sitting in amazed silence, the Harvester began working for effect. He lay quietly, but in turn he answered a dozen birds so accurately they thought their mates were calling, so closer and closer they came. An oriole in orange and black heard his challenge, and flew up the river bank, answering at steady intervals for quite a time before it was visible, and in resorting to the last notes he could think of a quail whistled "Bob White" and a shitepoke, skulking along the river bank, stopped and cried: "Cowk, cowk!"

At his limit of calls the Harvester changed his notes and whistled or cried bits of bird talk in tone with every mellow accent and inflection he could manage. Gradually the excitement subsided, the birds flew and tilted closer, turned their sleek heads, peered with bright eyes, venturing on and on until the very bravest, the wren and the jay, were almost in touch. Then, tired of hunting, Belshazzar came racing, so the little feathered people scattered in precipitate flight.

"How do you like that kind of a noise?" inquired the Harvester.

"Of course you know that was the most exquisite sight I ever saw," she said. "I never shall forget it. I did not think there were that many different birds in the whole world. Of all the gaudy colours! And they came so close you could have touched them."

"Yes," said the Harvester calmly. "Birds are never afraid of me. At Medicine Woods, when I call them like that, many, most of them, in fact, eat from my hand. If you ever have looked at me enough to notice bulgy pockets, they are full of wheat. These birds are strangers, but I'll wager you that in a week I can make them take food from me. Of course, my own birds know me, because they are around every day. It is much easier to tame them in winter, when the snow has fallen and food is scarce, but it only takes a little while to win a bird's confidence at any season."

"Birds don't know what there is to be afraid of."

"Your pardon," said the Harvester, "but I am familiar with them, and that is not correct. They have more to fear than human beings. No one is going to kill you merely to see if he can shoot straight enough to hit. Your life is not in danger because you have magnificent hair that some woman would like for an ornament. You will not be stricken out in a flash because there are a few bits of meat on your frame some one wants to eat. No one will set a seductive trap for you, and, if you are tempted to enter it, shut you from freedom and natural diet, in a cage so small you can't turn around without touching bars. You are in a secure and free position compared with the birds. I also have observed that they know guns, many forms of traps, while all of them decide by the mere manner of a man's passing through the woods whether he is a friend or an enemy. Birds know more than many people realize. They do not always correctly estimate gun range, they are foolishly venturesome at times when they want food, but they know many more things than most people give them credit for understanding. The greatest trouble with the birds is they are too willing to trust us and be friendly, so they are often deceived."

"That sounds as if you were right," said the Girl.

"I am of the woods, so I know I am," he answered.

"Will you look at this now?"

The Harvester examined the drawing closely.

"Where did you learn?" he inquired.

"My mother.　She was educated to her finger tips.　She drew, painted, played beautifully, sang well, and she had read almost all the best books.　Besides what I learned at high school she taught me all I know.　Her embroidery always brought higher prices than mine, try as I might.　I never saw any one else make such a dainty accurate little stitch as she could."

"If this is not perfect, I don't know how to criticise it.　I can and will use it in my work.　But I have one luna cocoon remaining and I would give ten dollars for such a drawing of the moth before it flies.　It may open to-night or not for several days.　If your aunt should be worse so you cannot come to-morrow and the moth emerges, is there any way in which I could send it to you?"

"What could I do with it?"

"I thought perhaps you could take a piece of paper and the pencils with you, and secure an outline in your room. It need not be worked up with all the detail in this.　Merely a skeleton sketch would do.　Could I leave it at the house or send it with some one?"

"No!　Oh no!" she cried.　"Leave it here.　Put it in a box in the bushes where I hid the books.　What are you going to do with these things?"

"Hide them in the thicket and scatter leaves over them."

"What if it rains?"

"I have thought of that. I brought a few yards of oil-cloth to-day, so they will be safe and dry if it pours."

"Good!" she said. "Then if the moth comes out you bring it, and if I am not here, put it under the cloth and I will run up some time in the afternoon. But if I were you, I would not spread the rug until you know if I can remain. I have to steal every minute I am away, while any day uncle takes a notion to stay at home I dare not come."

"Try to come to-morrow. I am going to bring some medicine for your aunt."

"Put it under the cloth if I am not here; but I will come if I can. I must go now; I have been away far too long."

The Harvester picked up one of the drug pamphlets, laid the drawing beside it, and placed it with his other books. Then he drew out his pocket book, laid a five-dollar bill on the table and began folding up the chair and putting away the things. The Girl looked at the money with eager eyes.

"Is that honestly what you would pay at the arts and crafts place?"

"It is the customary price for my patterns."

"And are you sure this is as good?"

"I can bring you some I have paid that for, so you can see for yourself that it is better."

"I wish you would!" she cried eagerly. "I need that money. I would like to have it dearly, if I really have earned it, but I can't touch it if I have not."

"Won't you accept my word?"

"No. I will see the other drawings first; then if I think

mine are as good, I will be glad to take the money to‑
morrow."

"What if you can't come?"

"Put them under the oilcloth. I watch all the time. I
think Uncle Henry has trained even the boys so they don't
play in the river on his land. I never see a soul here; the
woods, house, and everything is desolate until he comes
home and then it is like——" she paused.

"I'll say it for you," said the Harvester promptly.
"Then it is like hell."

"At its worst," supplemented the Girl. Taking pencils
and a sheet of paper she went swiftly through the woods.
Before she left the shelter of the trees, the Harvester saw
her busy her hands with the front of her dress, so he knew
that she was concealing the drawing material. The
colour box was left. He said things as he put it with the
chair and table, covered them with the rug and oilcloth,
heaping on a layer of leaves.

Then he drove to the city. Betsy turned at the hospital
corner with no interference. He could face his friend that
day. Despite all discouragements he felt reassured. He
was progressing. Means of communication had been
established. If she did not come, he could leave a note to
tell her if the moth had not emerged and how sorry he was
to have missed seeing her.

"Hello, lover!" cried Doctor Carey as the Harvester
entered the office. "Are you married yet?"

"No. But I'm going to be," said the Harvester with
confidence.

"Have you asked her?"

"No. We are getting acquainted. She is too close to trouble, too ill, and too worried over a sick relative for me to intrude myself; it would be brutal, but it's a temptation. Doc, is there any way to compel a man to provide medical care for his wife?"

"Can he afford it?"

"Amply. Anything! Worth thousands in land and nobody knows what in money. It's Henry Jameson."

"The meanest man I ever knew. If he has a wife it's a marvel she has survived this long. Won't he provide for her?"

"I suppose he thinks he has when she has a bed to lie on and a roof to cover her. He won't supply food she can eat and medicine. He says she is lazy."

"What do you think?"

"I quote Miss Jameson. She says her aunt is slowly dying from overwork and neglect."

"David, doesn't it seem pretty good, when you say 'Miss Jameson?'"

"Loveliest sound on earth, except the remainder of it."

"What's that?"

"Ruth!"

"Jove! That is a beautiful name. Ruth Langston. It will go well, won't it?"

"Music that the birds, insects, Singing Water, the trees, and the breeze can't ever equal. I'm holding on with all my might, but it's tough, Doc. She's in such a dreadful place and position, and she needs so much. She is sick. Can't you give me a prescription for each of them?"

"You just bet I can," said the doctor, "if you can engineer their taking them."

"I suppose you'd hold their noses and pour stuff down them."

"I would if necessary."

"Well, it is."

"All right——I'll fix something, and you see that they use it."

"I can try," said the Harvester.

"Try! Pah! You aren't half a man!"

"That's a half more than being a woman, anyway."

"She called you feminine, did she?" cried the doctor, dancing and laughing. "She ought to see you harvesting skunk cabbage and blue flag or when you are angry."

The doctor left the room for half an hour.

"Try that on them according to directions," he said, handing over a couple of bottles on his return.

"Thank you!" said the Harvester, "I will!"

"That sounds manly enough."

"Oh pother! It's not that I'm not a man, or a laggard in love; but I'd like to know what you'd do to a girl dumb with grief over the recent loss of her mother, who was her only relative worth counting, sick from God knows what exposure and privation, and now a dying relative on her hands. What could you do?"

"I'd marry her and pick her out of it!"

"I wouldn't have her, if she'd leave a sick woman for me!"

"I wouldn't either. She must stick it out until her aunt grows better; then I'll go out there and show you how to court a girl."

"I guess not! You keep the girl you did court, courted, and you'll have your hands full. How does that appear to you?"

The Harvester held up the drawing of the moth.

The doctor turned to the light.

"Good work!" he cried. "Did she do that?"

"She did. In a little over an hour."

"Fine! She should have a chance."

"She is going to. She is going to have all the opportunity that is coming to her."

"Good for you, David! Any time I can help!"

The Harvester replaced the sketch and went to the wagon; but he left Belshazzar in charge, while he visited the largest dry goods store in Onabasha. There he held a conference with the floor walker. When he came out he carried a heaping load of boxes of every size and shape, with a label on each. He drove to Medicine Woods singing and whistling.

"She didn't want me to go, Belshazzar!" he chuckled to the dog. "She was more afraid of a cow than she was of me. I made some headway to-day, old boy. She doesn't seem to have a ray of an idea what I am there for, but she is going to trust me soon now; that is written in the books. Oh I hope she will be there to-morrow, and the luna will be out. Got half a notion to take the case and lay it in the warmest place I can find. But if it comes out and she isn't there, I'll be sorry. Better trust to luck."

The Harvester stabled Betsy, fed the stock, and visited with the birds. After supper he took his purchases and entered her room. He opened the drawers of the chest he had made, and selecting the labelled boxes he laid them in. But not a package did he open. Then he arose and radiated conceit of himself.

"I'll wager she will like those," he commented proudly, "because Kane promised me fairly that he would have the right things put up for a girl the size of the clerk I selected for him, and exactly what Ruth should have. That girl was slenderer and not quite so tall, but he said everything was made long on purpose. Now what else should I get?"

He turned to the dressing table and taking a note-book from his pocket made this list:

> Rugs for bed and bath room.
> Mattresses, pillows and bedding.
> Dresses for all occasions.
> All kinds of shoes and overshoes.

"There are gloves, too!" exclaimed the Harvester. "She has to have some, but how am I going to know what is right? Oh, but she needs shoes! High, low, slippers, everything! I wonder what that clerk wears. I don't believe shoes would be comfortable without being fitted, or at least the proper size. I wonder what kind of dresses she likes. I hope she's fond of white. A woman always appears loveliest in that. Maybe I'd better buy what I'm sure of and let her select the dresses. But I'd love to have this room crammed with girl-fixings when she comes. Doesn't seem as if she ever has had any little luxuries. I can't miss it on anything a woman uses. Let me think!" Slowly he wrote again: Parasols. Fans. Veils. Hats.

"I never can get them! I think that will keep me busy for a few days," said the Harvester as he closed the door softly, and went to look at the pupæ cases. Then he carved on the vine of the candlestick for her dressing table; with one arm around Belshazzar, re-read the story of John Muir's dog, went into the lake, and to bed.

CHAPTER XI

DEMONSTRATED COURTSHIP

WHEN the Harvester saw the Girl coming toward the woods, he spread the rug, opened and placed the table and chair, laid out the colour box, then another containing the last luna.

"Did the green one come out?" she asked, touching the box lightly.

"It did!" said the Harvester proudly, as if he were responsible for the performance. "It is an omen! It means that I am to have my long-coveted pattern for my best candlestick. It also clearly indicates that the gods of luck are with me for the day, so I get my way about everything. There won't be the least use in your asking 'why' or interposing objections. This is my clean sweep. I shall be fearfully dictatorial so you must submit, because the fates have pointed out that they favour me to-day. If you go contrary to their decrees you will have a bad time."

The Girl's smile was somewhat wan. She sank on a chair and picked up a pencil.

"Lay that down!" cried the Harvester. "You haven't had permission from the Dictator to begin drawing. You are to sit and rest a long time."

"Please may I speak?" asked the Girl.

The Harvester grew foolishly happy. Was she really

going to play the game? Of course he had hoped, but it
was hope without any foundation.

"You may," he said soberly.

"I am afraid that if you don't allow me to draw the
moth at once, I'll never get it done. I dislike to mention
it on your good day, but Aunt Molly is very restless. I
got a neighbour's little girl to watch her and call me if I'm
wanted. It's quite certain that I must go soon, so if you
would like the moth——"

"When luck is coming your way, never hurry it! You
always upset the bowl if you grow greedy and crowd. If
it is a gamble whether I get this moth, I'll take the chance;
but I won't change my foreordained programme. First,
you are to sit still ten minutes, shut your eyes, and rest. I
can't sing, but I can whistle. I'm going to entertain you
so you won't feel alone. Ready now!"

The Girl leaned her elbows on the table, closed her eyes,
and pressed her slender white hands over them.

"Please don't call the birds," she said. "I can't rest if
you do. It was so exciting trying to see all of them and to
guess what they were saying."

"No," said the Harvester gently. "This ten minutes is
for relaxation, you know. You ease every muscle, sink
limply on your chair, lean on the table, let go all over, and
don't think. Merely listen to me. I assure you it's going
to be perfectly lovely."

Watching intently he saw the strained muscles relaxing
at his suggestion and caught the smile over the last words
as he slid into a low whistle. It was an easy, slow, old-
fashioned tune, carrying along gently, with neither heights

nor depths, just monotonous, sleepy, soothing notes, that went on and on with a little ripple of change at times, only to return to the theme, until at last the Girl lifted her head.

"It's far past ten minutes," she said, "but that was a real rest. Truly, I am better prepared for work."

"Broke the rule, too!" said the Harvester. "It was for me to say when time was up. Can't you allow me to have my way for ten minutes?"

"I am so anxious to see and draw this moth," she answered. "But first of all you promised to bring the drawings you have been using."

"Now where does my programme come in?" inquired the Harvester. "You are spoiling everything. I refuse to have my lucky day interfered with; therefore we will ignore the suggestion until we reach the place where it is proper. Next comes refreshments."

He arose to clear the table. Then he spread on it a paper tray cloth with a gay border, and going into the thicket brought out a box and a big bucket containing a jug packed in ice. The Girl's eyes widened. She reached down, caught up a piece, holding it to drip a second, then started to put it in her mouth.

"Drop that!" commanded the Harvester. "That's a very unhealthful proceeding. Wait a minute."

From one end of the box he produced a tin of wafers, from the other a plate. Then he dug into the ice, lifting chilled fruit. From the jug he poured a combination that he made of the juices of oranges, pineapples, and lemons. He set the glass, rapidly frosting in the heat, and the fruit before the Girl.

"Now!" he said.

For one instant she stared at the table. Then she looked at him. In the depths of her dark eyes was an appeal he never forgot.

"I made that drink myself, so it's all right," he assured her. "There's a pretty stiff touch of pineapple in it. It cuts the cobwebs on a hot day. Please try it!"

"I can't!" cried the Girl with a half-sob. "Think of Aunt Molly!"

"Are you fond of her?"

"No. I never saw her until a few weeks ago. Since then I've seen mostly her poor, tired back. She lies in a heap facing the wall. But if she could have things like these, she needn't suffer. And if my mother could have had them she would be living to-day. Oh Man, I can't touch this."

"I see," said the Harvester.

He reached over, picked up the glass, and poured its contents into the jug. He repacked the fruit and closed the wafer box. Then he made a trip to the thicket and came out putting something into his pocket.

"Come on!" he said. "We are going to the house."

She stared at him. "I simply don't dare."

"Then I will go alone," said the Harvester, taking the bucket and starting.

The Girl followed him.

"Uncle Henry may come any minute," she urged.

"Well if he comes and acts unpleasantly, he will get what he richly deserves."

"And he will make me pay for it afterward."

"Oh no he won't!" said the Harvester. "I'll look out for that. This is my lucky day. He isn't going to come."

When he reached the back door he opened it, stepping inside. Of all the barren places of crude, disheartening ugliness the Harvester ever had seen, that was the worst.

"I want a glass and a spoon," he said.

The Girl brought them.

"Where is she?"

"In the next room."

At the sound of their voices a small girl came to the kitchen door.

"How do you do?" inquired the Harvester. "Is Mrs. Jameson asleep?"

"I don't know," answered the child. "She just lies there."

The Harvester gave her the glass. "Please fill that with water," he said. Then he picked up the bucket and went into the front room. When the child came with the water he took a bottle from his pocket, filled the spoon, and handed it to her.

"Hold that steadily," he said.

Then he slid his strong hands under the light frame, turning the face of the faded little creature toward him.

"I am a Medicine Man, Mrs. Jameson," he said casually. "I heard you were sick, so I came to see if a little of this stuff wouldn't brace you up. Open your lips."

He held out the spoon. The amazed woman swallowed the contents before she realized what she was doing. Then the Harvester ran a hand under her shoulders; lifting her gently he tossed her pillow with the other hand.

"You are a light little body, much like my mother," he commented.   "Now I have something else sick people sometimes enjoy."

He held the fruit juice to her lips as he slightly raised her on the pillow.   Her trembling fingers lifted, closing around the sparkling glass.

"Oh it's cool!" she gasped.

"It is," said the Harvester, "and sour!   I think you **can** take it.   Try!"

She drank so greedily he drew away the glass, urging caution, but the shaking fingers clung to him; the wavering voice begged for more.

"In a minute," said the Harvester gently.   But the fevered woman would not wait.   She drank the cooling liquid until she could take no more.   Then she watched him fill a small pitcher, pack it in a part of the ice and lay some fruit around it.

"Who, Ruth?" she panted.

"A Medicine Man who heard about you."

"What will Henry say?"

"He won't know," explained the Girl, smoothing the hot forehead.   "I'll put it in the cupboard, and slip it to you while he is out of the room.   It will make you strong and well."

"I don't want to be strong and well and suffer it all over again.   I want to rest.   Give me more of the cool drink. Give me all I want, then I'll go to sleep."

"It's wonderful," said the Girl.   "That's more than I've heard her talk since I came.   She is much stronger.   Please let her have it."

The Harvester assented.   He gave the child some of the fruit, telling her to sit beside the bed and hold the drink when it was asked for.   She agreed to be very careful and watchful.   Then he took the bucket, and accompanied by the Girl, returned to the woods.

"Now we must begin all over again," he said, as she seated herself at the table.   "Because of the walk in the heat, this time the programme is a little different."

He replaced the wafer box, opened it, filled the glass, and heaped the cold fruit.

"Your aunt is going to have a refreshing sleep now," he said, "so your mind can be free about her for an hour or two.   I am very sure your mother would not want you deprived of anything because she missed it, so you are to enjoy this, if you care for it.   At least try a sample."

The Girl lifted the glass to her lips with a trembling hand.

"I'm like Aunt Molly," she said; "I wish I could drink all I could swallow; then lie down and go to sleep forever. I suppose this is what they have in Heaven."

"No, it's what they drink all over earth at present, but I have a conceit of my own brand.   Some of it is too strong of one fruit or of the other; all too sweet for health.   This is compounded scientifically, so it's just right.   If you are not accustomed to cold drinks, go slowly."

"You can't scare me," said the Girl; "I'm going to drink all I want."

There was a note of excitement in the Harvester's laugh.

"You must have some, too!"

"After a while," he said.   "I was thirsty when I made it, so I don't care for any more now.   Try the fruit and those wafers. Of course they are not home made—they are the best I could do at a bakery. Take time enough to eat slowly. I'm going to tell you a tale while you lunch. It's about a Medicine Man named David Langston. It's a very peculiar story, but it's quite true. This man lives in the woods east of Onabasha, accompanied by his dog, horse, cow, and chickens, and a forest full of birds, flowers, and matchless trees. He has lived there in this manner for six long years. Every spring he and his dog have a seance and agree whether he shall go on gathering medicinal herbs and trying his hand at making medicine or go to the city to live as other men. Always the dog chooses to remain in the woods.

"Then every spring, on the day the first bluebird comes, the dog also decides whether the man shall go on alone or find a mate and bring her home for company. Each year the dog regularly has decided that they live as before. This spring, for some unforeseen reason, he changed his mind, and compelled the man, according to his vow in the beginning, to go courting. The man was so very angry at the idea of having a woman in his home, interfering with his work, disturbing his arrangements, and perhaps wanting to spend more money than he could afford, that he struck the dog for making that decision; struck him for the very first time in his life——I believe you'd like those apricots. Please try one."

"Go on with the story," said the Girl, sipping delicately but constantly at the frosty glass.

The Harvester arosè and refilled it. Then he dropped pieces of ice over the fruit.

"Where was I?" he inquired casually.

"Where you struck Belshazzar, and it's no wonder," answered the Girl.

Without taking time to ponder that, the Harvester continued:

"But that night the man had a wonderful, golden dream. A beautiful girl came to him, and she was so gracious and lovely that he was sufficiently punished for striking his dog, because he fell unalterably in love with her."

"Meaning you?" interrupted the Girl.

"Yes," said the Harvester, "meaning me. I——if you like——fell in love with the girl. She came so alluringly, and I was so close to her that I saw her better than I ever did any other girl, so I knew her for all time. When she went, my heart was gone."

"And you have lived without that important organ ever since?"

"Without even the ghost of it! She took it with her. Well, that dream was so real, that the next day I began building over my house, making furniture, and planting flowers for her; and every day, wherever I went, I watched for her."

"What nonsense!"

"I can't see it."

"You won't find a girl you dreamed about in a thousand years."

"Wrong!" cried the Harvester triumphantly. "Saw her in little less than three months, but she vanished and it took some time and difficult work before I located her again; but I've got her all solid now, so she doesn't escape."

"Is she a 'lovely and gracious lady?'"

"She is!" said the Harvester, emphatically.

"Young and beautiful, of course!"

"Indeed yes!"

"Please fill this glass. I told you what I was going to do."

The Harvester obeyed, then the Girl drank.

"Now won't you set aside these things and allow me to go to work?" she asked. "My call may come any minute, so I'll never forgive myself if I waste time, and don't draw your moth pattern for you."

"It's against my principles to hurry; besides, my story isn't finished."

"It is," said the Girl. "She is young and lovely, gentle and a lady, you have her 'all solid,' and she can't 'escape;' that's the end, of course. But if I were you, I wouldn't have her until I gave her a chance to get away, and saw whether she would if she could."

"Oh I am not a jailer," said the Harvester. "She shall be free if I cannot make her love me; but I can, and I will; I swear it."

"You are truly in earnest?"

"I am in deadly earnest."

"Honestly, you dreamed about a girl, and then found the very one?"

"Most certainly, I did."

"It sounds like the wildest romancing."

"It is the veriest reality."

"Well I hope you win her, and that she will be everything you desire."

"Thank you," said the Harvester. "It's written in the book of fate that I succeed. The very elements are with me. The South Wind carried a message to her for me. I am going to marry her, but you could make it much easier for me if you would."

"I! What could I do?" cried the Girl.

"You could cease being afraid of me. You could learn to trust me. You could try to like me, if you see anything likeable about me. That would encourage me so that I could tell you of my Dream Girl, and then you could show me how to win her. A woman always knows about those things better than a man. You could be the greatest help in all the world to me, if only you would."

"I couldn't possibly! I can't leave here. I have no proper clothing to appear before another girl. She would be shocked at my white face. That I could help you is the most improbable dream you have had."

"You must pardon me if I differ from you, and persist in thinking that you can be of invaluable assistance to me, if you will. But you can't influence my Dream Girl, if you fear and distrust me yourself. Promise me that you will help me that much, anyway."

"I'll do all I can. I only want to make you see that I am in no position to grant any favours, no matter how much I owe you or how I'd like to. Is the candlestick you are carving for her?"

"It is," said the Harvester. "I am making a pair of maple for a dressing table I built for her. It is unusually beautiful wood, so I hope she will like it."

"Please take these things away and let me begin. This

is the only thing I can see that I can do for you, and the moth will want to fly before I have finished."

The Harvester cleared the table and placed the box, while the Girl spread the paper, then began work eagerly.

"I wonder if I knew there were such exquisite things in all the world," she said. "I scarcely think I did. I am beginning to understand why you couldn't kill one. You could make a chair or a table; so you feel free to destroy them; but it takes ages and Almighty wisdom to evolve a creature like this, so you don't dare. I think no one else would if they really knew. Please talk while I work."

"Is there a particular subject you want discussed?"

"Anything but her. If I think too strongly of her, I can't work so well."

"Your ginseng is almost dry," said the Harvester. "I think I can bring you the money in a few days."

"So soon!" she cried.

"It dries day and night in an even temperature, and faster than you would believe. There's going to be between seven and eight pounds of it, when I make up what it has shrunk. It will go under the head of the finest wild roots. I can get eight for it sure."

"Oh what good news!" cried the Girl. "This is my lucky day, too. And the little girl isn't coming, so Aunt Molly must be asleep. Everything goes right! If only Uncle Henry wouldn't come home!"

"Let me fill your glass," proffered the Harvester.

"Just half way, then set it where I can see it," said the Girl. She worked with swift strokes, while there was a hint of colour in her face, as she looked at him. "I hope you won't think I'm greedy," she said, "but truly, that's the first thing I've had that I could taste in——I can't remember when."

"I'll bring a barrel to-morrow," offered the Harvester, "and a big piece of ice wrapped in coffee sacking."

"You mustn't think of such a thing! Ice is expensive and so are fruits."

"Ice costs me the time required to saw and pack it at my home. I almost live on the fruit I raise. I confess to a fondness for this drink. I have no other personal expenses, unless you count in books, and a very few clothes, such as I'm wearing; so I surely can afford all the fruit juice I want."

"For yourself, yes."

"Also for a couple of women or I am a mighty poor attempt at a man," said the Harvester. "This is my day, so you are not to talk, because it won't do any good. Things go my way."

"Please see what you think of this," she said.

The Harvester arose to bend over her.

"That will do finely," he answered. "You can stop. I don't require all those little details for carving, I merely want a good outline. It is finished. See here!"

He drew some folded papers from his pocket and laid them before her.

"Those are what I have been working from," he said.

The Girl took them, studying each carefully.

"If those are worth five dollars to you," she said gently, "why then I needn't hesitate to take as much for mine. They are superior."

"I should say so," laughed the Harvester as he picked up the drawing and laid down the money.

"If you would make it half that much I'd feel better about it," she said.

"How could I?" asked the Harvester. "Your fingers are well trained and extremely skilful. Because some one has not been paying you enough for your work is no reason why I should keep it up. From now on you must have what others get. As soon as you can arrange for work, I want to tell you about some designs I have studied out from different things, show you the plants and insects, then have you make some samples. I'll send them to proper places, and see what experts say about the ideas and drawing. Work in the woods is healthful, with proper precautions; it's easy compared with the exactions of being bound to sewing or embroidering in the confinement of a room; it's vividly interesting in the search for new subjects, changes of material, and differing harmonious combinations; it's truly artistic; while it brings the prices high-grade stuff always does."

"Almost you give me hope," said the Girl. "Almost, Man——almost! Since mother died, I haven't thought or planned beyond paying for the medicine she took and the shelter she lies in. Oh I didn't mean to say that——!"

She buried her face in her hands. The Harvester suffered until he scarcely knew how to endure it.

"Please finish," he begged. "You hadn't planned beyond the debt, you were saying——"

The Girl lifted her tired, strained face.

"Give me a little more of that delicious drink," she said. "I am ravenous for it. It puts new life in me. This and what you say bring a far away, misty vision of a clean, bright, peaceful room somewhere, and work one could love and live on in comfort; enough to give a desire to finish life to its natural end. Oh Man, you make me hope in spite of myself!"

"'Praise God from whom all blessings flow;'" quoted the Harvester reverently. "Now try one of these peaches. It's juicy and cold. Get that room right in focus in your brain, then nurture the idea. Its walls shall be bright as sunshine, its floor creamy white, and it shall open into a small garden, where only yellow flowers grow, and the birds shall sing. The first ray of sun that peeps over the hills of morning shall fall through its windows across your bed, and you shall work only as you please, after you've had months of play and rest; it's coming true the instant you can leave here. Dream of it, make up your mind to it, because it's coming. I have a streak of second sight, so I see it on the way."

"You are talking wildly," said the Girl, "else you are a good genie trying to conjure a room for me."

"This room I am talking of is ready whenever you want to take possession," said the Harvester. "Accept it as a reality, because I tell you I know where it is, that it is waiting, while you can earn your way into it with no obligation to any one."

The Girl stretched out her right hand, then slowly turned and opened and closed it. She glanced at the Harvester with a weary smile.

"From somewhere I feel a glimmering of the spirit, but Oh, dear Lord, the flesh is weak!" she said.

"That's where nourishing foods, appetizing drinks, plenty of pure, fresh air, and good water come in. Now we have talked enough for one day, and worked too much. The fruit and drink go with you. I will carry it to the house, and you can hide it in your room. I am going to put a bottle of tonic on top that the best surgeon in the state gave me for you. Try to eat something strengthening and then take a spoonful of this, and use all the fruit you want. I'll bring more to-morrow and put it here, with plenty of ice. Now suppose you let the moth go free," he suggested to avoid objections. "You must take my word for it, that it is perfectly harmless, lacking either sting or bite, and hold your hand before it, so that it will climb on your fingers. Then stand where a ray of sunshine falls and in a few minutes it will go out to live its life."

The Girl hesitated a second as she studied the clean-cut, interested face of the man; then she held out her hand, and he urged the moth to climb on her fingers. She stepped where a ray of strong light fell on the forest floor, holding the moth in it. The brightness also touched her transparent hand, her white face and the gleaming black hair. The Harvester choked down a rising surge of desire for her, then took a new grip on himself.

"Oh!" she cried breathlessly, as the clinging feet suddenly loosened while the luna slowly flew away among the trees. She turned to the Harvester. "You teach me wonders!" she cried. "You give life different meanings. You are not as other men."

"If that be true, it is because I am of the woods. The Almighty does not evolve all his wonders in animal, bird, and flower form; He keeps some to work out in the heart, if humanity only will go to His school, and allow Him to have dominion. Come now, you must go. I will come back and put away all the things and to-morrow I will bring your ginseng money. Any time you cannot come, if you want to tell me why, or if there is anything I can do for you, put a line under the oilcloth. I will carry the bucket."

"I am so afraid," she said.

"I will only go to the edge of the woods. You can see if there is any one at the house first. If not, you can send the child away; then I shall carry the bucket to the door for you, and it will furnish comfort for one night, at least."

They went to the cleared land, then the Girl passed on alone. Soon she reappeared. The Harvester saw the child going down the road. He set the bucket inside the door.

"Is there anything I can do for you?"

"Nothing but go, before you make trouble."

"Will you hide that stuff and walk back as far as the woods with me? There is something more I want to say to you."

The Girl staggered under the heavy load, so the man turned his head and pretended he did not see. Presently she came to him, and they returned to the line of the woods. Just as they entered the shade there was a flash before them; on a twig a few rods away a little gray bird alighted, while in precipitate pursuit came a flaming wonder of red, that in a burst of excited trills, broken whistles, and imploring gestures, perched beside her.

The Harvester drew the Girl behind some bushes.

"Watch!" he whispered. "You are going to see a sight so lovely and so rare it is vouchsafed to few mortals ever to behold."

"What are they fighting about?" she whispered.

"You are witnessing a cardinal bird declare his love," breathed the Harvester.

"Do cardinals love different birds?"

"No. The female is gray, because if she is coloured the same as the trees, branches and her nest, she will have more chance to bring off her young in safety. He is blood red, because he is the bravest, gayest, most ardent lover of the whole woods," explained the Harvester.

The Girl leaned forward breathlessly watching, while a slow surge of colour crept into her cheeks. The red bird twisted, whistled, rocked, tilted, and trilled, and the gray sat demurely watching him, as if only half convinced he really meant it. The gay lover began at the beginning, saying it all over again with more impassioned gestures than before; then he edged in touch and softly stroked her wing with his beak. She appeared startled, but did not fly. So again the fountain of half-whistled, half-trilled notes bubbled with the acme of pleading intonation, while that time he leaned and gently kissed her as she reached her bill for the caress. Then she fled in headlong flight; the streak of flame darting after her. The Girl caught her breath in a swift spasm of surprise and wonder. She turned to the Harvester.

"What was it you wanted to say to me?" she asked hurriedly.

The Harvester was not the man to miss the goods the gods provided. Truly this was his lucky day. Unhesitating he answered: "Precisely what he said to her. And if you observed closely, you noticed that she didn't ask him 'why.'"

Before she could open her lips, he was gone, his swift strides carrying him through the woods.

CHAPTER XII

"The Way of a Man with a Maid"

THE following day the Harvester lifted the oil-cloth, and picking up a folded note he read——
"Aunt Molly found rest in the night. She was more comfortable than she has been since I have known her. Close the end she whispered to me to thank you if I ever saw you again. She will be buried to-morrow. Past that, I dare not think."

The Harvester sat on the log, studying the lines. She would not come that day or the next. After a long time he put the note in his pocket, wrote an answer telling her he had been there; would come the following day on the chance of her wanting anything he could do, while the next he would bring the ginseng money, so she must be sure to meet him.

Then he went back to the wagon, turned Betsy, and drove around the Jameson land watching closely. There were several vehicles in the barn lot, and a couple of men sitting under the trees of the door yard. Faded bedding hung on the line; women moved through the rooms, but he could not see the Girl. Slowly he drove on until he came to the first house, where he stopped and went in. He saw the child of the previous day, and as she came forward her mother appeared in the doorway.

The Harvester explained who he was, that he was examining the woods in search of some almost extinct herbs he needed in his business. Then he told of having been at the adjoining farm the day before and about the sick woman. He added that later she had died. He casually mentioned that a young woman there seemed pale and ill and wondered if the neighbours would see her through. He suggested that the place appeared as if the owner did not take much interest in it. When the woman finished with Henry Jameson, he said how very important it seemed to him that some good, kind-hearted soul should go and mother the poor girl. The woman thought she was the very person. Without knowing exactly how he did it, the Harvester left with her promise to remain with the Girl the coming two nights. The woman had her hands full of strange and delicious fruit without understanding why it had been given her, or why she had made those promises. She thought the Harvester a remarkably fine young man to take such interest in strangers, so she told him he was welcome to anything he could find on her place that would help with his medicines.

The Harvester just happened to be coming from the woods as the woman freshly dressed left the house, so he took her in the wagon and drove back to the Jameson place, because he was going that way. Then he returned to Medicine Woods and worked with all his might.

First he polished floors, cleaned windows, and arranged the rooms as best he could inside the cabin; then he gave a finishing touch to everything outside. He could not have told why he did it, but he thought it was because there was hope that now the Girl would come to Onabasha. If he found opportunity to bring her to the city, he hoped that possibly he might drive home with her and show Medicine Woods, so everything must be in order. Then he worked with flying fingers in the dry-house, putting up her ginseng for market. Never was weight so liberal.

The following morning he drove early to Onabasha and came home with a loaded wagon, the contents of which he scattered through the cabin where it seemed most suitable, but the greater part of it was for her. He glanced at the bare floors and walls of the outer rooms, thinking of trying to improve them, but he was afraid of not getting the right things.

"I don't know much about what is needed here," he said, "but I am perfectly safe in buying anything a girl ever used."

Then he returned to the city, explained the situation to the doctor, and selected the room he wanted in case the Girl could be persuaded to come to the hospital. After that he went to see the doctor's wife, and made arrangements for her to be ready for a guest, because there was a possibility he might want to call for help. He had another jug of fruit-juice and all the delicacies he could think of, also a big cake of ice, when he reached the woods. There were only a few words for him.

"I will come to-morrow at two, if at all possible; if not, keep the money until I can."

There was nothing to do except to place his offering under the oilcloth and wait, but he simply was compelled

to add a line to say he would be there, also to express the
hope that she was comfortable as possible and thinking of
the sunshine room.

At noon the following day he bathed, shaved, and
dressed in fresh, clean clothing.　He stopped in Onabasha
for more fruit, then drove to the Jameson woods.　He was
waiting and watching the usual path the Girl followed,
when her step sounded on the other side.　The Harvester
arose and turned.　Her pallor was alarming.　She stepped
on the rug he had spread, sinking almost breathless on the
chair.

"Why do you come a new way that fills you with fear?"
asked the Harvester.

"It seems as if Uncle Henry is watching me every
minute, and I didn't dare come where he could see.　I
must not remain a second.　You must take these things
away and go at once.　He is dreadful."

"So am I," said the Harvester, "when affairs go too
everlastingly wrong.　I am not afraid of any man living.
What are you planning to do?"

"I want to ask you, are you sure about the prices of my
drawing and the ginseng?"

"Absolutely," said the Harvester.　"As for the ginseng
it went in fresh and early, best wild roots, so it brought
eight a pound.　There were eight pounds when I made up
weight and here is your money."

He handed her a long envelope addressed to her.

"What is the amount?" she asked.

"Sixty-four dollars."

"I can't believe it."

"You have it in your fingers."

"You know that I would like to thank you properly, if I had words to express myself."

"Never mind that," said the Harvester. "Tell me what you are planning. Say that you will come to the hospital for the long, perfect rest now."

"It is absolutely impossible. Don't weary me by mentioning it. I cannot."

"Will you tell me what you intend doing?"

"I must," she said, "for it depends entirely on your word. I am going to get Uncle Henry's supper, and then go and remain the night with the neighbour who has been helping me. In the morning, when he leaves, she is coming with her wagon for my trunk. She is going to drive with me to Onabasha, find me a cheap room and lend me a few things, until I can buy what I need. I am going to use fourteen dollars of this and my drawing money for what I am forced to buy, then pay fifty on my debt. I will send you my address when I am ready for work."

She clutched the envelope, then for the first time looked at him.

"Very well," said the Harvester. "I could take you to the wife of my best friend, the chief surgeon of the city hospital, where everything would be ease and rest until you are strong; she would love to have you."

The Girl dropped her hands wearily.

"Don't tire me with it!" she cried. "I am almost falling despite the stimulus of food and drink I can touch. I never can thank you properly for that. I won't be able to work hard enough to show you how much I appreciate

what you have done for me.   But you don't understand.
A woman, even a poverty-poor woman, if she be delicately
born and reared, cannot go to another woman on a man's
whim; when she lacks even the barest necessities.   I don't
refuse to meet your friends.   I shall love to, when I can be
so dressed that I will not shame you.   Until that time
comes, if you are the gentleman you appear to be, you will
wait without urging me further."

"I must be a man, in order to be a gentleman," said the
Harvester.   "And it is because the man in me is in hot re-
bellion against more loneliness, pain, and suffering for you,
that the conventions become chains I do not care how soon
or how roughly I break.   If only you could be induced to
say the word, I tell you I could bring one of God's gentlest
women to you."

"And probably she would come in a dainty gown, in her
carriage or motor, then be disgusted, astonished, and
secretly sorry for you.   As for me, I do not require her
pity.   I will be glad to know the beautiful, refined, and
gentle woman you are so certain of, but not until I am
better dressed and more attractive in appearance than
now.   If you will give me your address, I will write you
when I am ready for work."

Silently the Harvester wrote it.   "Will you give me permission to take these things to your neighbour for you?"
he asked.   "They would serve until you can do better, and
I have no earthly use for them."

She hesitated.   Then she laughed shortly.

"What a travesty' my efforts at pride are with you!"
she cried.   "I begin by trying to preserve some proper dig-

nity; then end by confessing abject poverty. I yet have
the ten you paid me the other day, but twenty-four dollars
are not much to set up housekeeping on, so I would be
gladder than I can say for these very things."

"Thank you," said the Harvester. "I will take them
when I go. Is there anything else?"

"I think not."

"Will you have a drink?"

"Yes, if you have more with you. I believe it is really
cooling my blood."

"Are you taking the medicine?"

"Yes," she said, "and I am truly stronger. I know I
appear ghastly to you, but it's loss of sleep, trying to lay
away poor Aunt Molly decently, and——"

"And fear of Uncle Henry," added the Harvester.

"Yes," said the Girl. "That most of all! He thinks
I am going to stay here, to take her place. I can't tell him
I am not, and how I am to hide from him when I am gone,
I don't know. I am afraid of him."

"Has he any claim on you?"

"Shelter for the past three months."

"Are you of age?"

"I am almost twenty-four," she said.

"Then suppose you leave Uncle Henry to me," suggested the Harvester.

"Why?"

"Careful now! The red bird told you why!" said the
man. "I will not urge it upon you now, but keep it
steadily in the back of your head that there is a sunshine
room all ready and waiting for you, while I am going to

take you to it very soon.   As things are, I think you might allow me to tell you——"

She was on her feet in instant panic.   "I must go," she said.   "Uncle Henry is dogging me to promise to remain; I will not, so he is watching me.   I must go——"

"Can you give me your word of honour that you will go to the neighbour woman to-night; that you feel perfectly safe?"

She hesitated.   "Yes, I——I think so.   Yes, if he doesn't find out and grow angry.   Yes, I will be safe."

"How soon will you write me?"

"Just as soon as I am settled and rest a little."

"Do you mean several days?"

"Yes, several days."

"An eternity!" cried the Harvester with white lips.   "I cannot let you go.   Suppose you fall ill, fail to write me, and I do not know where you are, while there is no one to care for you."

"But can't you see that I don't know where I will be?   If it will satisfy you, I will write you to-morrow night to tell you where I am, then you can come later."

"Is that a promise?" asked the Harvester.

"It is," said the Girl.

"Then I will take these things to your neighbour and wait until to-morrow night.   You won't fail me?"

"I never in all my life saw a man so wild over designs," said the Girl, as she started toward the house.

"Don't forget that the design I'm craziest about is the same as the red bird's," the Harvester flung after her, but she hurried on, making no reply.

He folded the table and chair, rolled the rug, and

shouldering them picked up the bucket, then started down the river bank.

"David!"

Such a faint little call he never would have been sure he heard anything if Belshazzar had not stopped suddenly. The hair on the back of his neck arose as he turned with a growl in his throat. The Harvester dropped his load with a crash and ran in leaping bounds, but the dog was before him. Halfway to the house, Ruth Jameson swayed in the grip of her uncle. One hand clutched his coat front in a spasmodic grasp; with the other she covered her face.

The roar the Harvester sent up stayed the big, lifted fist, while the dog leaped for a throat hold, compelling the man to defend himself. The Harvester never knew how he covered the space until he stood between them, and saw the Girl draw back, snatching together the front of her dress.

"He took it from me!" she panted. "Make him, oh make him give back my money!"

Then for a few seconds things happened too rapidly to record. Once the Harvester tossed a torn envelope exposing money to the Girl, again a revolver, then both men panting and dishevelled were on their feet.

"Count your money, Ruth!" said the Harvester in a voice of deadly quiet.

"It is all here," said she.

"Her money?" cried Henry Jameson. "My money! She has been stealing the price of my cattle from my pockets. I thought I was short several times lately."

"You are lying," said the Harvester deliberately. "It

is her money. I just paid it to her. You were trying to take it from her, not the other way."

"Oh, she is in your pay?" leered the man.

"If you say an insulting word I think very probably I shall finish you," said the Harvester. "I can, with my naked hands, while all your neighbours will say it is a good job. You have felt my grip! I warn you!"

"Why is my niece taking money from you?"

"You have forfeited all right to know. Ruth, you cannot remain here. You must come with me. I will take you to Onabasha and find you a room."

A horrible laugh broke from the man.

"So that is the end of my saintly niece!" he said.

"Remember!" cried the Harvester, advancing a step. "Ruth, will you go to the rest I suggested for you?"

"I cannot."

"Will you go to Doctor Carey's wife?"

"Impossible!"

"Will you marry me and go to the shelter of my home with me?"

Wild-eyed she stared at him.

"Why?"

"Because I love you, and want life made easier for you, above anything else on earth."

"But your Dream Girl!"

"*You are the Dream Girl!* I thought the red bird told you for me! I didn't know it would be a shock. I believed I had made you understand."

By that time she was shaking with a nervous chill; the sight unmanned the Harvester.

"Come with me!" he urged. "We will decide what you want to do on the way. Only come, I beg you."

"First it was marry, now it's decide later," broke in Henry Jameson, crazed with anger. "Move a step and I'll strike you down. I'd better than see you disgraced——"

The Harvester advanced, Jameson stepped back.

"Ruth," said the Harvester, "I know how impossible this seems. It is giving you no chance at all. I had intended, when I found you, to court you tenderly as girl ever was wooed before. Come with me, and I'll do it yet. The new home was built for you. The sunshine room is ready and waiting for you. There is pure air, fresh water, nothing but rest and comfort. I'll nurse you back to health and strength, and you shall be courted until you come to me of your own accord."

"Impossible!" cried the girl.

"Only if you make it so. If you will come now, we can be married in a few hours, and you can be safe in your own home. I realize now that this is unexpected and shocking to you, but if you will come with me and allow me to restore you to health and strength, and if, say, in a year, you are convinced that you do not love me, I will set you free. If you will come, I swear to you that you shall be my wife first, and my honoured guest afterward, until such time as you either tell me you love me or that you never can. Will you come on those terms, Ruth?"

"I cannot!"

"It will end fear, uncertainty, and work, until you are strong and well. It will give you home, rest, and love, that you will find is worth your consideration. I will keep my word; of that you may be sure."

"No," she cried. "No! But take back this money! Keep it until I tell you to whom to pay it."

She started toward him, holding out the envelope.

Henry Jameson, with a dreadful oath, sprang for it, his contorted face a drawn snarl. The Harvester caught him in air and sent him reeling. He snatched the revolver from the Girl, then put the money in his pocket.

"Ruth, I can't leave you here," he said. "Oh my Dream Girl! Are you afraid of me yet? Won't you trust me? Won't you come?"

"No."

"You are right about that, my lady; you will come back to the house, that's what you'll do," said Henry Jameson, starting toward her.

"No!" cried the Girl, retreating. "Oh Heaven help me! What am I to do?"

"Ruth, you must come with me," said the Harvester. "I don't dare leave you here."

She stood between them, giving Henry Jameson one long, searching look. Then she turned to the Harvester.

"I am far less afraid of you. I will accept your offer," she said.

"Thank you!" said the Harvester. "I will keep my word. You shall have no regrets. Is there anything here you wish to take with you?"

"I want a little trunk of my mother's. It contains some things of hers."

"Will you show me where it is?"

She started toward the house; he followed, then Henry Jameson fell in line. The Harvester turned to him. "You remain where you are," he said. "I will take nothing but the trunk. I know what you are thinking, but you will not get your gun just now. I will return this revolver to-morrow."

"And the first thing I do with it will be to use it on you," said Henry Jameson.

"I'll report that threat to the police, so that they can see you properly hanged if you do," retorted the Harvester, as he followed the girl.

"Where is his gun?" he asked as he overtook her. When he reached the house he told her to watch the door. He went inside, broke the lock from the gun in the corner, found the trunk, swung it to his shoulder, passed Henry Jameson, and went back through the woods. The Harvester set the trunk in the wagon, helped the Girl in, then returned for the load he had dropped at her call. Then he took the lines and started to Onabasha.

The Girl beside him was almost fainting. He stopped to give her a drink, trying to encourage her.

"Brace up the best you can, Ruth," he said. "You must go with me for a license; that is the law. Afterward, I'll make it just as easy for you as possible. I will do everything. In a few hours you will be comfortable in your room. You brave girl! This must come out right! You have suffered more than your share. I will have peace for you the remainder of the way."

She lifted shaking hands, trying to arrange her hair and dress. As they neared the city she spoke.

"What will they ask me?"

"I don't know. But I am sure the law requires you to appear in person now. I can take you somewhere and find out first."

"That will take time. I want to reach my room. What would you think?"

"If you are of age, where you were born, if you are a native of this country, what your father and mother died of, how old they were, and such questions as that. I'll help you all I can. You know those things, don't you?"

"Yes. But I must tell you——"

"I don't want to be told anything," said the Harvester. "Save your strength. All I want to know is any way in which I can make this easier for you. Nothing else matters. I will tell you what I think; if you have any objections, make them. I will drive to the bank, get a draft for what you owe, and have that off your mind. Then we will get the license. After that I'll take you to the side door, slip you in the elevator and to the fitting room of a store where I know the manager, and you shall have some pretty clothing while I arrange for a minister, then I'll come for you with a carriage. That isn't the kind of wedding you or any other girl should have, but there are times when a man only can do his best. You will help me, won't you?"

"Anything you choose. It doesn't matter——only be quick as possible."

"There are a few details to which I must attend," said the Harvester, "and the time will go faster trying on dresses than waiting alone. When you are properly clothed you will feel better. What did you say the amount you owe is?"

"You may get a draft for fifty dollars. I will **pay the** remainder when I earn it."

"Ruth, won't you give me the pleasure of taking you home free from the worry of that debt?"

"I am not going to 'worry.' I am going to work and pay it."

"Very well," said the Harvester. "This is the bank. We will stop here."

As they went in, he handed her a slip of paper.

"Write the name and address on that?" he said.

When the slip was returned to him, without a glance he folded and slid it under a wicket. "Write a draft for fifty dollars payable to that party, and send to that address, from Miss Ruth Jameson," he said.

Then he turned to her.

"That is over. See how easy it is! Now we will go to the court house. It is very close. Try not to think. Just move and speak."

"Hello, Langston!" said the clerk. "What can we do for you here?"

"Show this girl every consideration," whispered the Harvester, as he advanced. "I want a marriage license in your best time. I will answer first."

With the document in his possession, they went to the store he designated, where he found the Girl a chair in the fitting room, while he went to see the manager.

"I want one of your most sensible and accommodating

clerks," said the Harvester, "and I would like a few words with her."

When she was presented he scrutinized her carefully, deciding she would do.

"I have many thanks and something more substantial for a woman who will help me to carry through a slightly unusual project with sympathy and ability," he said, "and the manager has selected you.   Are you willing?"

"If I can," said the clerk.

"She has put up your other orders," interposed the manager; "were they satisfactory?"

"I don't know," said the Harvester.   "They have not yet reached the one for whom they were intended.   What I want you to do," he said to the clerk, "is to go to the fitting room and dress the girl you find there for her wedding.   She had other plans, but death disarranged them, so she has only an hour in which to meet the event most girls love to linger over for months.   She has been ill, and is worn with watching; but some time she may look back to her wedding day with joy, so if you would help me to make the best of it for her, I would be under more obligations than I can express."

"I will do anything," said the clerk.

"Very well," said the Harvester.   "She has come from the country entirely unprepared.   She is delicate and refined.   Save her all the embarrassment you can.   Dress her beautifully in white.   Keep a memorandum slip of what you spend for my account."

"What is the limit?" asked the clerk.

"There is none," said the Harvester.   "Put the pretti-

est things on her you have in the right sizes, and if you are
a woman with a heart, be gentle!"

"Is she ready?" inquired the manager at the door an
hour later.

"I am," said the Girl, stepping through.

The astounded Harvester stood and stared, utterly oblivious of the curious people.

"Here, here, here!" suddenly he whistled it, in the
red bird's most entreating tones.

The Girl laughed and the colour in her face deepened.

"Let us go," she said.

"But what about you?" asked the manager of the
Harvester.

"Thunder!" cried the man, aghast. "I was so busy
getting everything else ready, I forgot all about myself.
I can't stand before a minister beside her, can I?"

"Well I should say not," said the manager.

"Indeed yes," said the Girl. "I never saw you in
any other clothing. You would be a stranger of whom
I'd be afraid."

"That settles it!" said the Harvester calmly. "Thank
all of you more than words can express. I will come in
the first of the week and tell you how we get along."

Then they went to the carriage and started for the
residence of a minister.

"Ruth, you are my Dream Girl to the tips of your
eyelashes," said the Harvester. "I almost wish you were
not. It wouldn't keep me thinking so much of the remainder of that dream. You are the loveliest sight I
ever saw."

"Do I really appear well?" asked the Girl, hungry for appreciation.

"Indeed you do!" said the Harvester. "I never could have guessed that such a miracle could be wrought. And you don't seem so tired. Were they good to you?"

"Wonderfully! I did not know there was kindness like that in all the world for a stranger. I did not feel lost or embarrassed, except the first few seconds when I didn't know what to do. Oh I thank you for this! You were right. Whatever comes in life I always shall love to remember 'that I was daintily dressed and appeared as well as I could when I was married. But I must tell you I am not real. They did everything on earth to me, three of them working at a time. I feel an increase in self-respect in some way. David, I do appear better?"

When she said "David," the Harvester looked out of the window, gulping down his delight. He leaned toward her.

"Shut your eyes and imagine you see the red bird," he said. "In my soul, I am saying to you again and again what he sang. You are wonderfully beautiful, Ruth, and more than wonderfully sweet. Will you answer me a question?"

"If I can."

"I love you with all my heart. Will you marry me?"

"I said I would."

"Then we are engaged, aren't we?"

"Yes."

"Please remove the glove from your left hand. I want

to put on your ring. This will have to be a very short engagement, but no one save ourselves need know."

"David, that isn't necessary."

"I have it here, and believe me, Ruth, it will help in a few minutes; while all your life you will be glad. It is a precious symbol that has a meaning. This wedding won't be hurt by putting all the sacredness into it we can. Please, Ruth!"

"On one condition."

"What is it?"

"That you will accept and wear my mother's wedding ring in exchange," she said. "It is all I have."

"Ruth, do you really wish that?"

"I do."

"I am more pleased than I can tell you. May I have it now?"

She removed her glove. The Harvester held her hand closely a second, then lifted it to his lips, passionately kissed it and slipped on a ring, the setting a big, lustrous pearl.

"I looked at some others," he said, "but nothing got a second glance save this. They knew you were coming down the ages, so they had the pearls ready. How beautiful it is on your hand! Wear that ring as if you had owned it for the long, happy year of betrothal every girl should have. You can start yours to-day. If by this time next year I have not won you to my heart and arms, I'm no man and not worthy of you. Ruth, you will try to love me, won't you?"

"I will try with all my heart," she said instantly.

"Thank you! I am perfectly happy with that. I never expected to marry you before a year, anyway. All the difference will be the blessed fact that instead of coming to see you somewhere else, I now can have you in my care, and court you every minute. You might as well make up your mind to capitulate soon. It's on the books that you do."

"If a time ever comes when I realize that I love you, I will come straight and tell you; believe me, I will."

"Thank you!" said the Harvester. "This is going to be a proper wedding after all. It will be over soon and you on the home way. Lord, Ruth——!"

The Girl smiled at him as he opened the carriage door, helped her up the steps and rang the bell.

"Be brave now!" he whispered. "Don't lose your lovely colour. These people will be as kind as the others."

The minister was gentle and wasted no time. His wife and daughter, who appeared for witnesses, kissed Ruth, and congratulated her. She and the Harvester stood, took the vows, exchanged rings, and returned to the carriage, a man and his wife by the laws of man.

"Drive to Seaton's café," the Harvester said.

"Oh David, let us go home!"

"This is so good I hate to stop it for something you may not like so well. I ordered lunch and if we don't eat it I will have to pay for it anyway. You wouldn't want me to be extravagant, would you?"

"No," said the Girl, "and besides, since you mention it, I believe I am hungry."

"Good!" cried the Harvester. "I hoped so! Ruth,

you wouldn't allow me to hold your hand until we reach the café? It might save me from bursting with joy."

"Yes," she said. "But I must take off my lovely gloves first. I want to keep them forever."

"I'd hate the glove being removed dreadfully," said the Harvester, his eyes dancing.

"I'm sorry I am so thin and shaky," said the Girl "I will be steady and plump soon, won't I?"

"On your life you will," said the Harvester, taking the hand gently.

Now there are a number of things a man deeply in love can think of to do with a woman's white hand. He can stroke it, press it tenderly, and lay it against his lips or his heart. The Harvester lacked experience in these arts; yet by some wonderful instinct all of these things occurred to him. There was real colour in the Girl's cheeks by the time he helped her into the café. They were guided to a small room, cool and restful, close a window, beside which grew a tree covered with talking leaves. A waiting attendant, who seemed perfectly adept, brought in steaming bouillon, fragrant tea, broiled chicken, properly cooked vegetables, a wonderful salad, then delicious ices and cold fruit. The happy Harvester leaned back, watching the Girl daintily manage almost as much food as he wanted to see her eat.

When they had finished: "Now we are going home," he said. "Will you try to like it, Ruth?"

"Indeed I will," she promised. "As soon as I grow accustomed to the dreadful stillness, and learn what things will not bite me, I'll do better."

"I'll have to ask you to wait a minute," he said. "I forgot to hire a man to take Betsy home."

"Aren't you going to drive her yourself?"

"No ma'am! We are going in a carriage or a motor," said the Harvester.

"Indeed we are not!" contradicted the Girl. "You have had this all your way so far. I am going home behind Betsy, with Belshazzar at my knee."

"But your dress! People will think I am crazy to put a lovely woman like you in a spring wagon."

"Let them!" said the Girl placidly. "Why should we bother about other people? I am going with Betsy and Belshazzar."

The Harvester had been thinking that he adored her, that it was impossible to love her more, but every minute was proving to him that he was capable of feeling so profound it startled him. To carry the Girl, his bride, through the valley and up the hill in the little spring wagon drawn by Betsy—that would have been his ideal way. But he had supposed that she would be afraid of soiling her dress, or embarrassed to ride in such a conveyance. Instead it was her choice. Yes, he could love her more. Hourly she was proving that.

"Come this way a few steps," he said. "Betsy is here."

The Girl laid her face against the nose of the faithful old animal, then stroked her head and neck. She held her skirts as the Harvester helped her into the wagon. She took the seat, and the dog went wild with joy.

"Come on, Bel," she softly commanded.

The dog hesitated, looking at the Harvester for permission.

"You may come here and put your head on my knee," said the Girl.

"Belshazzar, you lucky dog, you are privileged to sit there and lay your head on the lady's lap," said the Harvester, while the dog quivered with joy.

Then the man picked up the lines, gave a backward glance to the bed of the wagon, high piled with large bundles, then turned Betsy toward Medicine Woods. Through the crowded streets and toward the country they drove, when a big red car passed, a man called to them, then reversed and slowly began backing beside the wagon. The Harvester stopped.

"That is my best friend, Doctor Carey, of the hospital, Ruth," he said hastily. "May I tell him? Will you shake hands with him?"

"Certainly!" said the Girl.

"Is it really you, David?" the doctor peered with gleaming eyes from under the car top.

"Really!" cried the Harvester, as man greets man with a full heart when he is sure of sympathy. "Come give us your best send-off, Doc! We were married an hour ago. We are headed for Medicine Woods. Doctor Carey, this is Mrs. Langston."

"Mighty glad to know you!" cried the doctor, reaching a happy hand.

The Girl cordially smiled on him.

"How did this happen?" demanded the doctor. "Why

didn't you let us know? This is hardly **fair of you, David**
You might have let us share with you."

"That is to be explained," said the Harvester. "This
was decided on very suddenly, and rather sadly, on account of the death of Mrs. Jameson. I forced Ruth to
marry me and come with me. I grow rather frightened
when I think of it, but it was the only way I knew. She
absolutely refused my other plans. You see before you
a wild man carrying away a woman to his cave."

"Don't believe him, Doctor!" laughed the Girl. "If
you know him, you will understand that to offer all he
had was like him, when he saw my necessity. You will
come to see us soon?"

"I'll come right now," said the doctor. "I'll bring
my wife and arrive by the time you do."

"Oh no you won't!" said the Harvester. "Do you observe the bed of this wagon? This happened all 'unbeknownst' to us. We have to set up housekeeping this
evening. We will notify you when we are ready for visitors. You subside and wait until you are sent for."

"Why David!" cried the astonished Girl.

"That's the law!" said the Harvester tersely. "Good-
bye, Doc; we'll be ready for you in a day or two."

He leaned down, holding out his hand. The grip that
caught it said all any words could convey; then Betsy
started up the hill.

CHAPTER XIII

WHEN THE DREAM CAME TRUE

AT FIRST the road lay between fertile farms dotted with shocked wheat, covered with undulant seas of ripening oats, and forests of growing corn. The larks were trailing melody above the shorn and growing fields, the quail were ingathering beside the fences, from the forests on graceful wings slipped the nighthawks and sailed and soared, dropping so low that the half moons formed by white spots on their spread wings showed plainly.

"Why is this country so different from the other side of the city?" asked the Girl.

"It is older," replied the Harvester, "and it lies higher. This was settled and well cultivated when that was a swamp. But as a farming proposition, the money is in the lowland like your uncle's. The crops raised there are enormous compared with the yield of these fields."

"I see," said she. "But this is much better to look at and the air is different."

"I don't allow any air to surpass that of Medicine Woods," said the Harvester, "by especial arrangement with the powers that be."

Then they dipped into a little depression and followed a longer valley that was ragged and unkempt compared with the road between cultivated fields. The Harvester was busy trying to plan what to do first, and working his brain to think if he had everything the Girl would require for her comfort; so he drove silently through the deepening shadows. She shuddered and awoke him suddenly. He glanced at her from the corner of his eye.

Her thoughts had gone on a journey, also, and the way had been rough, for her face wore a strained appearance. The hands lying bare in her lap were tightly gripped, so that the nails and knuckles were blue. The Harvester hastily sought for the cause of the transformation. A few minutes ago she had seemed at ease and comfortable, now she was close open panic. With brain alert he searched for the reason. Then it began to come to him. The unaccustomed silence and depression of the country might have been the beginning. Coming from the city and crowds of people to the gloomy valley with a man almost a stranger, going she knew not where, to conditions she knew not what, with the experiences of the day vivid before her. The black valley road was not prepossessing, with its border of green pools, through which grew swamp bushes and straggling vines. The Harvester looked carefully at the road, then ceased to marvel at the Girl. But he disliked to let her know he understood, so he gave one last glance at those gripped hands and casually held out the lines.

"Will you take these just a second?" he asked. "Don't let them touch your dress. We must not lose any of our load, because it's mostly things that will make you more comfortable."

He arose, and turning, pretended to see that everything was all right.   Then he resumed his seat.

"I am a little ashamed of this stretch through here,"
he said apologetically.   "I could have managed to have
it cleared and in better shape long ago, but in a way
it yields a snug profit, and so far I've preferred the money.
The land is not mine, but I could grub out this growth
entirely, instead of taking only what I need."

"Is there stuff here you use?" the Girl aroused herself
to ask.   The Harvester saw the look of relief that crossed
her face at the sound of his voice.

"Well I should say yes," he laughed.   "Those bushes,
numerous everywhere, with the hanging yellow-green
balls, those, in bark and root, go into fever medicines.
They are not so much used now, but sometimes I have
a call, so when I do, I pass the beds on my——on our
land, and come down here to get what is needed.   That
bush," he indicated with the whip, "blooms exquisitely
in the spring.   It is a relative of flowering dogwood; the
one of its many names I like best is silky cornel.   Isn't
that pretty?"

"Yes," she said, "it is beautiful."

"I've planted some for you in a hedge along the driveway so next spring you can gather all you want.   I think
you'll like the odour.   The bark brings more than true
dogwood.   If I get a call from some house that uses it,
I save mine and use this.   Around the edge are hop trees.
I realize something from them, and also the false and true
bitter-sweet that run riot here.   Both of them have pretty
leaves, while the berries of the true hang all winter and

the colour is gorgeous. I've set your hedge closely with them. When it has grown a few months it's going to furnish flowers in the spring, a million different, wonderful leaves and berries in the summer, many fruits the birds love in the fall, and bright berries, queer seed pods, and nuts all winter."

"You planted it for me?"

"Yes. I think it will be beautiful in a season or two; it isn't so bad now. I hope it will call myriads of birds to keep you company. When you cross this stretch of road hereafter, don't see fetid water and straggling bushes and vines; say to yourself, this helps to fill orders!"

"I am perfectly tolerant of it now," she said. "You make everything different. I will come with you and help collect the roots and barks you want. Which bush did you say relieved the poor souls scorching with fever?"

The Harvester drew on the lines, Betsy swerved to the edge of the road, while he leaned and broke a branch.

"This one," he answered. "Buttonbush, because those balls resemble round buttons. Aren't they peculiar? See how waxy and gracefully cut and set the leaves are. Go on, Betsy, get us home before night. We appear our best early in the morning, when the sun tops Medicine Woods and begins to light us up, or in the evening, just when she drops behind Onabasha back there, and strikes us with a few level rays. Will you take the lines until I open this gate?"

She laid the twig in her lap on the white gloves and took the lines. As the gate swung wide, Betsy walked through, stopping at the usual place.

"Now my girl," said the Harvester, "cross yourself, lean back, and take your ease. This side that gate you are at home. From here on belongs to us."

"To you, you mean," said the Girl.

"To us, I mean," declared the Harvester. "Don't you know that the 'worldly goods bestowal' clause in a marriage ceremony is a partial reality. It doesn't give you 'all my worldly goods,' but it gives you one-third. Which will you take, the hill, lake, marsh, or a part of all of them."

"Oh, is there water?"

"Did I forget to mention that I was formerly sole owner and proprietor of the lake of Lost Loons, also a brook of Singing Water, having many cold springs? The lake covers about one-third of our land. My neighbours would allow me ditch outlet to the river, but they say I'm too lazy to take it."

"Lazy! Do they mean drain your lake into the river?"

"They do," said the Harvester, "and make the bed into a cornfield."

"But you wouldn't?" She turned to him with confidence.

"I haven't so far, but of course, when you see it, if you prefer it in a corn—— Let's play a game! Turn your head so," he indicated with the whip, "close your eyes; now open them when I say ready."

"All right!"

"Now!" said the Harvester.

"Oh," cried the Girl. "Stop! Please stop!"

They were at the foot of a small levee that ran to the

bridge crossing Singing Water. On the left lay the valley through which the stream swept from its hurried rush down the hill, a marshy thicket of vines, shrubs, and bushes, the banks impassable with water growth. Everywhere flamed foxfire and cardinal flower, thousands of wild tiger lilies lifted gorgeous orange-red trumpets, beside pearl-white turtle head and moon daisies, while all the creek bank was a coral line with the first opening bloom of big pink mallows. Rank jewel flower poured gold from dainty cornucopias and lavender beard-tongue offered honey to a million bumbling bees; water smart-weed spread a glowing pink background, and twining amber dodder topped the marsh in lacy mist with its delicate white bloom. Straight before them a white-sanded road climbed to the bridge and up a gentle hill between the young hedge of small trees and bushes, where again flowers and bright colours rioted and led to the cabin yet invisible. On the right, the hill, crowned with gigantic forest trees, sloped to the lake; midway the building stood, and from it, among scattering trees all the way to the water's edge, were immense beds of vivid colour. Like a scarf of gold flung across the face of earth waved the misty senna; while beside the road running down the hill, in a sunny, open space arose tree-like specimens of thrifty magenta pokeberry. On the hill crept the masses of colour, changing from dry soil to water growth.

High around the blue-green surface of the lake waved lacy heads of wild rice, lower cat-tails, bulrushes, and marsh grasses; arrowhead lilies lifted spines of pearly bloom, while yellow water lilies and blue water hyacinths intermingled; here and there grew a pink stretch of water smartweed and the dangling gold of jewel flower. Over the water, bordering the edge, starry faces of white pond lilies floated. Blue flags waved graceful leaves, willows grew in clumps, and vines clambered everywhere.

Among the growth of the lake shore, duck, coot, and grebe voices commingled in the last chattering hastened splash of securing supper before bedtime; crying killdeers crossed the water, while overhead the nighthawks massed in circling companies. Betsy climbed the hill and at every step the Girl cried: "Slower! please go slower!" With wide eyes she stared around her.

"*Why didn't you tell me it would be like this?*" she demanded in awed tones.

"Have I had opportunity to describe much of anything?" asked the Harvester. "Besides, I was born and reared here, and while it has been a garden of bloom for the past six years only, it always has been a picture; but one forgets to say much about a sight seen every day and that requires the work this does."

"That white mist down there, what is it?"

"Pearls grown by the Almighty," answered the Harvester. "Flowers that I hope you will love. They are like you. Tall and slender, graceful, pearl white and pearl pure——those are the arrowhead lilies."

"And the wonderful purplish-red there on the bank? Oh, I could kneel and pray before colour like that!"

"Pokeberry!" said the Harvester. "Roots bring five cents a pound. Good blood purifier."

"Man!" cried the Girl. "How can you? I'm not

going to ask what another colour is.   I'll just worship
what I like in silence."

"Will you forgive me if I tell you what a woman whose
judgment I respect says about that colour?"

"Perhaps!"

"She says, 'God proves that He loves it best of all the
tints in His workshop by using it first and most sparingly.'
Now are you going to punish me by keeping silent?"

"I couldn't if I tried."

Then they came upon the bridge crossing Singing
Water, and there was a long view of its border, rippling
bed, and marshy banks; while on the other hand the lake
resembled a richly incrusted sapphire.

"Is the house close?"

"Only a few rods, at the turn of the drive."

"Please help me down.   I want to remain a while.   I
don't care what else there is to see.   Nothing can equal
this.   I wish I could bring down a bed and sleep here.
I'd like to draw and paint here.   I understand now what
you mean about designs.   Why, there must be thousands!
I can't go on.   I never saw anything so appealing in all
my life."

Now the Harvester's mother had planned that bridge,
while he had built it with much care.   From bark-covered
railings to oak floor and comfortable benches along the
sides it was intended to be a part of the landscape.

"I'll send Belshazzar to the cabin with the wagon,"
he said, "so you can see better."

"But you must not!" she cried.   "I can't walk.   I
wouldn't soil these beautiful shoes for anything."

"Why don't you change them?" inquired the Harvester.

"I am afraid I forgot everything I had," said the Girl.

"There are shoes somewhere in this load. I thought of them in getting other things for you, but I had no ideas as to size, so I told that clerk to-day when she got your measure to put in every kind you'd need."

"You are horribly extravagant," she said. "But if you have them here, perhaps I could use one pair."

The Harvester hunted until he found a large box, and opening it on the bench he disclosed almost every variety of shoe, walking shoe and slipper, a girl ever owned, as well as sandals and high overshoes.

"For pity's sake!" cried the Girl. "Cover that box! You frighten me. You'll never get them paid for. You must take them straight back."

"Never take anything back," said the Harvester. "'Be sure you are right, then go ahead,' is my motto. Now I know these are your correct size and that for differing occasions you will want just such shoes as other girls have, so here they are. Simple as life! I think these will serve because they are for street wear, yet they are white inside." He produced a pair of canvas walking shoes and kneeling before her held out his hand.

When he had finished, he loaded the box on the wagon, gave the hitching strap to Belshazzar, and told him to lead Betsy to the cabin and hold her until he came. Then he turned to the Girl.

"Now," he said, "look as long as you choose. But remember that the law gives you part of this and your lover, which same am I, gives you the remainder, so you are privileged to come here at any hour as often as you please. If you miss anything this evening, you have all time to come in which to re-examine it."

"I'd like to live right here on this bridge," she said. "I wish it had a roof."

"Roof it to-morrow," offered the Harvester. "Simple matter of a few pillars already cut, joists joined, and some slab shingles left from the cabin. Anything else your ladyship can suggest?"

"That you be sensible."

"I was born that way," explained the Harvester, "and I've cultivated the faculty until I've developed real genius. Talking of sense, there never was a proper marriage in which the man didn't give the woman a present. You seem likely to be more appreciative of this bridge than anything else I have, so right here and now would be the appropriate place to offer you my wedding gift. I didn't have much time, but I couldn't have found anything more suitable if I'd taken a year." He held out a small, white velvet case. "Doesn't that look as if it were made for a bride?"

"It does," answered the Girl. "But I can't take it. You are not doing right. Marrying as we did, you never can believe that I love you; maybe it won't ever happen that I do. I have no right to accept gifts and expensive clothing from you. In the first place, if the love you ask never comes, there is no possible way in which I can repay you. In the second, these things you are offering are not suitable for life and work in the woods. In the third, I think you are being extravagant, and I couldn't forgive myself if I allowed that."

"You divide your statements like a preacher, don't you?" asked the Harvester ingenuously. "Now sit thee here and gaze on the placid lake and quiet your troubled spirit, while I demolish your 'perfectly good' arguments. In the first place, you are now my wife, so you have a right to take anything I offer, if you care for it or can use it in any manner. In the second, you must recognize a difference in our positions. What seems nothing to you means all the world to me, and you are less than human if you deprive me of the joy of expressing feelings I am in honour bound to keep in my heart, by these little material offerings. In the third place, I inherited over six hundred acres of land and water, please observe the water——it is now in evidence on your left. All my life I have been taught to be frugal, economical, and to work. All I've earned either has gone back into land, into the bank, or into books, very plain food, and such clothing as you now see me wearing. Just the value of this place as it stands, with its big trees, its drug crops yielding all the year around, would be difficult to estimate; and I don't mind telling you that on the top of that hill there is a gold mine, and it's mine——ours since four o'clock."

"A gold mine!"

"Acres and acres of wild ginseng, seven years of age and ready to harvest. Do you remember what your few pounds brought?"

"Why it's worth thousands!"

"Exactly! For your peace of mind I might add that

all I have done or got is paid for, except what I bought to-day, and I will write a check for that as soon as the bill is made out. My bank account never will feel it. Truly, Ruth, I am not doing or going to do anything extravagant. I can't afford to give you diamond necklaces, yachts, and trips to Europe; but you can have the contents of this box and a motor boat on the lake, a horse and carriage, and a trip——say to New York, perfectly well. Please take it."

"I wish you wouldn't ask me. I would be happier not to."

"Yes, but I do ask you," persisted the Harvester. "You are not the only one to be considered. I have some rights also, while I'm not so self-effacing that I won't insist upon them. From your standpoint I am almost a stranger. You have spent no time considering me in near relations; I realize that. You feel as if you were driven here for a refuge, which is true. I said to Belshazzar one day that I must remember that you had no dream, so had spent no time loving me, and I do. I know how this wedding seems to you, but it's going to mean something different and better soon, please God. I can see your side; now suppose you take a look at mine. I did have a dream, it was my dream, and beyond the sum of any delight I ever conceived. On the strength of it I rebuilt my home and remodelled these premises. Then I saw you, and from that day I worked early and late. I lost you and I never stopped until I found you; I would have courted and won you, but the fates intervened so here you are! It's now my delight to court and win you. If you knew the difference between having a dream that stirred the least fibre of your being and facing the world in a demand for realization of it; then finding what you coveted in the palm of your hand, as it were, you would know what is in my heart, and why expression of some kind is necessary to me now, and why I'll explode if it is denied. It will lower the tension, if you will accept this as a matter of fact; as if you rather expected and liked it, if you can."

The Harvester set his finger on the spring.

"Don't!" she said. "I'll never have the courage if you do. Give it to me in the case, and let me open it. Despite your unanswerable arguments, I am quite sure that is the only way in which I can take it."

The Harvester gave her the box.

"My wedding gift!" she exclaimed, more to herself than to him. "Why should I be the buffet of all the unkind fates kept in store for a girl my whole life; then suddenly be offered home, beautiful gifts, and wonderful loving kindness by a stranger?"

The Harvester ran his fingers through his crisp hair, pulled it into a peak, stepped to the seat and sitting on the railing, he lifted his elbows, tilted his head, and began a motley outpouring of half-spoken, half-whistled trills and imploring cries. There was enough similarity that the Girl instantly recognized the red bird. Out of breath the Harvester dropped to the seat beside her.

"And don't you keep forgetting it!" he cried. "Now open that box and put on the trinket; because I want to take you to the cabin when the sun falls level on the drive."

She opened the case, exposing a thread of gold that appeared too slender for the weight of an exquisite pendant, set with shimmering pearls.

"If you will look down there," the Harvester pointed over the railing to the arrowhead lilies touched with the fading light, "you will see that they are similar."

"They are!" cried the Girl. "How lovely! Which is more beautiful I do not know. And you won't like it if I say I must not."

She held the open case toward the Harvester.

"'Possession is nine points in the law,'" he quoted. "You have taken it already, it is in your hands; now make the gift perfect for me by putting it on and saying nothing more."

"My wedding gift!" repeated the Girl. Slowly she lifted the beautiful ornament, holding it in the light. "I'm so glad you just force me to take it," she said. "Any half-normal girl would be delighted. I do accept it. And what's more, I am going to keep and wear it and my ring at suitable times all my life, in memory of what you have done to be kind to me on this awful day."

"Thank you!" said the Harvester. "That is a flash of the proper spirit. Allow me to put it on you."

"No!" said the Girl. "Not yet! After a while! I want to hold it in my hands, where I can see it!"

"Now there is one other thing," said the Harvester. "If I had known for any length of time that this day was coming and bringing you, as most men know when a girl is to be given into their care, I could have made it different. As it is, I've done the best I knew. All your after life I hope you will believe this: that if you missed anything to-day that would have made it easier for you or more pleasant, the reason was because of my ignorance of women and the conventions, and lack of time. I want you to know and to feel that in my heart those vows I took were real. This is undoubtedly all the marrying I shall ever want to do. I am old-fashioned in my ways, and deeply imbued with the spirit of the woods, which means unending evolution along the same lines.

"To me you are my revered and beloved wife, my mate now; so I am sure and nothing will change me. This is the day of my marriage to the only woman I ever have thought of wedding, and to me it is joy unspeakable. With other men such a day ends differently from the close of this with me. Because I have done and will continue to do the level best I know for you, this oration is the prologue to asking you for one gift to me from you, a wedding gift. I don't want it unless you can bestow it ungrudgingly, and truly want me to have it. If you can, I will have all from this day I hope for at the hands of fate. May I have the gift I ask of you, Ruth?"

She lifted startled eyes to his face.

"Tell me what it is?" she breathed.

"It may seem much to you," said the Harvester; "to me it appears only a gracious act, from a wonderful woman, if you will give me freely, one real kiss. I've never had one, save from a Dream Girl Ruth, and you will have to make yours pretty good if it is anything like hers. You are woman enough to know that most men crush their brides in their arms and take a thousand. I'll put my hands behind me and never move a muscle, and I won't ask for more, if you will crown my wedding day with only one touch of your lips. Will you kiss me only once, Ruth?"

The Girl lifted a piteous face down which big tears suddenly rolled.

"Oh Man, you shame me!" she cried. "What kind of a heart have I that it fails to respond to such a plea? Have I been overworked and starved so long there is no feeling in me? I don't understand why I don't take you in my arms and kiss you a hundred times, but you see I don't. It doesn't seem as if I ever could."

"Never mind," said the Harvester gently. "It was merely a fancy of mine, bred from my dream and unreasonable, perhaps. I am sorry I mentioned it. The sun is on the stoop now; I want you to enter your home in its light. Come!"

He half lifted her from the bench. "I am going to help you up the drive as I used to assist mother," he said, fighting to keep his voice natural. "Clasp your hands before you and draw your elbows to your sides. Now let me take one in each palm, and you will scoot up this drive as if you were on wheels."

"But I don't want to 'scoot,'" she said unsteadily. "I must go slowly and not miss anything."

"On the contrary, you don't want to do any such thing——you should leave most of it for to-morrow."

"I had forgotten to-morrow. It seems as if the day would end it and set me adrift again."

"You are going to awake in the gold room with the sun shining on your face in the morning, and it's going to keep

on all your life. Now if you've got a smile in your an-
atomy, bring it to the surface, for just beyond this tree
lies happiness for you."

His voice was clear and steady now, his confidence
something contagious. There was a lovely smile on her
face as she looked at him, and stepped into the line of
light crossing the driveway; then she stopped and cried,
"Oh lovely! Lovely! Lovely!" over and over.

The cabin of large, peeled, golden oak logs, oiled to
preserve them, nestled like a big mushroom on the side
of the hill. Above and behind the building the trees
arose in a green setting. The roof was stained to their
shades. The wide veranda was enclosed in screening,
over which wonderful vines climbed in places, and round
it grew ferns and deep-wood plants. Inside hung big
baskets of wild growth; there was a wide swinging seat,
with a back rest, supported by heavy chains. There
were chairs and a table of bent saplings and hickory
withes. Two full stories the building arose; the western
sun warmed it almost to orange-yellow, while graceful
vines crept toward the roof.

The Girl looked at the rapidly rising hedge on each
side of her, at the white floor of the drive, and long and
long at the cabin.

"You did all this since February?" she asked.

"Even to transforming the landscape," he answered.

"Oh I wish it were not coming night!" she cried. "I
don't want the dark to come, until you have told me the
name of every tree and shrub of that wonderful hedge,
and every plant and vine of the veranda; I want to follow

up the driveway and see that beautiful little creek—listen
to it chuckle and laugh! Is it always glad like that? See
the ferns and things that grow on the other side of it!
Why, there are big beds of them. And lilies of the valley
by the acre! What is that yellow around the corner?"

"Never mind that now," said the Harvester, guiding
her up the steps, along the gravelled walk to the screen
that he opened, and over a flood of gold light she crossed
the veranda, to enter the door.

"Now here it appears bare," said the Harvester, "because I didn't know what should go on the walls or what
rugs to get or about the windows. The table, chairs, and
couch I made myself with some help from a carpenter.
They are solid black walnut and will age finely."

"They are beautiful," said the Girl, touching the table
top. "Please put the necklace on me now, I must use my
eyes and hands for other things."

She held out the box so the Harvester lifted the pendant
and clasped the chain around her neck. She glanced
at the lustrous pearls, then the fingers of one hand softly
closed over them. She went through the long, wide living-
room, examining the chairs and mantel, stopping to touch
and exclaim over its array of half-finished candlesticks.
At the door of his room she paused. "And this?" she
questioned.

"Mine," said the Harvester, turning the knob. "I'll
give you one peep to satisfy your curiosity, and show
you the location of the bridge over which you came to me
in my dream. All the remainder is yours. I reserve only
this."

"Will the 'goblins git me' if I come here?"

"Not goblins, but a man alive; so heed your warning. After you have seen it, keep away."

The floor was cement, three of the walls heavy screening with mosquito wire inside, the roof slab shingled. On the inner wall was a bookcase, below it a desk, at one side a gun cabinet, at the other a bath in a small alcove beside a closet. The room contained two chairs like those of the veranda. The bed was a low oak couch covered with a thick mattress of hemlock twigs, topped with sweet fern, on which the sun shone all day. On a chair at the foot were spread some white sheets, a blanket, and an oilcloth. The sun beat in, the wind drifted through. One lying on the couch could see down the bright hill, and sweep the lake to the opposite bank without lifting the head. The Harvester drew the Girl to the bedside.

"Now straight in a line from here," he said, "across the lake to that big, scraggy oak, every clear night the moon builds a bridge of molten gold, and once you walked it, my girl, and came straight to me, alone and unafraid; and you were gracious and lovely beyond anything a man ever dreamed of before. I'll have that to think of to-night. Now come see the dining-room, kitchen, and hand-made sunshine."

He led her into what had been the front room of the old cabin, now a large, long dining-room having on each side wide windows with deep seats. The fireplace back-wall was against that of the living-room, but here the mantel was bare. All the wood-work, chairs, the dining table, cupboards, and carving table were golden oak.

Only a few rugs and furnishings and a woman's touch were required to make it an unusual and beautiful room. The kitchen was shining with a white hard-wood floor, white wood-work, and pale green walls. It was a light, airy, sanitary place, supplied with a pump, sink, hot and cold water faucets, refrigerator, and every modern convenience possible to the country.

Then the Harvester almost carried the Girl up the stairs and showed her three large sleeping rooms, empty and bare save for some packing cases.

"I didn't know about these, so I didn't do anything. When you find time to plan, tell me what you want, and I'll make or buy it. They are good-sized, cool rooms. They all have closets and pipes from the furnace, so they will be comfortable in winter. Now there is your place remaining. I'll leave you while I stable Betsy and feed the stock." He guided her to the door opening from the living-room to the east. "This is the sunshine spot," he said. "It is bathed in morning light, and sheltered by afternoon shade. Singing Water is across the drive there to talk to you always. It comes pelting down so fast it never freezes, so it makes music all winter, while the birds are so numerous you'll have to go to bed early for they'll wake you by dawn. I noticed this room was going to be full of sunshine when I built it, and I craved only brightness for you, so I coaxed all of it to stay that I could. Every stroke is the work of my hands, and all of the furniture. I hope you will like it. This is the room of which I've been telling you, Ruth. Go in and take possession, and I'll entreat God and all His ministering angels to send you the sunshine and joy." He opened the door, guided her inside, closed it, and went swiftly to his work.

The Girl stood looking around her with amazed eyes. The floor was pale yellow wood, polished until it shone like a table top. The casings, table, chairs, dressing table, chest of drawers, and bed were solid curly maple. The doors were big polished slabs of it, each containing enough material to veneer all the furniture in the room. The walls were of plaster, tinted yellow, and the windows with yellow shades were curtained in dainty white. She could hear the Harvester carrying the load from the wagon to the front porch, the clamour of the barnyard; and as she went to the north window to see the view, a shining peacock strutted down the walk and went to the Harvester's hand for grain, while scores of white doves circled over his head. She stepped on deep rugs of yellow goat skins, and, glancing at the windows on either side, she opened the door.

Outside it lay a porch with a railing, but no roof. On each post stood a box filled with yellow wood-flowers and trailing vines of pale green. A big tree rising through one corner of the floor supplied the cover. A gate opened to a walk leading to the driveway, and on either side lay a patch of sod, outlined by a deep hedge of bright gold. In it senna, cone-flowers, black-eyed Susans, golden-rod, wild sunflowers, and jewel flower grew, while some of it, enough to form a yellow line, was already in bloom. Around the porch and down the walk were beds of yellow violets, pixie moss, and every tiny gold flower of the woods. The

Girl leaned against the tree, looking around her, then staggered inside and dropped on the couch.

"What planning! What work!" she sobbed. "What taste! Why he's a poet! What wonderful beauty! He's an artist with earth for his canvas, and growing things for colours."

She lay there staring at the walls, the beautiful woodwork and furniture, the dressing table with its array of toilet articles, a low chair before it, and the thick rug for her feet. Over and over she looked at everything, then closed her eyes and lay quietly, too weary and overwhelmed to think. By and by came tapping at the door, so she sprang up and crossing to the dressing table straightened her hair and composed her face.

"Ajax demands to see you!" cried a gay voice.

The Girl stepped outside.

"Don't be frightened if he screams at you," warned the Harvester as she passed him. "He detests a stranger so he always cries and sulks."

It was a question what was in the head of the bird as he saw the strange looking creature invading his domain, for he did scream, a wild, high, strident wail that delighted the Harvester inexpressibly, because it sent the Girl headlong into his arms.

"Oh good gracious!" she cried. "Has such a beautiful bird got a noise in it like that? Why I've fed them in parks and I never heard one explode before."

"But you see you are in the woods now, and this is not a park bird. It will be the test of your power to see how soon you can coax him to your hand."

"How do I work to win him?"

"I am afraid I can't tell you that," said the Harvester. "I had to invent a plan for myself. It required a long time and much petting, and my methods might not avail for you. It will interest you to study that out. But the member of the family it is positively essential that you win to a life and death allegiance is Belshazzar. If you can make him love you, he will protect you at every turn. He will go before you into the forest and all the crawling, creeping things will get out of his way. He will nose around the flowers you want to gather, and if he growls and the hair on the back of his neck rises, never forget that you must heed that warning. A few times I have not stopped for it, and I always have been sorry. So far as anything animate or uncertain footing is concerned, you are always perfectly safe if you obey him. About touching plants and flowers, you must confine yourself to those you are certain you know, until I can teach you. There are wonderfully attractive things here, but some of them are rank poison. You won't handle plants you don't know, until you learn, Ruth?"

"I will not," she promised instantly.

She went to the seat under the porch tree and leaning against the trunk she studied the hill, the rippling course of Singing Water where it turned and curved before the cabin, and started across the vivid little marsh toward the lake. Then she looked at the Harvester. He seated himself on the low railing and smiled at her.

"You are very tired?" he asked.

"No," she said. "You are right about the air being

better up here.   It is stimulating instead of depressing."

"So far as pure air, location, and water are concerned," said the Harvester, "I consider this place ideal. The lake is large enough to cool the air and raise sufficient moisture to dampen it, and too small to make it really cold and disagreeable. The slope of the hill gives perfect drainage. The heaviest rains do not wet the earth for more than three hours. North, south, and west breezes sweep the cool air from the water to the cabin in summer. The same suns warm us here on the winter hillside. My violets, spring beauties, anemones, and dutchman's breeches here are always two weeks ahead of those in the woods. I am not afraid of your not liking the location or the air. As for the cabin, if you don't care for that, it's very simple. I'll transform it into a laboratory and dry-house, and build you whatever you want, within my means, over there on the hill just across Singing Water and facing the valley toward Onabasha. That's a perfect location. The thing that worries me is what you are going to do for company, especially while I am away."

"Don't trouble yourself about anything," she said. "Just say in your heart, 'she is going to be stronger than she ever has been in her life in this lovely place, and she has more right now than she ever had or hoped to have.' For one thing, I am going to study your books. I never have had time before. While we sewed or embroidered, mother talked by the hour of the great writers of the world, told me what they wrote, and how they expressed themselves, but I got to read very little for myself."

"Books are my company," said the Harvester.

"Do your friends come often?"

"Almost never! Doc and his wife come most. If you look out some day and see a white-haired, bent old woman, with a face as sweet as dawn, coming up the bank of Singing Water, that will be my mother's friend, Granny Moreland, who joins us on the north. She is frank and brusque, so she says what she thinks with unmistakable distinctness, but her heart is big and tender and her philosophy keeps her sweet and kindly despite the ache of rheumatism and the weight of seventy years."

"I'd love to have her come," said the Girl. "Is that all?"

"Yes."

"Why?"

"Your favourite word," laughed the Harvester. "The reason lies with me, or rather with my mother. Some day I will tell you the whole story, and the cause. I think now I can encompass it in this: the place is an experiment. When medicinal herbs, roots, and barks became so scarce that some of the most important were almost extinct, it occurred to me that it would be a good idea to stop travelling miles and poaching on the woods of other people, and turn our land into an herb garden. For four years before mother went, and six since, I've worked with all my might, and results are beginning to take shape. While I've been at it, of course, my neighbours had an inkling of what was going on, so I've been called a fool, lazy, and a fanatic, because I did not fell the trees and plow for corn. You readily can see I'm a little short of corn ground out there," he waved toward the marsh and lake, "and up there," he indicated the steep hill and wood. "But somewhere on this land I've been able to find muck for mallows, water for flags and willows, shade for ferns, lilies, and ginseng, rocky, sunny spaces for mullein, and open, fertile beds for Bouncing Bet—— just for examples. God never evolved a place better suited for an herb farm; from woods to water and all that goes between, it is perfect."

"And indescribably lovely," added the Girl.

"Yes, I think it is," said the Harvester. "But in the days when I didn't know how it was coming out, I was sensitive about it; so I kept quiet and worked, and allowed the other fellow to do the talking. After a while the ginseng bed grew a treasure worth guarding, so I didn't care for any one to know how much I had or where it was, as a matter of precaution. Ginseng and money are synonymous, and I was forced to be away some of the time."

"Would any one take it?"

"Certainly!" said the Harvester. "If they knew it was there, and what it is worth. Then, as I've told you, much of the stuff here must not be handled except by experts, and I didn't want people coming in my absence and taking risks. The remainder of my reason for living so alone is cowardice, pure and simple."

"Cowardice? You! Oh no!"

"Thank you!" said the Harvester. "But it is! Some day I'll tell you of a very solemn oath I've had to keep. It hasn't been easy. You wouldn't understand, at least not now. If the day ever comes when I think you will, I'll tell

you.   Just now I can express it by that one word.   I didn't
dare fail or I felt I would be lost as my father was before me.
So I remained away from the city and its temptations and
men of my age, and worked in the woods until I was tired
enough to drop, read books that helped, tinkered with the
carving, and sometimes I had an idea, so I went into that
little building behind the dry-house, took out my different
herbs, and tried my hand at compounding a new cure for
some of the pains of humanity.   It isn't bad work, Ruth.
It keeps a fellow at a fairly decent level, while some good
may come of it.   Carey is trying several formulæ for me,
and if they work I'll carry them higher.   If you want
money, Girl, I know how to get it for you."

"Don't you want it?"

"Not one cent more than I've got," said the Harvester
emphatically.   "When any man accumulates more than
he can earn with his own hands, he begins to enrich himself
at the expense of the youth, the sweat, the blood, the joy
of his fellow men.   I can go to the city, take a look, and
see what money does, as a rule, and it's another thing I'm
afraid of.   You will find me a dreadful coward on those
two points.   I don't want to know society and its ways.
I see what it does to other men; it would be presumption
to reckon myself stronger.   So I live alone.   As for money,
I've watched the cross cuts and the quick and easy ways
to accumulate it; but I've had something in me that held
me to the slow, sure, clean work of my own hands, and it's
yielded me enough for one, for two even, in a reasonable
degree.   So I've worked, read, compounded, and carved.
If I couldn't wear myself down enough to sleep by any

other method, I went into the lake, and swam across and back; and that is guaranteed to put any man to rest, clean and unashamed."

"Six years," said the Girl softly, as she studied him. "I think it has set a mark on you. I believe I can trace it. Your forehead, brow, and eyes bear the lines and the appearance of all experience, all comprehension, but your lips are those of a very young lad. I shouldn't be surprised if I had that kiss ready for you, and I really believe I can make it worth while."

"Oh good Lord!" cried the Harvester, turning a backward somersault over the railing and starting in big bounds up the drive toward the stable. He passed around it and into the woods at a rush. A few seconds later from somewhere on the top of the hill his strong, deep voice swept down: "Glory, glory hallelujah!"

By and by he came soberly to the barn and paused to stroke Betsy's nose. "Stop chewing grass and listen to me," he said. "She's here, Betsy! She's in our cabin. She's going to remain, you can stake your oats on that. She's going to be the loveliest and sweetest girl in all the world, and because you're a beast, I'll tell you something a man never could know. Down with your ear, you critter! She's going to kiss me, Betsy! This very night, before I lay me, her lips meet mine, and maybe you think that won't be glorious. I supposed it would be a year, anyway, but it's now! Ain't you glad you are an animal, Betsy, and can keep secrets for a fool man who can't?" He walked down the driveway, and before the Girl had a chance to speak, he said: "I wonder if I had not better

carry those things into your room, and arrange your bed
for you?"

"I can," she said.

"Oh no!" exclaimed the Harvester. "You can't lift
the mattress and heavy covers. Hold the door and tell
me how." He laid a big bundle on the floor, opened it,
and took out the shoes. "Your shoe box is in the closet
there."

"I didn't know what that door was, so I didn't open it."

"That is a part of my arrangements for you," said
the Harvester. "Here is a closet with shelves for your
covers and other things. They are bare because I didn't
know what should be put on them. This is the shoe box
here in the corner; I'll put these in it now." He knelt
and in a row set the shoes in the curly maple box and closed
it. "There you are for all kinds of places and weather.
This adjoining is your bathroom. I put in towels, soaps,
and everything I could think of, and there is hot water
ready for you——rain water, too."

The Girl followed to see a shining little bathroom,
with its white porcelain tub and wash bowl, enamelled
woodwork, dainty green walls, and white curtains. She
could see no accessory she knew of that was missing. The
Harvester had gone back to the sunshine room, and was
kneeling on the floor beside the bundle. He began opening boxes and handing her dresses.

"There are skirt, coat, and waist hangers on the hooks,"
he said. "I only got a few things to start on, because I
didn't know what you would like. Instead of being so
careful with that dress, why don't you take it off, and put

on a common one? Then we will have something to eat, and go to the top of the hill to see the moon bridge the lake."

While she hung the dresses and selected the one to wear, he placed the mattress, spread the padding and sheets, and encased the pillow. Then he bent and pressed the springs with his hands. "I think you will find that soft and easy enough for health," he said. "All the personal belongings I had that clerk put up for you are in that chest of drawers there. I put the little boxes in the top and went down. You can empty and arrange them to-morrow. Just hunt out what you will need now. There should be everything a girl uses there somewhere. I told them to be very careful about that. If the things are not right or not to your taste, you can take them back as soon as you are rested, and they will exchange them for you. If there is anything I have missed that you can think of that you need to-night, tell me and I'll go and get it."

The Girl turned toward him.

"You couldn't be making sport of me," she said, "but Man! Can't you see that I don't know what to do with half you have here? I never saw such things closely before. I don't know what they are for. I don't know how to use them. My mother would have known, but I do not. You overwhelm me! Fifty times I've tried to tell you that a room of my very own, such a room as this will be when to-morrow's sun comes in, and these, and these, and these," she turned from the chest of boxes to the dressing table, bed, closet, and bath, "all these for me, and you know absolutely nothing about me——I get a big lump in my throat, and the words that do come all seem so meaningless, I am perfectly ashamed to say them. Oh Man, why do you do it?"

"I thought it was about time to spring another 'why' on me," said the Harvester. "Thank God, I am now in a position where I can tell you 'why!' I do it because you are the girl of my dream, my mate by every law of Heaven and earth. All men build as well as they know when the one woman of the universe lays her spell on them. I did all this for myself——merely as a kind of expression of what it would be in my heart to do if I could do what I'd like. Put on the easiest dress you can find while I go and set out something to eat."

She stood with arms high piled with the prettiest dresses that could be selected hurriedly, the tears running down her white cheeks and smiled through them at him.

"There wouldn't be any of that liquid amber would there?" she asked.

"Quarts!" cried the Harvester. "I'll bring some. . . . Does it really hit the spot, Ruth?" he questioned as he handed her the glass.

She heaped the dresses on the bed and took it.

"It really does. I am afraid I am using too much."

"I think it can't hurt you. To-morrow we will ask Doc. How soon will you be ready for lunch?"

"I don't want a bite."

"You will when you see and smell it," said the Harvester. "I am an expert cook. It's my chiefest accomplishment. You should taste the dishes I improvise. But there won't be much to-night, because I want you to see the moon rise over the lake." He went away. The Girl removed her dress, spreading it on the couch. Then she bathed her face and hands. When she saw the discoloured cloth, it proved that she had been painted; this made her very indignant. Yet she could not be altogether angry, for that flush of colour had saved the Harvester from being pitied by his friend. She stood a long time before the mirror, staring at her gaunt, colourless face; then she went to the dressing table and committed a crime. She found a box of cream and rubbed it on for a foundation. Then she opened some pink powder, and carefully dusted her cheeks.

"I am utterly ashamed," she said to the image in the mirror, "but he has done so much for me, he is so, so——I don't know a word big enough——that I can't bear him to see how ghastly I am, how little worth it. Perhaps the food, better air, and outdoor exercise will give me strength and colour soon. Until it does I'm afraid I'm going to help out all I can with this. It is wonderful how it changes one. I really appear like a girl instead of a bony old woman."

Then she looked over the dresses, selected a pretty white princesse, slipped it on, and went to the kitchen. But the Harvester would not have her there. He seated her at the dining table, beside the window overlooking the lake, lighted a pair of his home-made candles in his finest sticks, and placed before her bread, butter, cold meat, milk, and fruit, and together they ate their first meal in their home.

"If I had known," said the Harvester, "Granny Moreland is a famous cook. She is a Southern woman, who can fry chicken and make some especial dishes to surpass any one I ever knew. She would have been so pleased to come over and get us an all-right supper."

"I'd much rather be by ourselves," said the Girl.

"Well, you can bank on it, I would," agreed the Harvester. "For instance, if any one were here, I might feel restrained about telling you that you are exactly the beautiful, flushed Dream Girl I have adored for months, while your dress is most becoming. You are a picture to blind the eyes of a lonely bachelor, Ruth."

"Oh why did you say that?" wailed the Girl. "Now I've got to feel like a sneak or tell you——and I didn't want you to know."

"Don't you ever tell me or any one else anything you don't want to," said the Harvester roundly. "It's nobody's business!"

"But I must! I can't begin with deception. I was fool enough to think you wouldn't notice. Man, they painted me! I didn't know they were doing it, but when it all washed off, I looked so ghastly I almost frightened myself. I hunted through the boxes they put up for you and found some pink powder——"

"But don't all the daintiest women powder these days, and consider it indispensable? The clerk said so. I bought it for you to use."

"Yes, just powder, but Man, I put on a lot of cold cream first to stick the powder good and thick. Oh I wish I hadn't!"

"Well since you've told it, is your conscience perfectly at ease? No you don't! You sit where you are! You are lovely, and if you don't use enough powder to cover the paleness, until your colour returns, I'll hold you and put it on. I know you feel better when you appear so that every one must admire you."

"Yes, but I'm a fraud!"

"You are no such thing!" cried the Harvester hotly. "There hasn't a woman in ten thousand got any such rope of hair. I have been seeing the papers on the hair question, too. No one will believe it's real. If they think your hair is false, when it is natural, they won't be any more fooled when they think your colour is real, and it isn't. Very soon it will be so no one need ever know the difference. You go on and fix up your level best. To see yourself appearing well will make you ambitious to become so as soon as possible."

"Harvester-man," said the Girl, gazing at him with wet luminous eyes, "for the sake of other women, I could wish that all men had an oath to keep, and had been reared in the woods."

"Here is the place we adjourn to the moon!" cried the Harvester. "I don't know of anything that can cure a sudden accession of swell head like gazing at the heavens. One finds his place among the atoms naturally and instantaneously with the eyes on the night sky. Should you have a wrap? You should! The mists from the lake are cool. I don't believe there is one among my orders. I forgot that. But upstairs with mother's clothing there are several shawls and shoulder capes. All of them were washed and carefully packed. Would you use one, Ruth?"

"Why not give it to me? Wouldn't she like me to use her things better than to have them in moth balls?"

The Harvester looked at her wonderingly.

"I can't tell how pleased she would be," he said.

"Where are her belongings?" asked the Girl. "I could use them to help furnish the house, then it wouldn't appear so strange to you."

"All the washed things are in those boxes upstairs; also some fine skins I've saved on the chance of wanting them. Her dishes are in the bottom of the china closet there; she was mighty proud of them. The furniture and carpets were so old and abused I burned them. I'll go bring a wrap." He took the candle and climbed the stairs, soon returning with a little white wool shawl and a big pink coverlet. "Got this for her Christmas one time," he said. "She'd never had a white one so she thought it was pretty." He folded it around the Girl's shoulders, then picked up the coverlet.

"You're never going to take that to the woods!" she cried.

"Why not?"

She took it in her hands to find a corner.

"Just as I thought! It's a genuine Peter Hartman! It's one of the things that money can't buy, or rather, one that takes a mint of money to own. They are heirlooms. They are not manufactured any more. At the art store where I worked they'd give you fifty dollars for that. It is not faded or worn a particle. It would be lovely in my room; you mustn't take a treasure like that out of doors."

"Ruth, are you in earnest?" demanded the Harvester. "I believe there are six of them upstairs."

"Plutocrat!" cried the Girl. "What colours?"

"More of this pinkish red, blue, and pale green."

"Famous! May I have them to help furnish with?"

"Certainly! Anything you can find, any way on earth you want it, only in my room. That is taboo, as I told you. What am I going to take to-night?"

"Isn't the rug you had in the woods in the wagon yet? Use that!"

"Of course! The very thing! Bel, proceed!"

"Are you going to leave the house like this?"

"Why not?"

"Suppose some one breaks in!"

"Nothing worth carrying away, except what you have on. No one to get in. There is a big swamp back of our woods, marsh in front, we're up here where we can see the drive and bridge. There is nothing possible from any direction. Never locked the cabin in my life, except your room, and that was because it was sacred, not that there was any danger. Clear the way, Bel!"

"Clear it of what?"

"Katydids, hoptoads, and other carnivorous animals."

"Now you are making fun of me! Clear it of what?"

"A coon that might go shuffling across, an opossum, or a snake going to the lake. Now are you frightened so that you will not go?"

"No. The path is broad and white. Surely you and Bel can take care of me."

"If you will trust us we can."

"Well, I am trusting you."

"You are indeed," said the Harvester. "Now see if you think this is pretty."

He indicated the hill sloping toward the lake. The path wound among massive trees, between whose branches patches of moonlight filtered. Around the lake shore and climbing the hill were thickets of bushes. The water lay shining in the light, a gentle wind ruffled the surface in undulant waves, while on the opposite bank arose the line of big trees. Under a giant oak widely branching, on the top of the hill, the Harvester spread the rug and held one end of it against the tree trunk to protect the Girl's dress. Then he sat a short distance away and began to talk. He mingled some sense with a quantity of nonsense, and appreciated every hint of a laugh he heard. The day had been no amusing matter for a girl absolutely alone among strange people and scenes. Anything more foreign to her previous environment or expectations he could not imagine. So he talked to prevent her from thinking, and worked for a laugh as he usually laboured for bread.

"Now we must go," he said at last. "If there is the malaria I strongly suspect in your system, this night air is bad for you. I only wanted you to see the lake the first night in your new home, and if it won't shock you, I brought you here because this is my holy of holies. Can you guess why I wanted you to come, Ruth?"

"If I wasn't so stupid with alternate burning and chills, and so deadened to every proper sensibility, I suppose I should," she answered, "but I'm not brilliant. I don't know, unless it is because you knew it would be the loveliest place I ever saw. Surely there is no other spot in the world quite so beautiful."

"Then would it seem strange to you," asked the Harvester, going to the Girl and gently putting his arms around her, "would it seem strange to you, that a woman who once homed here and thought it the prettiest place on earth, chose to remain for her eternal sleep, rather than to rest in a distant city of stranger dead?"

He felt the Girl tremble against him.

"Where is she?"

"Very close," said the Harvester. "Under this oak. She used to say that she had a speaking acquaintance with every tree on our land, and of them all she loved this big one the best. She liked to come here in winter, to feel the sting of the wind sweeping across the lake, while in summer this was her place to read and to think. So when she slept the unwaking sleep, Ruth, I came here and made her bed with my own hands; then carried her to it, covered her, and she sleeps well. I never have regretted her going. Life did not bring her joy. She was very tired. She used to say that after her soul had fled, if I would lay her here, perhaps the big roots would reach down to her, and from her frail frame gather slight nourishment so that her body would live again in talking leaves that would shelter me in summer and whisper her love in winter. Of all Medicine Woods this is the dearest spot to me. Can you love it too, Ruth?"

"Oh I can!" cried the Girl; "I do now! Just to see the

place and hear that is enough. I wish, oh to my soul I
wish——"

"You wish what?" whispered the Harvester gently.

"I dare not! I was wild to think of it. I would be
ungrateful to ask it."

"You would be ungracious if you didn't ask anything
that would give me the joy of pleasing you. How long
is it going to require for you to learn, Ruth, that to make
up for some of the difficulties life has brought you would
give me more happiness than anything else could? Tell
me now."

"No!"

He gathered her closer. "Ruth, there is no reason why
you should be actively unkind to me. What is it you
wish?"

She struggled from his arms and stood alone in white
moonlight, staring across the lake, along the shore, deep
into the perfumed forest, and then at the mound she now
could distinguish under the giant tree. Suddenly she
went to him and with shaking hands gripped his arm.

"My mother!" she panted. "Oh she was a beautiful
woman, delicately reared, and her heart was broken. By
the inch she went to a dreadful end I could not avert or
allay, while in poverty and grime I fought for a way to
save her body from further horror, and it's all so dreadful.
I thought all feeling in me was dried and still, but I am not
quite calloused yet. I suffer it over with every breath.
It is never entirely out of my mind. Oh Man, if only you
would lift her from the horrible place she lies, where briers
run riot and cattle trample and the unmerciful sun beats!

Oh if only you'd lift her from it, and bring her here! I
believe it would take away some of the horror, the shame,
and the heartache. I believe I could go to sleep without
hearing the voice of her suffering, if I knew she was lying
on this hill, under your beautiful tree, close the dear
mother you love. Oh Man, would you——?"

The Harvester crushed the Girl in his arms while shud-
dering sobs shook his big frame, and choked his voice.

"Ruth, for God's sake, be quiet!" he cried. "Why I'd
be glad to! I'll go anywhere you tell me, and bring
her."

She stared at him with strained face.

"You——you wouldn't!" she breathed.

"Ruth, child," said the Harvester, "I tell you I'd be
happy. Look at my side of this! I'm in search of bands
to bind you to me and to this place. Could you tell me
a stronger than to have the mother you idolized lie here for
her long sleep? Why Girl, you can't know the deep and
abiding joy it would give me to bring her. I'd feel I had
you almost secure. Where is she, Ruth?"

"In that old unkept cemetery south of Onabasha,
where it costs no money to lay away your loved ones."

"Close here! Why I'll go to-morrow! I supposed she
was in the city."

She straightened and drew away from him.

"How could I? I had nothing. I could not have
paid even her fare and brought her here in the cheapest
box the decency of man would allow him to make if her
doctor had not given me the money I owe. Now do you
understand why I must earn and pay it myself! Save

for him, it was charity or her delicate body to horrors.
Money never can repay him."

"Ruth, the day you came to Onabasha was she with
you?"

"In the express car," said the Girl.

"Where did you go when you left the train shed?"

"Straight to the baggage room, where Uncle Henry
was waiting. Men brought and put her in his wagon.
He drove with me to the place, other men lowered her,
and that was all."

"You poor Girl!" cried the Harvester. "This time
to-morrow night she shall sleep in luxury under this oak,
so help me God! Ruth, can you spare me? May I go
at once? I can't rest, myself."

"You will?" cried the Girl. "You will? Oh Man, I
can't ever, ever tell you!"

"Don't try," said the Harvester. "Call it settled.
I will start early in the morning. I know that little ceme-
tery. The man whose land it is on can point me the spot.
She is probably the last one laid there. Come now, Ruth.
Go to the room I made for you, and sleep deeply and in
peace. Will you try to rest?"

"Oh David!" she exulted. "Only think! Here where
it's clean and cool; beside the lake, where leaves fall gently
and I can come and sit close to her and bring flowers; and
she never will be alone, for your dear mother is here. Oh
David!"

"It is better. I can't thank you enough for thinking
of it. Come now, let me help you."

He half carried her down the hill. Then he made the

cabin a glamour of light by putting candles in the sticks he had carved and placing them everywhere.

"There is a lighting plant in the basement," he said, "but I had not expected to use it until winter, so I have no acetylene. Candles were our grandmothers' lights and they are the best anyway. Go bathe your face, Ruth, and wash away all trace of tears. Put on the pink powder, and in a few weeks you will have colour to outdo the wildest rose. You must be as gay as you can the remainder of this night."

"I will!" cried the Girl. "I will! Oh I didn't know a thing on earth could make me happy! I didn't know I really could be glad. Oh if the ice in my heart would melt, and the wall break down, and the girlhood I've never known would come yet! Oh David, if it would!"

"Before the Lord it shall!" vowed the Harvester. "It shall come with the fulness of joy right here in Medicine Woods. Think it! Believe it! Keep it before you! Work for it! Happiness is worth while! All of us have a right to it! It shall be yours and soon."

"I will try! I will!" promised the Girl. "I'll go right now and I'll put on the blessed pink powder so thickly you'll never know what is under it, and soon it won't be needed at all."

She was laughing as she left the room. The Harvester restlessly walked the floor a few minutes, then sat with a note-book and began entering items.

When the Girl returned, he brought the pillow from her bed, folded the coverlet, and she lay in the big swing. He covered her with the white shawl, and while Singing

Water sang its loudest, katydids exulted over the delightful act of their ancestor, and a million gauze-winged creatures of night hummed against the screen, in a voice soft and low he told her in a steady stream, as he swayed her back and forth, what each sound of the night was, how and why it was made, all the way from the rumbling buzz of the June bug to the screech of the owl or the splash of the bass in the lake. All of it, as it appealed to him, was the story of steady evolution, the natural processes of reproduction, the joy of life and its battles, and the conquest of the strong in nature. At his hands every sound was stripped of terror. The leaping bass was exulting in life, the screeching owl was telling its mate it had found a fat mouse for the children, the nighthawk was courting, the big bullfrogs booming around the lake were serenading the moon. There was not a thing to fear or a voice left with an unsympathetic note in it. She was half asleep when at last he helped her to her room, set a pitcher of frosty, clinking drink on her table, locked her door and window screens inside, spread Belshazzar's blanket on her porch, and set his door wide open, that he might hear if she called; then said good night and went back to his memorandum book.

"No bad beginning," he muttered softly, "no bad beginning, but I'd almost give my right hand if she hadn't forgotten——"

In her room th exhausted girl slipped the pins from her hair and sank on the low chair before the dressing table. She picked up the shining, silver backed brush and stared at the monogram, R. J. L., entwined on it.

"My soul!" she exclaimed. "*Was he so sure as that?*"

She dropped the brush and with tired hands pushed back the heavy braids. Then she arose and going to the chest of drawers began lifting lids to find a night robe. As she searched the boxes she found every dainty, pretty undergarment a girl ever used and at last the robes. She shook out a long white one, slipped into it, and walked to the bed. That stood as he had arranged it, white, clean, and dainty.

"Everything for me!" she said softly. "Everything for me! Shall there be nothing for him? Oh he makes it easy, easy!"

She stepped to the closet, picked down a lavender silk kimono and drawing it over her gown she gathered it around her, and opening the bathroom door, she stepped into a hall leading to the dining-room. As she entered the living-room the Harvester bent over his book. Her step was very close when he heard it and turned his head. In an instant she touched his shoulders. The Harvester dropped the pencil, and palm downward laid his hands on the table, his promise strong in his heart. The Girl slid a shaking palm under his chin, leaned his head against her breast, and dropped a sweet, tear-wet face on his. With all the strength of her frail arms she gripped him a second, then gave the kiss, into which she tried to put all she could find no words to express.

CHAPTER XIV

SNOWY WINGS

THE Harvester sat at the table in deep thought, until the lights in the Girl's room were darkened and everything was quiet. Then he locked the screens inside and went into the night. The moon flooded all the hillside, so that coarse print could have been read with keen eyes in its light. A restlessness, born of exultation he could not allay or control, was on him. She had not forgotten! After this, the dream would be effaced by reality. It was the beginning. He scarcely had dared hope for so much. Surely it presaged the love with which she some day would come to him and crown his life. He walked softly up and down the drive, passing her windows, unable to think of sleep. Over and over he dwelt on the incidents of the day, so inevitably he came to his promise.

"Merciful Heaven!" he muttered. "How can such things happen? The poor, overworked, suffering girl! It will give her some comfort. It has to be done. I believe I will do the worst part of it while she sleeps."

He went to the cabin, crept very close one of her windows and listened intently. Surely no mortal awake could lie motionless so long. She must be sleeping. He patted Belshazzar, whispered, "Watch, boy, watch for

your life!" and then crossed to the dry-house. Beside
it he found a big roll of coffee sacks that he used in collecting roots, and going to the barn, he took a spade and
mattock. Then he climbed the hill to the oak; in the
white moonlight laid off his measurements and began
work. His heart was very tender as he lifted the earth,
and threw it into the tops of the big bags he had propped
open. "I'll line it with a couple of sheets and finish the
edge with pond lilies and ferns," he planned, "and I'll
drag this earth from sight, and cover it with brush until I
need it."

Sometimes he paused in his work to rest a few minutes,
then he stood and glanced around him. Several times
he went down the hill and slipped to a window, but he
could not hear a sound. When his work was finished, he
stood before the oak, scraping clinging earth from the
mattock with which he had cut roots he had been compelled to remove. He was tired now and he thought he
would go to his room and sleep until daybreak. As he
turned the implement he remembered how through it he
had found her, and now he was using it in her service.
He smiled as he worked, half listening to the steady roll
of sound encompassing him. A cool breath swept from
the lake, so he wondered if it found her wet, hot cheek. A
wild duck in the rushes below gave an alarm signal. It
ran in subdued voice, note by note, along the shore. The
Harvester gripped the mattock and stood motionless.
Wild things had taught him so many lessons he heeded
their warnings instinctively. Perhaps it was a mink or
muskrat approaching the rushes. Listening intently,

he heard a stealthy step coming up the path behind him.

The Harvester waited. He soundlessly moved around the trunk of the big tree. An instant more the night prowler stopped squarely at the head of the open grave, then jumped back with an oath. He stood tense a second, advanced, scratched a match and dropped it into the depths of the opening. That instant the Harvester recognized Henry Jameson. With a spring he landed between the man's shoulders and sent him, face down, headlong into the grave. He snatched one of the sacks of earth, and tipping it, emptied the contents on the head and shoulders of the prostrate man. Then he dropped on him and feeling across his back took an ugly, big revolver from a pocket. He swung to the surface and waited until Henry Jameson crawled from under the weight of earth and began to rise; then, at each attempt, he knocked him down. At last he caught the exhausted man by the collar and dragged him to the path, where he dropped him and stood gloating.

"So!" he said; "It's you! Coming to execute your threat, are you? What's the matter with my finishing you, loading your carcass with a few stones into this sack, and dropping you in the deepest part of the lake."

There was no reply.

"Ain't you a little hasty?" asked the Harvester. "Isn't it rather cold blooded to come sneaking when you thought I'd be asleep? Don't you think it would be low down to kill a man on his wedding day?"

Jameson arose cautiously and faced the Harvester.

"Who have you killed?" he panted.

"No one," answered the Harvester. "This is for the victim of a member of your family, but I never dreamed I'd have the joy of planting any of you in it first, even temporarily. Did you rest well? What I should have done was to fill it in, and leave you at the bottom."

Jameson retreated a few steps. The Harvester laughed and advanced the same distance.

"Now then," he said, "explain what you are doing on my premises, a few hours after your threat, and armed with another revolver before I could return the one I took from you this afternoon. You must grow them on bushes at your place, they seem so numerous. Speak up! What are you doing here?"

There was no answer.

"There are three things it might be," mused the Harvester: "You might think to harm me, but you're watched on that score and I don't believe you'd enjoy the result sure to follow. You might contemplate trying to steal Ruth's money again, but we'll pass that up. You might want to go through my woods to inform yourself as to what I have of value there. But in all probability, you are after me. Well, here I am. Go ahead! Do what you came to!" The Harvester stepped toward the lake bank and Jameson, turning to watch him, exposed a face ghastly through its grime. "Look here!" cried the Harvester, sickening. "We will end this right now. I was rather busy this afternoon, but I wasn't too hurried to take that little weapon of yours to the chief of police and tell him where and how I got it and what occurred. He was to return it to you to-morrow with his ultimatum. When I have added the history of to-night, reinforced by another gun, he will understand your intentions and know where you belong. You should be confined, but because your name is the same as the Girl's, and there is of your blood in her veins, I'll give you one more chance. I'll let you go this time, but I'll report you, and deliver this implement to be added to your collection at headquarters. And I tell you, and I'll tell them, that if ever I find you on my premises again, I'll finish you on sight. Is that clear?"

Jameson nodded.

"What I should do is to plump you squarely into confinement, as I could easily enough, but that's not my way. I am going to let you off, but you go knowing the law. One thing more: don't leave with any distorted ideas in your head. I saw Ruth the day she stepped from the cars in Onabasha and I loved her. I wanted to court and marry her, as any man would the girl he loves, but you spoiled that with your woman killing brutality. So I married her in Onabasha this afternoon. You can see the records at the county clerk's office and interview the minister who performed the ceremony, if you doubt me. Ruth is in her room, comfortable as I can make her, asleep and unafraid, thank God! This grave is for her mother. The Girl wants her lifted from the horrible place you put her, and laid where it is sheltered and pleasant. Now, I'll see you off my land. Hurry yourself!"

With the Harvester following, Henry Jameson went back over the path he had come, until he reached and mounted the horse he had ridden. As the Harvester watched him, Jameson turned in the saddle and spoke for the second time.

"What will you give me in cold cash to tell you who she is, and where her mother's people are?"

The Harvester leaped for the bridle and missed. Jameson bent over the horse and lashed it to a run. Halfway to the oak the Harvester remembered the revolver, but being unaccustomed to weapons, he had forgotten it when he needed it most. He replaced the earth in the sack and dragged it away, then plunged into the lake, and afterward went to bed, where he slept soundly until dawn. First, he slipped into the living-room and wrote a note to the Girl. Then he fed Belshazzar and ate a hearty breakfast. He stationed the dog at her door, gave him the note, and went to the oak. There he arranged everything neatly and as he desired, and then hitching Betsy he quietly guided her down the drive and over the road to Onabasha. He went to an undertaking establishment, made all his arrangements, and then called up and talked with the minister who had performed the marriage ceremony the previous day.

The sun shining in her face awoke Ruth, she revelled in the light. "Maybe it will colour me faster than the powder," she thought. "How peculiar for him to say what he did! I always thought men detested it. But he is not like any one else." She lay looking around the beautiful room and wondering where the Harvester was. She could not hear him. Then, slowly and painfully, she dragged her aching limbs from the bed and went to the

door. The dog was gone from the porch and she could not
see the man at the stable. She selected a frock and putting
it on opened the door. Belshazzar arose and offered this
letter:

DEAR RUTH:

I have gone to keep my promise. You are locked in
with Bel. Please obey me and do not step outside the
door until four o'clock. Then put on a pretty white
dress, and with the dog, come to the bridge to meet me.
I hope you will not suffer and fret. Put away your
clothing, arrange the rooms to keep busy, or better yet,
lie in the swing and rest. There is food in the ice chest,
pantry, and cellar. Forgive me for leaving you to-day,
but I thought you would feel easier to have this over. I
am so glad to bring your mother here. I hope it will
make you happy enough to meet us with a smile. Do
not forget the pink box until the reality comes.

With love,   DAVID.

The Girl went to the kitchen and found food. She
offered to share with Belshazzar, but she could see from
his indifference he was not hungry. Then she returned
to the room flooded with light, and filled with treasures,
and tried to decide how she would arrange her clothing.
She spent hours opening boxes and putting dainty, pretty
garments in the drawers, hanging the dresses, and placing the toilet articles. Often she wearily dropped to the
chairs and couches, or gazed from door and windows at
the pictures they framed. "I wonder why he doesn't
want me to go outside," she thought. "I wouldn't be
afraid in the least, with Bel. I'd just love to go across
to that wonderful little river of Singing Water and sit

in the shade; but I won't open the door until four o'clock."
When she thought of where he had gone, and why, the
swift tears filled her eyes, but she forced them back and
resolutely went to investigate the dining-room. Then
for two hours she was a home builder, with a touch of
that homing instinct found in the heart of every good
woman. First, she looked where the Harvester had said
the dishes were, and suddenly sat on the floor exulting.
There were a quantity of old chipped and cracked white
ware and some gorgeous baking powder prizes; but there
were also big blue, green, and pink bowls, several large
lustre plates, and a complete tea set without chip or
blemish, two beautiful pitchers, and a number of willow
pieces. She set the green bowl on the dining table, the
blue on the living-room, and took the pink herself, while
a beautiful yellow one she placed in the dining-room window seat.

"Oh, if I only dared fill them with those lovely flowers!"
She stood in the window and gazed longingly toward the
lake. "I know what colour I'd like to put in each of
them," she said, "but I promised not to touch anything,
and the ones I want most I never saw before, and I'm
not to go out anyway. I can't see the sense in that,
when I'm not at all afraid, but if he does this wonderful
thing for me I must do what he asks. Oh mother, mother!
Are you really coming to this beautiful place and to rest
at last?"

She sank to the window seat and lay trembling, but
she bravely restrained the tears. After a time she remembered the upstairs and went to see the coverlets.

She found half a dozen beautiful ones, and smiled as she examined the stiffly conventionalized birds facing each other in the border designs, and in one corner of each blanket she read, woven in the cloth:

Peter and John
Hartman
Wooster,
Ohio,
1837

She took a blue and a green one, several fine skins from the fur box the Harvester had told her about, then went downstairs. It required all her strength to push the heavy tables before the fireplaces. She spread papers on them to stand on, and tacked a skin above each mantel. She set all of the candlesticks, except those she wanted to use, in the lower part of an empty bookcase. A pair of black walnut she placed on the living-room mantel, together with a big blue plate, a yellow one, and an old brass candlestick. She admired the effect very much. She put the blue coverlet on the couch, and arranged the blue bowl and some books on the table. Here and there she hung a skin across a chair back, or laid it in a wide window seat. Having exhausted all her resources, she returned to the dining-room, spread a skin before the hearth and in each window seat, set a pink and green lustre plate on the mantel, and a pair of oak candlesticks, and arranged the lustre tea set on the side table. The pink coverlet she took for herself, and after resting a time she was surprised on going back to the rooms to see how homelike they appeared.

At three o'clock she dressed and at almost four unlocked the screen, called Belshazzar to her side, and slowly
went down the drive to the bridge. She had used the
pink powder, put on a beautiful white dress, carefully
arranged her hair, and wore the pearl ornament. Once
her fingers strayed to the pendant and she said softly:
"I think both he and mother would like me to wear
it."

At the foot of the hill she stopped at a bench and sat
in the shade waiting. Belshazzar stretched beside her,
and gazed at her with questioning, friendly dog eyes.
The Girl looked from Singing Water to the lake, and
up the hill to make sure it was real. She tried to quiet
her quivering muscles and nerves. He had asked her
to meet him with a smile. How could she? He could
not have understood what it meant when he made the
request. There never would be any way to make him
realize; indeed, why should he? The smile must be
ready. He had loved his mother deeply; yet he had said
he did not grieve to lay her to rest. Earth had not been
kind. Then why should she sorrow for her mother?
Again life had been not only unkind, but bitterly cruel.

Belshazzar arose, watching down the drive. The Girl
looked also. Through the gate and up the levee came a
strange procession. First walked the Harvester alone,
with bared head, carrying an armload of white lilies. A
carriage containing a man and several women followed.
Then came a white hearse with snowy plumes, and behind
that another carriage filled with people, then Betsy followed drawing men in the spring wagon. The Girl arose

and as she stepped to the drive she swayed uncertainly an instant.

"Gracious Heaven!" she gasped. "He is bringing her in white, and with flowers and song!"

Then she lifted her head; with a smile on her lips she went to meet him. As she reached his side, he tenderly put an arm around her, and came on steadily.

"Courage Girl!" he whispered. "Be as brave as she was!"

Around the driveway and up the hill he half carried her, to a seat he had placed under the oak.. Before her lay the white-lined grave. The Harvester arranged his lilies around it. The teams stopped at the barn and men came up the hill bearing a white burden. Behind them followed the minister who yesterday had performed their marriage ceremony, and after him a choir of trained singers softly chanting:

"Blessed are the dead who die in the Lord,
  For they shall cease from their labours."

"But David," panted the Girl. "It was mean and poor. That is not she!"

"Hush!" said the Harvester. "It is your mother. The location was high and dry; it has been only a short time. We wrapped her in white silk, laid her on a soft cushion and pillow, and housed her securely. She can sleep well now, Ruth. Listen!"

Covered with white lilies, slowly the casket sank into earth. At its head stood the minister and as it began to disappear, the white doves, frightened by the strange conveyances at the stable, came circling above. The minister looked up. He lifted a clear tenor, and softly and purely he sang, while at a wave of his hand the choir joined him:

"Oh, come angel band! Oh, come, and around me stand!
Oh, bear me away on your snowy wings to my immortal home!"

He uttered a low benediction, and singing, the people turned and went downhill. The Harvester gathered the Girl in his arms, carrying her to the lake. He laid her in his boat and taking the oars sent it along the bank in the shade, through cool, green places.

"Now cry all you choose!" he said.

The overstrained Girl covered her face and sobbed wildly. After a time he began talking to her gently, so before she realized it, she was listening.

"Death has been kinder to her than life, Ruth," he said. "She is lying as you saw her last, I think. We lifted her very tenderly, wrapped her carefully, and brought her gently as we could. Now they shall rest together, those little mothers of ours, to whom men were not kind; in their long sleep we must forget, as they have forgotten, and forgive, as no doubt they have forgiven. Don't you want to take some lilies to them before we go to the cabin? Right there on your left are unusually large ones."

The Girl gathered the white flowers. When the last vehicle crossed the bridge, the Harvester tied the boat, helping her up the hill. The old oak stretched its wide arms above two mounds, both moss covered and scattered with flowers. The Girl added her lilies, then went to the Harvester, sinking at his feet.

"Ruth, you shall not!" cried the man. "I simply will not have that. Come now, I will bring you back this evening."

He helped her to the swing on the veranda. He sat beside her while she rested; then they went into the cabin for supper. Soon he had her telling what she had found, while he made notes of what would yet be required to transform the cabin into a home. The Harvester left it to her to decide whether he should roof the bridge the next day or make a trip for furnishings. She said he had better buy what they needed, then she could make the cabin homelike while he worked on the bridge.

CHAPTER XV

The Harvester Interprets Life

SO THEY went through the rooms together; the Girl suggested the furnishings she thought necessary, while the Harvester wrote the list. The following morning he was eager to have her company, but she was very tired, and begged to be allowed to wait in the swing, so again he drove away, leaving her with Belshazzar on guard. When he had gone, she went through the cabin arranging the furniture the best she could, then dressed and went to the swinging couch. It was so wide and heavy a light wind rocked it gently, while from it she faced the fern and lily carpeted hillside, the majesty of big trees of a thousand years, or heard the music of Singing Water as it sparkled diamond-like where the sun rays struck its flow.

There were squirrels barking and racing in the big trees or over the ground. They crossed the sodded space of lawn and came to the top step for nuts, eating them from cunning paws. They were living life according to the laws of their nature. She knew that their sharp, startling bark was not to frighten her, but to warn straying intruders of other species of their kindred from a nest, because the Harvester had told her so. He had said

their racing here and there in wild scramble was a game
of tag which she found most interesting to observe.

Birds of brilliant colour flashed everywhere, singing
in wild joy, or tilted on the rising hedge before her, hunting
berries and seeds.   Their bubbling, spontaneous song was
an instinctive outpouring of their joy over mating time,
nests, young, much food, and running water.   Their
social, inquiring, short cry was to locate a mate, or to call
her to good feeding.   The sharp wild scream was when a
hawk passed over, a weasel lurked in the thicket, or a
black snake sunned on the bushes.   She remembered these
things, while listening intently, trying to interpret every
sound as the Harvester did.

Birds of wide wing hung as if nailed to the sky, or
wheeled and sailed in grandeur.   They were searching
the landscape below to locate a hare or snake in the waving grass or carrion in the fields.   The wonderful exhi-
bitions of wing power were their expression of exultation
in life, just as the song sparrow threatened to rupture
his throat as he swung on the hedge, while the red bird
somewhere in the thicket whistled so forcefully it sounded
as if the notes might hurt him.

On the lake bass splashed in a game with each other.
Grebes chattered, because they were very social.   Ducks
dived and gobbled for roots and worms of the lake shore,
congratulating each other when they were lucky.

Killdeer cried for slaughter, in plaintive tones, as their
white breasts gleamed silver-like across the sky.   They
insisted on the death of their ancient enemies, because
the deer had trampled nests around the shore, roiled the

water, spoiled the food hunting, and had been unmindful of the laws of feathered folk from the beginning.

Behind the barn imperial cocks crowed challenges of defiance to each other and all the world, because they once had worn royal turbans on their heads, and ruled the forests, even the elephants and lions. Happy hens cackled when they deposited an egg, or wandered through their park singing the spring egg song.

Upon the barn Ajax spread and exulted in glittering plumage, while screaming viciously. He was sending a wireless plea to the forests of Ceylon for a gray mate to come share the ridge pole with him, to help him wage red war on the sickening love making of the white doves he hated.

Everything was beautiful, some of it was amusing, all instructive, and intensely interesting. The Girl wanted to know about the brown, yellow, and black butterflies sailing from flower to flower. She watched big black and gold bees come from the forest for pollen or listened to their monotonous bumbling. Her first humming bird poised in air, to sip nectar before her astonished eyes. It was marvellous, but more wonderful to the Girl than anything she saw or heard was the fact that because of the Harvester's teachings she now could trace through all of it the ordained processes of the evolution of life. Everything was right in its way, all necessary to human welfare, so there was nothing to fear, but marvels to learn and pictures to appreciate. She would have taken Belshazzar and gone out, but the Harvester had exacted a promise that she would not. He could see that she was

coming gradually to a sane and natural view of life and
living things, so he did not want some sound or creature
to frighten her, thus spoiling what he had accomplished.
So she swayed in the swing, trying to interpret sights and
sounds as he did.

Before an hour she realized that she was coming speedily
into sympathy with the wild life around her; for instead
of shivering and shrinking at unaccustomed sounds, she
was listening especially for them, trying to arrive at a sane
interpretation; instead of the senseless roar of commerce, manufacture, and life of a city, she was beginning
to appreciate sounds that varied, that carried the Song
of Life in unceasing measure and absorbing meaning,
while she was more than thankful for the fresh, pure air,
and the blessed, God-given light. It seemed to the Girl
that there was enough sunshine at Medicine Woods for
the whole world.

"Bel," she said to the dog standing beside her, "it's a
shame to separate you from the Medicine Man and pen
you here with me. It's a wonder you don't bite off my
head or run away to find him. He's gone to bring more
things to make life beautiful. I wanted to go with him,
but oh Bel, there's something dreadfully wrong with me.
I was afraid I'd fall on the streets and frighten and shame
him. I'm so weak, I scarcely can walk straight across one
of these big, cool rooms that he has built for me. He can
make everything beautiful, Bel, a home, rooms, clothing,
grounds, and life——above everything else he can make life
beautiful. He's so splendid and wonderful, with his wide
understanding and sane interpretation and God-like sym-

pathy and patience. Why Belshazzar, he can do the greatest thing in all the world! He can make you forget that the grave annihilates your dear ones by hideous processes, and set you to thinking instead that they come back to you in whispering leaves and flower perfumes. If I didn't owe him so much that I ought to pay, if this were not so alluringly beautiful, I'd like to go to the oak and lie beside those dear women resting there, and give my tired body to furnish sap for strength and leaves for music. He can take its bitterest sting——from death, Bel——and that's the most wonderful thing——in life, Bel——" Her voice became silent, her eyes closed; the dog stretched himself beside her on guard. It was so the Harvester found them when he drove home from the city. He heaped his load in the dining-room, stabled Betsy, carried the things he had brought where he thought they belonged, then prepared food. When she awakened she came to him.

"How is it going, Girl?" asked the Harvester.

"It has been lovely!"

"Do you really mean that your heart is warming a little to things here?"

"Indeed I do! I can't tell you what a morning I've had. There have been such myriad things to see and hear. Oh Harvester, can you ever teach me what all of it means?"

"I can right now," said the Harvester promptly. "It means two things, so simple any little child can understand——the love of God and the evolution of life. I am not precisely clear as to what I mean when I say God. I don't know whether it is spirit, matter, or force; it is that big thing that brings forth worlds, establishes their orbits, and gives us heat, light, food, and water. To me, that is God and His love. Just that we are given birth, sheltered, provisioned, and endowed for our work. Evolution is the natural consequence of this. It is the plan steadily unfolding. If I were you, I wouldn't bother my head over these questions; they never have been scientifically explained to the beginning; I doubt if they ever will be, because they start with the origin of matter which is too far beyond man for him to penetrate. Enjoy to the depths of your soul——that's worship. Be thankful for everything ——that's praising God as the birds praise him. And 'do unto others'——that's all there is of love and religion combined."

"You should tell the world that!"

"No! It isn't my vocation," said the Harvester. "My work is to provide pain-killer. I don't believe, Ruth, that there is any one on the footstool who is doing a better job along that line. I am boastfully proud of it——proud of sending in the packages that kill fever, refresh poor blood, and strengthen weak hearts; unadulterated, honest weight, fresh, and scrupulously clean. My neighbours have a different name for it; I call it a man's work."

"Every one who understands must," said the Girl. "I wish I could help with that. I feel as if it would do more to wipe out the pain I've suffered and seen her endure than anything else. Man, when I grow strong enough I want to help you. I believe that I am going to love it here."

"Don't ever suppress your feelings, Ruth!" hastily cried the Harvester. "It will be very bad for you. You will become wrought up, and 'het up,' as Granny Moreland says, which will make you very ill. When we drive the fever from your blood, the ache from your bones, the poison of wrong conditions from your soul, and good, healthy, red corpuscles begin pumping through your heart like a windmill, you can stake your life you're going to love it here. And the location and work are not all you're going to care for either, honey. Now just wait! That was not 'nominated in the bond.' I'm allowed to talk. I never agreed not to *say* things. What I promised was not to *do* them. So as I said, honey, sit at this table, and eat the food I've cooked; soon the furniture van will be here, and you shall tell me where and how."

"Oh if I were only stronger, David!"

"You are!" said the Harvester. "You are much better than you were yesterday. You can talk, and that's all that's necessary. The rooms are ready for furniture. The men will carry it where you want it. A decorator is coming to hang the curtains. By night we will be settled; you can lie in the swing while I read to you a story so wonderful that the wildest fairy tale you ever heard never touched it."

"What will it be, David?"

"Eat all the red raspberries and cream, bread and butter, and drink all the milk you can. There are blood, beefsteak, and bones in it. As I was saying, you have come here a stranger to a strange land. The first thing is for you to understand and love the woods. Before

you can do that you should master the history of one
tree; just the same as you must learn to know and love
me before your childhood trust in all mankind returns
again. Understand? Well, the fates knew you were on
the way, coming trembling down the brink, Ruth, so
they put it into the heart of a great man to write largely
of a wonderful tree, especially for your benefit. After
it had fallen he took it apart, split it in sections, and year
by year spread out history for all the world to read. It
made a classic story filled with unsurpassed wonders.
It was a pine of a thousand years, close the age of our
mother tree, Ruth. When we have learned from Enos
Mills how to wrest secrets from the hearts of centuries,
we will climb the hill and measure our oak; then I will
estimate, and you shall write, and we will make a record
for our tree."

"Oh I'd like that!"

"So would I," said the Harvester. "And a million
other things I can think of that we can learn together.
It won't require long for me to teach you all I know, by
that time your hand will be clasped in mine, and our
'hearts will beat as one,' so you will give me a kiss every
night and morning, and a few during the day for interest,
then we will go on in life together and learn songs, miracles,
and wonders until the old oak calls us. We will ascend
the hill gladly and offer up our bodies, while our children
will lay flowers over our hearts, and gather the herbs and
paint the pictures, Amen. I hear a van on the bridge.
Just you go to your room and lie down until I get things
unloaded and where they belong. Then you and the

decorator can make us so homelike, that to-morrow we will begin to live.   Won't that be great, Ruth?"

"With you, yes, I think it will."

"That will do for this time," said the Harvester.   "Lie and rest until I say ready."

As he went to meet the men, she could hear him singing lustily: "Praise God, from whom all blessings flow."

"What a child he is!" she said.   "And what a man!"

For an hour heavy feet sounded through the cabin carrying furniture to different rooms.   Then with a floor brush in one hand, and a polishing cloth in the other, the Harvester tapped at her door and helped the Girl upstairs.   He had divided the space into three large, square sleeping chambers.   In each he had set up a white iron bed, a dressing table, and wash stand, and placed two straight-backed and one rocking chair, all white.   The walls were tinted lightly with green added to the plaster. There were a mattress and a stack of bedding on each bed, a large rug and several small ones on the floors.   He led her to the rocking chair in the middle room, where she could see through the open doors of the other two.

"Now," said the Harvester, "I didn't know whether the room with two windows toward the lake and one on the marsh, or two facing the woods and one front, was the guest chamber.   It seemed about an even throw whether a visitor would prefer woods or water, so I made them both guest chambers, and got things alike for them. Now if we are entertaining two, one can't feel more highly honoured than the other.   Was that a scheme?"

"Fine!   I don't see how it could be surpassed."

"'Be sure you are right, then go ahead,'" quoted the Harvester. "Now I'll make the beds and Mr. Rogers can hang the curtains. Is white correct for sleeping rooms? Won't that wash best and always be fresh?"

"It will," said the Girl. "White wash curtains are much the nicest."

"Make them short, Mr. Rogers; keep them off the floor," advised the Harvester. "And simple——don't arrange anything elaborate that will tire a woman to keep in order. Whack them off the right length and pin them to the poles."

"How about that, Mrs. Langston?" asked Rogers.

"I am quite sure that is the very best thing to do."

"Now about this?" inquired the Harvester. "Do I put on sheets and fix these beds ready to use?"

"I would not," said the Girl. "I would spread the pad and the counterpane and lay the sheets and pillows in the closet until they are wanted. They can be sunned and the bed made delightfully fresh."

"Of course," said the Harvester.

When he had finished, he spread a cover on the dressing table and laid out white toilet articles and grouped a white wash set with green decorations on the stand. Then he brushed the floor, spread a big green rug in the middle and small ones before the bed, stand, and table, and coming out closed the door.

"Guest chamber with lake view is now ready for company," announced the Harvester. "Repeat the operation on the woods room, finished also. Why do people make work of things and string them out eternally and fuss so much? Isn't this simple and easy, Ruth?"

"Yes, if you can afford it," said the Girl.

"Forbear!" cried the Harvester. "We have the goods, the dealer has my check. Excuse me ten minutes, until I furnish another room."

The laughing Girl could catch glimpses of him busy over beds and dresser, floor and rugs; then he came where she sat.

"Woods guest chamber ready," he said. "Now we come to the interior apartment, that from its view might be called the marsh room. Aside from being two windows short, it is exactly similar to the others. It occurred to me that, in order to make up for the loss of those windows; also because I may be compelled to ask some obliging woman to occupy it in case your health is precarious at any time, and in view of the further fact that if any woman could be found, who would kindly and willingly care for us, my gratitude would be inexpressible; on account of all these things, I got a shade the *best* furnishings for this room."

The Girl stared at him with blank face.

"You see," said the Harvester, "this is a question of ethics. Now what is a guest? A thing of a day! A person who disturbs your routine and interferes with important concerns. Why should any one be grateful for company? Why should time and money be lavished on visitors? They come. You overwork yourself. They go. You are glad of it. You return the visit, because it's the only way to have back at them; but why pamper

them unnecessarily? Now a good housekeeper means
more than words can express. Comfort, kindness, sanitary living, care in illness! Here's to the prospective
housekeeper of Medicine Woods! Rogers, hang those
ruffled embroidered curtains. Observe that whereas mere
guest beds are plain white, this has a touch of brass.
Where guest rugs are floor coverings, this is a work of art.
Where guest brushes are celluloid, these are enamelled,
while the dresser cover is hand embroidered. Let me also
call your attention to the chairs touched with gold, cush-
ioned for ease, and a decorated pitcher and bowl. Watch
the bounce of these springs and the thickness of this mattress and pad, and notice that where guests, however welcome, get a down cover of sateen, the lady of the house
has silkaline. Won't she prepare us a breakfast after a
night in this room?"

"David, are you in earnest?" gasped the Girl.

"Don't these things prove it?" asked the Harvester.
"No woman shall enter my home, when my necessities
are so great I have to hire her to come, and take the
worst in the house. After my wife, she gets the best,
every time. Whenever I need help, the woman who will
come and serve me is what I'd call the real guest of the
house. Friend? Where are your friends when trouble
comes? It always brings a crowd on account of the excitement, and there is noise and racing; but if your soul
is saved alive, it is by a steady, trained hand you pay to
help you. Friends come and go, but a good housekeeper
remains, she is a business proposition—one that if conducted rightly for both parties and on a strictly common-

sense basis, gives you living comfort. Now that we have disposed of the guests who go and the one that remains, we will arrange for ourselves."

"David, did you ever know any one who treated a housekeeper as you say you would?"

"No. And I never knew any one who raised medicinal stuff for a living, but I'm making a gilt-edged success of it, and I will of a housekeeper, too."

"It doesn't seem——"

"That's the bedrock of all the trouble on the earth," interrupted the Harvester. "We are a nation and a part of a world that spends our time on 'seeming.' Our whole outer crust is 'seeming.' When we get beneath the surface and strike the *being*, then we live as we are privileged by the Almighty. I don't think I give a tinker how anything *seems*. What concerns me is how it *is*. It doesn't 'seem' possible to you to hire a woman to come into your home to take charge of its cleanliness and the food you eat—the very foundation of life—and treat her as an honoured guest, and give her the best comfort you have to offer. The cold room, the old covers, the bare floor, and the cast off furniture are for her. No wonder, as a rule, she gives what she gets. She dignifies her labour in the same ratio that you do. Wait until we need a housekeeper, then gaze with awe on the one I shall raise to your hand."

"I wonder——"

"Don't! It's wearing! Come tell me how to make our living-room less bare than it appears at present."

They went downstairs and began work on the room.

The Girl was placed on a couch and made comfortable; then the Harvester looked around.

"That bundle there, Rogers, is the curtains we bought for this room. If you and my wife think they are not right, we will not hang them."

The decorator opened the package and took out curtains of tan-coloured goods with borders of blue and brown.

"Those are not expensive," said the Harvester, "but to me a window appears bare with only a shade, so I thought we'd try these. When they become soiled we'll burn them and buy some fresh ones."

"Good idea!" laughed the Girl. "As a house decorator you surpass yourself as a Medicine Man."

"Fix these as you did those upstairs," ordered the Harvester. "We don't want any fol-de-rols. Put the bottom even with the sill and shear them off at the top."

"No, I am going to arrange these," said the decorator, "you go on with your part."

"All right! First, I'll lay the big rug."

He cleared the floor, spread a large rug with a rich brown centre and a wide blue border. Smaller ones of similar design and colour were placed before each of the doors leading from the room.

"Now for the hearth," said the Harvester, "I got this tan goat skin. Doesn't that look fairly well?"

It certainly did; so the Girl and the decorator hastened to agree. The Harvester replaced the table and chairs; then sat on the couch at the Girl's feet.

"I call this almost finished," he remarked. "All we need now is a bouquet and something on the walls which

is serious business. What goes on them usually remains
for a long time, so it should be selected with care. Ruth,
have you a picture of your mother?"

"None since she was my mother. I have some lovely
girl photographs."

"Good!" cried the Harvester. "Exactly the thing!
I have a picture of my mother when she was a pretty
girl. We will select the best of yours and have them
enlarged in those beautiful brown prints they make in
these days, then we'll frame one for each side of the mantel. After that you can decorate the other walls as you
see things you want. Fifteen minutes gone; we are ready
to march to the dining-room. Oh I forgot my pillows!
Here are half a dozen tan, brown, and blue for this room.
Ruth, you arrange them."

The Girl heaped four on the couch, dropped one beside
the hearth, and laid another in a big chair.

"Now I don't know what you will think of this," said
the Harvester. "I found it in a magazine at the library.
I copied this whole room. The plan was to have the floor,
furniture, and casings of golden oak and the walls pale
green. Then it said get yellow curtains bordered with
green and a green rug with yellow figures, so I got them.
I had green leather cushions made for the window seats,
and these pillows go on them. Hang the saffron curtains,
Rogers, and we will finish in good shape for dinner by six.
By the way, Ruth, when will you select your dishes? It
will take a big set to fill all these shelves and you shall
have exactly what you want."

"I can use those you have very well."

"Oh no you can't!" cried the Harvester. "I may live and work in the woods, but I am not so benighted that I don't own and read the best books and magazines, and subscribe for a few papers. I patronize the library and see what is in the stores. My money will buy just as much as any man's, if I do wear khaki trousers. Kindly notice the word. Save in deference to your ladyship I probably would have said pants. You see how *élite* I can be if I try. And it not only extends to my wardrobe, to a 'yaller' and green dining-room, but it takes in the 'chany' as well. I have looked up that, too. You want china, cut glass, silver cutlery, and linen. Ye! Ye! You needn't think I don't know anything but how to dig in the dirt. I have been studying this especially, so I know exactly what to get."

"Come here," said the Girl, making a place for him beside her. "Now let me tell you what I think. We are going to live in the woods, and our home is a log cabin— —"

"With acetylene lights, a furnace, baths, and hot and cold water——" interpolated the Harvester.

"Anyway," said she, "if you are going to let me have what I would like, I'd prefer a set of tulip yellow dishes with the Dutch little figures on them. I don't know what they cost, but certainly they are not so expensive as cut glass and china."

"Is that earnest or is it because you think I am spending too much money?"

"It is what I want. Everything else is different; why should we have dishes like city folk? I'd dearly love to have the Dutch ones, and a white cloth with a yellow border, glass where it is necessary, and silver knives, forks, and spoons."

"That would be great, all right!" endorsed the decorator. "And you have got a priceless old lustre tea set there, and your willow ware is as fine as I ever saw. If I were you, I wouldn't buy a dish with what you have, except the yellow set."

"Great day!" ejaculated the Harvester. "Will you tell me why my great-grandmother's old pink and green teapot is priceless?"

The Girl explained pink lustre. "That set in the shop I knew in Chicago would sell for from three to five hundred dollars. Truly it would! I've seen one little pink and green pitcher like yours bring nine dollars there. And you've not only got the full tea set, but water and dip pitchers, two bowls, and two bread plates. They are priceless, because the secret of making them is lost; they take on beauty with age, and they were your great-grandmother's."

The Harvester reached over to shake hands.

"Ruth, I'm so glad you've got them!" he bubbled. "Now elucidate on my willow ware. What is it? Where is it? Why have I willow ware and am not informed. Did my ancestors buy better than they knew, or worse? Is willow ware a crime for which I should hide my head, or is it further riches thrust upon me? I thought I had investigated the subject of proper dishes quite thoroughly; but I am very certain I saw no mention of lustre or willow. I thought, in my ignorance, that lustre was a dress, and willow a tree. Have I been deceived? Why is a blue pitcher willow ware?"

"Bring that platter from the mantel," suggested the Girl, "and I will show you."

The Harvester obeyed, watching the finger that traced the design.

"That's a healthy willow tree!" he commented. "If Loon Lake couldn't go ahead of that it should be drained. And will you please tell me why this precious platter from which I have eaten much stewed chicken, fried ham, and in youthful days, sopped the gravy——will you tell me why this relic of my ancestors is called a willow plate, when there are a majority of orange trees so extremely fruitful they have neglected to grow a leaf? Why is it not an orange plate? Look at that boat! And in plain sight of it, two pagodas, a summer house, a water-sweep, and a pair of corpulent swallows; you would have me believe that a couple are eloping in broad daylight."

"Perhaps it's night! And those birds are doves."

"Never!" cried the Harvester. "There is a total absence of shadows. There is no moon. Each orange tree is conveniently split in halves, so you can see to count the fruit accurately; the birds are in flight. Only a swallow or a stork can fly in decorations, either by day or by night. And for any sake look at that elopement! He goes ahead carrying a cane, she comes behind lugging the baggage, another man with a cane brings up the rear. They are not running away. They have been married ten years at least. In a proper elopement, they forget there are such things as jewels and they always carry each other. I've often looked up the statistics and it's the only authorized version. As I regard this treasure, I grow faint when I remember with what unnecessary force my father bore down when he carved the ham. I'll bet a cooky he split those orange trees. Now me——I'll never dare touch knife to it again. I'll always carve the meat on the broiler, and gently lift it to this platter with a fork. Or am I not to be allowed to dine from my ancestral treasure again?"

"Not in a green and yellow room," laughed the Girl. "I'll tell you what I think. If I had a tea table to match the living-room furniture, standing beside the hearth, a chafing dish to cook in, and the willow ware to eat from, we could have little tea parties in there, when we aren't very hungry or to treat a visitor. It would help make that room 'homey,' and it's wonderful how they harmonize with the other things."

"How much willow ware have I got to 'bestow' on you?" inquired the Harvester. "Suppose you show me all of it. A guilty feeling arises in my breast; I fear me I have committed high crimes!"

"Oh Man! You didn't break or lose any of those dishes, did you?"

"Show me!" insisted the Harvester.

The Girl arose, opened the cupboard he had designed for her china, and set before him a teapot, cream pitcher, two plates, a bowl, a pitcher, the meat platter, and a sugar bowl. "If there were all of the cups, saucers, and plates, I know where they would bring five hundred dollars," she said.

"Ruth, are you getting even with me for poking fun at them, or are you in earnest?" asked the Harvester.

"I mean every word of it."

"You really want a small, black walnut table made especially for those old dishes?"

"Not if you are too busy. I could use it with beautiful effect, while I can't tell you how proud I'd be of them."

The Harvester's face flushed. "Excuse me," he said, rising. "I have now finished furnishing a house; I will go and take a peep at the engine." He went into the kitchen and hearing the rattle of dishes the Girl followed in time to see him hastily slide something into his pocket. He picked up half a dozen old white plates, saucers, and several cups, starting toward the evaporator. He heard her coming.

"Look here, honey," he said, turning, "you don't want to see the dry-house now. I have terrific heat to do some rapid work. I'll be gone only a few minutes. You better boss the decorator. . . . I'm afraid that wasn't very diplomatic," he muttered. "It savoured a little of being sent back. But if what she says is right, and she should know if they handle such stuff at that art store, she will feel considerably better not to see this." He set his load at the door, drew an old blue saucer from his pocket and made a careful examination. He pulled some leaves from a bush, pushed a greasy cloth out of the saucer, wiped it the best he could, and held it to light. "That is a crime!" he commented. "Saucer from your maternal ancestors' tea set used for a grease dish. I am afraid I'd better sink it in the lake. She'd feel worse to see it than never to know. Wish I could clean off the grease! I could do better if it were hot. I can set it on the engine."

The Harvester placed the saucer on the engine, entered the dry-house, and closed the door. In the stifling air he began pouring seed from beautiful, big willow plates to old white ones.

"About the time I have ruined you," he said to a white plate, "some one will pop up and discover that the art of making you is lost so you are priceless, then I'll have been guilty of another blunder. Now there are the dishes mother got with baking powder. She thought they were grand. I know plenty well she prized them more than these blue ones or she wouldn't have saved them and used these for every day. There they set, all so carefully taken care of, and the Girl doesn't even look at them. Thank Heaven, there are the four remaining plates all right, anyway! Now I've got seed in some of the saucers; one is there; where on earth is the last one? And where, oh unkind fates! are the cups?"

He found more saucers, setting them with the plates. As he passed the engine he noticed the saucer on it was bubbling grease, literally exuding it from the particles of clay. "Hooray!" cried the Harvester. He took it up, rubbed off all the grease, and imagined it was brighter. "If 'a little is good, more is better,'" quoted the Harvester.

Then he slipped out, dripping perspiration, glanced toward the cabin, and ran into the workroom. The first object he saw was a willow cup half full of red paint, stuck and dried as if to remain forever. He took his knife and tried to whittle it off, but noticing that he was scratching the cup he filled it with turpentine, set it under a work bench, turned a tin pan over it, and covered it with shavings. A few steps farther brought one in sight, filled with carpet tacks. He searched everywhere, but could find no more, so he went to the laboratory. Beside his wash bowl at the door stood the last willow saucer. He had used it for years as a soap dish. He scraped the contents on the bench and filled the dish with water. Four cups held medicinal seeds and were in good condition. He lacked one, although he could not remember of ever having broken it. Gathering his collection, he carried his treasures into the workroom, then went to the barn to feed. As he was leaving the stable he uttered a joyous exclamation and snatched from a window sill a willow cup, gummed and smeared with harness oil.

"The full set, by hokey!" marvelled the Harvester. "Now if I only can clean them, I'll be ready to make her tea table, whatever that is. My, I hope she will stay away until I get these in better shape!" He filled the last cup with turpentine, set it with the other under the work bench, stacked the remaining pieces, polished the saucer he was baking, and went to bring a dish pan and towel.

As he stood busily working over the dishes, with light step the Girl came to the door. She took one long look and understood. She turned swiftly going back to the cabin, but her shoulders were shaking. Presently the Harvester came in and explained that after finishing in the dry-house he had gone to do the feeding. He suggested that before it grew dark they should go through the rooms to see how they appeared, then gather the flowers

the Girl wanted. Then they went to the hillside sloping
to the lake. For the dining-room, the Girl wanted yellow
water lilies, so the Harvester brought his old boat and
gathered enough to fill the green bowl. For the living-
room, she used wild ragged robins in the blue bowl, while
on one end of the mantel set a pitcher of senna and on the
other arrowhead lilies. For her room, she selected big,
blushy mallows that grew all along Singing Water and
around the lake.

"Isn't that slightly peculiar?" questioned the Harvester.

"Take a peep," said the Girl, opening her door.

She had spread the pink coverlet on her couch, so when
she set the big pink bowl filled with mallows on the table
the effect was exquisite.

"I think perhaps that's a little Frenchy," she said, "and
you may have to be educated to it; but salmon pink and
buttercup yellow are colours I love in combination."

She closed the door and went to the swing, where she
liked to rest, look, and listen. The Harvester suggested
reading to her, but she shook her head.

"Wait until winter," she said, "when the days are
longer and cold, and the snow buries everything, and then
read. Now tell me about my hedge and the things you
have planted in it."

The Harvester went out and collected a bunch of twigs.
He handed her a big, evenly proportioned leaf of ovate
shape, and explained: "This is burning bush, so called
because it has pink berries that hang from long, graceful
stems all winter, and when fully open they expose a

flame-red seed pod. It was for this colour on gray and white days that I planted it. In the woods I grow it in thickets. The root bark brings twenty cents a pound, at the very least. It is good fever medicine."

"Is it poison?"

"No. I didn't set anything acutely poisonous in your hedge. I wanted it to be a mass of bloom you were free to cut for the cabin all spring, an attraction to birds in summer, and bright with colour in winter. To draw the feathered tribe, I planted alder, wild cherry, and grape-vines. This is cherry. The bark is almost as beautiful as birch. I raise it for tonics and the birds love the cherries. This fern-like leaf is from mountain ash; when it attains a few years' growth it will flame with colour all winter in big clusters of scarlet berries. That I grow in the woods is a picture in snow time, while the bark is one of my standard articles."

The Girl raised on her elbow to look at the hedge.

"I see it," she said. "The berries are green now. I suppose they change colour as they ripen."

"Yes," said the Harvester. "And you must not confuse them with sumac. The leaves are somewhat similar, but the heads differ in colour and shape. The sumac and buckeye you must not touch, until we learn what they will do to you. To some they are slightly poisonous, to others not. I couldn't help putting in a few buckeyes on account of the big buds in early spring. You will like the colour if you are fond of pink and yellow in combination, while the red-brown nuts in grayish-yellow, prickly hulls, and the leaf clusters are beautiful, but you must use care. I put in witch hazel for variety, it's mighty good medicine, too; so is spice brush, and it has leaves that colour brightly, and red berries. These selections were all made for a purpose. Now here is wafer ash; it is for music as well as medicine. I have invoked all good fairies to come and dwell in this hedge, so I had to provide an orchestra for their dances. This tree grows a hundred tiny castanets in a bunch; when they ripen and become dry the wind shakes fine music from them. Yes, they are medicine; that is, the bark of the roots is. Almost without exception everything here has medicinal properties. The tulip poplar will bear you the loveliest flowers of all, while its root bark, taken in winter, makes a good fever remedy."

"How would it do to eat some of the leaves and see if they wouldn't take the feverishness from me?"

"It wouldn't do at all," said the Harvester. "We are well enough fixed to allow Doc to come now; he is the one to allay the fever."

"Oh no!" she cried. "No! I don't want to see a doctor. I will be all right soon. You said I was better."

"You are," said the Harvester. "Much better! We will have you strong and well soon. You should have come in time for a dose of sassafras. Your hedge is filled with that, because of its peculiar leaves and odour. I put in dogwood for the white display around the little green bloom, lots of alder for bloom and berries, haws for blossoms and fruit for the squirrels, wild crab apples for the exquisite bloom and perfume, button bush for the buttons, a few pokeberry plants for the colour, and I tried some mallows, but I doubt if it's wet enough for them. I set pecks of vine roots, that are coming nicely, and ferns along the front edge. In two years that hedge will make a picture that will do your eyes good."

"Can you think of anything at all you forgot?"

"Yes indeed!" said the Harvester. "The woods are full of trees I have not used; some because I overlooked them, some I didn't want. A hedge like this, in perfection, is the work of years. Some species must be cut back, some encouraged, but soon it will be lovely, and its colour and fruit attract every bird of the heavens, and butterflies and insects of all varieties. I set several common cherry trees for the robins and some blackberry and raspberry vines for the orioles. The bloom is pretty while the birds you'll have will be a treat to see and hear, if we keep away cats, don't fire guns, scatter food, and move quietly among them. With our water added, there is nothing impossible in the way of making friends with feathered folk."

"There is one thing I don't understand," said the Girl. "You wouldn't risk breaking the wing of a moth by keeping it when you wanted a drawing very much; you don't seem to kill birds and animals that other people do. You almost worship a tree; now how can you peel bark to sell or dig up beautiful bushes by the root."

"Perhaps I've talked too much about the woods," said the Harvester gently. "I've longed inexpressibly for sympathetic company here, because I feel rooted for life, so I am more than anxious that you should care for it. I may have made you feel that my greatest interest is in the woods; that I am not consistent when I call on

my trees and plants to yield of their store for my purposes.
Above everything else, the human proposition comes first,
Ruth. I do love my trees, bushes, and flowers, because
they keep me at the fountain of life, and teach me lessons
no book ever hints at; but above everything come my fellow men. All I do is for them. My heart is filled with
feeling for the things you see around you here, but it
would be joy to me to uproot the most beautiful plant I
have if by so doing I could save you pain. Other men
have wives they love as well, little children they have fath-
ered, big bodies useful to the world, that are sometimes
crippled with disease. There is nothing I would not give
to allay the pain of humanity. It is not inconsistent to
offer any growing thing you soon can replace, to cure suffering. Get that idea out of your head! You said you
could worship at the shrine of the pokeberry bed, you feel
holier before the arrowhead lilies, your face takes on an appearance of reverence when you see pink mallow blooms.
Which of them would you have hesitated a second in uprooting if you could have offered it to subdue fever or pain
in the body of the little mother you loved?"

"Oh I see!" cried the Girl. "Like everything else
you make this different. You worship all this beauty
and grace, wrought by your hands, but you carry your
treasure to the market place for the good of suffering
humanity. Oh Man! I love the work you do!"

"Good!" cried the Harvester. "Good! And Ruth-
girl, while you are about it, see if you can't combine the
man with his occupation a little."

CHAPTER XVI

Granny Moreland's Visit

THE following morning the Girl was awakened by wheels on the gravel outside her window. She lifted her head to see Betsy passing with a load of lumber. Shortly afterward the sound of hammer and saw came to her, so she knew that Singing Water bridge was being roofed to provide shade for her. She dressed and went to the kitchen to find a dainty breakfast waiting, so she ate what she could, then washed the dishes and swept. By that time she was so tired she dropped on a dining-room window seat, looking toward the bridge. She could catch glimpses of the Harvester as he worked. She watched his deft ease in handling heavy timbers, and the assurance with which he builded. Sometimes he stood with tilted head to study his work a minute, then swiftly proceeded. Occasionally he glanced toward the cabin, at last he came swinging up the drive. He entered the kitchen quietly, but when he saw the Girl in the window he sat at her feet.

"Oh but this is a morning, Ruth!" he said.

She looked at him closely. He radiated health and good cheer. His tanned cheeks were flushed red with exercise, while the hair on his temples was damp.

"You have been breaking the rules," he said. "It

is the law that I am to do the work until you are well and strong again. Why did you tire yourself?"

"I am so perfectly useless! I see so many things that I would enjoy doing. Oh you can do everything else, make me well! Make me strong!"

"How can I, when you won't do as I tell you?"

"I will! Indeed I will!"

"Then no more attempts to stand over dishes and clean big floors. You mustn't overwork yourself at anything. The instant you feel in the least tired you must lie down and rest."

"But Man! I'm tired every minute, with a dead, dull ache. I feel as if I never would be rested again in all the world."

The Harvester took one of her hands, felt its fevered palm, fluttering wrist pulse, then noticed that the brilliant red of her lips had extended to spots on her cheeks. He formed his resolution.

"Can't work on that bridge any more until I drive in for some big nails," he said. "Do you mind being left alone for an hour?"

"Not at all, if Bel will stay with me. I'll lie in the swing."

"All right!" answered the Harvester. "I'll help you get settled. Is there anything you want from town?"

"No, not a thing!"

"Oh but you are modest!" cried the Harvester. "I can sit here and name fifty things I want for you."

"Oh but you are extravagant!" imitated the Girl. "Please, please, Man, don't! Can't you see I have so

much now I don't know what to do with it? Sometimes
I almost forget the ache, just lying and looking at all the
wonderful riches that have come to me so suddenly. I
can't believe they won't vanish as they came. By the
hour in the night I look at my lovely room. I just fight
my eyes to keep them from closing for fear they'll open in
that stifling garret to the heat of day and work I have not
strength to do. I know all this will prove to be a dream
yet, a wilder one than yours."

The face of the Harvester was very anxious.

"Please remember my dream came true," he said,
"and sooner than I had the least hope that it would.
I'm wide awake or I couldn't be building bridges; while
you are real, if I know flesh and blood when I touch it."

"If I were well, strong, and attractive, I could understand," she said. "Then I could work in the house, at
the drawings, help with the herbs, and I'd feel as if I had
some right to be here."

"All that is coming," said the Harvester. "Take
a little more time. You can't expect to sin steadily
against the laws of health for years, and recover in a
day. You will be all right much sooner than you think
possible."

"Oh I hope so!" said the Girl. "But sometimes I
doubt it. How I could come here to put such a burden
on a stranger, I can't see. I scarcely can remember what
awful stress drove me. I had no courage. I should
have finished in my garret as my mother did. I must
have some of my father's coward blood in me. She never
would have come. I never should!"

"If it didn't make any real difference to you, and meant all the world to me, I don't see why you shouldn't humour me.   I can't begin to tell you how happy I am to have you here.   I could shout and sing all day."

"It requires very little to make some people happy."

"You are not much, but you are going to be more soon," laughed the Harvester, as he gently picked up the Girl and carried her to the swing, where he covered her, kissed her hot hand, then whistled for Belshazzar.   He pulled the table close and set a pitcher of iced fruit juice on it. Then he left her.

"Betsy, this is mighty serious business," said the Harvester.   "The Girl is scorching or I don't know fever. I wonder—well, one thing is sure——she is bound to be better off in pure, cool air and with everything I can do to be kind, than in Henry Jameson's attic with everything he could do to be mean.   Pleasant men those Jamesons!   Wonder if the Girl's father was much like her Uncle Henry?   I think not or her refined and lovely mother never would have married him.   Come to think of it, that's no law, Betsy.   I've seen beautiful and delicate women fall under some mysterious spell, and yoke their lives with rank degenerates.   Whatever he was, they have paid the price.   Maybe the wife deserved it, and bore it in silence because she knew she did, but it's bitter hard on Ruth.   Girls should be taught to think at least one generation ahead when they marry.   I wonder what Doc will say, Betsy!   He will have to come and see for himself.   I don't know how she will feel about that.   I had hoped I could pull her through with care,

food, and tonics, but I don't dare go any farther alone.
Betsy, that's a thin, hot, little hand to hold a man's only
chance for happiness."

"Well, bridegroom! I've been counting the days!"
said Doctor Carey. "The Missus and I made it up this
morning that we had waited as long as we would. We
are coming to-night. David——"

"It's all right, Doc," said the Harvester. "Don't
you dare think anything is wrong or that I am not the
proudest, happiest man in this world, because I appear
anxious. I am not trying to conceal it from you. You
know we both agreed at first that Ruth should be in the
hospital, Doc. Well, she should! She is what would
be a lovely woman if she were not full of the poison of
wrong food and air, overwork, and social conditions that
have warped her. She is all I dreamed of and more,
but I've come after you. I hoped she would begin to gain
strength at once on changed conditions. As yet I can't
see any difference. She needs a doctor, but I hate for her
to know it. Could you come out this afternoon, and pretend as if it were a visit? Bring Mrs. Carey, then watch
the Girl. If you need an examination, I think she will
obey me. If you can avoid it, fix what she should have
and send it back to me by a messenger. I don't like to
leave her when she is so ill."

"I'll come at once, David."

"Then she will know that I came for you; that will
frighten her. You can do more good to wait until afternoon, and pretend you are making a social call. I'd have
brought her in, but I have no proper conveyance yet.

I'm promised something soon, perhaps it is ready now. Good-bye! Be sure to come!"

The Harvester drove to a livery barn and examined a little horse, a shining black creature that seemed gentle and spirited. He thought favourably of it. A few days before he had selected a smart carriage, so with this outfit tied behind the wagon he returned to Medicine Woods. He left the horse at the bridge, stabled Betsy, and then returned for the new conveyance, driving it to the hitching post. At the sound of unexpected wheels the Girl lifted her head, staring at the turnout.

"Come on!" cried the Harvester, opening the screen. "We are going to the woods to initiate your carriage."

She went with cries of surprised wonder.

"This is how you travel to Onabasha to do your shopping, to call on Mrs. Carey and the friends you will make, and visit the library. When I've tried out Mr. Horse enough to prove him reliable as guaranteed, he is yours, for your purposes only. When you grow wonderfully well and strong, we'll sell him and buy you a real live horse and a stanhope, such as city ladies have; and there must be a saddle so that you can ride."

"Oh I'd love that!" cried the Girl. "I always wanted to ride! Where are we going?"

"To show you Medicine Woods," said the Harvester. "I've been waiting for this. You see there are several hundred acres of trees, thickets, shrubs, and herb beds up there, so if the wagon road that winds between them were stretched straight it would be many miles in length. We have a cool, shaded, perfumed driveway all our own.

Let me get you a drink before you start and the little
shawl. It's chilly there compared with here. Now are
you comfortable and ready?"

"Yes," said the Girl. "Hurry! I've just longed to go,
but I didn't like to ask."

"I am sorry," said the Harvester. "Living here for
years alone and never having had a sister, how am I to
know what a girl would like if you don't tell me? I knew
it would be too tiresome for you to walk, so I was waiting
to find a reliable horse and a suitable carriage."

"You won't scratch or spoil it up there?"

"I'll lower the top. It is not so wide as the wagon;
nothing will touch it."

"This is just so lovely, and such a wonderful treat, do
you observe that I'm not saying a word about extrava-
gance?" asked the Girl, as she leaned back in the carriage
to inhale the invigorating wood air.

The horse climbed the hill, when the Harvester guided
him down long, dim roads through deep forest, while
he explained what large thickets of bushes were, why he
grew them, how he collected the roots or bark, for what
each was used and its value. Excited red birds darted
among the bushes, as the Harvester answered their cry.
Blackbirds protested against the unusual intrusion of
strange objects, and a brown thrush slipped from a late
nest close the road, wailing in anxiety.

One after another the Harvester introduced the Girl
to the best trees, and pointed out which brought large
prices for lumber and which had medicinal bark and roots.
On and on they slowly drove through the woods, past the

big beds of cranesbill, violets, and lilies. He showed her
where the mushrooms were most numerous, then for the
first time told the story of how he had sold them and the
violets from door to door in Onabasha in his search for
her. The amazed Girl sat staring at him. He told of
Doctor Carey having seen her once, and inquired as they
passed the bed if the yellow violets had revived. He
stopped to search, finding a few late ones, deep among the
leaves.

"Oh if I only had known that!" cried the Girl, "I would
have kept them forever."

"No need," said the Harvester. "I now present you
with the white and yellow violet beds. Next spring you
shall fill your room. Won't that be a treat?"

"One money never could buy!" cried the Girl.

"Seems to be my strong point," commented the Harvester. "The most I have to offer worth while is something you can't buy. There is a fine fairy platform.
They can spare you one. I'll get it."

The Harvester broke from a tree a large fan-shaped
fungus, the surface satin fine, the base mossy, and explained to the Girl that these were the ballrooms of the
woods, the floors on which the little people dance in the
moonlight at their great celebrations. Then he added a
piece of woolly dog moss, showing her how each separate
spine was like a perfect little evergreen tree. "That is
where the fairies get their Christmas pines," he explained.

"Do you honestly believe in fairies?"

"Surely!" exclaimed the Harvester. "Who would tell
me when the maples are dripping sap, and the mushrooms

springing up, if the fairies didn't whisper in the night?
Who paints the flower faces, colours the leaves, enamels
the ripening fruit with bloom, and frosts the window
pane to let me know that it is time to prepare for winter?
Of course!   They are my friends and everyday helpers.
And the winds are good to me.   They carry down news
when tree bloom is out, when the pollen sifts gold from
the bushes, and it's time to collect spring roots.   The
first bluebird always brings me a message.   Sometimes he
comes by the middle of February, again not until late
March.   On his day, Belshazzar decides my fate for a
year.   Six years we've played that game; now it is ended
in blessed reality.   In the woods and at my work I remain
until I die, with a few outside tries at medicine making.
I am putting up some compounds in which I really have
faith.   Of course they have got to await their time to be
tested, but I believe in them.   I have grown stuff so carefully, gathered it according to rules, washed it decently,
and dried and mixed it with such scrupulous care.   Night
after night I've sat over the books until midnight and
later, studying combinations; and day after day I've
stood in the laboratory testing and trying, and two or
three will prove effective, or I've a disappointment coming."

"You haven't wasted time!   I'd much rather take
medicines you make than any at the pharmacies.   Several
times I've thought I'd ask you if you wouldn't give me
some of yours.   The prescription Doctor Carey sent
does no good.   I've almost drunk it, yet I am constantly
tired.   You make me something from these tonics and

stimulants you've been telling me about.   Surely you **can** help me!"

"I've got one combination that's going to save life, in my expectations.   But Ruth, it never has been tried, so I couldn't experiment on the very light of my eyes with it.   If I should give you something and you'd grow worse as a result—I am a strong man, my girl, but I couldn't endure that.   I'd never dare.   But dear, I am expecting Carey and his wife out any time; probably they will come to-day, it's so beautiful; and when they do, for my sake, won't you talk with him, tell him exactly what made you ill, then take what he gives you?   He's a great man.   He was recently President of the National Associa-tion·of Surgeons.   Long ago he abandoned general prac-tice, but he will prescribe for you; all his art is at your command.   It's quite an honour, Ruth.   He performs many miracles, and saves life every day.   He had not seen you, what he gave me was only by guess.   He may not think it right after he meets you."

"Then I am really ill?"

"No.   You only have the germs of illness in your blood, and if you will help me that much we can eliminate them; then it is you for housekeeper, with first assistant in me, the drawing tools, paint box, and all the woods for sub-jects.   So, as I was going to tell you, Belshazzar and I have played our game for the last time.   That decision was ultimate.   Here I will work, live, and die.   Here, please God, strong and happy, you shall live with me. Ruth, you must recover quickly.   You will consult the doctor?"

"Yes, and I wish he would hurry," said the Girl. "He can't make me new too soon to suit me. If I had a strong body, oh Man, I just feel as if you could find a soul somewhere in it that would respond to all these wonders you have brought me among. Oh! make me well, then I'll try as woman never did before to bring you happiness to pay for it."

"Careful now," warned the Harvester. "There is to be no talk of obligations between you and me. Your presence here and your growing trust in me are all I ask at the hands of fate at present. Long ago I learned to 'labour and to wait.' By the way——here's my most difficult labour and my longest wait. This is the precious ginseng bed."

"How pretty!" exclaimed the Girl.

Covering acres of wood floor, among the big trees, stretched the lacy green carpet. On slender, upright stalks waved three large leaves, each made up of five-stemmed, ovate little leaves, round at the base, sharply pointed at the tip. A cluster of from ten to twenty small green berries, that would turn red later, arose above. The Harvester lifted a plant to show the Girl that the Chinese name, Jin-chen, meaning man-like, originated because the divided root resembled legs. Away through the woods spread the big bed, the growth waving lightly in the wind, the peculiar odour filling the air.

"I am going to wait to gather the crop until the seeds are ripe," said the Harvester, "then bury some as I dig a root. My father said that was the way of the Indians. It's a mighty good plan. The seeds are so delicate, they are difficult to gather and preserve properly. Instead of collecting and selling all of them to start rivals in the business, I shall replant my beds. I must find half a dozen assistants to harvest this crop in that way, which will be difficult, because it will come when my neighbours are busy with corn."

"Maybe I can help you."

"Not with ginseng digging," laughed the Harvester. "That is not woman's work. You may sit in an especially attractive place while you boss the job."

"Oh dear!" cried the Girl. "I want to walk."

Gradually they had climbed the summit of the hill, descended on the other side, then followed the road through the woods until they reached the brier patches, fruit trees, and the garden of vegetables, with big beds of sage, rue, wormwood, hoarhound, and boneset. From there to the lake sloped the sunny fields of mullein and catnip; the earth was molten gold with dandelion creeping everywhere.

"Too hot to-day," cautioned the Harvester. "Too rough walking. Wait until fall, then I shall have a treat there for you. Another flower I want you to love because I do."

"I will," said the Girl. "I feel it in my heart."

"Well I am glad you feel something besides the ache of fever," said the Harvester. Then noticing her tired face he added: "Now this little horse had quite a trip from town, while the wheels cut deeply into this woods soil and make difficult pulling, so I wonder if I had not better put him in the stable and let him become ac-

quainted with Betsy.   I don't know what she will think.
She has had sole possession for years.   Maybe she will be
jealous; perhaps she will be as delighted for company
as her master.   Ruth, if you could have heard what I
said to Belshazzar when he decided I was to go courting
this year, and seen what I did to him, and then take a
look at me now——merciful powers, I hope the dog doesn't
remember!   If he does, no wonder he forms a new allegiance so easily.   Have you observed that lately, when I
whistle, he starts; then turns back to see if you want
him?   He thinks as much of you as he does of me right
now."

"Oh no!" cried the Girl.   "That couldn't be possible.
You told me I must make friends with him, so I have
given him food, and tried to win him."

"You sit in the carriage until I put away the horse; it
will save you being alone while I work."

She leaned her head against the carriage top the Harvester had raised to screen her, and watched him stable
the horse.   Evidently he was very fond of animals, for
he talked as if it were a child he was undressing and kept
giving it extra strokes and pats as he led it away.   Ajax
disliked the newcomer instantly, noticed the carriage and
the woman's dress, so screamed his ugliest.   The Girl
smiled.   As the Harvester appeared she inquired: "Is
Ajax now sending a wireless to Ceylon asking for a mate?"

The Harvester saw a gleam of mischief in the usually
dull dark eyes that delighted him.

"That is the customary supposition when he finds
voice," he said.   "But since this has become your home,

you are bound to learn some of my secrets. One of them I try to guard is the fact that Ajax has a temper. No, my dear, he is not always sending a wireless, I am sorry to say. As a matter of fact he is venting his displeasure at any difference in our conditions. He hates change. He learned that from me. I will enjoy seeing him come for favour a year from now, as I learned to come for it, even when I didn't get much, and the road lay west of Onabasha. Ajax, stop that! There's no use to object. You know you think that horse is nice company for you, and that two can feed you more than one. Cease crying things you don't mean, and learn to love the people I do. Come on, old boy!"

The peacock came, but with feathers closely pressed and stepping daintily. As the bird advanced, the Harvester retreated, until he stood beside the Girl; then he slipped some grain to her hand and she offered it. But Ajax would not be coaxed. He haughtily turned and marched away, screaming at intervals.

"Nasty temper!" commented the Harvester. "Never mind! He soon will become accustomed to you, then he will love you as Belshazzar does. Feed the doves instead. They are friendly enough in all conscience. Do you notice that there is not a coloured feather among them? The squab that is hatched with one you may have for breakfast. Now let's go find something to eat, then I will finish the bridge so you can rest there to-night to watch the sun set on Singing Water."

So they went into the cabin and prepared food; then the Harvester told the Girl to make herself so pretty that she would be a picture and come talk to him while he finished the roof. She went to her room, found a pale lavender linen dress and put it on, dusted the pink powder thickly, then went where a wide bench made an inviting place in the shade. There she sat to watch her lightly expressed whim take shape.

"Soon as this is finished," said the Harvester, "I am going to begin on that tea table. I can make it in a little while, if you want it to match the other furniture."

"I do," said the Girl.

"Wonder if you could draw a plan showing how it should appear. I am rather shy on tea tables."

"I think I can."

The Harvester brought paper, pencil, and a shingle for a drawing pad.

"Now remember one thing," he said. "If you are in earnest about using those old blue dishes, this must be a big, healthy table. A little one will appear top heavy with them. It would be a good idea to set out what you want to use, arranged as you would like them, then let me take the top measurements that way."

"All right! I'll only indicate how it should be. We will find the size later. I could almost weep because that wonderful set is broken. If I had all of it I'd be so proud!"

The Girl bent over the drawing. The Harvester worked with his attention divided between her, the bridge, and the road. At last he saw the big red car creeping up the valley.

"Seems to be some one coming, Ruth! Guess it must be Doc. I'll go open the gate?"

"Yes," said the Girl. "I'm so glad. You won't forget to ask him to help me if he can?"

The Harvester wheeled hastily. "I won't forget!" he said, as he hurried to the gate. The car ran slowly; the Girl could see him swing to the step to talk as they advanced. When they reached her they stopped and all of them came forward. She went to meet them. She shook hands with Mrs. Carey, then with the doctor.

"I am so glad you have come," she said.

"I hope you are not lonesome already," laughed the doctor.

"I think any one with brains to appreciate half of this never could become lonely here," answered the Girl. "No, it isn't that."

"A-ha!" cried the doctor, turning to his wife. "You see that the beautiful young lady remembers me, and has been wishing I would come. I always said you didn't half appreciate me. What a place you are making, David! I'll run the car to the shade and join you."

For a long time they talked under the trees, then they went to see the new home and all its furnishings.

"Now this is what I call comfort," said the doctor. "David, build us a house exactly similar to this over there on the hill, and let us live out here also. I'd love it. Would you, Clara?"

"I don't know. I never lived in the country. One thing is sure: if I tried it, I'd prefer this to any other place I ever saw. David, won't you take me far enough up the hill that I can look from the top to the lake?"

"Certainly," said the Harvester. "Excuse us a little while, Ruth!"

As soon as they were gone the Girl turned to the doctor. "Doctor Carey, David says you are great. Won't you exercise your art on me? I am not at all well, and oh! I'd so love to be strong and sound."

"Will you tell me," asked the doctor, "just enough to show me what caused the trouble?"

"Bad air and water, poor light and food at irregular times, overwork and deep sorrow; every wrong condition of life you could imagine, with not a ray of hope in the distance, until now. For the sake of the Harvester, I would be well again. Please, please try to cure me!"

So they talked until the doctor thought he knew all he desired; then they went to see the gold flower garden.

"I call this simply superb," said he, taking a seat beneath the tree roof of her porch. "Young woman, I don't know what I'll do to you if you don't speedily grow strong here. This is the prettiest place I ever saw."

"Isn't he wonderful?" asked the Girl, looking up the hill, where the tall form of the Harvester could be seen moving around. "Only to see him, you would think him the essence of manly strength and force. And he is! So strong! Into the lake at all hours, at the dry-house, on the hill, grubbing roots, lifting big pillars to support a bridge roof, yet with it all a fancy as delicate as any dreaming girl. Doctor, the fairies paint the flowers, colour the fruit, and frost the windows for him; the winds carry pollen to tell him when his growing things are ready for the dry-house. I don't suppose I can tell you anything new about him; but isn't he a perpetual surprise? Never like any one else! And no matter how he startles me in the beginning, he always ends by convincing me that he is right."

"I never loved any other man as I do him," said the doctor. "I ushered him into the world when I was a young man just beginning to practise. I've known him ever since. I know few men so scrupulously clean. Try to get well and make him happy, Mrs. Langston. He so deserves it."

"You may be sure I will," answered the Girl.

After the visitors had gone, the Harvester told her to place the old blue dishes as she would like to arrange them on her table, so he could get a correct idea of the size, then he left to put a few finishing strokes on the bridge cover. She went into the dining-room and opened the china closet. She knew from her peep in the work-room that there would be more pieces than she had seen before, but she did not think or hope that a full half dozen tea set and plates, bowl, platter, and pitcher would be waiting for her.

"Why Ruth, what made you tire yourself to come down? I intended to return in a few minutes."

"Oh Man!" cried the laughing Girl, as she clung pant-ingly to a bridge pillar for support, "I just had to come to tell you. There are fairies! Really truly ones! They have found the remainder of the willow dishes for me. Now there are so many it isn't going to be a table at all. It must be a little cupboard especially for them, in that space between the mantel and the bookcase. There should be a shining brass tea canister, and a wafer box like the arts people make. I'll pour tea and tend the chafing dish while you can toast the bread with a long fork over the coals. We will have suppers on the living-room table. It will be such fun!"

"Be seated!" cried the Harvester. "Ruth, that's the longest speech I ever heard you make, while it sounded, praise the Lord, like a girl. Did Doc say he would fix something for you?"

"Yes, such a lot of things! I am going to shut my eyes, open my mouth and swallow all of them. I'm going to be born again and forget all I ever knew before I came here. Soon I will be tagging you everywhere, begging you to suggest designs for my pencil, and I'll simply force life to come right for you."

"Sounds good!" he said. "But, Ruth, I'm a little dubious about force work. Life won't come right unless you learn to love me, and love is a stubborn, contrary bulldog element of our nature that won't be driven an inch. It wanders as the wind, and strikes us as it will. You'll arrive at what I hope for much sooner if you forget it in amusing yourself and being as happy as you can. Then, perhaps all unknown to you, a little spark of tenderness for me will light in your breast; if it ever does we will buy a fanning mill and raise a flame or know why."

"And there won't be any force in that?"

"What you can't compel is the start. It's all right to push any growth after you have something to work on."

"That reminds me," said the Girl, "there is a question I want to ask you."

"Go ahead!" said the Harvester, glancing at her as he hewed a joist.

She turned away her face, looking across the lake for a long time.

"Is it a difficult question, Ruth?" inquired the Harvester to help her.

"Yes," said the Girl. "I don't know how to make you see."

"Take any kind of a plunge. I'm not usually dense."

"It is really quite simple after all. It's about a girl ——a girl I knew very well in Chicago. She had a problem——and it worried her dreadfully, so I just wondered what you would think of it."

The Harvester shifted his position until he could watch the side of the averted face.

"You'll have to tell me, before I can tell you," he suggested.

"She was a girl who never had anything from life but work and worry. Of course, that's the only kind I'd know! One day when the work was most difficult, and worry cut deepest, and she really thought she was losing her mind, a man came by and helped her. He lifted her out; rescued all that was possible for a man to save to her in honour, then went his way. There wasn't anything more. Probably there never would be. His heart was great, so he stooped to pity her gently and passed on. After a time another man came by, a good and noble man. He offered her love so wonderful she hadn't brains to comprehend how or why it was."

The Girl's voice trailed off as if she were too weary to

speak further, while she leaned her head against a pillar, gazing with dull eyes across the lake.

"And your question," suggested the Harvester at last. She aroused herself. "Oh, the question! Why this—— if in time, after she had tried and tried, love to equal his simply would not come——would——would she be wrong to *pretend* she cared, to do the very best she could, and hope for real love some day? Oh David, would she?"

The Harvester's face was whiter than the Girl's. He pounded the chisel into the joist savagely.

"Would she, David?"

"Let me understand you clearly," said the man in a dry, breathless voice. "Did she love this first man to whom she came under obligations?"

The Girl sat gazing across the lake while the tortured Harvester stared at her.

"I don't know," she said at last. "I don't know whether she knew what love was or ever could. She never before had known a man; her heart was as undeveloped and starved as her body. I don't think she realized love, but there was a *something*. Every time she would feel most grateful and long for the love that was offered her, that 'something' would awake and hurt her almost beyond endurance. Yet she knew he never would come. She knew he did not care for her. I don't know that she felt she wanted him, but she was under such obligations to him that it seemed as if she must wait to see if he might not possibly come, and if he did she should be free."

"If he came, she preferred him?"

"There was a debt she had to pay——if he asked it I don't know whether she preferred him. I do know she had no idea that he would come, but the *possibility* was always before her. If he didn't come in time, would she be wrong in giving all she had to the man who loved her?"

The Harvester's laugh was short and sharp.

"She had nothing to give, Ruth! Talk about wormwood, colocynth apples, and hemlock! What sort of husks would that be to offer a man who gave honest love? Lie to him! Pretend feeling she didn't experience. Endure him for the sake of what he offered her? Well I don't know how calmly any other man would take that proceeding, Ruth, but tell your friend for me, that if I offered a woman the deep, lasting, and only loving passion of my heart, and she gave back a lie and indifferent lips, I'd drop her into the deepest hole of my lake and take my punishment cheerfully."

"But if it would make him happy? He deserves every happiness, and he need never know!"

The Harvester's laugh raised to an angry roar.

"You simpleton!" he cried roughly. "Do you know so little of human passion in the heart that you think love can be a successful assumption? Good Lord, Ruth! Do you think a man is made of wood or stone, that a woman's lips in her first kiss wouldn't tell him the truth? Why Girl, you might as well try to spread your tired arms and fly across the lake as to attempt to pretend a love you do not feel. You never could!"

"I said a girl I knew!"

"'A Girl you knew,' then! Any woman! The idea is

monstrous. Tell her so and forget it. You almost scared
the life out of me for a minute, Ruth. I thought it was
going to be you. But I remember your debt is to be paid
with the first money you earn, while you cannot have the
slightest idea what love is, if you honestly ask if it can be
simulated. No, ma'am! It can't! Not possibly! Not
ever! And when the day comes that its fires light your
heart, you will come to me, and tell of a flood of delight
that is tingling from the soles of your feet through every
nerve and fibre of your body, and you will laugh with me
at the time when you asked if it could be imitated success-
fully. No, ma'am! Now let me serve a good supper, and
see you eat like a farmer."

All evening the Harvester was so gay he kept the Girl
laughing, so at last she asked him the cause.

"Relief, honey! Relief!" cried the man. "You had
me paralyzed for a minute, Ruth. I thought you were
trying to tell me that there was some one so possessing
your heart that it failed every time you tried to think
about caring for me. If you hadn't convinced me before
you finished that love never has touched you I'd be the
saddest man in the world to-night, Ruth."

The Girl stared at him with wide eyes then silently
turned away.

Then for a week they worked out life together in the
woods. The Harvester was the housekeeper and the
cook. He added to his store many delicious broths and
stimulants he brought from the city. They drove every
day through the cool woods, often rowed on the lake in
the evenings, walked up the hill to the oak and scattered

fresh flowers on the two mounds there, or sat beside them talking for a time. The Harvester kept up his work with the herbs, and the little closet for the blue dishes was finished. They celebrated installing them by having supper on the living-room table, with the teapot on one end, and the pitcher full of bell-flowers on the other.

The Girl took everything prescribed for her, bathed, slept when she could, and worked for health with all the force of her frail being, but as the days went by it seemed to the Harvester her weight grew lighter, her hands hotter, and she drove herself to a gayety almost delirious. He thought he would have preferred a dull, stupid sleep of malaria. There was colour in plenty on her cheeks now, and sometimes he found her wrapped in the white shawl at noon on the warmest days Medicine Woods knew in early August; while on cool nights she wore the thinnest clothing and begged to be taken on the lake. The Careys came out every other evening and the doctor watched and worked, but he did not get the results he desired. His medicines were not effective.

"David," he said one evening, "I don't like the looks of this. Your wife has fever I can't break. It is eating the little store of vitality she has right out of her, so some of these days she is coming down with a crash. She should yield to the remedies I am giving her. She acts to me like a woman driven wild by trouble she is concealing. Do you know anything that worries her?"

"No," said the Harvester, "but I'll try to find out if it will help you in your work."

After they were gone he left the Girl lying in the swing,

guarded by the dog, and went across the marsh on the
excuse that he was going to a bed of thorn apple at the
foot of the hill.   There he sat on a log and tried to think.
With the mists of night closing around him, ghosts arose
he fain would have escaped.   "What will you give me in
cold cash to tell you who she is, and who her people are?"
Times untold in the past two weeks he had smothered,
swallowed, and choked it down.   That question she had
wanted to ask——was it for a girl she had known, or was
it for herself?   Days of thought had deepened the first
slight impression he so bravely had put aside, not into
certainty, but a great fear that she had meant herself.
If she did, what was he to do?   Who was the man?
There was a debt she had to pay if he asked it?   What
debt could a woman pay a man that did not involve
money?   Crouched on a log he suffered and twisted in
agonizing thought.   At last he arose, returning to the
cabin.   He carried a few frosty, blue-green leaves of velvet
softness and unusual cutting, prickly thorn apples full of
seeds, and some of the smoother, more yellowish-green
leaves of the jimson weed, to give excuse for his absence.

"Don't touch them," he warned as he came to her.
"They are poison and have disagreeable odour.   But
we are importing them for medicinal purposes.   On the
far side of the marsh, where the ground rises, there is a
waste place just suited to them, and as long as they will
seed and flourish with no care at all, I might as well have
the price as the foreign people who raise them.   They
don't bring enough to make them worth cultivating, but
when they grow alone and with no care, I can make

money on the time required to clip the leaves and dry the seeds. I must go wash before I come close to you."

The next day he had business in the city. Again she lay in the swing, talking to the dog while the Harvester was gone. She was startled as Belshazzar arose with a gruff bark. She looked down the driveway, but no one was coming. Then she followed the dog's eyes and saw a queer, little old woman coming up the bank of Singing Water from the north. She remembered what the Harvester had said, so rising she opened the screen and went down the path. As the Girl advanced she noticed the scrupulous cleanliness of the calico dress and gingham apron; the snowy hair framing a bronzed face with dancing dark eyes.

"Are you David's new wife?" asked Granny Moreland with laughing inflection.

"Yes," said the Girl. "Come in. He told me to expect you. I am so sorry he is away, but we can get acquainted without him. Let me help you."

"I don't know but that ought to be the other way about. You don't look very strong, child."

"I am not well," said the Girl, "but it's lovely here, and the air is so fine I am going to be better soon. Take this chair until you rest a little; then you shall see our pretty home, all the furniture and my dresses."

"Yes, I want to see things. My, but David has tried himself! I heard he was just tearin' up Jack over here, and I could get the sound of the hammerin'. One day he asked me to come see about his beddin'. He had that Lizy Crofter to wash for him, but if I hadn't jest stood

over her his blankets would have been ruined. She's no
more respect for fine goods than a pig would have for
cream pie. I hate to see woollens abused, as if they were
human. My, but things is fancy here since what David
planted is growin'! Did you ever live in the country
before?"

"No."

"Where do you hail from?"

"Well not from the direction of hail," laughed the Girl.
"I lived in Chicago, but we were——were not rich, so I
didn't know the luxury of the city; just the lonely, difficult
part."

"Do you call Chicago lonely?"

"A thousand times more so than Medicine Woods.
Here I know the trees will whisper to me, and the water
laughs and sings all day, while the birds almost split their
throats making music for me; but I can imagine no loneliness on earth that will begin to compare with being among
the crowds of a large city and no one has a word or look
for you. I miss the sea of faces and the roar of life; at
first I was almost wild with the silence, but now I don't
find it still any more; the Harvester is teaching me what
each sound means and they seem to be countless."

"You think, then, you'll like it here?"

"I do, indeed! Any one would. Even more than
the beautiful location, I love the interesting part of the
Harvester's occupation. I really think that gathering
material to make medicines that will allay pain is the
very greatest of all the great work a man can do."

"Good!" cried Granny Moreland, her dark eyes snapping. "I've always said it! I've tried to encourage David in it. And he's just capital at puttin' some of his stuff in shape, and combinin' it in as good medicine as you ever took. This spring I was all crippled up with the rheumatiz until I wanted to holler every time I had to move, and sometimes it got so aggravatin' I'm not right sure but I done it. 'Long comes David and says, 'I can fix you somethin',' and bless you, if the boy didn't take the tucks out of me, until here I am, and tickled to pieces that I can get here. This time last year I didn't care if I lived or not. Now seems as if I'm caperish as a three weeks' lamb. I don't see how a man could do a bigger thing than to stir up life in you like that."

"I think this place makes an especial appeal to me, because, shortly before I came, I had to give up my mother. She was very ill and suffered horribly. Every time I see David going to his little laboratory on the hill to work a while I slip away and ask God to help him to fix something that will ease the pain of humanity as I should like to have seen her relieved."

"Why you poor child! No wonder you are lookin' so thin and peaked!"

"Oh I'll soon be over that," said the Girl. "I am much better than when I came. I'll be coming over to trade pie with you before long. David says you are my nearest neighbour, so we must be close friends."

"Well bless your big heart! Now who ever heard of a pretty young thing like you wantin' to be friends with a plain old country woman?"

"Why I think you are lovely!" cried the Girl. "And

all of us are on the way to age, so we must remember
that we will want kindness then more than at any other
time. David says you knew his mother. Sometime won't
you tell me all about her? You must very soon. The
Harvester adored her, and Doctor Carey says she was the
noblest woman he ever knew. It's a big contract to take
her place. Maybe if you would tell me all you can remember I could profit by much of it."

Granny Moreland watched the Girl keenly.

"She wa'ant no ordinary woman, that's sure," she
commented. "And she didn't make no common man
out of her son, either. I've always contended she took
the job too serious, and wore herself out at it, but she certainly done the work up prime. If she's above cloud lean-
in' over the ramparts lookin' down——though it gets me
as to what foundation they use or where they get the
stuff to build the ramparts——but if they is ramparts,
and she's peekin' over them, she must take a lot of solid
satisfaction in seeing that David is not only the man she
fought and died to make him, but he's give her quite a
margin to spread herself on. She 'lowed to make him a
big man, but you got to know him close and plenty 'fore it
strikes you jest what his size is. I've watched him pretty
sharp, and tried to help what I could since Marthy went,
for I'm frank to say I'd ruther see David happy than to
be happy myself. I've had my fling. The rest of the way
I'm willin' to take what comes, with the best grace I can
muster, and wear a smilin' face to betoken the joy I have
had; but it cuts me sore to see the young sufferin'."

"Do you think David is unhappy?" asked the Girl.

"I don't see how he could be!" cried the old lady. "Of course he ain't! 'Pears as if he's got everythin' to make him the proudest, best satisfied of men. I'll own I was mighty anxious to see you. I know the kind o' woman it would take to make David miserable, and it seems sometimes as if men——that is good men——are plumb, stone blind when it comes to pickin' a woman. They jest hitch up with everlastin' misery easy as dew rolling off a cabbage leaf. It's sech a blessed sight to see you, and hear your voice and know you're the woman anybody can see you be. Why I'm so happy when I set here and con-tem'-plate you, I want to cackle like a pullet announcin' her first egg. Ain't this porch the purtiest place?"

"Come see everything," invited the Girl, rising.

Granny Moreland followed with alacrity.

"Bare floors!" she cried. "Wouldn't that best you? I saw they was finished capital when I was over, but I 'lowed they'd be covered afore you come. Don't you like nice, flowery Brissels carpets, honey?"

"No I don't," said the Girl. "You see, when rugs are dusty they can be rolled, carried outside, and cleaned. The walls can be wiped, the floors polished, and that way a house is always fresh. I can keep this shining, germ proof, and truly clean with half the work and none of the danger of heavy carpets and curtains."

"I don't doubt but them is true words," said Granny Moreland earnestly. "Work must be easier and sooner done than it was in my day, or people jest couldn't have houses the size of this or the time to gad that women have now. From the looks of the streets of Onabasha,

you wouldn't think a woman 'ud had a baby to tend, a
dinner pot a-bilin', or a bakin' of bread sence the flood.
And the country is jest as bad as the city. We're a apin'
them to beat the monkeys at a show. I hardly got a
neighbour that ain't got figgered Brissels carpet, a furnace,
a windmill, a pianny, and her own horse and buggy.
Several's got autermobiles, and the young folks are visitin'
around a-ridin' the trolleys, goin' to college, and copyin'
city ways. Amos Peters, next to us, goes bareheaded in
the hay field, and wears gloves to pitch and plow in. I
tell him he reminds me of these city women that only
wears the lower half of a waist and no sleeves, and a yard
of fine goods moppin' the floors. Well if that don't beat
the nation! Ain't them Marthy's old blue dishes?"

"Let me show you!" The Girl opened the little cupboard and exhibited the willow ware. The eyes of the
old woman began to sparkle.

"Foundation or no foundation, I do hope them ramparts is a go!" she cried. "If Marthy Langston is
squintin' over them and she sees her old chany put in a
fine cupboard, her little shawl round as purty a girl as
ever stepped, and knows her boy is gittin' what he deserves, good Lord, she'll be like to oust the Almighty,
and set on the throne herself! 'Bout everythin' in life
was a disappointment to her, 'cept David. Now if she
could see this! Won't I rub it into the neighbours? And
my boys' wives!"

"I don't understand," said the bewildered Girl.

"'Course you don't, honey," explained the visitor.
"It's like this: I don't know anybody, man or woman,

in these parts, that ain't rampagin' for *change*. They ain't one of them that would live in a log cabin, though they's not a house in twenty miles of here that fits its surroundin's and looks so homelike as this. They run up big, fancy brick and frame things, all turns and gables and gay as frosted picnic pie, and work and slave to git these very carpets you say ain't healthy, and the chairs you say you wouldn't give house room, an' they use their grandmother's chany for bakin', scraps, and grease dishes, and hide it if they's visitors. All of them strainin' after something they can't afford, and that ain't healthy when they git it, because somebody else is doin' the same thing. Mary Peters says she is afeared of her life in their new steam wagon, and she says Andy gits so narvous runnin' it, he jest keeps on a-jerkin' and drivin' all night, and she thinks he'll soon go to smash himself, if the machine doesn't beat him. But they are keepin' it up, because Graceston's is, and so it goes all over the country. Now I call it a slap right in the face to have a Chicagy woman come to the country to live, and enjoy a log cabin, bare floors, and her man's grandmother's dishes. If there ain't Marthy's old blue coverlid also carefully spread on a splinter new sofy. Landy, I can't wait to get to my son John's! He's got a woman that would take two coppers off the collection plate while she was purtendin' to put on one, if she could, and then spend them for a brass pin or a string of glass beads. Won't her eyes bung when I tell her about this? She wanted my Peter Hartman kiver for her ironin' board. Show me the rest!"

"This is the dining-room," said the Girl.

Granny Moreland stepped in, sending her keen eyes ranging over the floor, walls, and furnishings. She sank on a chair and said with a chuckle: "Now you go on and tell me all about it, honey. Jest what things are and why you fixed them, and how they are used."

The Girl did her best, while the old woman nodded in delighted approval.

"It's the purtiest thing I ever saw," she announced. "A minute ago, I'd 'a' said them blue walls back there, jest like October skies in Indian summer, and the brown rugs, like leaves in the woods, couldn't be beat; but this green and yaller is purtier yet. That blue room will keep the best lookin' part of fall on all winter, and with a roarin' wood fire, it'll be capital, and no mistake; but this here is spring, jest spring eternal, an' that's best of all. Looks like it was about time the leaves was bustin' and things pushin' up. It wouldn't surprise me a mite to see a flock of swallers come sailin' right through these winders. And here's a place big enough to lay down and rest a spell right handy to the kitchen, where a-body gits tiredest, without runnin' half a mile to find a bed, and in the mornin' you can look down to the 'still waters'; and in the afternoon, when the sun gits around here, you can pull that blind and 'lift your eyes to the hills,' like David of the Bible says. My, didn't he say the purtiest things! I never read nothin' could touch him!"

"Have you seen the Psalms arranged in verse as we would write it now?"

"You don't mean to tell me David's been put into real poetry?"

"Yes. Some Bibles have all the poetical books in our forms of verse."

"Well! Sometimes I git kind o' knocked out! As a rule I hold to old ways. I think they're the healthiest and the most faver'ble to the soul. But they's some changes come along, that's got sech hard common sense to riccomend them, that I wonder the past generations didn't see sooner. Now take this! An hour ago I'd told you I'd read my father's Bible to the end of my days. But if they's a new one that's got David, Solomon, and Job in nateral form, I'll have one, and I'll git a joy I never expected out of life. I ain't got so much poetry in me, but it always riled me to read, '7. The law of the Lord is perfect, covertin' the soul. 8. The statutes of the Lord are right. 9. The fear of the Lord is clean.' And so it goes on, 'bout as much figgers as they is poetry. Always did worry me. So if they make Bibles 'cordin' to common sense, I'll have one to-morrow if I have to walk to Onabasha to get it. Lawsy me! if you ain't gathered up Marthy's old pink tea set, and give it a show, too! Did you do that to please David, or do you honestly think them is nice dishes?"

"I think they are beautiful," laughed the Girl, sinking to a chair. "I am not sure that it did please him. He had been studying the subject, but something saved him from buying anything until I came. I'd have felt dreadfully if he had gotten what he wanted."

"What did he want, honey?" asked the old lady in an awestruck whisper.

"Egg-shell china and cut glass."

"And you wouldn't let him! Woman! What do you want?"

"A set of tulip-yellow dishes, with Dutch little figures on them. They are so quaint and they would harmonize perfectly with this room."

The old lady laughed gleefully.

"My! I wouldn't 'a' missed this for a dollar," she cried. "It jest does my soul good. More'n that, if you really like Marthy's dishes and are going to take care of them and use them right, I'll give you mine, too. I ain't never had a girl. I've always hoped she'd 'a' had some jedgment of her own, and not been eternally apin', if I had, but the Lord may 'a' saved me many a disappointment by sendin' all mine boys. Not that I'm layin' the babies on to the Lord at all——I jest got into the habit of sayin' that, 'cos everybody else does, but all mine, I had a purty good idy how I got them. If a girl of mine wouldn't 'a' had more sense, raised right with me, I'd 'a' been purty bad cut up over it. Of course, I can't be held responsible for the girls my boys married, but t'other day Emmeline ——that's John's wife——John is the youngest, and I sort o' cling to him——Emmeline she says to me, 'Mother, can't I have this old pink and green teapot?' My heart warmed right up to the child, so I says, 'What do you want it for, Emmeline?' And she says, 'To draw the tea in.' Cracky Dinah! That fool woman meant to set my grandmother's weddin' present from her pa and ma, dishes same as Marthy Washington used, on the stove to bile the tea in. I jest snorted! 'No,' says I, 'you can't! 'Fore I die,' says I, 'I'll meet up with some woman that'll love dishes and know how to treat them.' I think jest about as much of David as I do my own boys, and I don't make no bones of the fact that he's a heap more of a man. I'd jest as soon my dishes went to his children as to John's. I'll give you every piece I got, if you'll take keer of them."

"Would it be right?" wavered the girl.

"Right! Why, I'm jest tellin' you the fool wimmen would bile tea in them, make grease sassers of them, and use them to dish up the bakin' on! Wouldn't you a heap rather see them go into a cupboard like David's ma's is in, where they'd be taken keer of, if they was yours? I guess you would!"

"Well if you feel that way, and really want us to have them, I know David will build another little cupboard on the other side of the fireplace to put yours in, and I can't tell you how I'd love and care for them."

"I'll jest do it!" said Granny Moreland. "I got about as many blue ones as Marthy had an' mine are purtier than hers. And my lustre is brighter, for I didn't use it so much. Is this the kitchen? Well if I ever saw sech a cool, white place to cook in before! Ain't David the beatenest hand to think up things? He got the start of that takin' keer of his ma all his life. He sort of learned what a woman uses, and how it's handiest. Not that other men don't know; it's jest that they are too mortal selfish and keerless to fix things. Well this is great! Now when you bile cabbage and the wash, always open your winders wide and let the steam out, so it won't spile your walls."

"I'll be very careful," promised the Girl. "Now come see my bathroom, closet and bedroom."

"Well as I live! Ain't this fine. I'll bet a purty that if I'd 'a' had a room and a trough like this to soak in when I was wore to a frazzle, I wouldn't 'a' got all twisted up with rheumatiz like I am. It jest looks restful to see. I never washed in a place like this in all my days. Must feel grand to be wet all over at once! Now everybody ought to have sech a room and use it at all hours, like David does the lake. Did you ever see his beat to go swimmin'? He's always in splashin'! Been at it all his life. I used to be skeered when he was a little tyke. He soaked so much 'peared like he'd wash all the substance out of him, but it only made him strong."

"Has he ever been ill?"

"Not that I know of, and I reckon I'd knowed it if he had. Well what a clothespress! I never saw so many dresses at once. Ain't they purty? Oh I wish I was young, and could have one like that yaller. And I'd like to have one like your lavender right now. My! You are lucky to have so many nice clothes. It's a good thing most girls haven't got them, or they'd stand primpin' all day tryin' to decide which one to put on. I don't see how you tell yourself."

"I wear the one that best hides how pale I am," answered the Girl. "I use the colours now. When I grow plump and rosy, I'll wear the white."

Granny Moreland dropped on the couch to assure herself that it was Martha's pink Peter Hartman. Then she examined the sunshine room.

"Well I got to go back to the start," she said at last. "This beats the dinin'-room. This *is* the purtiest thing I ever saw. Oh I do hope they ain't so run to white in Heaven as some folks seem to think! Used to be scandalized if a-body took anythin' but a white flower to a funeral. Now they tell me that when Jedge Stilton's youngest girl come from New York to her pa's buryin' she fetched about a wash tub of blood-red roses. Put them all over him, too! Said he loved red roses livin', so he was goin' to have them when he passed over. Now if they are lettin' up a little on white on earth, mebby some of the stylish ones will carry the fashion over yander. If Heaven is like this, I won't spend none of my time frettin' about the foundations. I'll jest forget there is any, even if we do always have to be so perticler to get them solid on earth. Talk of gold harps! Can't you almost hear them? And listen to the birds and that water! Say, you won't get lonesome here, will you?"

"Indeed no!" answered the Girl. "Wouldn't you like to lie on my beautiful couch that the Harvester made with his own hands, and I'll spread Mother Langston's coverlet over you and let you look at all my pretty things while I slip away a few minutes to something I'd like to do?"

"I'd love to!" said the old woman. "I never had a chance at such fine things. David told me he was makin' your room all himself, and that he was goin' to fill it chuck full of everythin' a girl ever used, and I see he done it right an' proper. Away last March he told me he was buildin' for you, an' I hankered so to have a woman

"'Oh, I do hope they ain't so run to white in Heaven as some folks seem to think!'"

here again, even though I never s'posed she'd be soch-
iable like you, that I egged him on jest all I could. I
never would 'a' s'posed the boy could marry like this——
all by himself."

The Girl went to the ice chest to bring some of the
fruit juice, chilled berries, then to the pantry for bread and
wafers to make a dainty little lunch that she placed on
the veranda table; then she and Granny Moreland talked,
until the visitor said that she must go. The Girl went
with her to the little bridge crossing Singing Water on the
north. There the old lady took her hand.

"Honey," she said, "I'm goin' to tell you somethin'.
I am so happy I can purt near fly. Last night I was
comin' down the pike over there chasin' home a contrary
old gander of mine, when I looked over on your land and
I see David settin' on a log with his head between his
hands a lookin' like grim death, if I ever see it. My
heart plum stopped. Says I, 'she's a failure! She's a
bustin' the boy's heart! I'll go straight over and tell
her so.' I didn't dare bespeak him, but I was on nettles
all night. I jest laid a-studyin' and a-studyin', and I
says, 'Come mornin' I'll go straight and give her a curry-
combin' that'll do her good.' So I started a-feelin' pretty
grim, and here you came to meet me, and wiped it all out
of my heart in a flash. It did look like the boy was
grievin'; but I know now he was jest thinkin' up what to
put together to take the ache out of some poor old carcass
like mine. It never could have been about you. Like a
half blind old fool I thought the boy was sufferin', and
here he was only studyin'! Like as not he was thinkin'

what to do next to show you how he loves you. What an old silly I was! I'll sleep like a log to-night to pay up for it. Good-bye, honey! You better go back and lay down a spell. You do look mortal tired."

The Girl said good-bye and staggering a few steps sank on a log and sat staring at the sky.

"Oh he was suffering, and about me!" she gasped. A chill began to shake her and feverish blood to race through her veins. "He does and gives everything; I do and give nothing! Oh why didn't I stay at Uncle Henry's until it ended? It wouldn't have been so bad as this. What shall I do? Oh what shall I do? Oh mother, mother! if I'd only had the courage you did."

She arose, climbed the hill, passed the cabin and went to the oak. There she sank shivering to earth, laying her face among the mosses. The frightened Harvester found her at almost dusk when he came from the city with the Dutch dishes, and helped a man launch a gay little motor boat for her on the lake.

"Why Ruth! Ruth-girl!" he exclaimed, kneeling beside her.

She lifted a strained, distorted face.

"Don't touch me! Don't come near me!" she cried. "It is not true that I am better. I am not! I am worse! I never will be better. And before I go I've got to tell you of the debt I owe; then you will hate me, and then I will be glad! Glad, I tell you! Glad! When you despise me, then I can go, and know that some day you will love a girl worthy of you. Oh I want you to hate me! I am fit for nothing else."

She fell forward sobbing wildly while the Harvester tried in vain to quiet her. At last he said: "Well then tell me, Ruth. Remember I don't want to hear what you have to say. I will believe nothing against you, not even from your own lips, when you are feverish and excited as now, but if it will quiet you, tell me and have it over. See, I will sit here and listen, and when you have finished I'll pick you up and carry you to your room, and I am not sure but I will kiss you over and over. What is it you want to tell me, Ruth?"

She sat up panting and pushed back the heavy coils of hair.

"I've got to begin away at the beginning to make you see," she said. "The first thing I can remember is a small, such a small room, and mother sewing and sometimes a man I called father. He was like Henry Jameson made over tall and smooth, and more, oh, much more heartless! He was gone long at a time, and always we had most to eat, and went oftener to the parks, and were happiest with him away. When I was big enough to understand, mother told me that she had met him and cared for him when she was an inexperienced girl. She must have been very, very young, for she was only a girl as I first remember her, and oh! so lovely, but with the saddest face I ever saw. She said she had a good home and every luxury, and her parents adored her; but they knew life and men, so they would not allow him in their home. She left it with him, and he married her and tried to force them to accept him, but they would not. At first she bore it. Later she found him out, and appealed to them, but they were away or would not forgive. She was a proud thing, and would not beg more after she had said she was wrong, and would they take her back.

"As I grew up we were girls together. We embroidered, I drew, and sometimes we had little treats and good times. My father did not come often, so we got along the best we could. Always it was worse on her, because she was not so strong as I, and her heart was secretly breaking for her mother, while she was afraid he would come back any hour. She was tortured that she could not educate me more than to put me through the high school. She wore herself out doing that, but she was wild for me to be reared and trained right. So every day she crouched over delicate laces and embroidery. Before and after school I carried them and got more; vacation we worked together. But living grew higher, she became ill, and could not work, I hadn't her skill, while the drawings didn't bring much, and I'd no tools——"

"Ruth, for mercy sake let me take you in my arms. If you must tell this to find peace, let me hold you."

"Never again," said the Girl. "You won't want to in a minute. You must hear this, because I can't bear it any longer. It isn't fair to let you grieve and think me worth loving. Anyway, I couldn't earn what she did. I was afraid, for a great city is heartless to the poor. One morning she fainted and couldn't get up. I can see the awful look in her eyes now. She knew what was coming. I didn't. I tried to be grave and to work. Oh it's no use to go on with that! It was just worse and worse. She was lovely and delicate, she was my mother, and I adored her. Oh Man! You won't judge harshly?"

"No!" cried the Harvester, "I won't judge at all, Ruth. I see now. Get it over if you must tell me."

"One day she had been dreadfully ill for a long time and there was no food or work or money. The last scrap was pawned; she simply would not let me notify the charities or tell me who or where her people were. She said she had sinned against them and broken their hearts; probably they were dead, so I was desperate. I walked all day from house to house where I had delivered work, but it was no use; no one wanted anything I could do. I went back frantic, to find her gnawing her fingers and gibbering in delirium. She did not know me, so for the first time she implored me for food.

"Then I locked the door and went on the street and I asked a woman. She laughed and said she'd report me and I'd be locked up for begging. Then I saw a man I passed sometimes. I thought he lived close. I went straight to him, and told him my mother was very ill, and asked him to help her. He told me to go to the proper authorities. I told him I didn't know who they were or where; I had no money and she was a woman of refinement, and never would forgive me. I offered, if he would come to see her, get her some beef tea, and take care of her while she lived, that afterward——"

The Girl's frail form shook in a storm of sobs. At last she lifted her eyes to the Harvester's. "There must be a God, and somewhere at the last extremity He must come in. The man went with me. He was a young doctor who had an office a few blocks away, so he knew what to do. He hadn't much himself, but for several weeks he divided. She was more comfortable and not hungry when she went. When it was over I dressed her the best I could in my graduation dress, folded her hands, and kissed her good-bye, then told him I was ready to fulfill my offer; and oh Man!——He said he had forgotten!"

"God!" panted the Harvester.

"We couldn't bury her there. But I remembered my father had said he had a brother in the country; once he had been to see us when I was very small, so the doctor telegraphed him. He answered that his wife was sick, and if I were able to work I could come. He would bury her, and give me a home. The doctor borrowed the money and bought the coffin you found her in. He couldn't do better or he would, for he had learned to love her. He paid our fares and took us to the train. Before I started I went on my knees to him and worshipped him as the Almighty. I am sure I told him that I always would be indebted to him, and any time he required I would pay. The rest you know."

"Have you heard from him, Ruth?"

"No."

"It *was* yourself the other day on the bridge?"

"Yes."

"Did he love you?"

"Not that I know of. No! Nobody but you would love a girl who appeared as I did then."

The Harvester strove to keep a set face, but his lips drew back from his teeth.

"Ruth, do you love him?"

"Love!" cried the Girl. "A pale, expressionless word! Adore would come closer! I tell you she was delirious with hunger, and he fed her. She was suffering horrors, and he eased the pain. She was lifeless, and he kept her poor tired body from the dissecting table. I would have fulfilled my offer, and gone straight into the lake, but he spared me, Man! He spared me! Worship is a good word. I think I worship him. I tried to tell you. Before you got that license, I wanted you to know."

"I remember," said the Harvester. "But no man could have guessed that a girl with your face had agony like that in her heart, not even when he read deep trouble."

"I should have told you then! I should have forced you to hear! I was wild with fear of Uncle Henry, and I had nowhere to go. Now you know! Go away, and the end will come soon."

The Harvester arose and walked a few steps toward the lake, where he paused stricken, but fighting for control. For him the light had gone out. There was nothing beyond. The one passion of his life must live on, satisfied with a touch from lips that loved another man. Broken sobbing came to him. He did not even have time to suffer. Stumblingly he turned to the Girl, picked her up, and sat on the bench holding her closely.

"Stop it, Ruth!" he said unsteadily. "Stop this! Why should you suffer so? I simply will not have it. I will save you against yourself and the world. You shall have all happiness yet; I swear it, my girl! You are all right. He was a noble man, and he spared you

because he loved you, of course. I will make you well
and rosy again; then I will go and find him, and arrange
everything for you. I have spared you, also; if he doesn't
want you to remain here with me, Mrs. Carey would be
glad to have you until I can free you. Judges are human.
It will be a simple matter. Hush, Ruth, listen to me!
You shall be free! At once, if you say so! You shall
have him! I will go and bring him here, then I will go
away. Ruth, darling, stop crying and hear me. You
will grow better, now that you have told me. It is this
secret that has made you feverish and kept you ill. Ruth,
you shall have happiness yet, if I have got to circle the
globe and scale the walls of Heaven to find it for you."

She struggled from his arms and ran toward the lake.
When the Harvester caught her, she screamed wildly,
and struck him with her thin white hands. He lifted and
carried her to the laboratory, where he gave her a few
drops from a bottle and soon she became quiet. Then
he took her to the sunshine room, laid her on the bed,
locked the screens and her door, called Belshazzar to watch,
and ran to the stable. A few minutes later with distended
nostrils and indignant heart Betsy, under the flail of an un-
sparing lash, pounded down the hill toward Onabasha.

CHAPTER XVII

LOVE INVADES SCIENCE

THE Harvester placed the key in the door, then turned to Doctor Carey and the nurse.

"I drugged her into unconsciousness before I left, but she may have returned, at least partially. Miss Barnet, will you kindly see if she is ready for the doctor? You needn't be in the least afraid. She has no strength, even in delirium."

He opened the door, his head averted. The nurse hurried into the room. The Girl on the bed was beginning to toss, moan, and mutter. Skilful hands straightened her, arranged the covers, then the doctor was called. In the living-room the Harvester paced in misery too deep for consecutive thought. As consciousness returned, the Girl grew wilder, so the nurse could not follow the doctor's directions and care for her. Then Doctor Carey called the Harvester. He went in and sitting beside the bed took the feverish, wildly beating hands in his strong, cool ones, and began stroking them and talking.

"Easy, honey," he murmured softly. "Lie quietly while I tell you. You mustn't tire yourself. You are wasting strength you need to fight the fever. I'll hold your hands tight, I'll stroke your head for you. Lie quietly, dear, and Doctor Carey and his head nurse are

353

going to make you well in a little while. That's right! Let me do the moving; you lie and rest. Only rest and rest, until all the pain is gone, and the strong days come, and they are going to bring great joy, love, and peace, to my dear, dear girl. Even the moans take strength. Try just to lie quietly and rest. You can't hear Singing Water if you don't listen, Ruth."

"She doesn't realize that it is you or know what you say, David," said Doctor Carey gently.

"I understand," said the Harvester. "But if you will observe, you will see that she is quiet when I stroke her head and hands, and if you notice closely you will grant that she gets a word occasionally. If it is the right one, it helps. She knows my voice and touch, and she is less nervous and afraid with me. Watch a minute!"

The Harvester took both of the Girl's fluttering hands in one of his and with long, light strokes gently brushed them, then her head, and face, then her hands again, while in a low, monotonous, half sing-song voice he crooned: "Rest, Ruth, rest! It is night now. The moon is bridging Loon Lake, and the whip-poor-will is crying. Listen, dear, don't you hear him crying? Still, Girl, still! Just as quiet! Lie so quietly. The whip-poor-will is going to tell his mate he loves her, loves her so dearly. He is going to tell her, when you listen. That's a dear girl. Now he is beginning. He says: 'Come over the lake and listen to the song I'm singing to you, my mate, my mate, my dear, dear mate,' and the big night moths are flying; and the katydids are crying, positive and sure they are crying, a thing that's past denying. Hear them crying? And the

ducks are cheeping, soft little murmurs while they're sleeping, sleeping. Resting, softly resting! Gently, Girl,
gently! Down the hill comes Singing Water, laughing,
laughing! Don't you hear it laughing? Listen to the
big owl courting; it sees the coon out hunting, it hears the
mink softly slipping, slipping, where the dews of night are
dripping. And the little birds are sleeping, so still they are
sleeping. Girls should be a-sleeping, like the birds
a-sleeping, for to-morrow joy comes creeping, joy and
life and love come creeping, creeping to my Girl. Gently,
gently, that's a dear girl, gently! Tired hands rest easy,
tired head lies still! That's the way to rest——"

On and on the even voice kept up the story. All over
and around the lake, the length of Singing Water, the
marsh folk found voices to tell of their lives, where it
was a story of joy, rest, and love. Up the hill ranged the
Harvester, through the forest where the squirrels slept,
the owl hunted, the fire-flies flickered, the fairies squeezed
flower leaves to make colour to paint the autumn foliage,
or danced on toadstool platforms. As long as his voice
murmured and his touch continued, so long the Girl lay
quietly, and the medicines could act. But no other
touch or voice would serve. If the Harvester left the room
five minutes, to show the nurse how to light the fire, and
where to find things, he returned to tossing, restless delirium.

"It's magic David," said Doctor Carey. "Magic!"

"It is love," said the Harvester. "Even crazed with
fever, she recognizes its voice and touch. You've got
your work cut out, Doc. Roll your sleeves and collect

your wits. Set your heart on winning. There is one thing shall not happen. Get that straight in your mind, right now. And you too, Miss Barnet! There is nothing like fighting for a certainty. You may think the Girl is desperately ill, and she is, but make up your minds that you are here to fight for her life, and to save it. Save, do you understand? If she is to go, I don't need either of you. I can let her do that myself. You are here on a mission of life. Keep it before you! Life and health for this Girl is the prize you are going to win. Dig into it, and I'll pay the bills, and extra besides. If money is any incentive, I'll give you all I've got for life and health for the Girl. Are you doing all you know?"

"I certainly am, David."

"But when day comes you'll have to go back to the hospital and we may not know how to meet crises that will arise. What then? We should have a competent physician in the house until this fever breaks."

"I had thought of that, David. I will arrange to send one of the men from the hospital who will be able to watch symptoms and come for me when needed."

"Won't do!" said the Harvester calmly. "She has no strength for waiting. You are to come when you can, and remain as long as possible. The case is yours; your decisions go, but I will select your assistant. I know the man I want."

"Who is he, David?"

"I'll tell you when I learn whether I can get him. Now I want you to give the Girl the strongest sedative you dare, take off your coat, roll your sleeves, and see

how well you can imitate my voice, and how much you
have profited by listening to my song. In other words,
before day calls, I want you to take my place so success-
fully that you deceive her, and give me time to make a
trip to town. There are a few things that must be done,
and I think I can work faster in the night. Will you?"

Doctor Carey bent over the bed. Gently he slipped
a practised hand under the Harvester's, gradually he took
possession of the thin hands, and his touch fell on the
masses of dark hair. As the Harvester arose the doctor
took the seat.

"You go on!" he ordered. "I'll do better alone."

The Harvester stepped back. The doctor's touch was
easy so the Girl lay quietly for an instant, then she moved
restlessly.

"You must be still now," he said gently. "The moon
is up, the lake is all white, and the birds are flying all
around. Lie still or you'll make yourself worse. Stiller
than that! If you don't you can't hear things courting.
The ducks are quacking, the bullfrogs are croaking, and
everything. Lie still, still, I tell you!"

"Oh good Lord, Doc!" groaned the Harvester.

The Girl wrenched her hands free while her head rolled
on the pillow.

"Harvester! Harvester!" she cried.

The doctor started to arise

"Sit still!" commanded the Harvester. "Take her
hands and go to work, idiot! Give her more sedative,
tell her I'm coming. That's the word, if she realizes
enough to call for me."

The doctor possessed himself of the flying hands; gently held and stroked them.

"The Harvester is coming," he said. "Wait just a minute, he's on the way. He is coming. I think I hear him. He will be here soon, very soon now. That's a good girl! Lie still for David. He won't like it if you toss and moan. Just as still, lie still so I can listen. I can't tell whether he is coming until you are quiet."

Then he said to the Harvester: "You see, I've got it now. I can manage her, but for pity sake, hurry man! Take the car! Jim is asleep on the back seat——Yes, yes, Girl! I'm listening for him. I think I hear him! I think he's coming!"

The Harvester ran to the car, awakened the driver and told him he had a clear road to Onabasha, to speed up.

"Where to?" asked the driver.

"Dickson, of the First National."

In a few minutes the car stopped before the residence. The Harvester made an attack on the front door. Presently the man came.

"Excuse me for routing you out at this time of night," said the Harvester, "but it's a case of necessity. I have an automobile here. I want you to go to the bank with me, and get me an address from your draft records. I know the rules, but I want the name of my wife's Chicago physician. She is delirious, so I must telephone him."

The cashier stepped out and closed the door. "Nine chances out of ten it will be in the vault," he said.

"That leaves one that it won't," answered the Harvester. "Sometimes I've looked in when passing in the night. I've noticed that the books are not always put away. I could see some on the rack to-night. I think it is there."

It was there, so the Harvester ordered the driver to hurry him to the telephone exchange. He called the Chicago Information office.

"I want Dr. Frank Harmon, whose office address is 1509 Columbia Street. I don't know the 'phone number."

Then came a long wait. After twenty minutes he heard the blessed buzzing whisper: "Here's your party."

"Doctor Harmon?"

"Yes."

"You remember Ruth Jameson, the daughter of a recent patient of yours?"

"I do."

"Well my name is Langston. The Girl is in my home and care. She is very ill with fever, and she has much confidence in you. This is Onabasha, on the Grand Rapids and Indiana. You take the Pennsylvania at seven o'clock, telegraph ahead that you are coming so that they will make connection for you, change at twelve-twenty at Fort Wayne, and I will meet you here. You will find your ticket and a check waiting you at the Chicago depot. Arrange to remain a week at least. You will be paid all expenses and regular prices for your time. Will you come?"

"Yes."

"All right. Make no failure. Good-bye."

The Harvester left an order with the telephone company to run a wire to Medicine Woods the first thing in the morning, then drove to the depot to arrange for the ticket and check. In less than an hour he was holding the Girl's hands and crooning over her.

"Jerusalem!" said Doctor Carey, rising stiffly. "I'd rather undertake to cut off your head and put it back on than to tackle another job like that. She's quite delirious, but she has flashes, and at such times she knows whom she wants; the rest of the time it's a jumble and some of it is rather gruesome. She's seen dreadful illness, hunger, and there's a debt she's wild about. I told you something was back of this. You've got to find out and set her mind at ease."

"I know all about it," said the Harvester. "But the crash came before I could convince her that it was all right and I could fix everything for her easily. If she only could understand me!"

"Did you find your man?"

"Yes. He will be here this afternoon."

"Quick work!"

"This takes quick work."

"Do you know anything about him?"

"Yes. He is a young fellow, just starting out. He is a fine, straight, manly man. I don't know how much he knows, but it will be enough to recognize your ability and standing, and to do what you tell him. I have perfect confidence in him. I want you to come back at one, and take my place until I go to meet him."

"I can bring him out."

"I have to see him myself. There are a few words to be said before he sees the Girl."

"David, what are you up to?"

"Being as honourable as I can. No man gets any too decent, but there is no law against doing as you would be done by, or being as straight as you know how. When I've talked to him, I'll know where I stand, then I'll have something to say to you."

"David, I'm afraid——"

"Then what do you suppose I am?" said the Harvester. "It's no use, Doc. Be still and take what comes! The manner in which you meet a crisis proves you a whining cur or a man. I have got lots of respect for a dog, as a dog; but I've none for a man as a dog. If you've gathered from the Girl's delirium that I've made a mistake, I hope you have confidence enough in me to believe I'll right it, and take my punishment without whining. Go away, you make her worse. Easy, Girl, the world is all right and every one is sleeping now, so you should be at rest. With the day the doctor will come, the good doctor you know and like, Ruth. You haven't forgotten your doctor, Ruth? The kind doctor who cared for you. He will make you well, Ruth; well and oh, so happy! Harmon, Harmon, Doctor Harmon is coming to you, Girl; then you will be so happy!"

"Why you blame idiot!" cried Doctor Carey in a harsh temper. "Have you lost all the sense you ever had? Stop that gibber! She wants to hear about the birds and Singing Water. Go on with that woods line of talk; she likes that away the best. This stuff is making her restless. See!"

"You mean you are," said the Harvester wearily.

"Please leave us alone. I know the words that will bring comfort. You don't."

He began the story all over again, but now there ran through it a continual refrain. "Your doctor is coming, the good doctor you know. He will make you well and strong, and he will make life so lovely for you."

He was talking without pause or rest when Doctor Carey returned in the afternoon to take his place. He brought Mrs. Carey with him. She tried a woman's powers of soothing another woman, and almost drove the Girl to fighting frenzy. So the doctor made another attempt, while the Harvester raced down the hill to the city. He went to the car shed as the train pulled in, and stood at one side while the people hurried through the gate

"I think I'll know him," muttered the Harvester grimly. "I think the masculine element in me will pop up instinctively at the sight of this man who will take my Dream Girl from me. Oh good God! Are You sure You *are* good?"

In his brown khaki trousers and shirt, his head bare, his bronze face limned with agony he made no attempt to conceal, the Harvester with feet planted firmly, and tightly folded arms, his head tipped slightly to one side, braced himself as he sent his keen gray eyes searching the crowd. Far away he selected his man. He was young, strong, criminally handsome, clean and alert; there was discernible anxiety on his face, while it touched the Harvester's heart that he was coming just as swiftly as he could force his way. As he passed the gates the Harvester reached his side.

"Doctor Harmon, I think," he said.

"Yes."

"This way! If you have luggage, I will send for it later." The Harvester hurried to the car. "Take the shortest cut and cover space," he said to the driver.

Doctor Harmon removed his hat, ran his fingers through dark waving hair and yielded his body to the swing of the car. Neither man attempted to talk. Once the Harvester leaned forward and told the driver to stop on the bridge, and then sat silently. As the car slowed down, they alighted.

"Drive on and tell Doc we are here, and will be up soon," said the Harvester. Then he turned to the stranger. "Doctor Harmon, there's little time for words. This is my place, and here I grow herbs for medicinal houses."

"I have heard of you, and heard your stuff recommended," said the doctor.

"Good!" exclaimed the Harvester. "That saves time. I stopped here to make a required explanation to you. The day you sent Ruth Jameson to Onabasha, I saw her leave the train and recognized in her my ideal woman. I lost her in the crowd and it took some time to locate her. I found her about a month ago. She was miserable. If you saw what her father did to her and her mother in Chicago, you should have seen what his brother was doing here. The end came one day in my presence, when I paid her for ginseng she had found to settle her debt to you. He robbed her by force. I took the money from him, then he threatened her. She was ill then from heat,

overwork, wrong food——every misery you can imagine
heaped upon the dreadful conditions in which she came.
It had been my intention to court and marry her if I
possibly could. That day she had nowhere to go; she was
wild with fear; the fever that is scorching her now was
in her veins then. I did an insane thing. I begged her
to marry me at once and come here for rest and protection.
I swore that if she would, she should not be my wife, but
my honoured guest, until she learned to love me and released me from my vow. She tried to tell me something;
I had no idea it was anything that would make any real
difference, so I wouldn't listen. Last night, when the
fever was beginning to do its worst, she told me of your
entrance into her life and what it meant to her. Then I
saw that I had made a mistake. You were her choice, the
man she could love, not me, so I took the liberty of sending
for you. I want you to cure her, court her, marry her,
and make her happy. God knows she has had her share
of suffering. You recognize her as a girl of refinement?"

"I do."

"You grant that in health she would be lovelier than
most women, do you not?"

"She was more beautiful than most in sickness and
distress."

"Good!" cried the Harvester. "She has been here
two weeks. I give you my word, my promise to her has
been kept faithfully. As soon as I can leave her to attend to it, she shall have her freedom. That will be easy.
Will you marry her?"

The doctor hesitated.

"What is it?" asked the Harvester.

"Well to be frank," said Doctor Harmon, "it is money! I'm only getting a start. I borrowed funds for my schooling and what I used for her. She is in every way attractive enough to be desired by any man, but how am I to provide a home and support her and pay these debts? I'll try it, but I am afraid it will be taking her back to wrong conditions again."

"If you knew that she owned a comfortable cottage in the suburbs, where it is cool and clean, and had, say a hundred a month of her own for the coming three years, could you see your way?"

"That would make all the difference in the world. I thought seriously of writing her. I wanted to, but I concluded I'd better work as hard as I could for some practice first. I had no idea she would not be comfortably cared for at her uncle's."

"I see," said the Harvester. "If I had kept out, life would have come right for her."

"On the contrary," said the doctor, "it appears very probable that she would not be living."

"It is understood between us, then, that you will court and marry her so soon as she is strong enough?"

"It is understood," agreed the doctor.

"Will you honour me by taking my hand?" asked the Harvester. "I scarcely had hoped to find so much of a man. Now come to your room and get ready for the stiffest piece of work you ever attempted."

The Harvester led the way to the guest chamber overlooking the lake, and installed its first occupant. Then he hurried to the Girl. It took him ten strenuous minutes to make his touch and presence known and to work quiet. All over he began crooning his story of rest, joy, and love. He broke off with a few words to introduce Doctor Harmon to the Careys and the nurse; then calmly continued while the other men stood watching him.

"Seems rather cut out for it," commented Doctor Harmon.

"I never yet have seen him attempt anything that he didn't appear cut out for," answered Doctor Carey.

"Will she know me?" inquired the young man, approaching the bed.

When the Girl's eyes fell on him she lay staring at him. Suddenly with a wild cry she struggled to rise.

"You have come!" she cried. "Oh I knew you would come! I felt you would come! I cannot pay you now! Oh why didn't you come sooner?"

The young doctor leaned over, taking one of the white hands from the Harvester.

"Why you did pay, Ruth! How did you come to forget? Don't you remember the draft you sent me? I didn't come for money; I came to visit you, to nurse you, to do all I can to make you well. I am going to take care of you now so finely you'll be out on the lake and among the flowers soon. I've got some medicine that makes every one well. It's going to make you strong, and there's something else that's going to make you happy; and me, I'm going to be the proudest man alive."

He reached over and took possession of the other hand, stroking them softly, while the Girl lay tensely staring at him, gradually yielding to his touch and voice. The Harvester arose, and passing around the bed, he placed a chair for Doctor Harmon and motioning for Doctor Carey left the room. He went to the shore to his swimming pool, wearily dropped on the bench, and stared across the water.

"Well thank God it worked, anyway!" he muttered.

"What's that popinjay doing here?" thundered Doctor Carey. "Got some medicine that cures everybody. Going to make her well, is he? Make the cows, and the ducks, and the chickens, and the shitepokes well, and happy——no name for it! After this we are all going to be well and happy! You look it right now, David! What under Heaven have you done?"

"Left my wife with the man she loves, and to whom I release her, my dear friend," said the Harvester. "And it's so easy for me that you needn't give any thought to making it a little harder."

"David, forgive me!" cried Doctor Carey. "I don't understand this. Will you tell me what it means?"

"Means that I took advantage of the Girl's illness, utter loneliness, and fear, and forced her into marrying me for shelter and care, when she loved and wanted another man, who was preparing to come to her. He is her Chicago doctor, and fine in every fibre, as you can see. There is only one thing on earth for me to do; that is to get out of their way, and I'll do it as soon as she is well; but I vow I won't leave her poor, tired body until she is, not even for him. I thought sure I could teach her to love me! Oh, but this is bitter Doc!"

"You are a consummate fool to bring him here!" cried Doctor Carey. "If she is too sick to realize the situation now, she will be different when she is normal again. Any sane girl that wouldn't love you, David, ain't fit for anything!"

"Yes, I'm a whale of a lover!" said the Harvester grimly. "Nice mess I've made of it. But there is no real harm done. Thank God, Harmon was not the only white man."

"David, what do you mean?"

"Is it between us, Doc?"

"Yes."

"For all time?"

"It is."

The Harvester told him. He ended: "Give the fellow his dues, Doc. He had her at his mercy, utterly alone and unprotected, in a big city. There was not a living soul to hold him to account. He added to his burdens, borrowed more money, and sent her here. He thought she was coming to the country where she would be safe and well cared for until he could support her. I did the remainder. Now I must undo it, that's all! But you have got to go in there and practise with him. You've got to show him every courtesy of the profession. You must go a little over the rules, and teach him all you can. You will have to stifle your feelings, and be as much of a man as it is in you to be, at your level best."

"I'm no good at stifling my feelings!"

"Then you'll have to learn," said the Harvester. "If you'd lived through my years of repression in the woods

you'd do the fellow credit.   As I see it, his side of this is
nearly as fine as you make it.   I tell you she was utterly
stricken, alone, and beautiful.   She sought his assistance.
When the end came he thought only of her.   Won't you
give a young fellow in a place like Chicago some credit
for that?   Can't you get through you what it means?"

Doctor Carey stood frowning in deep thought, but the
lines of his face gradually changed.

"I suppose I've got to stomach him," he said.

The nurse came down the gravel path.   "Mr. Langston,
Doctor Harmon asked me to call you," she said.

"What does he want, Molly?" asked the doctor.

"Wants to turn over his job," chuckled the nurse.
"He held it about seven minutes in peace; then she began
to fret and call for the Harvester.   He just sweat blood
to pacify her, but he couldn't make it.   He tried to hold
her, to make love to her, but she struggled and cried,
'David,' until he had to give it up and send me."

"Molly," said Doctor Carey, "we've known the Harvester a long time, and he is our friend, isn't he?"

"Of course!" said the nurse.

"We know this is the first woman he ever loved, probably ever will, as he is made.   Now we don't like this
stranger butting in here; we resent it, Molly.   We are on
the side of our friend, so we want him to win.   I'll grant
that this fellow is fine, that he has done well, but what's
the use in tearing up arrangements already made?   And
so suitable!   Now Molly, you are my best nurse, and a
good reliable aid in times like this.   I gave you instructions an hour ago.   I'll add this to them.   *You are on the*

Harvester's side. Do you understand? In this, and the days to come, you'll have a thousand chances to put in a lick with a sick woman. Put them in as I tell you."

"Yes, Doctor Carey."

"And Molly! You are something besides my best nurse. You're a smashing pretty girl, and your occupation should make you especially attractive to a young doctor. I'm sure this fellow is all right, so while you are doing your best with your patient for the Harvester, why not have a try for yourself with the doctor? It couldn't do any harm, and it might straighten out matters. Anyway, you think it over."

The nurse began to laugh.

"He is up there doing his best with her," she said.

The doctor threw out his hands in a gesture of disdain, so the nurse laughed again; but her cheeks were pink, her eyes flashing as she returned to duty.

"Random shot, but it might hit something, you never can tell," commented the doctor.

The Harvester entered the Girl's room and stood still. She was fretting and raising her temperature rapidly. Before he reached the door his heart gave one great leap at the sound of her voice calling his name. He knew what to do, but he hesitated.

"She seems to have become accustomed to you, and at times does not remember me," said Doctor Harmon. "I think you had better take her again until she grows quiet."

The Harvester stepped to the bed and looked the doctor in the eye.

"I am afraid I left out one important feature in our little talk on the bridge," he said. "I neglected to tell you that in your fight for this woman's life and love you have a rival. I am he. She is my wife, and with the last fibre of my being I adore her. If you win, and she wants you to take her away, I will help you; but my heart goes with her forever. If by any chance it should occur that I have been mistaken or misinterpreted her delirium or that she has been deceived and finds she prefers me and Medicine Woods, to you and Chicago, when she has had opportunity to measure us man against man, you must understand that I claim her. So I say to you frankly, take her if you can, but don't imagine that I am passive. I'll help you if I know she wants you, but I fight you every inch of the way. Only it has got to be square and open. Do you understand?"

"You are certainly sufficiently clear."

"No man who is half a man sees the last chance of happiness go from his life without putting up the stiffest battle he knows," said the Harvester grimly. "Ruth-girl, you are raising the fever again. You must be quiet."

With infinite tenderness he possessed himself of her hands, then began stroking her hair, while in a low and soothing voice the story of the birds, flowers, lake, and woods continued. To keep it from growing monotonous the Harvester branched out, putting in everything he knew. In the days that followed he held a position none could take from him. While the doctors fought the fever, he worked for rest and quiet, soothing the tortured body as best he could, that the medicines might act

But the fever was stubborn; the remedies were slow; long before the dreaded coming day the doctors and nurse were quietly saying to each other that when the crisis came the heart would fail. There would not be enough vitality to sustain life. But they did not dare tell the Harvester. Day and night he sat beside the maple bed or stretched sleeping a few minutes on the couch while the Girl slept. With faith never faltering and courage unequalled, he warned them to have their remedies and appliances ready.

"I don't say it's going to be easy," he said. "I merely state that it must be done. And I'll also mention that, when the hour comes, the man who discovers that he could do something if he had digitalis, or a remedy he should have had ready and has forgotten, that man had better keep from my sight. Make your preparations now. Talk the case over. Fill your hypodermics. Clean your air pumps. Get your hot-water bottles ready. Have system. Label your stuff large and set it conveniently. You see what is coming, be prepared!"

One day, while the Girl lay in a half-drugged, feverish sleep, the Harvester went for a swim. He dressed a little sooner than was expected and in crossing the living-room he heard Doctor Harmon say to Doctor Carey on the veranda: "What are we going to do with him when the end comes?"

The Harvester stepped to the door. "That won't be the question," he said grimly. "It will be what will *he* do with us?"

Then, with an almost imperceptible movement, he

caught Doctor Harmon at the waist line, lifted and dangled him as a baby, then stood him on the floor. "Didn't hardly expect that much muscle, did you?" he inquired lightly. "And I'm not in what you could call condition, either. Instead of wasting any time on fool questions like that, you two go over your stuff and ask each other, have we got every last appliance known to physics and surgery? Have we got duplicates on hand in case we break delicate instruments like hypodermic syringes and that sort of thing? Engage yourselves with questions pertaining to life; that is your business. Instead of planning what you'll do in failure, bolster your souls against it. Granny Moreland beats you two put together in grip and courage."

The Harvester returned to his task, so the fight went on. At last the hour came when the temperature fell lower and lower. The feeble pulses flickered, then grew indiscernible; a gray pallor spread over the Girl, while a cold sweat stood on her temples.

"Now!" said the Harvester. "Exercise your calling! Fight like men or devils, but win you must."

They did work. They administered stimulants; applied heat to the chilled body; fans swept the room with vitalized air; hypodermics were used; every last resort known to science was given a full test, yet the weak heart throbbed slower and slower, while life ran out with each breath. The Harvester stood waiting with set jaws. He could detect no change for the better. At last he picked up a chilled hand, but could discover no pulse, while the gray nails and the dark tips told a story of arrested circulation.   He laid down the hand and faced the men.

"This is what you'd call the crisis, Doc?" he asked gently.

"Yes."

"Are you stemming it? Are you stemming it? Are you sure she is holding her own?"

Doctor Carey looked at him silently.

"Have you done all you can do?" asked the Harvester.

"Yes."

"You believe her going out?"

"Yes."

The Harvester turned to Doctor Harmon.   "Do you concur in that?"

"Yes."

Then to the nurse, "And you?"

"Yes."

"Then," said the Harvester, "all of you are useless. Get out of here.   I don't want your atmosphere.   If you can believe only in death, leave us!   She is my wife, and if this is the end she belongs to me.   I will do as I choose with her.   All of you go!"

The Harvester stepped to the bathroom door to call Granny Moreland.   "Granny," he said, "science has turned tail, leaving me in extremity.   Fill your hot-water bottles and come in here with your heart big with hope and help me save my Dream Girl.   She is breathing, Granny; we've got to make her keep it up, that's all—— merely keep her breathing."

He returned to the sunshine room, placed a small table beside the bed; on it a glass of water, spoon, and a hypodermic syringe. When Granny Moreland came he said: "Now you begin on her feet and rub with long, sweeping, upward strokes to drive the blood to her heart."

Around the Girl he piled hot-water bottles and breathlessly hung over her, rubbing her hands. He wiped the perspiration from her forehead; then dropped by her bed and for a second laid his face on her cold palm.

"If I am wrong, Heaven forgive me," he prayed. "And you, oh, my darling Dream Girl, forgive me, but I am forced to try——God helping me! Amen."

He arose, took a small bottle from his pocket, filled the spoon with water, then measured into it three drops of liquid as yellow as gold. Then he held the spoon to the blue lips, with his fingers worked apart the set teeth, and poured the medicine down her throat. Then they rubbed and muttered snatches of prayer for fifteen minutes when the Harvester administered another three drops. It might have been fancy, but it seemed to him her jaws were not so stiff. Faster flew his hands while he sent Granny Moreland to refill the hot bottles. When he gave the Girl the third dose he injected some of the liquid over her heart and of the glycerine the doctors had left, in the extremities. He released more air, then began rubbing again.

The second hour started in the same way, but ended with slowly relaxing muscles and faint tinges of colour in the white cheeks. The feet were not so cold; when the Harvester held the spoon he knew that the Girl made an effort to swallow, while he could see her eyelids tremble. Thereupon he pointed these signs to Granny, imploring her to rub and pray, and pray and rub, while he worked until the perspiration rolled down his gray face. At the end of the second hour he began decreasing the doses and shortening the time, while again he commenced in a low rumble his song of life and health, to encourage the Girl as consciousness returned.

Occasionally Doctor Carey opened the door slightly, peeping in to see if he were wanted, but he received no invitation to enter. The last time he left with the impression that the Harvester was raving, while he worked over a lifeless body. He had the Girl warmly covered as he bent over her face and hands. At her feet crouched Granny Moreland, rubbing, still rubbing, beneath the covers, while in a steady stream the Harvester was pouring out his song. If the doctor had listened an instant longer he would have recognized that the tone and the words had changed. Now it was, "Gently, breathe gently, Girl! Slowly, steadily, easily! Deeper, a little deeper, Ruth! Brave Girl, never another so wonderful! That's my Dream Girl coming from the shadows, coming to life's sunshine, coming to hope, coming to love! Deeper, just a little deeper! Smoothly and evenly! You are making it, Girl! You are making it! By all that is holy and glorious! Stick to it, Ruth, hold tight to me! I'll help you, dear! You are coming, coming back to life and love. Don't worry yourself trying too hard, if only you can send every breath as deeply as the last one, you can make it. You brave girl! You wonderful Dream Girl! Ah, Ruth, the name of this is victory!"

An hour before Doctor Carey had said to Doctor Harmon and the nurse, as he softly closed the door: "It is over. The Harvester is raving. We'll give him more time to see if he won't realize it himself. That will be easier for him than for us to try to tell him."

Now he opened the door, stared a second, and coming to the opposite side of the bed, he leaned over the Girl. Then he felt her feet. They were warm and slightly damp. A surprised look crept over his face. He gently reached for a hand that the Harvester yielded to him. It was warm, the blue tips becoming rosy, the wrist pulse discernible. Then he bent closer, touched her face, and saw the tremulous eyelids. He turned back the cover, and held his ear over her heart. When he straightened, "As God lives, she's got a chance, David!" he exulted in an awed whisper.

The Harvester lifted a graven face, down which the sweat of agony rolled, while his lips parted in a twitching smile. "Then this is where love beats the doctors, Carey!" he said.

"It is where love ventured something science dared not. Love didn't do all of this. In the name of the Almighty, what did you give her, David?"

"Life!" cried the Harvester. "Life! Come on, Ruth, come on! Out of the valley come to me! You are well now, Girl! It's all over! The last trace of fever is gone, the last of the dull ache. Can you swallow just two more drops of bottled sunshine, Ruth?"

The flickering lids slowly opened, then the big black eyes looked straight into the Harvester's. He met them steadily, smiling encouragement.

"Hang on to each breath, dear heart!" he urged. "The fever is gone. The pain is over! Long life and the love you crave are for you. You've only to keep breathing a few more hours and the battle is yours. Glorious Girl! Noble! You are doing finely! Ruth, do you know me?"

Her lips moved.

"Don't try to speak," said the Harvester. "Don't waste breath on a word. Save the good oxygen to strengthen your tired body. But if you do know me, maybe you could smile, Ruth!"

She could barely smile, that was all. Feeble, flickering, transient, but as it crossed the living face the Harvester lifted her hands, kissing them over and over, back, palm, and finger tips.

"Now just one more drop, honey; then a long rest. Will you try it again for me?"

She assented, so the Harvester took the bottle from his pocket, poured the drop, and held the spoon to willing lips. The big eyes were on him with a question. The Harvester understood.

"Yes, it's mine! It's got sixty years of wonderful life in it, every one of them full of love and happiness for my dear Dream Girl. Can you take it, Ruth?"

Her lips parted, the wine of life passed between. She smiled faintly, then her eyelids dropped shut, but presently they opened again.

"David!"

"My Dream Girl!"

"Harvester?"

"Yes!"

"Medicine Man?"

"Don't, Ruth!   Save every breath to help your heart."

"Life?"

"Life it is, Girl!" exulted the Harvester.   "Long life! Love! Home! The man you love! Every happiness that ever came to a girl! Nothing shall be denied you! Nothing shall be lacking! It's all in your hands now, Ruth. We've all done everything we can; you must do the remainder. It's your work to send every breath as deeply as you can. Doc, release another tank of air. Are her feet warm, Granny? Let the nurse take your place now. And, honey, go to sleep! I'll keep watch for you. I'll measure each breath you draw. If they shorten or weaken, I'll wake you for more medicine. You can trust me! Always you can trust me, Ruth."

The Girl smiled, then fell into a light, even slumber. Granny Moreland stumbled to the couch, and rolled on it sobbing with nervous exhaustion. Doctor Carey called the nurse to take her place. Then he came to the Harvester's side and whispered: "Let me, David!"

The Harvester looked up with his queer grin, but he made no motion to arise.

"Won't you trust me, David? I'll watch as if it were my own wife."

"I wouldn't trust any man on earth, for the coming three hours," replied the Harvester. "If she keeps this up that long, she is safe. Go and rest until I call you."

He again bent over the Girl, one hand on her left wrist, the other over her heart, his eyes on her lips, watching the depth and strength of her every breath. Regularly he administered the medicine he was giving her. Sometimes she took it half asleep; again she gave him a smile that to the Harvester was the supreme thing of earth or Heaven. Toward the end of the long vigil, in exhaustion he slipped to the floor, laid his head on the side of the bed, so for a second his hand relaxed and he fell asleep. The Girl awakened as his touch loosened, on looking down she saw his huddled body. A second later the Harvester awoke with a guilty start to find her fingers twisted in the shock of hair on the top of his head.

"Poor stranded Girl," he muttered. "She's clinging to me for life. You can stake all you are worth she's going to get it!"

Then he gently relaxed her grip, gave her the last dose he felt necessary, yielded his place to Doctor Carey and staggered up the hill. As the sun peeped over Medicine Woods he stretched himself between the two mounds under the oak, while for a few minutes his body was rent with the awful, torn sobbing of a strong man. Belshazzar whining pitifully nosed the twisting figure. A chattering little marsh wren tilted on a bush and scolded. A blue jay perched above, trying to decide whether there were cause for an alarm signal. A snake coming from the water to hunt birds ran close to him, then changing its course, went weaving away among the mosses. Gradually the pent forces spent themselves, so for hours the Harvester lay in the deep sleep of exhaustion, while stretched beside him, Belshazzar guarded with anxious dog eyes.

CHAPTER XVIII

The Better Man

IN THE middle of the afternoon the Harvester arose, went into the lake, ate a hearty dinner, then took up his watch again. For two days and nights he kept his place, until he had the Girl out of danger, and where careful nursing was all that was required to insure life and health. As he sat beside her the last day, his physical endurance strained to the breaking point, she laid her hand over his, looking long and steadily into his eyes.

"There are so many things I want to know," she said.

The Harvester's firm fingers closed over hers. "Ruth, have you ever been sorry that you trusted me?"

"Never!" said the Girl instantly.

"Then suppose you keep it up," said he. "Whatever it is that you want to know, don't use an iota of strength to talk or to think about it now. Just say to yourself, he loves me well enough to do what is right, and I know that he will. All you have to do is to be patient until you grow stronger than you ever have been in your life; then you shall have exactly what you want, Ruth. Sleep like a baby for a week or two. Then, slowly and gradually, we will build up such a constitution for you that you shall ride, drive, row, swim, dance, play, and have all that your girlhood has missed in fun and frolic, and all that your womanhood craves in love and companionship. Happiness has come at last, Ruth. Take it from me. Everything you crave is yours. The love you want, the home, and the life. As soon as you are strong enough, you shall know all about it. Your business is to drink stimulants and sleep now, dear."

"So tired of this bed!"

"It won't be long until you can lie on the couch or the veranda swing again."

"Glory!" said the Girl. "David, I must have been sick for a long time. I can't remember everything."

"Don't try, I tell you. Life is coming out right for you; that's all you need know now."

"And for you, David?"

"Whenever things are right for you, they are for me."

"Don't you ever think of yourself?"

"Not when I am with you."

"Ah! Then I shall have to grow strong very soon and think of you."

The Harvester's smile was pathetic.

"Never mind me!" he said. "Only get well."

"David, was there a little horse?"

"There certainly was and is," said the Harvester. "You had not named him yet, but in a few days I can lead him to the window."

"Was there something said about a boat?"

"Two of them."

"Two?"

"Yes. A row boat for you, and a launch that will

take you all over the lake with only the exertion of steering on your part."

"David, I want my pendant and ring. I am so tired of lying here, I want to play with them."

"Where do you keep them, Ruth?"

"In the willow teapot. I thought no one would look there."

The Harvester laughed as he brought the little boxes. He had to open them, but the Girl put on the ring and asked him if he would not help her with the pendant. He slipped the thread around her neck, clasping it. With a sigh of satisfaction she took the ornament in one hand and closed her eyes.

"You won't allow them to take it from me?"

"Indeed no! There is no reason why you should not have that thread around your neck if you want it."

"I am going to sleep now. I want two things. May I have them?"

"You may," said the Harvester promptly, "provided they are not to eat."

"No," said the Girl. "I've suffered and made others trouble. I won't bother you by asking for anything more than is brought me. This is different. You are completely worn out. Your face frightens me, David, while white hairs that were not there a few days ago have come along your temples. I can see them."

"You gave me a mighty serious scare, Ruth."

"I know," said the Girl. "Forgive me. I didn't mean to. I want you to leave me to Doctor Harmon or the nurse while you sleep a week. Then I will be ready for the swing, and to hear more about the trees and birds."

"I can keep it up if you really need me, but if you don't I am sleepy. So, if you feel safe, I think I will go."

"Oh I am safe enough," said the Girl. "It isn't that. I'm so lonely. I've made up my mind not to grieve for mother, but I miss her so now. I feel so friendless."

"But honey," said the Harvester, "you mustn't do that! Don't you see how all of us love you? Here is Granny shutting up her house and living here, just to be with you. The nurse will do anything you say. Here is the man you know best, and think so much of, staying in the cabin; happy to give you all his time. The Careys come every day, and will do their best to comfort you, while always I am here for you to fall back on."

"Yes, I'm falling right now," said the Girl. "I almost wish I had the fever again. No one has touched me for days. I feel as if every one were afraid of me."

The Harvester was puzzled. "Well, Ruth, I'm doing the best I know," he said. "What is it you want?"

"Nothing!" answered the Girl with slightly dejected inflection. "Say good-bye to me, then go sleep your week. I'll be very good. You shall take me for a drive up the hill when you awaken. Won't that be fine?"

"Say good-bye to me!" She felt a "little lonely!" They all acted as if they were "afraid" of her. The Harvester indulged in a flashing mental review, arriving at a decision. He knelt beside the bed, took both slender, cool hands, covering them with kisses. Then he slid a hand under the pillow and raised the tired head.

"If I am to say good-bye, I must do it in my own way,

Ruth," he said. Thereupon he began at the tumbled mass of hair and kissed from her forehead to her lips, kisses warm and tender. "Now you go to sleep, and grow strong enough by the time I come back to tell me whom you love best," he said, then went from the room without waiting for a reply.

With short intervals for food or dips in the lake the Harvester very nearly slept the week. When he finally felt himself again, he bathed, shaved, dressed freshly, and went to see the Girl. He had to touch her to be sure she was real. She was extremely weak and tremulous, but her face and hands were fuller, her colour was good, she was ravenously hungry. Doctor Harmon said she was a little tyrant; the nurse that she was plain cross. The first thing the Harvester noticed was that the dull blue look in the depth of the dark eyes was gone.

"Well I never would have believed it!" he cried. "Doctor Harmon, you are a great physician! You have made her all over new; in a few more days she will be on the veranda. This is great!"

"Do I appear so much better to you, Harvester?" asked the Girl.

"Has no one thought to show you?" cried the Harvester. "Here, let me!"

He stepped to her dressing table, picked up a mirror, holding it before her so that she could see herself.

"Seems to me I am dreadfully white and thin yet!"

"If you had seen what I saw ten days ago, my Girl, you would think you appear like a pink, rosy angel now, or a wonderful dream."

"Truly, do I in the least resemble a dream, David?"

"You are a dream. The loveliest one a man ever had. With three months of right care and exercise you'll be the beautiful woman nature intended. I'm so proud of you. You are being so brave! Only lie there in patience a few more days, then out you come again to life; life that will thrill your being with joy."

"All right," said the Girl, "I will. David are you attending to your herbs?"

"Not for a few weeks."

"You are very much behind?"

"No. Nothing important. I don't make enough to count on what is ready now. I can soon gather jimson leaves and seed to fill orders, the hemlock is about right to take the fruit, the mustard is yet in pod, while the senna and wormseed can be attended later. I can catch up in two days."

"What about——about the big bed on the hill?"

The Harvester experienced an inward thrill of delight. She was so impressed with the value of the ginseng she would not mention it, even before the man she loved—— no more than that——"adored"——"worshipped!" He smiled at her in understanding.

"I'll have to take a peep at that and report," he said.

"Are you rested now?"

"Indeed yes!"

"You are dreadfully thin."

"I always am. I'll pick up when I go back to work."

"David, I want you to go to work now."

"Can you spare me?"

"Haven't we done well these past few days?"

"I can't tell you how well."

"Then please go gather everything you need to fill orders except the big bed; by that time maybe you could take another week off, then I could go to the hill top and on the lake. I'm so anxious to put my feet on the earth. They feel so dead."

"Are your feet rubbed to help the circulation?"

"They are rubbed shiny and almost skinned, David. No one ever had better care, of that I am sure. Go gather what you should have."

"All right," said the Harvester. As he started to leave the room he took one last look at the Girl to see if he could detect anything he could suggest for her comfort. He read a message in her eyes. Instantly there was an answering flash in his. "I'll be back in a minute," he said. "I just noticed *discorea villosa* has the finest rattle boxes formed. I've been waiting to show you. And the hop tree has its castanets all green and gold. In a few more weeks it will begin to play for you. I'll bring you some."

Soon he returned with the queer seed formations. As he bent above her, with his back to Doctor Harmon, he whispered: "What is it?"

Her lips barely formed the one word: "Hurry!"

The Harvester straightened. "All comfortable, Ruth?"

"Yes."

"You understand, of course, that there is not the slightest necessity for my going to work if you really want me for anything, even if it's nothing more than to have me within calling distance, in case you *should* want something. The whole lot I can gather now won't amount to twenty dollars. It's merely a matter of pride with me to have what is called for. I'd much rather remain, if you can use me in any way at all."

"Twenty dollars is considerable, when expenses are as heavy as now, while it's worth more than any money to you not to fail when orders come. I have learned that, so David, I don't want you to either. You must fill all demands as usual. I wouldn't forgive myself this winter if you should be forced to send orders only partly filled because I fell ill and hindered you. Please go and gather all you possibly will need of everything you take at this season, only—remember!"

"There is no danger of my forgetting. If you are going to send me away to work, you will allow me to kiss your hand before I go, fair lady?" He did it fervently.

"One word with you, Harmon," he said as he started.

Doctor Harmon followed him to the gold garden.

"I merely want to mention that this is your inning," said the Harvester. "Find out if you are essential to the Girl's happiness as soon as you can. The day she tells me so, I will file her petition and take a trip to the city to study some little chemical quirks that bother me. That's all." The Harvester went to the dry-house for bags and clipping shears, while the doctor returned to the sunshine room.

"Ruth," he said, "do you know that the Harvester is the squarest man I ever met?"

"Is he?" asked the Girl.

"He is! He certainly is!"

"You must remember that I have little acquaintance with men," said she. "You are the first one I ever knew; the only one except him."

"Well I *try* to be square," said Doctor Harmon, "but that is where Langston has me beaten a mile. I have to try. He doesn't. He was born that way."

"His environment is so different," she said. "Perhaps if he were in a big city, he would have to try also."

"Won't do!" said the doctor. "He chose his location. So did I. He is a stronger physical man than I ever was or ever will be. The struggle that bound him to the woods and to research, that made him the master of forces that give back life, when a man like Carey says it is the end, proves him a master. The tumult in his soul must have been like a cyclone in his forest, when he turned his back on the world and stuck to the woods. Carey told me about it. Some day you must hear. It's a story a woman ought to know in order to arrive at proper values. You never will understand the man until you know that he is clean where most of us are blackened with ugly sins we have no right on God's footstool to commit with not so much reason as he. Every man should be as he is, but very few are. Carey says Langston's mother was a wonderful element in the formation of his character; but all mothers are anxious, yet none of them can build with no foundation and no soul timber. She had material for a man, or she couldn't have made one."

"I see what you mean."

"So far as any inexperienced girl ever sees," said the

doctor. "Some day if you live to fifty you will know, but you can't comprehend it now."

"If you think I lived all my life in Chicago's poverty spots and don't know unbridled human nature!"

"I found you and your mother unusually innocent women. You may understand some things. I hope you do. It will help you to decide who is the real man among the men who come into your life. There are some men, Ruth, who are fit to mate with a woman, to perpetuate themselves and their mental and moral forces in children who will be like them; there are others who are not. It is these 'others' who are responsible for the sin of the world, the sickness and suffering. Any time you are sure you have a chance at a moral man, square and honest, in control of his brain and body, if you are a wise woman, Ruth, stick to him as the limpet to the rock."

"You mean stick to the Harvester?"

"If you are a wise woman!"

"When was a woman ever wise?"

"A few have been. They are the only care-free, really happy ones of the world, the only wives without a big, poison, blue-bottle fly in their ointment."

"I detest flies!" said the Girl.

"So do I," said the doctor. "For this reason I say to you choose the ointment that never had one in it. Take the man who is 'master of his fate, captain of his soul.' Stick to the Harvester! He is infinitely the better man!"

"Well have you seen anything to indicate that I wasn't sticking?" asked the Girl.

"No. And for your sake I hope I never shall."

She laughed softly.

"You do love him, Ruth?"

"As I did my mother, yes. There is not a trace in my heart of the thing he calls love."

"You have been stunted, warped, and the fountains of life never have opened. It will come with right conditions of living."

"Do you think so?"

"I know so. At least there is no one else you love, Ruth?"

"No one except you."

"And do you feel about me just as you do him?"

"No! It is different. What I owe him is for myself. What I owe you is for my mother. You saw! You know! You understand what you did for her, and what it meant to me. The Harvester must be the finest man on earth, but when I try to think of either God or Heaven, your face intervenes."

"That's all right, Ruth, I'm so glad you told me," said Doctor Harmon. "I can make it all perfectly clear to you. You just go on and worship me all you please. It's bound to make a cleaner, better man of me. What you feel for me will hold me to a higher moral level all my life than I ever have known before; but never forget that you are not going to live in Heaven. You will be here at least sixty years yet, so when you come to think of selecting a partner for the relations of the world, you stick to the finest man you know; see?"

"I do!" said the Girl. "I saw you kiss Molly a week

ago. She is lovely, so I hope you will be perfectly happy. It won't interfere with my worshipping you; not the least in the world. Go ahead and be joyful!"

The doctor sprang to his feet in crimson confusion. The Girl lay laughing at him.

"Don't!" she cried. "It's all right! It takes a weight off my soul as heavy as a mountain. I do adore you, as I said. But every hour since I left Chicago a big, black cloud has hung over me. I didn't feel free. I didn't feel absolved. I felt that my obligations to you were so heavy that when I had settled the last of the money debt I was in honour bound——"

"Don't, Ruth! Forget those dreadful times, as I told you then! Think only of a happy future!"

"Let me finish," said the Girl. "Let me get this out of my system with the other poison. From the day I came here, I've whispered in my heart: 'I am not free!' But if you love another woman! If you are going to take her to your heart and to your lips, why that is my release. Oh Man, speak the words! Tell me I am free indeed!"

"Ruth, be quiet, for mercy sake! You'll raise a temperature, and the Harvester will pitch me into the lake. You are free, child, of course! You always have been. I understood the awful pressure that was on you with the very first glimpse I had of your mother. Who was she, Ruth?"

"She never would tell me."

"She thought you would appeal to her people?"

"She knew I would! I couldn't have helped it."

"Would you like to know?"

"I never want to. It is too late. I infinitely prefer to remain in ignorance. Talk of something else."

"Let me read a wonderful book I found on the Harvester's shelves."

"Anything there will contain wonders, because he only buys what appeals to him, and it takes a great book to do that. I am going to learn. He will teach me, and when I come within comprehending distance of him, then we are going on together."

"What an attractive place this is!"

"Isn't it? I have seen only enough to understand the plan. I scarcely can wait to set my feet on earth and go into detail. Granny Moreland says that when spring comes over the hill, and brings up the flowers in the big woods, she'd rather walk through them than to read Revelation. She says it gives her an idea of Heaven she can come closer realizing and it seems more stable. You know she worries about the foundations. She can't understand what supports Heaven. But up there in Medicine Woods the old dear gets so near her God that some day she is going to realize that her idea of Heaven there is quite as near right as marble streets and gold pillars and vastly more probable. The day I reach that hill top again, Heaven begins for me. Do you know the wonderful thing the Harvester did up there?"

"Under the oak?"

"Yes."

"Carey told me. It was marvellous."

"Not such a marvel as another the doctor couldn't have

known. The Harvester made passing out so natural, so easy, so a part of elemental forces, that I almost have forgotten her tortured body. When I think of her now, it is to wonder if next summer I can distinguish her whisper among the leaves. Before you go, I'll take you up there and tell you what he says, and show you what he means, so you will feel it also."

"What if I shouldn't go?"

"What do you mean?"

"Doctor Carey has offered me a splendid position in his hospital. There would be work all day, instead of waiting all day in the hope of working an hour. There would be a living in it for two from the word go. There would be better air, longer life, more to be got out of it, and if I can make good, Carey's work to take up as he grows old."

"Take it! Take it quickly!" cried the Girl. "Don't wait a minute! You might wear out your heart in Chicago for twenty years or forever, and not have an opportunity to do one-half so much good. Take it at once!"

"I am waiting to learn what you and Langston think."

"He will say take it."

"Then I shall be too happy for words. Ruth, you have not only paid the debt, but you have brought me the greatest joy a man ever had. And there is no need to wait the years I thought I must. He can tell in a year if I can do the work; I know I can now; so it's all settled, if Langston agrees."

"He will," said the Girl. "Let me tell him!"

"I wish you would," said the doctor. "I don't know just how to go at it."

Then for two days the Harvester and Belshazzar gathered herbs and spread them on the drying trays. On the afternoon of the third, close three, the doctor came to the door. "Langston," he said, "we have a call for you. We can't keep Ruth quiet much longer. She is tired. We want to change her bed completely. She won't allow either of us to lift her. She says we hurt her. Will you come and try it?"

"You'll have to give me time to dip and get into clean clothing," he said. "I've been keeping away, because I was working on time, so ⊥ smell to strangulation of stramonium and senna."

"Can't give you ten seconds," said the doctor. "Her temper is getting brittle. She is cross as the proverbial fever patient. If you don't come at once she will imagine you don't want to, and refuse to be moved at all."

"Coming!" cried the Harvester, as he plunged his hands in the wash bowl and soused his face. A second later he appeared on the porch. "Ruth," he said, "I am steeped in the odours of the dry-house. Can't you wait until I bathe and dress?"

"No, I can't," said a fretful voice. "I can't endure this bed another minute."

"Then let Doctor Harmon lift you. He is so fresh and clean." The Harvester glanced enviously at the shaven face and white trousers and shirt of the doctor.

"I just hate fresh, clean men. I want to smell herbs, and put my feet in the dirt and my hands in the water."

The Harvester came at a rush. He brought a big easy chair from the living-room, straightened the cover, and bent above the Girl. He picked her up lightly, gently, and easing her to his body settled in the chair. She laid her face on his shoulder, and heaved a deep sigh of content.

"Be careful with my back, Man," she said. "I think my spine is almost worn through."

"Poor girl," said the Harvester. "That bed should be softer."

"It should not!" contradicted the Girl. "It should be much harder. I'm tired of soft beds. I want to lie on the earth, with my head on a root; and I wish it would rain dirt on me. I am bathed threadbare. I want to be all streaky."

"I understand," said the Harvester. "Harmon, bring me a pad and pencil a minute, I must write an order for some things I want. Will you call up town and have them sent out immediately?"

On the pad he wrote: "Telephone Carey to get the highest grade curled-hair mattress, a new pad, and pillow, and bring them flying in the car. Call Granny and the girl and empty the room. Clean, air, and fumigate it thoroughly. Arrange the furniture differently, and help me into the living-room with Ruth." He handed the pad to the doctor.

"Please attend to that," he said, and to the Girl: "Now we go on a journey. Doc, you and Molly take the corners of the rug we are on and slide us into the other room until you get this aired and freshened."

In the living-room the Girl took one long look at the surroundings, then suddenly relaxed. She cuddled against the Harvester and lifting a tremulous white hand, drew it across his unshaven cheek.

"Feels so good," she said. "I'm sick and tired of immaculate men."

The Harvester laughed, tucking her feet in the cover. The Girl lay with her cheek against the rough khaki, palpitant with the excitement of being moved.

"Isn't it great?" she panted.

He caught the hand that had touched his cheek in a tender grip, and laughed a deep rumble of exultation.

"There's no name for it, honey," he said. "But don't try to talk until you have a long rest. Changing positions after you have lain so long may be making unusual work for your heart. Am I hurting your back?"

"No," said the Girl. "This is the first time I have been comfortable in ages. Am I tiring you?"

"Yes," laughed the Harvester. "You are almost as heavy as a large sack of leaves, but not quite equal to a bridge pillar or a log. Be sure to think of that, and worry considerably. You are in danger of straining my muscles to the last degree, my heart included."

"Where is your heart?" whispered the Girl.

"Right under your cheek," answered the Harvester. "But for Heaven's sake, don't intimate that you are taking any interest in it, or it will go to pounding until your head will bounce. It's one member of my body that I can't control where you are concerned."

"I thought you didn't like me any more."

"Careful!" warned the Harvester. "You are yet too close Heaven to fib like that, Ruth. What have I done to indicate that I don't love you more than ever?"

"Stayed away nearly every minute for three awful days, and wouldn't come without being dragged; and now you're wishing they would hurry and fix that bed, so you can put me down and go back to your rank old herbs again."

"Well of all the black prevarications! I went when you sent me, and came when you called. I'd willingly give up my hope of what Granny calls 'salvation' to hold you as I am for an hour, and you know it."

"It's going to be much longer than that," said the Girl, nestling to him. "I asked for you because you never hurt me, and they always do. I knew you were so strong that my weight now wouldn't be a load for one of your hands, and I am not going back to that bed until I am so tired that I will be glad to lie down."

For a long time she was so silent the Harvester thought her going to sleep; and having learned that for him joy was probably transient, he deliberately got all he could. He closely held the hand she had not withdrawn, often lifting it to his lips. Sometimes he stroked the heavy braid, gently ran his hands across the tired shoulders, or eased her into a different position.

"There is something I want to ask you," she said. "I promised Doctor Harmon I would."

Instantly the heart of the Harvester gave a leap that jarred the head resting on it.

"You don't like him?" questioned the Girl.

"I do!" declared the Harvester. "I like him immensely. There is not a fine, manly good-looking feature about him that I have missed. I don't fail to do him justice on every point."

"I'm so glad! Then you will want him to remain."

"Here?" asked the Harvester with a light, hot breath.

"In Onabasha! Doctor Carey has offered him the place of chief assistant at the hospital. There is a good salary and the chance of taking up the doctor's work as he grows older. It means plenty to do at once, healthful atmosphere, congenial society——everything to a young man. He only had a call once in a while in Chicago, often among people who received more than they paid, like me, and he was very lonely. I think it would be great for him."

"And for you, Ruth?"

"It doesn't make the least difference to me; but for his sake, because I think so much of him, I would like to see him have the place."

"You still think so much of him, Ruth?"

"More, if possible," said the Girl. "Added to all I owed him before, he has come here and worked for days to save me. Nothing alters the fact that he did all he could, most graciously and gladly. It wasn't his fault that it took a bigger man."

"What do you mean, Ruth?"

"Oh they have worn themselves out!" cried the Girl impatiently. "First, Granny Moreland told me every least little detail of how I went out, and you resurrected me. I knew what she said was true, because she worked with you. Then Doctor Carey told me, then Mrs. Carey,

and Doctor Harmon, and Molly; even Granny's little assistant has left the kitchen to tell me that I owe my life
to you. All of them might as well have saved breath. I
knew all the time that if ever I came out of this, or had a
chance to be like other women, it would be your work,
and I'm glad it is. I'd hate to be under obligations to
some people I know, but I feel honoured to be indebted to
you."

"I'm mighty sorry they worried you. I had no idea——"

"They didn't 'worry' me! I am merely telling you
that I knew it all the time; that's all!"

"Forget that!" said the Harvester. "Come back to
our subject. What was it you wanted, dear?"

"To know if you have any objections to Doctor Harmon remaining in Onabasha?"

"Certainly not! It will be a fine thing for him."

"Will it make any difference to you in any way?"

"Ruth, that's probing too deep," said the Harvester.

"I don't see why!"

"I'm glad of it!"

"Why?"

"I'd least rather show my littleness to you than to any
one else on earth."

"Then you have some feeling about it?"

"Perhaps a trifle. I'll get over it. Give me time to
adjust myself. Doctor Harmon shall have the place, of
course. Don't worry about that!"

"He will be so happy!"

"And you, Ruth?"

"I'll be happy too!"

"Then it's all right," said the Harvester.

He laid down her hand, drew the cover over it, and slightly shifted her position to rest her. The door opened, and Doctor Harmon announced that the room was ready. It was shining and fresh. The bed was now turned with its head to the north, so that from it one could see the big trees in Medicine Woods, the sweep of the hillside, the sparkle of mallow-bordered Singing Water, the driveway and the gold flower garden. Everything was so changed that the room had quite a different appearance. The instant he laid her on it the Girl said: "This bed is not mine."

"Yes it is," said the Harvester. "You see, we were a little excited sometimes, for we spilled a few quarts of perfectly good medicine on your mattress. It was hopelessly smelly and ruined; so I am going to cremate it; this is your splinter new one and a fresh pad and pillow. Now you try them and see if they are not much harder and more comfortable."

"This is just perfect!" she sighed, as she sank into the bed.

The Harvester bent over her to straighten the cover, when suddenly she reached both arms around his neck, and gripped him with all her strength.

"Thank you!" she said.

"May I hold you to-morrow?" whispered the Harvester, emboldened by this.

"Please do," said the Girl.

The Harvester, with dog to heel, went to the oak to think. "Belshazzar, kommen Sie!" said the man, dropping on the seat and holding out his hand. The dog laid his muzzle in the firm grip.

"Bel," said the Harvester, "I am all at sea. One day I think maybe I have a chance, the next——none at all. I had an hour of solid comfort to-day, now I'm in the sweat box again. It's a little selfish streak in me, Bel, that hates to see Harmon go into the hospital and take my place with the Careys. They are my best and only friends. He is young, social, handsome, and will be ever present. In three months he will become so popular that I might as well be off the earth. I wish I didn't think it, but I'm so small that I do. Then there is my Dream Girl, Bel. The girl you found for me, old fellow. There never was another like her. She has my heart for all time. And he has hers. That hospital plan is the best thing in the world for her. It will keep her where Carey can have an eye on her, where the air is better, where she can have company without the city crush, where she is close the country, with a good living assured. Bel, it's the nicest arrangement you ever saw for every one we know, except us."

The Harvester laughed shortly. "Bel," he said, "tell me! If a man lived a hundred years, could he have the heartache all the way? Seems like I've had it almost that long now. In fact, I've had it such ages I'd be lonesome without it. This is some more of my very own medicine, so I shouldn't make a wry face over taking it. I knew what would happen when I sent for him, yet I didn't hesitate. I must not now.

"Only I got to stop one thing, Bel. I told him I would

play square, and I have. But here it ends. After this, I must step back and be big brother. Lots of fun in this brother business, Bel. But maybe I am cut out for it. Anyway it's written! But if it is, how did she come to allow me such privileges as I took to-day? That wasn't professional by any means. It was the stiffest love-making I knew how to do, Bel, and she didn't object by the quiver of an eyelash. God knows I was watching closely enough for any sign that I was distasteful. And I might have been well enough. Rough, herb-stained old clothes, unshaven, everything to offend a dainty girl. She said I might hold her again to-morrow. And, Bel, what the nation did she hug me like that for, if she's going to marry him? Boy, I see my way clear to an hour more. While I'm at it, just to surprise myself, I believe I'll take it like other men. I think I'll go on a little bender, and make what probably will be the last day a plumb good one. Something worth remembering is better than nothing at all, Bel! He hasn't told me that he has won. She didn't *say* she was going to marry him, and she did say he hurt her, so she wanted me. Bel, how about the grimness of it, if she should marry him and then discover that he hurts her, and she still wants me. Lord God Almighty, if you have any mercy at all, never put me up against that," prayed the Harvester, "for my heart is water where she is concerned."

The Harvester arose, and going to the lake, he cut an armload of big, pink mallows, covered each mound with fresh flowers, whistled to the dog, and went to his work. Many things had accumulated, so he cleaned the barn, carried herbs from the dry-house to the storeroom, and put everything into shape. Close noon the next day he went to Onabasha, and was gone three hours. He came back barbered in the latest style, and carrying a big bundle. When the hour for arranging the bed came, he was yet in his room, but he sent word he would be there in a second.

As he crossed the living-room he pulled a chair to the veranda, placing a footstool before it. Then he stepped into the sunshine room. A quizzical expression crossed the face of Doctor Harmon as he closed the book he was reading aloud to the Girl and arose. Wholly unembarrassed the Harvester smiled.

"Have I got this rigging anywhere near right?" he inquired.

"David, what have you done?" gasped the Girl.

"I didn't feel anywhere near up to the 'mark of my high calling' yesterday," quoted the Harvester. "I don't know how I appear, but I'm clean as shaving, soap and hot water will make me, while my clothing will not smell offensively. Now come out of that bed for a happy hour. Where is that big coverlet? You are going on the veranda to-day."

"You look just like every one else," complained Doctor Harmon.

"You look perfectly lovely," declared the Girl.

"The swale sends you this invitation to come and see star-shine at the foot of mullein hill," said the Harvester, offering a bouquet. It was a loose bunch of long-stemmed, delicate flowers, each an inch across, and having five pearl-white petals lightly striped with pale green. Five long gold anthers arose; at their base gold stamens and a green pistil. The leaves were heart-shaped, of frosty, whitish-green, resembling felt. The Harvester bent to offer them.

"Have some Grass of Parnassus, my dear," he said.

The Girl waved them away. "Go stand over there by the door and slowly turn around. I want to see you."

The Harvester obeyed. He was freshly and carefully shaven. His hair was closely cropped at the base of the head, long, heavy, and slightly waving on top. He wore a white silk shirt, with a rolling collar and tie, white trousers, belt, hose, and shoes, while his hands were manicured with care.

"Have I made a mess of it, or do I appear anything like other men?" he asked, eagerly.

The Girl lifted her eyes to Doctor Harmon and smiled.

"Do you observe anything messy?" she inquired.

"You needn't fish for compliments quite so obviously," he answered. "I'll pay them without being asked. I do not. He is quite correct, and infinitely better looking than the average. Distinguished is a proper word for the gentleman in my opinion. But why, in Heaven's name, have we never had the pleasure of seeing you thus before?"

"Look here, Doc," said the Harvester, "do you mean that you like looking at me mercly because I am dressed this way?"

"I do indeed," said the doctor. "It is good to see you with the garb of work laid aside, and the stamp of cleanliness and ease upon you."

"By gum, that is rubbing it in a little too rough!" cried the Harvester. "I bathe oftener than you do. My clothing is always clean when I start out. Of course, in my work I come hourly in contact with muck, water, and herb juices."

"It's understood that is unavoidable," said Doctor Harmon.

"And if cleanliness is made an issue, I'd rather roll in any of it than put my finger tips into the daily work of a surgeon," added the Harvester, while the Girl giggled.

"That's enough, Medicine Man!" she said. "You did not make a 'mess' of it, or anything else you ever attempted. As for appearing like other men, thank Heaven, you do not. You look a whole world bigger, better and finer. Come, carry me out quickly. I am wild to go. Please put my lovely flowers in water, Molly, only give me a few to hold."

The Harvester arranged the pink coverlet, picked up the Girl, and carried her to the living-room. "We will rest here a little," he said, "and then, if you feel equal to it, we will try the veranda. Are you easy now?"

She nestled her face against the soft shirt and smiled at him. She lifted her hand, laid it on his smooth cheek and then the crisp hair.

"Oh Man!" she cried. "Thank God you didn't give me up, too! I want life! I want *life!*"

The Harvester tightened his grip just a trifle. "Then I thank God, too," he said. "Can you tell me how you are, dear? Is there any difference?"

"Yes," she answered. "I grow tired lying so long,

but there isn't the ghost of an ache in my bones. I can just feel pure, delicious blood running in my veins. My hands and feet are always warm, and my head cool."

The Harvester's face drew very close. "How about your heart, honey?" he whispered. "Anything new there?"

"Yes, I am all over new inside and out. I want to shout, run, sing, and swim. Oh I'd give anything to have you dip me in the lake right now."

"Soon, Girl! That will come soon," prophesied the Harvester.

"I scarcely can wait. And you did say a saddle, didn't you? Won't it be great to come galloping up the levee, when the leaves are red and the frost is in the air. Oh am I going fast enough?"

"Much faster than I expected," said the Harvester. "You are surprising all of us, me most of any. Ruth, you almost make me hope that you regard this as home. Honey, you are thinking of me a little these days?"

The hand that had fallen from his hair lay on his shoulder. Now it slid around his neck, gripping him with all its strength.

"Heaps and heaps!" she said. "All I get a chance to, for being bothered and fussed over, and everlastingly read mushy stuff that's intended for some one else. Please take me to the veranda now; I want to tell you something."

His head swam, but the Harvester set his feet firmly, arose, and carried his Dream Girl back to outdoor life. When he reached the chair, she begged him to go a few steps farther to the bench on the lake shore.

"I am afraid," said the man.

"It's so warm. There can't be any difference in the air. Just a minute."

The Harvester went to the bench, and seating himself, drew the cover closely around her.

"Don't speak a word for a long time," he said. "Just rest. If I tire you too much and spoil everything, I will be desperate."

He clasped her to him, laid his cheek against her hair, his lips on her forehead. He held her hand, kissing it over and over, while again he watched but could find no resentment. The cool, pungent breeze swept from the lake, and the voices of wild life chattered at their feet. Sometimes the water folks splashed, while a big black and gold butterfly mistook the Girl's dark hair for a perching place and settled on it, slowly opening its wonderful wings.

"Lie quietly, Girl," whispered the Harvester. "You are wearing a living jewel, an ornament above price on your hair. Maybe you can see it when it goes. There!"

"Oh I did!" she cried. "How I love it here! Before long may I lie in the dining-room window a while so I can see the water? I like the hill, but I love the lake more."

"Now if you just would love me," said the Harvester, "you would have all Medicine Woods in your heart."

"Don't hurry me so!" said the Girl. "You gave me a year; and it's only a few weeks. I've not been myself, and I'm not now. I mustn't make any mistake. All I know for sure is that I want you most, that I can rest best

with you, and I miss you every minute you are gone. I
think that should satisfy you."

"That would be enough for any reasonable man," said
the Harvester angrily. "Forgive me, Ruth, I have been
cruel. I forget how frail and weak you are. It is having
Harmon here that makes me unnatural. It almost drives
me to frenzy to know that he may take you from me."

"Then send him away!"

"*Send him away?*"

"Yes, send him away! I am tired to death of his
poetry, and seeing him moon around. Send both of them
away quickly!"

The Harvester gulped, blinked, and surreptitiously felt
for her pulse.

"Oh, I've not developed fever again," she said. "I'm
all right. But it must be a fearful expense to have both
of them here by the week, and I'm so tired of them.
Granny says she can take care of me just as well, and the
girl who helps her can cook. No one but you shall lift
me, if I don't get my nose out until I can walk alone.
Both of them are perfectly useless; I'd much rather you'd
send them away."

"There, there! Of course!" said the Harvester soothingly. "I'll do it as soon as I possibly dare. You don't
understand, honey. You are yet delicate beyond measure, internally. The fever burned so long. Every morsel
you eat is measured and cooked in sterilized vessels, so
I'd be scared of my life to have the girl undertake it."

"Why she is doing it straight along now! She and
Granny! Molly isn't out of Doctor Harmon's sight long

enough to cook anything. Granny says there is 'a lot of buncombe about what they do, and she is going to tell them so right to their teeth some of these days, if they badger her much more.' I wish she would, and you, too."

The Harvester gathered the Girl to him in one crushing bear hug.

"For the love of Heaven, Ruth, you drive me crazy! Answer me only one question. When you told me that you 'adored and worshipped' Doctor Harmon, did you mean it, or was that the delirium of fever?"

"I don't know *what* I told you! If I said I 'adored' him, it was the truth. I did! I do! I always shall! So do I adore the Almighty, but that's no sign I want him to read poetry to me, or be around all the time when I am wild for a minute with you. I can worship Doctor Harmon in Chicago or Onabasha quite as well. Fire him! If you don't, I will!"

"Good Lord!" cried the Harvester, helpless until the Girl had to cling to him to prevent rolling from his nerveless arms. "Ruth, Ruth, will you feel my pulse?"

"No, I won't! But you are going to drop me. Take me back to my beautiful bed, then send them away."

"A minute! Give me a minute!" gasped the Harvester. "I couldn't lift a baby just now. Ruth, dear, I thought you *loved* the man."

"What made you think so?"

"You did!"

"I didn't either! I never said I loved him. I said I was under obligations to him; but they are as well repaid as they ever can be. I said I adored him, and I tell you I do! Give him what we owe him, both of us, in money, then send them away. If you'd seen as much of them as I have, you'd be tired of them, too. Please, please, David!"

"Yes," said the Harvester, arising in a sudden tide of effulgent joy. "Yes, Girl, as quickly as I can with decency. I——I'll send them on the lake, and I'll take care of you."

"You won't read poetry to me?"

"I will not."

"You won't moon at me?"

"No!"

"Then hurry! But have them take your boat. I am going to have the first ride in mine."

"Indeed you are, and soon, too!" said the Harvester, marching up the hill as if he were leading hosts to battle. He laid the Girl on the bed, covering her and calling Granny Moreland to sit beside her a few minutes. He went into the gold garden and suggested that the doctor and the nurse go rowing until supper time. They went with alacrity. When they started he returned to the Girl, and sitting beside her, he told Granny to take a nap. Then he began to talk about wild music, and how it was made, what the different odours sweeping down the hill were, when the red leaves would come, the nuts rattle down, and the frost fairies enamel the windows, so soon she was sound asleep. When Granny came back, the Harvester walked around the lake shore to be alone and think quietly, for he was almost too bewildered for full realization.

As he followed the footpath he heard voices, and looking down, he saw the boat lying in the shade while beneath a big tree on the bank sat the doctor and the nurse. His arm was around her, her head was on his shoulder; she was saying very distinctly: "How long will it be until we can go without offending him?"

CHAPTER XIX

A VERTICAL SPINE

BY MIDDLE September the last trace of illness had been removed from the premises, while it was rapidly disappearing from the face and form of the Girl. She was showing a beautiful roundness, there was lovely colour on her cheeks and lips. In her dark eyes sparkled a touch of mischief. Rigidly she followed the rules laid down for diet and exercise. As strength flowed through her body, while no trace of pain tormented her, she began revelling in new and delightful sensations. She loved to pull her boat, drive over the wood road, study the books, cook, rearrange furniture, and go with the Harvester everywhere.

But that was greatly the management of the man. He was so afraid that something might happen to undo all the wonders accomplished in the Girl, and again whiten her face with pain, that he scarcely allowed her from his sight. He remained in the cabin, helping when she worked, then drove with her and a big blanket to the woods, arranged her chair and table, found some attractive subject, and while the wind ravelled her hair and flushed her cheeks, her fingers drew designs. At noon they went to the cabin to lunch, then the Girl took a nap, while the Harvester spread his morning's reaping on the shelves to dry. They returned to the woods until five o'clock; then home again and the Girl dressed and prepared supper, while the Harvester arranged his stores and fed the stock. Then he put on white clothing for the evening. The Girl rested while he washed the dishes, then they explored the lake in the little motor boat, or drove to the city for supplies, or to see their friends.

"Are you even with your usual work at this time of the year?" she asked as they sat at breakfast.

"I am," said the Harvester. "The only things that have been crowded out are the candlesticks. They will have to remain on the shelf until the herbs and roots are all in, and the long winter evenings come. Then I'll use the luna pattern and finish yours first of all."

"What are you going to do to-day?"

"Start on a regular fall campaign. Some of it for the sake of having it; some because there is good money in it. Will you come?"

"Indeed yes. May I help, or shall I take my drawing along?"

"Bring your drawing. Next fall you may help, but as yet you are too close suffering for me to see you do anything that might be even a slight risk. I can't endure it."

"Baby!" she jeered.

"Christen me anything you please," laughed the Harvester. "I'm short on names anyway."

He went to harness Betsy, while the Girl washed the dishes, straightened the rooms, and collected her drawing material. Then she walked up the hill, wearing a shirt and short skirt of khaki, stout shoes, and a straw hat

that shaded her face.   She climbed into the wagon, laid
the drawing box on the seat, and caught the lines as the
Harvester flung them to her.   He went swinging ahead,
Belshazzar to heel, the Girl driving after.

The Harvester stopped halfway up the hill, and beside
a large, shaded bed spread the rug, then set up the little
table and chair for the Girl.

"Want a plant to draw?" he asked.   "This is very
important to us.   It has a string of names as long as a
princess, but I call it goldenseal, because the roots are
yellow.   The chemists ask for hydrastis.   That sounds
formidable, but it's a cousin of buttercups.   The woods
of Ohio and Indiana produce the finest that ever grew,
but it is so nearly extinct now that the trade can be supplied by cultivation only.   I suspect I'm responsible
for its disappearance around here.   I used to get a dollar
fifty a pound, so most of my clothes and books when a
boy I owe to it.   Now I get two for my finest grade, that
accounts for the size of these beds."

"It's pretty!" said the Girl, studying a plant aver-
aging a foot in height.   On a slender, round, purplish
stem arose one big, rough leaf, heavily veined, and having
from five to nine lobes.   Opposite was a similar leaf, but
very small, and a head of scarlet berries resembling a big
raspberry in shape.   The Harvester shook the soil from
the yellow roots, and held up the plant.

"You won't enjoy the odour," he said.

"Well I like the leaves.   I can use them some way.
They are so unusual.   What wonderful colour in the
roots!"

"One of its names is Indian paint," explained the Harvester. "Probably it furnished the squaws of these woods with colouring matter. Now let's see what we can get from it. You draw the plant while I dig the roots."

For a time the Girl bent over her work and the Harvester was busy. Belshazzar ranged the woods chasing chipmunks. The birds came asking questions. When the drawing was completed, other subjects were found. The Girl talked almost constantly, her face alive with interest. The May-apple beds lay close, so she drew from them. She learned the uses and prices of the plant, then made drawings of cohosh, moonseed and bloodroot. That was so wonderful in its root colour, the Harvester filled the little cup with water and she began to paint. Intensely absorbed she bent above the big, notched, silvery leaves and the blood-red roots, testing and trying to match them exactly. Every few minutes the Harvester leaned over her shoulder to see how she was progressing and to offer suggestions. When she finished she picked up a trailing vine of moonseed.

"You have this on the porch," she said. "I think it is lovely. There is no end to the beautiful combinations of leaves, and these are such pretty grape-like clusters; but if you touch them the slightest you soil the wonderful surface."

"And that makes the fairies very sad," said the Harvester. "They love that vine best of any, because they paint its fruit with the most care. 'Bloom' the scientists call it. You see it on cultivated plums, grapes, and

apples, but never in any such perfection as on moonseed
and black haws in the woods. You should be able to design a number of pretty things from the cohosh leaves
and berries, also. You scarcely can get a start this fall,
but early in the spring you can begin, and follow the
season. If your work comes out well this winter, I'll send
some of it to the big publishing houses. You can make
book and magazine covers and decorations, if you would
like."

"'If I would like!' How modest! You know perfectly
well that if I could make a design that would be accepted,
and used on a book or magazine, I would almost fly. Oh
do you suppose I could?"

"I don't 'suppose' anything about it, I know," said
the Harvester. "It is not possible that the public can
be any more tired of wild roses, golden-rod, and swallows
than the poor art editors who accept them because they
can't help themselves. Dangle something fresh and new
under their noses and see them snap. The next time I go
to Onabasha I'll get you some popular magazines, so you
can compare what is being used with what you see here,
and judge for yourself how glad they would be for a change.
And potteries, arts and crafts shops, and wall paper factories, they'd be crazy for the designs I could furnish them.
As for money, there's more in it than the herbs, if I only
could draw."

"I can do that," said the Girl. "Trail the vine and
give me an idea how to scale it. I'll just make studies
now, then this winter I'll conventionalize them and work
them into patterns. Won't that be fun?"

"That's more than fun, Ruth," said the Harvester solemnly. "That is creation. That touches the provinces of the Almighty. That is taking His unknown wonders and making them into pleasure and benefit for thousands, not to mention filling your face with awe divine, and lighting your eyes with interest and ambition. That is life, Ruth. You are beginning to live right now."

"I see," said the Girl. "I understand! I am!"

"You get your subjects now. When the harvest is over I'll show you what I have in my head, so before Christmas the fun will begin."

"What next?"

"Sketch a sarsaparilla plant and this yam vine. It grows on your veranda too——the rattle box, you remember. The leaves and seed pods are wonderful. You can do any number of new things with them."

He brought her samples of ginger leaves, Indian hemp, queen-of-the-meadow, cone-flower, burdock, baneberry, and Indian turnip, as he harvested them in turn. When they came to the large beds of orange pleurisy root the Girl cried out with pleasure.

"We will take its prosaic features first," said the Harvester. "It is good medicine, so worth handling. Forget that! The Bird Woman calls it butterfly flower. That's better. Now try to analyze a single bloom and you will see why there's poetry coming."

He knelt beside the Girl, separating the blooms to point out their marvellous colour and construction. She leaned against his shoulder, watching with breathless interest. As his bare head brought its mop of damp wind-rumpled hair close, she ran her fingers through it, and with her handkerchief wiped his forehead.

"Sometimes I almost wish you'd get sick," she said.

"In the name of common sense, why?"

"Oh it is born in the heart of a woman to want to mother something," answered the Girl. "I feel that I would like to take care of you, as if you were a little fellow. David, I know why your mother fought to make you the man she desired. You must have been charming when small. I can shut my eyes and see the boy you were. I should have loved you as she did."

"How about the man I am?" inquired the Harvester promptly. "Any leanings toward him yet, Ruth?"

"It's getting worser and worser every day and hour," said the Girl. "I don't understand it at all. I wouldn't try to live without you. I don't want you to leave my sight. Everything you do is the way I would have it. Nothing you ever say shocks or offends me. I'd love to render you any personal service. I want to take you in my arms and hug you tight half a dozen times a day as a reward for the kind and lovely things you do for me."

A dull red flamed up the neck and over the face of the Harvester. One arm lifted to the chair back, the other dropped across the table, so that the Girl was almost encircled.

"For the love of mercy, Ruth, why haven't I had a hint of this before?" he cried.

"You said you'd hate me. You said you'd drop me into the deepest part of the lake if I deceived you; so if I have to tell the truth, why, that is all of it. I think it is nonsense about some wonderful feeling that is going to take possession of your heart when you love any one. I love you so much I'd gladly suffer to save you pain or sorrow. But there are no thrills; it's just steady, sober, common sense that I should love you, so I do. Why can't you be satisfied with what I can give, David?"

"Because it's husks and ashes," said the Harvester grimly. "You drive me to desperation, Ruth. I am almost wild for your love, but what you offer me is plain, straight affection, nothing more. There isn't a trace of the feeling that should exist between man and wife in it. Some men might be satisfied to be your husband, and be regarded as a father or brother. I am not. The red-bird didn't want a sister, Ruth, he was asking for a mate. So am I. That's as plain as I know how to put it. There is some way to awaken you into a living, loving woman, and, please God, I'll find it yet, but I'm slow about it; there's no question of that. Never you mind! Don't worry! Some of these days I have faith to believe it will sweep you as a tide sweeps the shore; then I hope God will be good enough to let me be where you will land in my arms."

The Girl sat looking at him between narrowed lids. Suddenly she took his head between her hands, drew his face to hers and deliberately kissed him. Then she drew away and searched his eyes.

"There!" she challenged. "What is the matter with that?"

The Harvester's colour slowly faded to a sickly white.

"Ruth, you try me almost beyond human endurance,"

he said. "'What's the matter with that?'" He arose,
stepped back, folded his arms, and stared at her. "'What's
the matter with that?'" he repeated. "Never was I so
sorely tempted in all my life as I am now to lie to you,
to say there is nothing, to take you in my arms and try
to awaken you to what I mean by love. But suppose I
do——and fail! Then comes the agony of slow endurance
for me, with the possibility that any day you may meet
the man who can arouse in you the feelings I cannot.
That would mean my oath broken, and my heart as well;
while soon you would dislike me beyond tolerance, even.
I dare not risk it! The matter is, that was the loving
caress of a ten-year-old girl to a big brother. That's all!
Not much, but a mighty big defect when it is offered a
strong man as fuel on which to feed consuming passion."

"'Consuming passion,'" repeated the Girl. "David
you never lie, and you never exaggerate. Do you honestly mean that there is something——oh, there is! I
can see it! You are really suffering, and if I come to you,
and try my best to comfort you, you'll only call it baby
affection that you don't want. David, what am I going
to do?"

"You are going to the cabin," said the Harvester, "to
cook us a big supper. I am dreadfully hungry. I'll be
along presently. Don't worry, Ruth, you are all right!
That kiss was lovely. Tell me that you are not angry
with me."

Her eyes were wet as she smiled at him.

"If there is a bigger brute than a man anywhere on the
footstool, I should like to meet it," said the Harvester,

"and see what it appears like. Go along, honey; I'll be there as soon as I load."

He drove to the dry-house, washed and spread his reaping on the big trays, fed the stock, dressed in the white clothing, then entered the kitchen. That the Girl had been crying was obvious, but he overlooked it, helped with the work, and then they took a boat ride. When they returned he proposed that she should select her favourite likeness of her mother, so the next time he went to the city he could take it with his, and order the enlargements he had planned. To save carrying a lighted lamp into the closet he brought her little trunk to the living-room, where she opened it and hunted the pictures. There were several. All of them were of a young, elegantly dressed woman of great beauty. The Harvester studied them long.

"Who was she, Ruth?" he asked at last.

"I don't know, and have no desire to learn."

"Can you explain how the girl here represented came to marry a brother of Henry Jameson?"

"Yes. I was past twelve when my father came the last time, so I remember him distinctly. If Uncle Henry were properly clothed, he is not a bad man in appearance, unless he is very angry. He can use proper language, if he chooses. My father was the best in him, refined and intensified. He was much taller, very good looking, while he dressed and spoke well. They were born and grew to manhood in the East, and came out here at the same time. Where Uncle Henry is a trickster and a trader in stock, my father went a step higher; he tricked and traded in men

——and women! Mother told me this much once. He saw her somewhere and admired her. He learned who she was, went to her father's law office and pretended he was representing some great business in the West, until he was welcomed as a promising client. He hung around and when she came in one day her father was forced to introduce them. The remainder is the same world-old story ——a good looking, glib-tongued man, plying every art known to an expert, on an innocent girl."

"Is he dead, Ruth?"

"We thought so. We hoped so."

"Your mother did not feel that her people might be suffering for her as she was for them?"

"Not after she appealed to them twice and received no reply."

"Perhaps they tried to find her. Maybe she has a father or mother who is longing for word from her now. Are you very sure you are right in not wanting to know?"

"She never gave me a hint from which I could tell who or where they were. In so gentle a woman as my mother that only could mean she did not want them to know of her. Neither do I. This is the photograph I prefer; please use it."

"I'll put back the trunk in the morning, when I can see better," said the Harvester.

The Girl closed it, then soon went to bed. But there was no sleep for the man. He went into the night, and for hours he paced the driveway. Then he sat on the step and looked at Belshazzar before him.

"Life's growing easier every minute, Bel," said the

Harvester. "Here's my Dream Girl, lovely as the most golden instant of that wonderful dream, offering me—— offering me, Bel——in my present pass, the lips and the love of my little sister who never was born. And I've hurt Ruth's feelings, and sent her to bed with a heartache, trying to make her see that it won't do. It won't, Bel! If I can't have genuine love, I don't want anything. I told her so as plainly as I could find words, and set her crying, and made her unhappy to end a wonderful day. But in some way she has got to learn that propinquity, tolerance, approval, affection, even——is not love. I can't take the risk, after all these years of waiting for the real thing. If I did, and love never came, I should end——well, I know how I should end——and that would spoil her life. I simply have got to brace up, Bel, and keep on trying. She thinks it is nonsense about thrills, and some wonderful feeling that takes possession of you. Lord, Bel! There isn't much nonsense about the thing that rages in my brain, heart, soul, and body. It strikes me as the gravest reality that ever overtook a man. She is growing attached to me. 'Couldn't live without me,' Bel, that is what she said. Maybe it would be a scheme to bring Granny here to stay with her, and take a few months in some city this winter on those chemical points that trouble me. There is an old saying about 'absence making the heart grow fonder.' Maybe separation is the thing to work the trick. I've tried about everything else I know.

"But I'm in too much of a hurry! What a fool a man is! A few weeks ago, Bel, I said to myself that if Harmon were away and had no part in her life I'd be the happiest man alive. Happiest man alive! Bel, take a look at me now! Happy! Well, why shouldn't I be happy? She is here. She is growing in strength and beauty every hour. She cares more for me day by day. From an outside viewpoint it seems as if I had almost all a man could ask in reason. But when was a strong man in the grip of love ever reasonable? I think the Almighty took a pretty grave responsibility when He made men as He did. If I had been He, and understood the forces I was handling, I would have been too big a coward to do it. There is nothing for me, Bel, but to move on doing my level best; and if she doesn't awaken soon, I shall try the absent treatment. As sure as you are the most faithful dog a man ever owned, Bel, I'll try the absent treatment."

The Harvester arose and entered the cabin, stepping softly, for it was dark in the Girl's room. He could not hear a sound there. He turned up the lights in the living-room. As he did so the first thing he saw was the little trunk. He looked at it intently, then picked up a book. Every page he turned he glanced again at the trunk. At last he laid down the book and sat staring, his brain working rapidly. He ended by carrying the trunk to his room. He darkened the living-room, lighted his own, drew the rain screens, then piece by piece carefully examined the contents. There were the pictures, but the name of the photographer had been removed. There was not a word that would help in identification. He emptied it to the bottom. As he picked up the last piece his fingers struck in a peculiar way that did not give the impression of touching a solid surface. He felt over it carefully; when he examined with a candle he plainly could see where the cloth lining had been cut and lifted.

For a long time he knelt staring at it, then he deliberately inserted his knife blade and raised it. The cloth had been glued to a heavy sheet of pasteboard the exact size of the trunk bottom. Beneath it lay half a dozen yellow letters, and face down two tissue-wrapped photographs. The Harvester examined them first. They were of a man close forty, having a strong, aggressive face, on which pride and dominant will power were prominently indicated. The other was a reproduction of a dainty and delicate woman, with exquisitely tender and gentle features. Long the Harvester studied them. The names of the photographer and the city were missing. There was nothing except the faces. He could detect traces of the man in the poise of the Girl and the carriage of her head, also suggestions of the woman in the refined sweetness of her expression. Each picture represented wealth in dress and taste in pose. Finally he laid them together on the table, picked up one of the letters, and read it. Then he read all of them.

Before he finished, tears were running down his cheeks; soon his resolution was formed. These were the appeals of an adoring mother, crazed with fear for the safety of an only child, who unfortunately had fallen under the influence of a man the mother dreaded and feared, because of her knowledge of life and men of his character. They were one long, impassioned plea for the daughter not to trust a stranger, not to believe that vows of passion could be true when all else in life was false, not to trust her untried judgment of men and the world against the experience of her parents. But whether the tears that stained those sheets had fallen from the eyes of the suffering mother or the starved and deserted daughter, there was no way for the Harvester to know. One thing was clear: it was not possible for him to rest until he knew if that woman yet lived and bore such suffering. But every trace of address had been torn away, while there was nothing to indicate where or in what circumstances the letters had been written.

A long time the Harvester sat in deep thought. Then he returned all the letters save one. This with the pictures he made into a packet that he locked in his desk. The trunk he replaced, then went to bed. Early the next morning he drove to Onabasha and posted the parcel. The address it bore was that of the largest detective agency in the country. Then he bought an interesting book, a box of fruit, and hurried back to the Girl. He found her on the veranda, Belshazzar stretched close with one eye shut, the other on his charge, whose cheeks were flushed with lovely colour as she bent over her drawing material. The Harvester went to her with a rush, and slipping his fingers under her chin, tilted back her head against him.

"Got a kiss for me, honey?" he inquired.

"No sir," answered the Girl emphatically. "I gave you a perfectly lovely one yesterday, but you said it was not right. I am going to try just once more, if you say again that it won't do, I'm going back to Chicago or to my dear Uncle Henry, I haven't decided which."

Her lips were smiling, but her eyes were full of tears.

"Why thank you, Ruth! I think that is wonderful," said the Harvester. "I'll risk the next one. In the meantime, excuse me if I give you a demonstration of the real thing, merely to furnish you an idea of how it should be."

The Harvester delivered the sample, then went striding to the marsh. The dazed Girl sat staring at her work, trying to realize what had happened; for that was the first time the Harvester had kissed her on the lips. It was the material expression a strong man gives the woman he loves when his heart is surging at high tide. The Girl sat motionless, gazing at her study.

In the marsh she knew the Harvester was reaping queen-of-the-meadow, and around the high borders, elecampane and burdock. She could hear his voice in snatches of song or cheery whistle; notes that she divined were intended to keep her from worrying. Intermingled with them came the dog's bark of defiance as he digged for an escaping chipmunk, his note of pleading when he wanted a root cut with the mattock, his cry of discovery when he thought he had found something the Harvester would like, or his yelp of warning when he scented danger. The Girl looked down the drive to the lake or across at the hedge. Everywhere she saw glowing colour, with intermittent blue sky and green leaves, all of it a complete picture, from which nothing could be spared. She turned slowly and looked toward the marsh, trying to hear the words of the song above the ripple of Singing Water; to see the form of the man. Slowly she lifted her handkerchief and pressed it against her lips, as she whispered in an awed voice: "My gracious Heaven, is *that* the kind of a kiss he is expecting me to give *him?* Why, I couldn't ——not to save my life."

She placed her brushes in water, set the colour box on the paper, then went to the kitchen to prepare the noon lunch. As she worked the soft colour deepened in her cheeks, a new light glowed in her eyes, while she hummed over the tune that floated across the marsh. She was very busy when the Harvester came, but he spoke casually of his morning's work, ate heartily, and ordered her to take a nap while he washed roots and filled the trays; then they went to the woods together for the afternoon.

In the evening they came home to finish the day's work. As the night was chilly, the Harvester heaped some bark in the living-room fireplace, then lay on the rug before it, while the Girl sat in an easy chair watching him as he talked. He was telling her about some wonderful combinations he was going to compound for different ailments. He laughingly asked her if she wanted to live in a palace.

"Of course I could if I desired!" she suggested.

"You could!" cried the Harvester. "All that is necessary is to combine a few drugs in one remedy and float it. That is easy! The people will do the remainder."

"You talk as if you believe that," marvelled the Girl.

"Want it proved?" challenged the Harvester.

"No!" she cried in swift alarm. "What do we want with more than we have? What is there necessary to happiness that is not ours now? Maybe it is true that the

'love of money is the root of all evil.' Don't you ever get
a lot just to find out. You said the night I came here that
you didn't want more than you had, now I don't. I won't
have it! It might bring restlessness and discontent. I've
seen it make other people unhappy and separate them. I
don't want money, I want work. You make your remedies and offer them to suffering humanity for a living
profit, while I keep house and draw designs. I am perfectly happy, free, and unspeakably content. I never
dreamed that it was possible for me to be so glad; so filled
with the joy of life. There is only one thing on earth I
want. If I only could——"

"Could what, Ruth?"

"Could get that kiss right——"

"Forget it, I tell you!" he commanded. "Just so
long as you worry and fret, so long I've got to wait. If
you quit thinking about it, all 'unbeknownst' to yourself
you'll awake some morning with it on your lips. I can
see traces of it growing stronger every day. Very soon
now it's going to materialize; then get out of my way, for
I'll be a whirling, irresponsible lunatic, with the wild joy
of it. Oh I've got faith in that kiss of yours, Ruth! It's
on the way. The fates have booked it. There isn't a
reason on earth why I should be served so scurvy a trick
as to miss it, so I never will believe that I shall——"

"David," interrupted the Girl, "go on talking and
don't move a muscle, just reach over presently to fix the
fire or something; then turn naturally and look at the
window beside your door."

"——Shall miss it," said the Harvester steadily.

"That would be too unmerciful. What do you see, Ruth?"

"A face. If I am not greatly mistaken, it is my Uncle Henry and he appears like a perfect fiend. Oh David, I am afraid!"

"Be quiet and don't look," said the Harvester.

He turned, tossing a piece of bark on the fire. Then he reached for the poker, pushed it down and stirred the coals. He arose as he worked.

"Rise slowly and quietly and go to your room. Stay there until I call you."

With the Girl out of the way, the Harvester pottered over the fire; when the flame leaped he lifted a stick of wood, hesitated as if it were too small, and laying it down, started to bring a larger one. In the dining-room he caught a small stick from the wood box, softly stepped from the door, and ran around the house. But he awakened Belshazzar on the kitchen floor, so the dog barked and ran after him. By the time the Harvester reached the corner of his room the man leaped upon a horse and went racing down the drive. The Harvester flung the stick of wood, but missed the man and hit the horse. The dog sprang past the Harvester and vanished. There was the sound and flash of a revolver, and the rattle of the bridge as the horse crossed it. The dog came back unharmed. The Harvester ran to the telephone, called the Onabasha police, and asked them to send a mounted man to meet the intruder before he could reach a cross road; but they were too slow and missed him. However, the Girl was certain she had recognized her uncle. She was extremely nervous; but the Harvester only laughed and told her it was a trip made out of curiosity. Her uncle wanted to see if he could learn if she were well and happy. He finally convinced her that this was the case, although he was not very sanguine himself.

For the following three days the Harvester worked in the woods, but he kept the Girl with him every minute. By the end of that time he really had persuaded himself that it was merely curiosity. So through the cooling fall days they worked together. They were very happy. Before her wondering eyes the Harvester hung queer branches, burs, nuts, berries, and trailing vines with curious seed pods. There were masses of brilliant flowers, most of them strange to the Girl, many to the great average of humanity. While she sat bending over them, beside her the Harvester delved in the black earth of the woods, or the clay and sand of the open hillside, or the muck of the lake shore, and lifted large bagfuls of roots that he later drenched on the floating raft on the lake, and when they had drained he dried them. Some of them he did not wet, but scraped and wiped clean and dry. Often after she was sleeping, and long before she awoke in the morning, he was at work carrying heaped trays from the evaporator to the storeroom, or tying the roots, leaves, bark, and seeds into packages.

While he gathered trillium roots the Girl made drawings of the plant and learned its commercial value. She drew lady's slipper and Solomon's seal, learning their uses and prices; and carefully traced wild ginger leaves while nibbling the aromatic root. It was difficult to keep from protesting when the work carried them around the lake shore to the pokeberry beds, for the colour of these she loved. It required careful explanation as to the value of the roots and seeds as blood purifier, and the argument that in a few more days the frost would level the bed, to induce her to consent to its harvesting. But when the case was properly presented, she put aside her drawing and stained her slender fingers helping.

The sun was golden on the lake, the birds of the upland were clustering over reeds and rushes, for the sake of plentiful seed and convenient water. Many of them sang fitfully, the notes of almost all of them were melodious, so the days were long, happy dreams. There was but little left to gather until ginseng time. For that the Harvester had engaged several boys to help him, for the task of digging the roots, washing and drying them, burying part of the seeds and preparing the remainder for market seemed endless for one man to attempt. After a full day the Harvester lay before the fire, his head so close the Girl's knee that her fingers were in reach of his hair. Every time he mended the fire he moved, until he could feel the touch of her garments against him. Then he began to plan for the winter; how they would store food for the long, cold days, how much fuel would be required, when they would go to the city for their winter clothing, what they would read, and how they would work together at the drawings.

"I am almost too anxious to wait longer to get back to my carving," he said. "Whoever would have thought this spring that fall would come and find the birds talking of going, the caterpillars spinning winter quarters, the animals holing up, me getting ready for the cold, and your candlesticks not finished. Winter is when you really need them. Then there is solid cheer in numbers of candles and a roaring wood fire. The furnace is going to be a good thing to keep the floors and the bathroom warm, but an open fire of dry, crackling wood is the only rational source of heat in a home. You must watch for the fairy dances on the backwall, Ruth, and learn to trace goblin faces in the coals. Sometimes there is a panorama of temples and trees, while you will find exquisite colour in the smoke. Dry maple makes a lovely lavender, soft and fine as a floating veil, damp elm makes a blue, and hickory red and yellow. I almost can tell which wood is burning after the bark is gone, by the smoke and flame colour. When the little red fire fairies come out and dance on the backwall it is fun to figure what they are celebrating. By the way, Ruth, I have been a lamb for days. I hope you have observed! But I would sleep sounder to-night if you only could give me a hint whether that kiss is coming on at all." He tipped back his head to see her face. It was glorious in the red firelight; the big eyes never appeared so deep and dark. The tilted head struck her hand, and her fingers ran through his hair.

"You said to forget it," she reminded him, "and then it would come sooner."

"Which same translated means that it is not here yet. Well, I didn't expect it, so I am not disappointed; but begorry, I do wish it would materialize by Christmas. I think I will work for that. Wouldn't it make a day worth while, though? By the way, what do you want for Christmas, Ruth?"

"A doll," she answered.

The Harvester laughed. He tipped his head to see her face and suddenly grew quiet, for it was very serious.

"I am quite in earnest," she said. "I think the big dolls in the stores are beautiful, and I never owned only a teeny one. All my life I've wanted a big doll as badly as I ever longed for anything that was not absolutely necessary to keep me alive. In fact, a doll is essential to a happy childhood. The mother instinct is so ingrained in a girl that if she doesn't have dolls to love, even as a baby, she is deprived of a part of her natural rights. It's a pitiful thing to have been the little girl in the picture who stands outside the window and gazes with longing soul at the doll she is anxious to own and can't ever have. Harvester, I was always that little girl. I am quite in earnest. I want a big, beautiful doll more than anything else."

As she talked the Girl's fingers were idly threading the Harvester's hair. His head lightly touched her knee, so she shifted her position to afford him a comfortable resting place. With a thrill of delight that shook him, the man laid his head in her lap, his face glowing as a happy boy's.

"You shall have the loveliest doll that money can buy, Ruth," he promised. "What else do you want?"

"A roasted goose, plum pudding, and all those indigestible things that Christmas stories always tell about; and popcorn balls, candy, and everything I've always wanted and never had, and a long beautiful day with you. That's all!"

"Ruth, I'm so happy I almost wish I could go to Heaven right now before anything occurs to spoil this," said the Harvester.

The wheels of a car rattled across the bridge. He whirled to his knees, putting his arms around the Girl.

"Ruth," he said huskily. "I'll wager a thousand dollars I know what is coming. Hug me tight, quick! and give me the best kiss you can——any old kind of a one, so you touch my lips with yours before I've got to open that door and let in trouble."

The Girl threw her arms around his neck and with the imprint of her lips warm on his the Harvester crossed the room. He stepped out, closing the door behind him, and crossing the veranda, passed down the walk. He recognized the car as belonging to a garage in Onabasha. In it sat two men, one of whom spoke.

"Are you David Langston?"

"Yes," said the Harvester.

"Did you send a couple of photographs to a New York detective agency a few days ago with inquiries concerning some parties you wanted located?"

"I did," said the Harvester. "But I was not expecting any such immediate returns."

"Your questions touched on a case that long has been in the hands of the agency, so they telegraphed the parties. The following day the people had a letter, giving them the information they required, from another source."

"That is where Uncle Henry showed his fine Spencerian

hand," commented the Harvester. "It always will be a great satisfaction that I got my fist in first."

"Is Miss Jameson here?"

"No," said the Harvester. "My wife is at home. Her surname was Ruth Jameson, but we have been married since June. Did you wish to speak with Mrs. Langston?"

"I came for that purpose. My name is Kennedy. I am the law partner and the closest friend of the young lady's grandfather. News of her location has prostrated her grandmother so that he could not leave her. I was sent to bring the young woman."

"Oh!" said the Harvester. "Well you will have to interview her about that. One word first. She does not know that I sent those pictures and made that inquiry. One other word. She is just recovering from a case of fever, induced by wrong conditions of life before I met her. She is not so strong as she appears. Understand you are not to be abrupt. Go very gently! Her feelings and health must be guarded with care."

The Harvester opened the door. As she saw the stranger, the Girl's eyes widened, she arose and stood waiting.

"Ruth," said the Harvester, "this is a man who has been making quite a search for you, and at last he has you located."

The Harvester went to the Girl's side, to put a reinforcing arm around her.

"Perhaps he brings you some news that will make life most interesting and very lovely for you. Will you shake hands with Mr. Kennedy?"

The Girl suddenly straightened to unusual height.

"I will hear why he has been making 'quite a search for me,' and on whose authority he has me 'located,' first," she said.

A diabolical grin crossed the face of the Harvester.

"Then please be seated, Mr. Kennedy," he said, "and we will talk over the matter. As I understand, you are a representative of my wife's people."

The Girl stared at the Harvester.

"Take your chair, Ruth, and meet this as a matter of course," he advised casually. "You always have known that some day it must come. You couldn't look in the face of those photographs of your mother in her youth and not realize that somewhere hearts were aching and breaking, and brains were busy in a search for her."

The Girl stood rigid. "I want it distinctly understood," she said, "that I have no use on earth for my mother's people. They come too late. I absolutely refuse to see or to hold any communication with them."

"But young lady, that is very arbitrary!" cried Mr. Kennedy. "You don't understand! They are a couple of old people, who are slowly dying of broken hearts!'

"Not so badly broken or they wouldn't die slowly," commented the Girl grimly. "The heart that was really broken was my mother's. The torture of a starved, overworked body and hopeless brain was hers. There was nothing slow about her death, for she went out with only half a life spent, and much of that in acute agony, because of their negligence. David, you often have said that this is my home. I choose to take you at your word.

Will you kindly tell this man that he is not welcome in this house, and I wish him to leave it at once?"

The Harvester stepped back, while his face grew very white. "I can't, Ruth," he said gently.

"Why not?"

"Because I brought him here."

"You brought him here! You! David, are you crazy? You!"

"It is through me that he came."

The Girl caught the mantel for support.

"Then I stand alone again," she said. "Harvester, I had thought you were on my side."

"I am at your feet," said the man in a broken voice. "Ruth dear, will you let me explain?"

"There is only one explanation; with what you have done for me fresh in my mind, I can't put it into words."

"Ruth, hear me!"

"I must! You force me! But before you speak understand this: not now, or through all eternity, do I forgive the inexcusable neglect that drove my mother to what I witnessed and was helpless to avert."

"My dear! My dear!" said the Harvester, "I had hoped the woods had done a more perfect work in your heart. Your mother is lying in state now, Girl, safe from further suffering of any kind; and if I read aright, her tired face and shrivelled frame were eloquent of forgiveness. Ruth dear, if she so loved them that her heart was broken and she died for them, think what they are suffering! Have some mercy on them."

"Get this very clear, David," said the Girl. "She

died of hunger for food. Her heart was not so broken that she couldn't have lived a lifetime, and got much comfort out of it, if her body had not lacked sustenance. Oh I was so happy a minute ago. David, why did you do this thing?"

The Harvester picked up the Girl, placed her in a chair, kneeling beside her with his arms around her.

"Because of the *pain in the world*, Ruth," he said simply. "Your mother is sleeping in the long sleep that knows neither anger nor resentment; so I was forced to think of a gentle-faced, little old mother whose heart is daily one long ache, whose eyes are dim with tears, and a proud, broken old man who spends his time trying to comfort her, when his life is as desolate as hers."

"How do you know so wonderfully much about their aches and broken hearts?"

"Because I have seen their faces when they were happy, Ruth; so I know what suffering would do to them. There were pictures of them and letters in the bottom of your old trunk. I searched it the other night and found them; by what life has done to your mother and to you, I can judge what it is now bringing them. Never can you be truly happy Ruth, until you have forgiven them, and done what you can to comfort the remainder of their lives. I did it because of the pain in the world, my girl."

"What about my pain?"

"The only way on earth to cure it is through forgiveness. That, and that only, will ease it all away, and leave you happy and free for life and love. So long as you let this rancour eat in your heart, Ruth, you are not, and never can be, normal. You must forgive them, dear, hear what they have to say, and give them the comfort of seeing what they can discover of her in you. Then your heart will be at rest at last, your soul free, you can take your rightful place in life, and the love you crave will awaken in your heart. Ruth, dear, you are the acme of gentleness and justice. Be just and gentle now! Give them their chance! My heart aches, and always will ache for the pain you have known, but nursing and brooding over it will not cure it. It is going to take a heroic operation to cut it out, so I chose to be the surgeon. You have said that I once saved your body from pain Ruth, trust me now to free your soul."

"What do you want?"

"I want you to speak kindly to this man, who through my act has come here, to allow him to tell you why he came. Then I want you to do the kind and womanly thing your duty suggests that you should."

"David, I don't understand you!"

"That is no difference," said the Harvester. "The point is, do you *trust* me?"

The Girl hesitated. "Of course I do," she said at last.

"Then hear what your grandfather's friend has come to say for him; forget yourself in doing to others as you would have them——really, Ruth, that is all of religion or of life worth while. Go on, Mr. Kennedy."

The Harvester drew up a chair, seated himself beside the Girl, then taking one of her hands, he held it closely.

"I was sent here by my law partner and my closest friend, Mr. Alexander Herron, of Philadelphia," said the stranger.

"Both he and Mrs. Herron were bitterly opposed to your mother's marriage, because they knew life and human nature, while there never is but one end to men such as she married."

"You may omit that," said the Girl coldly. "Simply state why you are here."

"In response to an inquiry from your husband concerning the originals of some photographs he sent to a detective agency in New York. They have had the case for years, and recognizing the pictures as a clue, they telegraphed Mr. Herron. The prospect of news after years of fruitless searching so prostrated Mrs. Herron that he dared not leave her, so he sent me."

"Kindly tell me this," said the Girl. "Where were my mother's father and mother for the four years immediately following her marriage?"

"They went to Europe to avoid the humiliation of meeting their friends. There, in Italy, Mrs. Herron developed a fever; it was several years before she could be brought home. She retired from society, and has been confined to her room ever since. When they could return, a search was instituted at once for their daughter, but they never have been able to find a trace. They have hunted through every eastern city they thought might contain her."

"And overlooked a little insignificant place like Chicago, of course."

"I myself conducted a personal search there. I visited the home of every Jameson in the directory or who had mail at the office or of whom I could get a clue."

"I don't suppose two women in a little garret room would be in the directory, while there never was any mail."

"Did your mother ever appeal to her parents?"

"She did," said the Girl. "She admitted that she had been wrong, asked their forgiveness, and begged to go home. That was in the second year of her marriage, when she was in Cleveland. Afterward she went to Chicago, from there she wrote again."

"Her father and mother were in Italy fighting for the mother's life, two years after that. It is very easy to become lost in a large city. Criminals do it every day and are never found, even with the best detectives on their trail. I am very sorry about this. My friends will be broken-hearted. At any time they would have been more than delighted to have had their daughter return. A letter on the day following the message from the agency brought news that she was dead, and now their only hope for any small happiness at the close of years of suffering lies with you. I was sent to plead with you to return with me at once to make them a visit. Of course, their home is yours. You are their only heir, so they would be very happy if you were free, and would remain permanently with them."

"How do they know I will not be like the father they so detested?"

"They had sufficient cause to dislike him. They have every reason to love and welcome you. They are consumed with anxiety. Will you come?"

"No. This is for me to decide. I do not care for

them or their property. Always they have failed me when my distress was unspeakable. Now there is only one thing I ask of life, more than my husband has given me, and if that lay in his power I would have it. You may go back and tell them that I am perfectly happy. I have everything I need. They can give me nothing I want, not even their love. Perhaps, sometime, I will go to see them for a few days, if David will go with me."

"Young woman, do you realize that you are issuing a death sentence?" asked the lawyer gently.

"It is a just one."

"I do not believe your husband agrees with you. I know I do not. Mrs. Herron is a tiny old lady, with a feeble spark of vitality left; with all her strength she is clinging to life, pleading with it to give her word of her only child before she goes out unsatisfied. She knows that her daughter is gone, so now her hopes are fastened on you. If for only a few days, you certainly must go with me."

"I will not!"

The lawyer turned to the Harvester.

"She will be ready to start with you to-morrow morning, on the first train north," said the Harvester. "We will meet you at the station at cight."

"I——I am afraid I forgot to tell my driver to wait."

"You mean your instructions were not to let the Girl from your sight," said the Harvester. "Very well! We have comfortable rooms. I will show you to one. Please come this way."

The Harvester led the guest to the lake room and

arranged for the night. Then he went to the telephone and sent a message to an address he had been furnished, asking for an immediate reply. It went to Philadelphia, contained a description of the lawyer, and asked if he had been sent by Mr. Herron to escort his granddaughter to his home. When the Harvester returned to the living-room the Girl, white and defiant, waited before the fire. He knelt beside her to put his arms around her, but she repulsed him; so he sat on the rug and looked at her.

"No wonder you felt sure you knew what that was!" she cried bitterly.

"Ruth, if you will allow me to lift the bottom of that old trunk, and if you will read any one of the half-dozen letters I read, you will forgive me, and begin making preparations to go."

"It's a wonder you don't hold them before me and force me to read them," she said.

"Don't say anything you will be sorry for after you are gone, dear."

"I'm not going!"

"Oh yes you are!"

"Why?"

"Because it is right that you should, and right is inexorable. Also, because I very much wish you to; you will do it for me."

"Why do you want me to go?"

"I have three strong reasons: first, as I told you, it is the only thing that will cleanse your heart of bitterness and leave it free for the tenanting of a great and holy love. Next, I think they honestly made every effort to find your mother, and are now growing old in despair you can lighten, so you owe it to them and yourself to do it. Lastly, for my sake. I've tried everything I know, Ruth, but I can't make you love me, or bring you to a realizing sense of it if you do. So before I saw that chest, I had planned to harvest my big crop, trying with all my heart while I did it, and if love hadn't come then, I meant to get some one to stay with you, while I went away to give you a free perspective for a time. I meant to plead that I needed a few weeks with a famous chemist I know to prepare me better for my work. My real motive was to leave you, to let you see if absence could do anything for me in your heart. You've been very nearly the creature of my hands for months, my girl; whatever any one else may do, you're bound to miss me mightily, so I figured that with me away, perhaps you could solve the problem alone I seem to fail in helping you with. This is only a slight change of plans. You are going in my stead. I will harvest the ginseng and cure it, and then, if you are not at home, and the loneliness grows unbearable, I will take the chemistry course, until you decide when you will come, if ever."

"'If ever?'"

"Yes," said the Harvester. "I am growing accustomed to facing big propositions——I will not dodge this. The faces of the three of your people I have seen prove refinement. Their clothing indicates wealth. These long, lonely years mean that they will shower you with every outpouring of loving, hungry hearts. They will keep you if they can, my dear. I do not blame them. The life I propose for you is one of work, mostly for others, and the reward, in great part, consists of the joy in the soul of the creator of things that help in the world. I realize that you will find wealth, luxury, and lavish love. I know that I may lose you forever. If it is right and best for you, I hope I shall. I know exactly what I am risking, but I yet say, go."

"I don't see how you can, and love me as you prove you do."

"That is a little streak of the inevitableness of nature that the forest has ground into my soul. I'd rather cut off my right hand than take yours with it, in the parting that will come in the morning; but you are going, and I am sending you. So long as I am shaped like a human being, it is in me to dignify the possession of a vertical spine by acting as nearly like a man as I know how. I insist that you are my wife, because it crucifies me to think otherwise. I tell you to-night, Ruth, you are not and never have been. You are free as air. You married me without any love for me in your heart, and you pretended none. It was all my doing. If I find that I was wrong, I will free you without a thought of results to me. I am a secondary proposition. I thought then that you were alone and helpless. Before the Almighty, I did the best I could. But I know now that you are entitled to the love of relatives, wealth, and high social position, no doubt. If I allowed the passion in my heart to triumph over the reason of my brain, if I worked on your feelings and tied you to the woods, without knowing but that you might greatly prefer that other life you do not know, but to which you are entitled, I would go out and sink myself in Loon Lake."

"David, I love you. I do not want to go. Please, please let me remain with you."

"Not if you could say that realizing what it means, and give me the kiss right now I would stake my soul to win! Not by any bribe you can think of or any allurement you can offer. It is right that you go to those suffering old people. It is right you know what you are refusing for me, before you renounce it. It is right you take the position to which you are entitled, until you understand thoroughly whether this suits you better. When you know that life as well as this, the people you will meet as intimately as me, then you can decide for all time, and I can look you in the face with honest, unwavering eye. If by any chance your heart is in the woods, and you prefer me and the cabin to what they have to offer——to all eternity your place here is vacant, Ruth. My love is waiting for you; and if you come under those conditions, I never can have any regret. A clear conscience is worth restraining passion a few months to gain, besides, I always have got the fact to face that when you say 'I love,' and when I say 'I love,' it means two entirely different things. When you realize that the love of man for woman, and woman for man, is a thing that floods the heart, brain, soul, and body with a wonderful and all-pervading ecstasy, and if I happen to be the man who makes you realize it, then come tell me, and we will show God and His holy angels what earth means by the Heaven inspired word, 'radiance.'"

"David, there never will be any other man like you."

"The exigencies of life must develop many a finer and better."

"You still refuse me? You yet believe I do not love you?"

"Not with the love I ask, my girl. But if I did not believe it was germinating in your heart, that it would come pouring over me in a torrent some glad day, I doubt if I could allow you to go, Ruth! I am like any other man in selfishness and in the passions of the body."

"Selfishness! You haven't any idea what it means," said the Girl. "And what you call love——there I haven't. But I know how to appreciate you, so you may be positively sure that it will be only a few days until I shall come back to you."

"But I don't want you unless you can bring the love I crave. I am sending you to remain until that time, Ruth."

"But it may be months, Man!"

"Then stay months."

"But it may be——"

"It may be never! Then remain forever. That will be proof positive that your happiness does not lie in my hands."

"Why should I not consider you as you do me?"

"Because I love you, and you do not love me."

"You are cruel to yourself and to me. You talk about the pain in the world. What about the pain in my heart right now? And if I know you in the least, one degree more would make you cry aloud for mercy. Oh David, are we of no consideration at all?"

The muscles of the Harvester's face twisted an instant.

"This is where we lop off the small branches to grow perfect fruit later. This is where we do evil that good may result. This is where we suffer to-night in order we may appreciate fully the joy of love's dawning. If I am causing you pain, forgive me, dear heart. I would give my life to prevent it, but I am powerless. It is right! We cannot avoid doing it, if we ever would be happy."

He picked up the Girl, holding her crushed in his arms a long time. Then he set her inside her door and said: "Lay out what you want to take and I will help you pack, so that you can get some sleep. We must be ready early in the morning."

When the clothing to be worn was selected, the new trunk packed, and all arrangements made, the Girl sat in his arms before the fire as he had held her when she was ill; then he sent her to bed and went to the lake shore to fight it out alone. Only God, the stars and the faithful Belshazzar saw the agony of a strong man in his extremity.

Near dawn he heard the tinkle of the bell and went to receive his message and order a car for morning. Then he returned to the merciful darkness of night, pacing the driveway until light came peeping over the tree tops. He prepared breakfast, an hour later put the Girl on the train, then stood watching it until the last rift of smoke curled above the spires of the city.

CHAPTER XX

THE MAN IN THE BACKGROUND

THEN the Harvester returned to Medicine Woods to fight his battle alone. At first the pain seemed unendurable, but work always had been his panacea, it was his salvation now. He went through the cabin, folding bedding and storing it in closets, rolling rugs sprinkled with powdered alum, packing cushions, and taking window seats from the light.

"Our sleeping room and the kitchen will serve for us, Bel," he said. "We will put the other things away carefully, so they will be new when the Girl comes home."

The evening of the second day he was called to the telephone.

"There is a message from Philadelphia for you," said a voice. "It reads: 'Arrived safely. Thank you for making me come. Dear old people. Will write soon. With love, Ruth.' Have you got it?"

"No," lied the Harvester, grinning rapturously. "Repeat it slowly, and give me time to write it. Now! Go on!"

He carried the message to the back steps, reading it again and again.

"I supposed I'd have to wait at least four days," he said to Ajax as the bird circled before him. "This is from

451

the Girl, old man, and she is not forgetting us to begin with, anyway. She is there safely, she sees that they need her, they are lovable old people, she is going to write us about it soon, and she loves us all she knows how to love any one. That should be enough to keep us sane and sensible until her letter comes. There is no use to borrow trouble, so we will say everything in the world is right with us, and be as happy as we can on that until we find something we cannot avoid worrying over. In the meantime, we will have faith to believe that we have suffered our share, and the end will be happy for all of us. I am very glad the Girl has a home, and the right kind of people to care for her. Now, when she comes back to me, I needn't feel that she was forced, whether she wanted to or not, because she had nowhere to go. This will let me out with a clean conscience, which is the only thing on earth that allows a man to live in peace with himself. I'll go finish everything else; then I'll begin the ginseng harvest."

So the Harvester hitched Betsy and with Belshazzar at his feet he drove through the woods to the sarsaparilla beds. He noticed the beautiful lobed leaves, at which the rabbits had been nibbling, and the heads of lustrous purple-black berries as he began digging the roots that he sold for stimulants.

"I might have needed a dose of you now myself," the Harvester addressed a heap of uprooted plants, "if the electric wires hadn't brought me a better. Great invention that! Never before realized it fully! I thought to-day would be black as night, but that message changes the complexion of affairs mightily. So I'll dig you for people who really are in need of something to brace them up."

After the sarsaparilla was on the trays, he attacked the beds of Indian hemp, with its long graceful pods, and took his usual supply. Then he worked diligently on the warm hillside over the dandelion. When these were finished he brought half a dozen young men from the city and drilled them on handling ginseng. He was warm, dirty, and tired when he came from the beds the evening of the fourth day. He finished his work at the barn, prepared and ate his supper, slipped into clean clothing, and walked to the country road where it crossed the lane. There he opened his mail box. The letter he expected with the Philadelphia postmark was inside. He carried it to the bridge, and sitting in her favourite place, with the lake breeze threading his hair, opened his first letter from the Girl.

"My dear Friend, Lover, Husband," it began.

The Harvester turned the sheets face down across his knee, laid his hand on them, and stared meditatively at the lake. "'Friend,'" he commented. "Well, that's all right! I am her friend, as well as I know how to be. 'Lover.' I come in there, full force. I did my level best on that score, though I can't boast myself a howling success; a man can't do more than he knows; but if I had been familiar with all the wiles of expert, professional love-makers, they wouldn't have availed me in the Girl's condition. I had a peculiar case to handle in her, and not a particle of training. But if she says 'Lover,' I must have made some kind of a showing on the job. 'Hus band.'" A slow flush crept up the brawny neck and tinged the bronzed face. "That's a good word," said the Harvester, "and it must mean a wonderful thing——to some men. 'Who bides his time.' Well, I'm 'biding,' and if my time ever comes to be my Dream Girl's hus-band, I'll wager all I'm worth on one thing: I'll study the job from every point of the compass, and I'll see what showing I can make on being the kind of a husband that a woman clings to and loves at eighty."

Taking a deep breath the Harvester lifted the letter, and laying one hand on Belshazzar's head, he proceeded ——"I might as well admit in the beginning that I cried most of the way here. Some of it was because I was nervous and dreaded the people I would meet, and more on account of what I felt toward them, but most of it was because I did not want to leave you. I have been spoiled dreadfully! You have taught me so to depend on you——and for once I feel that I really can claim to have been an apt pupil——that it was like having the heart torn out of me to come. I want you to know this, because it will teach you that I have a little bit of appre-ciation of how good you are to me, and to all the world as well. I am glad that I almost cried myself sick over leaving you. I wish now I just had stood up in the car, and roared like a burned baby.

"But the tears I shed in fear of grandfather and grand-mother were wasted. They are a couple of dear old people. It would have been a crime to allow them to suf-fer more than they must of necessity. It all seems so

different when they talk; and when I see the home, luxuries, and friends my mother had, it appears utterly in-
comprehensible that she dared leave them for a stranger.
Probably the reason she did was because she was grandfather's daughter. He is gentle and tender some of the
time, but when anything irritates him, and something
does every few minutes, he breaks loose, and such another
explosion you never heard. It does not mean a thing,
and it seems to lower his tension enough to keep him from
bursting with palpitation of the heart or something, but
it is a strain for others. At first it frightened me dreadfully. Grandmother is so tiny and frail, so white in her
big bed, but when he is the very worst, she only smiles at
him, so I know he does not mean it. But, David, I
hope you never will get an idea that this would be a pleasant way for you to act, because it would not, and I never
would have the courage to offer you the love I have come
to find if you slammed a cane and yelled, 'demnation,' at
me. Grandmother says she does not mind at all, but I
wonder if she did not acquire the habit of lying in bed because it is easier to endure in a prostrate position.

"The house is so big I get lost; I do not know yet
which are servants and which friends; and there is a
steady stream of seamstresses and milliners making things
for me. Grandmother and father both think I will be
quite passable in appearance when I am what they call
'modishly dressed.' I think grandmother will forget
herself some day and leave her bed before she knows it,
in her eagerness to see how something appears. I could
not begin to tell you about all the lovely things to wear,

for every occasion under the sun, and they say these are only temporary, until some can be made especially for me.

"They divide the time in sections, and there is an hour to drive, I am to have a horse and ride later, and a time to shop, so long to visit grandmother, and set hours to sleep, dress, to be fitted, taken to see things, music lessons, and a dancing teacher. I think a longer day will have to be provided.

"I do not care anything about dancing. I know what would make me dance nicely enough for anything, but I am going to try the music, and see if I can learn just a few little songs and some old melodies for evening, when the work is done, the fire burns low, and you are resting on the rug. There is enough room for a piano between your door and the south wall and that corner seems vacant anyway. You would like it, David, I know, if I could play and sing just enough to put you to sleep nicely. It is in the back of my head that I will try to do every single thing, just as they want me to, for that will make them happy; but never forget that the instant I feel in my soul that your kiss is right on my lips, I am coming to you by lightning express; I told them so the first thing, and that I only came because you made me.

"They did not raise an objection, but I am not so dull that I cannot see they are trying to bind me to them from the very first with chains too strong to break. We had just one little clash. Grandfather was mightily pleased over what you told Mr. Kennedy about my never having been your wife, and that I was really free. There seems to be a man, the son of his partner, whom grandfather dearly loves, and he wants me to be friends with his friend. One can see at once what he is planning, because he said he was going to introduce me as Miss Jameson. I told him that would be creating a false impression, because I was a married woman; but he only laughed at me and went straight to doing it.

"Of course, I know why, but he is so terribly set I cannot stop him, so I shall have to tell people myself that I am a staid, old married lady. After all, I suppose I might as well let him go, if it pleases him. I shall know how to protect myself and any one else, from any mistakes concerning me; for in my heart I know what I know; what I cannot make you believe, but I will some day.

"I suspect you're harvesting the ginseng now. The roar and rush of the city seem strange, as if I never had heard it before, and I feel so crowded. I scarcely can sleep at night for the clamour of the cars, cabs, and throbbing life. Grandfather will not hear a word, and he just sputters and says 'demnation' when I try to tell him about you; but grandmother will listen, so I talk to her of you and Medicine Woods by the hour. She says she thinks you must be a wonderfully nice person. I haven't dared tell her yet the thing that will win her. She is so little and frail, and she has heart trouble so badly; but some day I shall tell her all about Chicago that I can, then of Uncle Henry, then about you and the oak, and that will make her love you as I do. There are so many things to do; they have sent for me three times. I shall tell them they must put you on the schedule, and give em so much time to write or I will upset the whole programme.

"I think you will like to know that Mr. Kennedy told grandfather all you said to him about my illness, for almost as soon as I came he brought a very wonderful man to my room. He asked many questions so I told him all about it, and what I had been doing. He made out a list of things to eat and exercises. I am being taken care of just as you did, so I will go on growing well and strong. The trouble is they are too good to me. I would just love to shuffle my feet in dead leaves, and lie on the grass this morning. I never got my swim in the lake. I will have to save that until next summer. He also told grandfather what you said about Uncle Henry. I think he was pleased that you tried to find him as soon as you knew. He let me see the letter Uncle Henry wrote; it was a vile thing——just such as he would write. It asked how much he would be willing to pay for information concerning his heir. I told grandfather all about it, and I saw the answer he wrote. I told him some things to say. One of them was that the honesty of a man without a price prevented the necessity of anything being paid to find me. The other was that you located my people yourself, and at once sent me to them against my wishes. I was determined he should know that. So Uncle Henry missed his revenge on you. He evidently thought he not only would hurt you by breaking up your home and separating us, but also he would get a reward for his work. He wrote some untrue things about you. I wish he hadn't, for grandfather can think of enough himself. But I will soon change that. Please, please take good care of all my things, my flowers and vines, and most of all tell Belshazzar to protect you with his life. And you be very good to my dear, dear lover. I will write again soon, Ruth."

When the Harvester had studied the letter until he could repeat it backward, he went to the cabin and answered it. Then he sent subscriptions for two of Philadelphia's big dailies, and harvested ginseng from dawn until black darkness. Never was such a crop grown in America. The beds had been made in the original home of the plant, so that it throve under perfectly natural conditions in the forest, but here and there branches had been thinned above, and nature helped by science below. This resulted in thick, pulpy roots of astonishing size and weight. As the Harvester lifted them he bent the tops and buried part of the seed for another crop. For weeks he worked over the bed. Then the last load went down the hill to the dry-house and the helpers were paid. Next the fall work was finished. Fuel and food were stored for winter, while the cold crept from the lake, swept down the hill and surrounded the cabin.

The Harvester finished long days in the dry-house and storeroom, then after supper he sat by the fire reading over the Girl's letters, carving on her candlesticks, or in the workroom, bending above the boards he was shaving and polishing for a gift he had planned for her Christmas. The Careys had him in their home for Thanksgiving. He told them all about sending the Girl away himself, read them some of her letters, and they talked with perfect assurance of how soon she would come home. The Harvester tried to think confidently, but as the days went by the letters became fewer, always with the excuse that there was no time to write, but with loving assurance that she was thinking of him and would do better soon.

However they came often enough that he had something new to tell his friends so that they did not suspect that waiting was a trial to him. A few days after Thanksgiving the gift that he had planned was finished. It was a big, burl-maple box, designed after the hope chests that he saw advertised in magazines. The wood was rare, cut in heavy slabs, polished inside and out, dovetailed corners with ornate brass bindings, hinges and lock, and hand-carved feet. On the inside of the lid cut on a brass plate was the inscription, "Ruth Langston, Christmas of Nineteen Hundred and Ten. David."

Then he began packing the chest. He put in the finished candlesticks and a box of candleberry dips he had made of delightfully spiced wax, coloured pale green. He ordered the doll weeks before from the largest store in Onabasha. The dealer brought on several that he might make a selection. He chose a large baby doll almost life size, then sent it to the dress-making department to be completely and exquisitely clothed. Long before the day he was picking kernels to glaze from nuts, drying corn to pop, and planning candies to be made of maple sugar. When he figured it was time to start the box, he worked carefully, filling spaces with chestnut and hazel burs, and finishing the tops of boxes with gaudy red and yellow leaves he had kept in their original brightness by packing them in sand. He put in scarlet berries of mountain ash and long twining sprays of yellow and red bitter-sweet berries, for her room. Then he carefully covered the chest with cloth, packed it in an outside box, and sent it to the Girl by express. As he came from the train shed, where he had helped with loading, he met Henry Jameson. Instantly the long arm of the Harvester reached for him. In a grip that could not be broken he caught the man by the back of the neck and dangled him. As he did so he roared with laughter.

"Dear Uncle Henry!" he cried. "How did you feel when you got your letter from Philadelphia? Wasn't it a crime that an honest man, which same refers to me, beat you? Didn't you gnash your teeth when you learned that instead of separating me from my wife I had found her people and sent her to them myself? Didn't it rend your soul to miss your little revenge and fail to get the good, fat reward you confidently expected? Ho! Ho! Thus are lofty souls downcast. I pity you, Henry Jameson, but not so much that I won't break your back if you meddle in my affairs again, and I am taking this opportunity to tell you so. Here you go out of my life, for if you appear in it once more I will finish you like a copperhead. Understand?" With a last shake the Harvester dropped him, and went into the express office, where several men had watched the proceedings.

"Been dipping in your affairs, has he?" asked the expressman.

"Trying it," laughed the Harvester. .

"Well he is just moving to Idaho, so you probably won't be bothered with him any more."

"Good news!" said the Harvester. He felt much relieved as he drove back to Medicine Woods.

The Careys had invited him, but he chose to spend Christmas alone. He had finished breakfast when the telephone bell rang, and the expressman told him there was a package for him from Philadelphia. The Harvester rode to the city at once. The package was so very small he slipped it into his pocket, then went to the doctor's to say Merry Christmas! To Mrs. Carey he gave a pretty lavender silk dress; to the doctor a new watch chain. Then he went to the hospital, where he left with Molly a set of china dishes from the Girl, and a fur-lined great coat, his gift to Doctor Harmon. He rode home and stabled Betsy, giving her an extra quart of oats, then going into the house he sat by the kitchen fire and opened the package.

In a nest of cotton lay a tissue-wrapped velvet box; inside that, in a leather pocket case, an ivory miniature of the Girl by an artist who knew how to reproduce life. It was an exquisite picture; a face of wonderful beauty. He looked at it for a long time; then called Belshazzar and carried it out to show Ajax. Then he put it into his breast pocket squarely over his heart, but he wore the case shiny the first day taking it out. Before noon he went to the mail box and found a long letter from the Girl, full of life, health, happiness, and with assurances of love for him, but no mention of coming home.

She seemed engrossed in the music lessons, riding,

dancing, pretty clothing, splendid balls, receptions, and parties of all kinds. The Harvester answered it with his heart full of love for her, and then waited. It was a long week before the reply came, and then it was short on account of so many things that must be done, but she insisted that she was well, happy, and having a fine time. After that the letters became less frequent and shorter. At times there would be stretches of almost two weeks with not a line; then only short notes to explain that she was too busy to write.

Through the dreary, cold days of January and February the Harvester invented work in the storeroom, in the workshop, at the candlesticks, sat long over great books, or spent hours in the little laboratory preparing and compounding drugs. In the evenings he carved or read. First of all he scanned the society columns of the papers he was taking, and almost every day he found the name of Miss Ruth Jameson, often a paragraph describing her dress and her beauty of face and charm of manner; while constantly the name of Mr. Herbert Kennedy appeared as her escort. At first the Harvester ignored this, saying to himself that he was glad she could have enjoyable times and congenial friends, and he was. But as the letters became fewer, paper paragraphs more frequent, and approaching spring worked its old insanity in the blood, gradually an ache crept into his heart again, and there were days when he could not work it out.

Every letter she wrote he answered just as warmly as he felt that he dared, but when they were so long coming and his heart was overflowing, he picked up a pen one night and wrote what he felt. He told her all about the ice-bound lake, the lonely crows in the big woods, the sap suckers' cry, and the gay cardinals' whistle. He told her about the cocoons dangling on bushes or rocking on twigs that he was cutting for her. He warned her that spring was coming, and soon she would begin to miss wonders for her pencil. Then he told her about the silent cabin, the empty rooms, and a lonely man. He begged her not to forget the kiss she had gone to find for him. He poured out his heart unrestrainedly, then folded the letter, sealed and addressed it to her, in care of the fire fairies, and pitched it into the ashes of the living-room fireplace. But expression made him feel better.

There was another longer wait for the next letter, but he had written her so many in the meantime that a little heap of them had accumulated as he passed through the living-room on his way to bed. He had supposed she would be gone until after Christmas when she left, but he never had thought of harvesting sassafras and opening the sugar camp alone. In those days his face appeared weary, while white hairs came again on his temples. Carey met him on the street and told him that he was going to the National Convention of Surgeons at New York in March, and asked him to go along and present his new medicine for consideration.

"All right," said the Harvester instantly, "I will go."

He went and interviewed Mrs. Carey; then visited the doctor's tailor, and a shoe store, buying everything required to put him in condition for travelling in good style,

and for the banquet he would be invited to attend.   Then
he got Mrs. Carey to coach him on spoons and forks,
and declared he was ready.   When the doctor saw that
the Harvester really would go, he sat down and wrote
the president of the association, telling him in brief outline of Medicine Woods and the man who had achieved a
wonderful work there, and of the compounding of the new
remedy.

As he expected, return mail brought an invitation for
the Harvester to address the association and describe his
work and methods and present his medicine.   The doctor went out in the car over sloppy roads with that letter,
locating the Harvester in the sugar camp.   He explained
the situation and to his surprise found his man intensely
interested.   He asked many questions as to the length of
time, and amount of detail required in a proper paper, so
the doctor told him.

"But if you want to make a clean sweep, David," he
said, "write your paper simply, then practise until it
comes easy before you speak."

That night the Harvester left work long enough to
get a notebook, and by the light of the camp fire, in company with the owls and coons, he wrote his outline.   One
division described his geographical location, another
traced his ancestry and education in wood lore.   One
was a tribute to the mother who moulded his character
and ground into him stability for his work.   The remainder described his methods in growing drugs, drying
and packing them; the end was a presentation for their
examination of the remedy that had given life where a

great surgeon had conceded death. Then he began amplification.

When the sugar making was over the Harvester commenced his regular spring work, but his mind was so busy over his paper that he did not have much time to realize just how badly his heart was beginning to ache. Neither did he consign so many letters to the fire fairies, for now he was writing of the best way to dry hydrastis and preserve ginseng seed. The day before time to start he drove to Onabasha to try on his clothing and have Mrs. Carey see if he had been right in his selections.

While he was gone, Granny Moreland, wearing a clean calico dress and carrying a juicy apple pie, came to the stretch of flooded marsh land; finding the path under water, she followed the road and crossing a field reached the levee which led to the bridge of Singing Water where it entered the lake. She rested a few minutes there, and then went to the cabin. She opened the front door, entered, and stood staring around her.

"Why things is all tore up here," she said. "Now ain't that sensible of David to put everything away and save it nice and careful until his woman gets back. Seems as if she's good and plenty long coming; seems as if her folks needs her mighty bad, or she's having a better time than the boy is or something."

She set the pie on the table, went through the cabin and up the hill a short distance, calling the Harvester. When she passed the barn she missed Betsy, so she knew he was in town. She returned to the living-room and sat looking at the pie as she rested.

"I'd best put you on the kitchen table," she mused. "Likely he will see you there first and eat you while you are fresh. I'd hate mortal bad for him to overlook you, and let you get stale, after all the care I've took with your crust, and all the sugar, cinnamon, and butter that's under your lid. You're a mighty nice pie, so you ort to be et hot. Now why under the sun is all them clean letters pitched in the fireplace?"

Granny knelt and selecting one, she blew off the ashes, and read: "To Ruth, in care of the fire fairies."

"What the Sam Hill is the idiot writin' his woman like that for?" cried Granny, bristling instantly. "And why is he puttin' pages and pages of good reading like this must have in it in care of the fire fairies? Too much alone, I guess! He's going wrong in his head. Nobody at themselves would do sech a fool trick as this. I believe I had better do something. Of course I had! These is writ to Ruth; she ort to have them. Wish't I knowed how she gets her mail, I'd send her some. Mebby three! I'd send a fat and a lean, and a middlin' so's that she'd have a sample of all the kinds they is. It's no way to write letters and pitch them in the ashes. It means the poor boy is honin' to say things he dassent, so he's writin' them out and never sendin' them at all. What's the little huzzy gone so long for, anyway? I'll fix her!"

Granny selected three letters, wiped away the ashes, and tucked the envelopes inside her dress.

"If I only knowed how to get at her," she muttered. She stared at the pie. "I guess you got to go back," she said, "and be et by me. Like as not I'll stall myself, for

I got one a-ready. But if David has got these fool things counted and misses any, and then finds that pie here, he'll s'picion me. Yes, I got to take you back, and hurry my stumps at that."

Granny arose with the pie, cast a lingering and covetous glance at the fireplace, stooped and took another letter; then started down the drive. Just as she reached the bridge she saw the Harvester coming up the levee. Instantly she threw the pie over the railing, then with a groan watched it strike the water and disappear.

"Lord of love!" she gasped, sinking to the seat, "that was one of grandmother's willer plates that I promised Ruth. 'Tain't likely I'll ever see hide ner hair of it again. But they wa'ant no place to put it, and I dassent let him know I'd been up to the cabin. Mebby I can fetch a boy some day and hire him to dive for it. How long can a plate be in water and not get spiled anyway? Now what'll I do? My head's all in a whirl! I'll bet my bosom is a sticking out with his letters 'til he'll notice and take them from me."

She gripped her hands across her chest, then sat staring at the Harvester as he stopped on the bridge. Seeing her attitude and distressed face, he sprang from the wagon.

"Why Granny, are you sick?" he cried anxiously.

"Yes!" gasped Granny Moreland. "Yes, David, I am! I'm a miserable woman. I never was in sech a shape in all my days."

"Let me help you to the cabin, and I'll see what I can do for you," offered the Harvester.

"No. This is jest out of your reach," said the old lady. "I want——I want to see Doctor Carey bad."

"Are you strong enough to ride in or shall I bring him?"

"I can go as well as not, David, if you'll take me."

"Let me run Betsy to the barn and get the Girl's phaeton. The wagon is too rough for you."

The Harvester leaped into the wagon, catching up the lines. As he disappeared around the curve of the driveway Granny snatched the letters from her dress front, thrusting them deep into one of her stockings.

"Now, drat you!" she cried. "Stick out all you please. Nobody will see you there."

In a few minutes the Harvester helped her into the carriage and drove rapidly toward the city.

"You needn't strain your critter," said Granny. "It's not so bad as that, David."

"Is your chest any better?"

"A sight better," said Granny. "Shakin' up a little 'pears to do me good."

"You never should have tried to walk. Suppose I hadn't been here. I'll have a telephone run to your house so you can call me after this."

Granny sat very straight suddenly.

"My! wouldn't that get away with some of my foxy neighbours," she said. "Me to have a 'phone like they do, an' be conversin' at all hours of the day with my son's folks and everybody. I'd be tickled to pieces."

"Then I'll never dare do it," said the Harvester, "because I can't keep house without you."

"Where's your own woman?" promptly inquired Granny.

"She can't leave her people. Her grandmother is sick."

"Grandmother your foot!" cried the old woman. "I've been hearing that song and dance from the neighbours, but you got to fool younger people than me on it, David. When did any grandmother ever part a pair of youngsters jest married, for months at a clip? I'd like to cast my eyes on that grandmother. She's a new breed! I was as good a mother as 'twas in my skin to be, and I'd like to see a child of mine do it for me; and as for my grandchildren, it hustles some of them to re-cog-nize me passing on the big road, 'specially if it's Peter's girl with a town beau."

The Harvester laughed. The old lady leaned toward him with a quaver in her voice, and asked softly: "Got ary friend that could help you, David?"

The man looked straight ahead in silence.

"Bamfoozle all the rest of them as much as you please, lad, but I stand to you in the place of your ma; so I ast you plainly——*got ary friend that could help?*"

"I can think of no way in which any one possibly could help me, dear," said the Harvester gently. "It is a matter I can't explain, but I know of nothing that any one could do."

"You mean you're tight-mouthed! You *could* tell me just like you would your ma, if she was up and comin'; but you can't quite put me in her place, and spit it out plain. Now mebby I can help you! Is it her fault or yourn?"

"Mine! Mine entirely!"

"Hum! What a fool question! I might a knowed it!
I never saw a lovinger, sweeter girl in these parts. I jest
worship the ground she treads on; and you, lad, you
hain't had a heart in your body sence first you saw her
face. If I had the stren'th, I'd haul you out of this keer-
idge and I'd hammer you meller, David Langston. What
in the name of sense have you gone and done to the purty,
lovin' child?"

The Harvester's face flushed, but a line around his
mouth whitened.

"Loosen up!" commanded Granny. "I got some rights
in this case that mebby you don't remember. You asked
me to help you get ready for her, so I done what you
wanted. You invited me to visit her, and I jest loved
her sweet, purty ways. You wanted me to shet up my
house and come over for weeks to help take keer of her,
and I done it gladly, for her pain and your sufferin' cut
me as if 'twas my livin' flesh and blood; so you can't
shet me out now. I'm in with you and her to the end.
What a blame fool thing have you gone and done to drive
away for months a girl that fair worshipped you?"

"That's exactly the trouble, Granny," said the Harvester. "She didn't! She merely respected and was
grateful to me, and she loved me as a friend; but I never
was any nearer her husband than I am yours."

"I've always knowed they was a screw loose somewhere," commented Granny. "And so you've sent her
off to her worldly folks in a big, wicked city to get weaned
away from you complete?"

"I sent her to let her see if absence would teach her

anything. I had months with her here, and I lay awake
at nights thinking up new plans to win her. I worked
for her love as I never worked for bread, but I couldn't
make it. So I let her go to see if separation would teach
her anything."

"Mercy me! Why you crazy critter! The child did
love you! She loved you 'nough an' plenty! She loved
you faithful and true! You was jest the light of her eyes.
I don't see how a girl could think more of a man. What
in the name of sense are you expecting months of separation to teach her, but to forget you, and mebby turn
her to some one else?"

"I hoped it would teach her what I call love, means,"
explained the Harvester.

"Why you dratted popinjay! If ever in all my born
days I wanted to take a man and jest lit'rally mop up
the airth with him, it's right here and now. 'Absence
teach her what you call love.' Idiot! That's your job!"

"But, Granny, I couldn't!"

"Wouldn't, you mean, no doubt! I hain't no manner
of a notion in my head but that child, depending on you,
and grateful as she was, and tender and loving, and all
sech as that——I hain't a doubt but she come to you
plain and told you she loved you with all her heart. What
more could you ast?"

"That she understand what love means before I can
accept what she offers."

"You puddin' head! You blunderbuss!" cried Granny.
"Understand what you mean by love. If you're going
to bar a woman from being a wife 'til she knows what

you mean by love, you'll stop about nine-tenths of the weddings in the world, and t'other tenth will be women that no decent-minded man would jine with."

"Granny, are you sure?"

"Well livin' through it, and up'ard of seventy years with other women, ort to teach me something.   The Girl offered you all any man needs to ast or git.   Her foundations was laid in faith and trust.   Her affections was caught by every loving, tender, thoughtful thing you did for her; and everybody knows you did a-plenty, David. I never see sech a master hand at courtin' as you be.   You had her lovin' you all any good woman knows how to love a man.   All you needed, to a-done was to take her in your arms, and make her your wife, and she'd 'a' waked up to what you meant by love."

"But suppose she never awakened?"

"Aw, bosh!   S'pose water won't wet!   S'pose fire won't burn!   S'pose the sun won't shine!   That's the law of nature, man!   If you think I hain't got no sense at all I jest dare you to ask Doctor Carey.   'Twouldn't take him long to comb the kinks out of you."

"I don't think you have left any, Granny," said the Harvester.   "I see what you mean, and in all probability you are right, but I can't send for the Girl."

"Name o' goodness why?"

"Because I sent her away against her will.   Now she is remaining so long that there is every probability she prefers the life she is living and the friends she has made there, to Medicine Woods and to me.   The only thing I can do is to await her decision."

"Oh good Lord!" groaned Granny. "You make me sick enough to kill. Touch up your nag and hustle me to Doc. You can't get me there quick enough to suit me."

At the hospital she faced Doctor Carey. "I think likely some of my innards has got to be cut out and mended," she said. "I'll jest take a few minutes of your time to examination me, and see what you can do."

In the private office she held the letters toward the doctor. "They hain't no manner of sickness ailin' me, Doc. The boy out there is in deep water. I knowed how much you thought of him, so I hoped you'd give me a lift. I went over to his place this mornin' to take him a pie, and I found his settin' room fireplace heapin' with letters he'd writ to Ruth about things his heart was jest so bustin' full of it eased him to write them down, and then he hadn't the horse sense and trust in her jedgment to send them on to her. I picked two fats, a lean, and a middlin' for samples, and I thought I'd send them some way, so I struck for home with them an' he ketched me plumb on the bridge. I had to throw my pie overboard, willer plate and all, and as God is my witness, I was so flustered the boy had good reason to think I was sick a-plenty; and soon as he noticed it, I thought of you spang off. I knowed you'd know her whereabouts, so I made him fetch me to you. On the way I jest dragged it from him that he'd sent her away his fool self, because she didn't sense what he meant by love, and she wa'ant beholden to him same degree and manner he was to her. Great day, Doc! Did you ever hear a piece of foolishness to come up with that? I told him to ast you! I told him you'd tell him that no clean, sweet-minded girl ever had known nor ever would know what love means to a man 'til he marries her and teaches her. Ain't it so, Doc?"

" It certainly is."

"Then will you grind it into him, clean to the marrer, and will you send these letters on to Ruthie?"

"Most certainly I will," said the doctor emphatically.

Granny opened the door and walked out: "I'm so relieved, David," she said. "He thinks they won't be no manner o' need to knife me. Likely he can fix up a few pills and send them out by mail so's that I'll be as good as new again. Now we must get right out of here and not take valuable time. What do I owe you, Doc?"

"Not a cent," said Doctor Carey. "Thank you very much for coming to me. You'll soon be all right again."

"I was some worried. Much obliged I am sure."

"One minute," said the doctor. "David, I am making up a list of friends to whom I am going to send programmes of the medical meeting, and I thought your wife might like to see you among the speakers, and your subject. What is her address?"

A slow red flushed the Harvester's cheeks. He opened his lips and hesitated. At last he said: "I think perhaps her people prefer that she receive mail under her maiden name while with them. Miss Ruth Jameson, care of Alexander Herron, 5770 Chestnut Street, Philadelphia, will reach her."

The doctor wrote the address, as if it were the most usual thing in the world, then asked the Harvester if he were ready to make the trip east. "I think we had best start to-night," he said. "We want a day to grow accustomed to our clothes and new surroundings before we run up squarely against serious business."

"I will be ready," promised the Harvester.

He took Granny home, set his house in order, installed the man he was leaving in charge, touched a match to the heap in the fireplace, and donning the new travelling suit, he went to Doctor Carey's.

Mrs. Carey added a few touches, warned him to remember about the forks and spoons, and not to forget to shave often, and saw them off. At the station Carey said to him: "You know, David, we can change at Wayne and go through Buffalo, or we can take the Pittsburg and go and come through Philadelphia."

"I am contemplating a trip to Philadelphia," said the Harvester, "but I believe I shall not be ready for, say a month yet. I have a theory which dies hard. If it does not work out the coming month, I will go, perhaps, but not now. Let us see how many kinds of a fool I make of myself in New York before I attempt the Quakers."

Almost to the city, the doctor smiled at the Harvester: "David, where did you get your infernal assurance?" he asked.

"In the woods," answered the Harvester placidly. "In doing clean work. With my fingers in the muck, with life literally teeming and boiling in sound and action, around, above, and beneath me, a right estimate of my place and province comes naturally. In daily handling stores on which humanity depends, I go even deeper than you surgeons and physicians. You are powerless unless

I reinforce your work with drugs on which you can rely. I do clean, honest work. I know its proper place and value to the world. That is why I called what I have to say, 'The Man in the Background.' There is no reason why I should shiver and shrink at meeting and explaining my work to my fellows. Every man has his vocation, and some of you in the limelight would cut a sorry figure if the man in the background should fail you at the critical moment. Don't worry about me, Doc. I am all serene. You won't find I possess either nerves or fear. 'Be sure you are right, and then go ahead,' is my law."

"Well I'll be confounded!" said the doctor.

In a large hall, peopled with thousands of medical men, the name of the Harvester was called the following day and his subject was announced. He arose in his place and began to talk.

"Take the platform," roared a hundred throats.

The Harvester hesitated.

"You must, David," whispered Carey.

The Harvester made his way forward, was guided through a side door, and a second later calmly walked down the big stage to the front, and stood at ease looking over his audience, as if to gauge its size and the pitch to which he should raise his voice. His lean frame loomed every inch of his six feet, his broad shoulders were square, his clean shaven face alert and afire.

"This scarcely seems compatible with my subject," he remarked casually. "I certainly appear very much in the foreground just at present, but perhaps that is quite as well. It may be time that I assert myself. I doubt if

there is a man among you who has not handled my products more or less; you may enjoy learning where and how
they are prepared, and understanding the manner in
which my work merges with yours. I think perhaps
the first thing is to paint you as good a word picture as
I can of my geographical location."

Then the Harvester named latitude and longitude
and degrees of temperature. He described the lake, the
marsh, the wooded hill, the swale, and open sunny fields.
He spoke of water, soil, shade, and geographical conditions.
"Here I was born," he said, "on land owned by my father
and grandfather before me, and previous to them, by the
Indians. My male ancestors, so far as I can trace them,
were men of the woods, hunters, trappers, herb gatherers.
My mother was from the country, educated for a teacher.
She had the most inexorable will of any woman I ever
have known. From my father I inherited my love for
muck on my boots, resin in my nostrils, the long trail,
the camp fire, forest sounds and silences in my soul.
From my mother I learned to read good books, to study
subjects that puzzled me, to tell the truth, to keep my soul
and body clean, and to pursue with courage the thing to
which I set my hand.

"There was not money enough to educate me as she
would; together we learned to find it in the forest. In
early days we sold ferns and wild flowers to city people,
harvested the sap of the maples in spring, and the nut
crop of the fall. Later, as we wanted more, we trapped
for skins, and collected herbs for the drug stores. This
opened to me a field I was peculiarly fitted to enter. I

knew woodcraft instinctively, I had the location of every
herb, root, bark, and seed that will endure my climate;
I had the determination to stick to my job, the right
books to assist me, and my mother's invincible will power
to uphold me where I wavered.

"As I look into your faces, men, I am struck with the
astounding thought that some woman bore the cold
sweat and pain of labour to give life to each of you.   I
hope few of you prolonged that agony as I did.   It was
in the heart of my mother to make me physically clean.
To that end she sent me daily into the lake, so long as it
was not ice covered, and put me at exercises intended to
bring full strength to every sinew and fibre of my body.
It was in her heart to make me morally clean, so she took
me to nature and drilled me in its forces and its methods of
reproducing life according to the law.   Her work was
good to a point that all men will recognize.   From there
on, for a few years, she held me, not because I was man
enough to stand, but because she was woman enough to
support me.   Without her no doubt I would have broken
the oath I took; with her I won the victory and reached
years of manhood and self-control as she would have had
me.   The struggle wore her out at half a lifetime, but as a
tribute to her memory I cannot face a body of men having
your opportunities without telling you that what was
possible to her and to me is possible to all mothers and men.
If she is above and hears me perhaps it will recompense
some of her shortened years if she knows I am pleading
with you, as men having the greatest influence of any
living, to tell and to teach the young that a clean life

is possible to them. The next time any of you are called upon to address a body of men tell them to learn for themselves and to teach their sons, and to hold them at the critical hour, even by sweat and blood, to a clean life; for in this way only can feeble-minded homes, almshouses, and the scarlet woman be abolished. In this way only can men arise to full physical and mental force, and become the fathers of a race to whom the struggle for clean manhood will not be the battle it is with us.

"By the distorted faces, by the misshapen bodies, by marks of degeneracy, recognizable to your practised eyes everywhere on the streets, by the agony of the mother who bore you, and later wept over you, I conjure you men to live up to your high and holy privilege, and tell all men that they can be clean, if they will. This in memory of the mother who shortened her days to make me a moral man. And if any among you is the craven to plead immorality as a safeguard to health, I ask, what about the health of the women you sacrifice to shield your precious bodies, and I offer my own as the best possible refutation of that cowardly lie. I never have been ill a moment in all my life, and strength never has failed me for work to which I set my hand.

"The rapidly decreasing supply of drugs and the adulterated importations early taught me that the day was coming when it would be an absolute necessity to raise our home supplies. So, while yet in my teens, I began collecting from the fields and woods for miles around such medicinal stuff as grew in my father's fields, marsh, and woods, and planting more wherever I found anything growing naturally in its prime. I merely enlarged nature's beds and preserved their natural condition. As the plants spread and the harvest increased, I built a dry-house on scientific principles, a large storeroom, and later a laboratory in which I have been learning to prepare some of my crude material for the market, combining ideas of my own in remedies, and at last producing one your president has just indicated that I come to submit to you as a final resort in certain conditions.

"My operations now have spread to close six hundred acres of almost solid medicinal growth, including a little lake, around the shores of which flourish a quadruple setting of water-loving herbs."

Occasionally he shifted his position or easily walked across the platform and faced his audience from a different direction. His voice was strong, deep, and rang clearly and earnestly. His audience sat on the front edge of their chairs, and listened to something new, with mouths half agape. A few times Carey turned from the speaker to face the audience. He agonized in his heart that it was a closed session, that his wife was not there to hear, and that the Girl was missing it.

By the bent backs and flying fingers of the reporters at their table in front he could see that to-morrow the world would read the Harvester's speech; and if it were true that the little mother had shortened her days to produce him, she had done earth a service for which many generations would call her blessed. For the doctor could look ahead, and he knew that this man would not escape. The call for him and his unimpeachable truth would come from everywhere, and his utterances would carry as far as newspapers and magazines were circulated. The good he would do would be past estimation.

The Harvester continued. He was describing the most delicate and difficult of herbs to secure. He was telling how they could be raised, prepared, kept, and compounded. He was discussing diseases that did not readily yield to treatment, pointing out what drugs were customarily employed and offering, if any of them had such cases, and would send to him, to forward samples of unadulterated stuff sufficient for a test comparison with what they were using. He was walking serenely and surely into the heart of every man before him.

Just at the point where it was the psychological time to close, he stopped, standing a long instant facing them, then he asked: "Did any man among you ever see the woman to whom he had given a strong man's first passion of love, slowly dying before him?"

One breathless instant he waited, then continued: "Gentlemen, I recently saw this in my own case. For days it was coming, so at night I shut myself in my laboratory, and from the very essence of the purest of my self-compounded drugs I distilled a stimulant into which I put a touch of heart remedy, a brace for weakening nerves, a vitalization of sluggish blood. As I worked, I thought in that thought which embodied the essence of prayer, so when my day and my hour came, and a man who has been the president of your honourable body, and is known to all of you, said it was death, I took this combination that I now present to you, and with the help of the Almighty and a woman above the price of rubies, I kept breath in the girl I love. To-day she is at full tide of womanhood. As a thank offering, the formula is yours. Test it as you will. Use it if you find it good. Gentlemen, I thank you!"

Carey sank in his chair, watching the Harvester cross the stage. As he disappeared the tumult began, and it lasted until the president arose and brought him back to make another bow. In an immaculate dress suit the Harvester sat that night on the right of the gray-haired president and responded to the toast, "The Harvester of the Woods." Then the reporters carried him away to be photographed, and to show him the gay sights of New York.

In the train the following day, speeding west, he said to Doctor Carey: "I feel as the old woman of Mother Goose who said: 'Lawk-a-mercy on us, can this be really I?'"

"You just bet it is!" cried the doctor. "And you have cut out work for yourself in good shape."

"What do you mean?"

"I mean that this is a beginning. You will be called upon to speak again and again."

"The point is, do you honestly think I helped any?"

"You did inestimable good. It only can help men to hear plain truth that is personal experience. As for that dope of yours, it will come closer raising the dead than anything I ever saw. Next case I see slipping, after I've done my best, I'm going to try it out for myself."

"All right! 'Phone me and I'll bring some fresh and help you."

At Buffalo the doctor left the car to buy a paper. As he had expected the portrait and speech of the Harvester were featured. The reporters had been gracious. They had done all that was just to a great event, then allowed themselves some latitude. He immediately mailed the paper to the Girl, and at Cleveland bought another for himself. When he showed it to the Harvester, as he glanced at it he observed: "Do I appear like that?" Then he continued talking with a man he had met who interested him.

CHAPTER XXI

THE COMING OF THE BLUEBIRD

THE Harvester stopped at the mail box on his way home; among the mass of matter it contained was something from the Girl. It was a scrap as long as his least finger and three times as wide; by the postmark it had lain four days in the box. On opening it, he found only her card with a line written across it, but the man went up the hill and into the cabin as if a cyclone were driving him, for he read: "Has your bluebird come?"

He threw his travelling bag on the floor, ran to the telephone, and called the station. "Take this message," he said. "Mrs. David Langston, care of Alexander Herron, 5770 Chestnut Street, Philadelphia. Found note after four days' absence. Bluebird long past due. The fairies have told it that my fate hereafter lies in your hands. As always. David."

The Harvester turned from the instrument and bent to embrace Belshazzar, leaping in ecstasy beside him.

"Understand that, Bel?" he asked. "I don't know but it means something. Maybe it doesn't——not a thing! And again, there is a chance——only the merest possibility——that it does. We'll risk it, Bel, and to begin on I have nailed it as hard as I knew how. Next, we will

485

clean the house——until it shines; then we will fill the
cupboard, so if anything does happen we won't be caught
napping. Yes, boy, we will take the chance! We can't
be any worse disappointed than we have been before and
survived it. Come along!''

He picked up the bag and arranged its contents, carefully brushed and folded, on his shelves and in his closet.
Then he removed the travelling suit, donned the old
brown clothes and went to the barn to see that his creatures had been cared for properly. Early the following
morning he awoke and after feeding and breakfasting
instead of going to harvest spice brush and alder he
stretched a line and hung the bedding from room after
room to air and sun. He swept, dusted, and washed
windows, made beds, and lastly polished the floors throughout the cabin. He set everything in order, then as a
finishing touch, filled vases, pitchers, and bowls with the
bloom of red bud and silky willow catkins. He searched
the south bank, but there was not a violet, even in the
most exposed places. The next day he worked scrubbing
the porches, straightening the lawn and hedges, even
sweeping the driveway to the bridge clear of wind-whirled
leaves and straw. He scouted around the dry-house and
laboratory, then spent several extra hours on the barn so
that when evening came everything was in perfect order.
Then he dressed, ate his supper and drove to the city.

He stopped at the mail box, but there was nothing
from the Girl. The Harvester did not know whether
he was sorry or glad. A letter might have said the same
thing. Nothing meant a delightful possibility; between

the two he preferred the latter. He whistled or sang as he drove to Onabasha, while Belshazzar looked at him with mystified eyes, for this was not the master he had known of late. He did not recognize the dress or the manner, but his dog heart was sympathetic to the man's every mood, for he remembered times when a drive down the levee always had been like this. To-night the Harvester's tongue was loosened and he talked in the old way.

"Only four words, Bel," he said. "And as I remarked before, they may mean the most wonderful thing on earth, and possibly nothing at all. But it is in the heart of man to hope, Bel, so we are going to live royally for a week or two, merely on hope, old boy. If anything should happen, we are ready, rooms shining, beds fresh, fireplaces filled and waiting a match, ice chest cool, and when we get back it will be stored. Also a secret, Bel: we are going to a florist and a fruit store. While we are at it, we will do the thing right; but we will stay away from Doc, until we are sure of something. He means well, but we don't like to be pitied, do we, Bel? Our friends don't manage their eyes and voices very well these days. Never mind! Our time will come yet. The bluebird will not fail us, but never before has it been so late."

On his return he filled the pantry shelves with packages, stored the ice chest, and set a basket of delicious fruit on the dining table. Two boxes remained. He opened the larger one, taking from it an armload of white lilies that he carried up the hill and divided between the mounds under the oak. Then he uncovered his head, and standing at the foot of them he looked among the boughs of the big tree, listening intently. After a time a soft, warm wind, catkin-scented, crept from the lake, and began a murmur among the clusters of brown leaves clinging to the branches.

"Mother," said the Harvester, "were you with me? Did I do it right? Did I tell them what you would have had me say for the boys? Are you glad now you held me to the narrow way? Do you want me to go before men if I am asked, as Doc says I will be, and tell them that the only way to abolish pain is for them to begin at the foundation by living clean lives? I don't know if I did any good, but they listened to me. Anyway, I did the best I knew. But that isn't strange; you ground it into me to do that every day, until it is almost an instinct. Mother, dear, can you tell me about the bluebird? Is that softest little rustle of all your voice? and does it say 'hope?' I think so, and I thank you for the word."

The man's gaze dropped to earth.

"And you other mother," he said, "have you any message for me? Up where you are can you sweep the world with understanding eyes and tell me why my bluebird does not come? Does it know that this year your child and not chance must settle my fate? Can you look across space and see if she is even thinking of me? But I know that! She had to be thinking of me when she wrote that line. Rather can you tell me——will she come? Do you think I am man enough to be trusted with her future, if she does? One thing I promise you: if such joy ever comes to me, I will know how to meet it gently, thankfully,

tenderly, please God.   Good night, little women.   I hope
you are sleeping well——"

He turned and went down the hill, entered the cabin
and took from the other box a mass of Parma violets.
He put these in the pink bowl, placing it on the table
beside the Girl's bed.   He stood for a time, then began
pulling single flowers from the bowl, dropping them over
the pillow and snowy spread.

"God, how I love her!" he whispered softly.

At last he went out and closed the door.   He was
tired and soon fell asleep with the night breeze stirring
his hair, while the glamour of moonlight flooding the lake
touched his face.   Clearly it etched the strong, manly
features, the fine brow and chin, and painted in unusual
tenderness the soft lines around the mouth.   The little
owl wavered its love story, a few frogs were piping; the
Harvester lay breathing the perfumed spring air deeply
and evenly.   Near midnight Belshazzar awakened him
by arising from the bedside and walking to the door.

"What is it, Bel?" inquired the Harvester.

The dog whined softly.   The man turned his head
toward the lake.   A ray of red light touched the opposite
embankment, then came wavering across the surface.
The Harvester sat up.   Two big, flaming eyes were
creeping up the levee.

"That," said the Harvester, "might be Doc coming
for me to help him try out my bottled sunshine, or it
might be my bluebird."

He tossed back the cover, swung his feet to the floor,
setting each in a slipper beside the bed, and arose, dressing

as he started for the door. As he opened the screen and stepped on the veranda a passenger car from the city stopped. The Harvester went down the walk to meet it. His heart turned over when he saw a woman's hand on the door.

"Permit me," he said, taking the handle and bringing it back with a sweep. A tall form arose, bent forward, then descended to the step. The full flare of moonlight fell on the glowing face of the Girl.

"Harvester, is it you?" she asked.

"Yes," gasped the man.

Two hands came fluttering out; he had presence of mind to step in range so that they rested on his shoulders.

"Has the bluebird come?"

"Not yet!"

"Then I am not too late?"

"Never too late to come to me, Ruth."

"I am welcome?"

"I have no words to tell you how welcome."

She swayed forward. The Harvester tried to reach her lips, but they brushed his cheek and touched his ear.

"I have brought one more kiss I want to try," she whispered.

The Harvester crushed her in his arms until he frightened himself for fear he had hurt her, murmuring an ecstasy of indistinct love words to her. Presently her feet touched the ground, she drew away from him.

"Harvester," she whispered, "I couldn't wait any longer; indeed I could not: but I couldn't leave grandfather and grandmother, and I didn't know what in the world to do, so I just brought them along. Are they welcome?"

"Aside from you, I would rather have them than any people on earth," said the Harvester.

There were two sounds in the car; one was an approving murmur; the other an undeniable snort. The Harvester felt the reassuring pressure of the Girl's hand.

"Please, Ruth," he said, "go turn on the light so that I can see to help grandmother."

A foot stamped before the front seat. "Madam Herron, if you please!" cried an acrid voice.

"'Madam Herron,'" said the Harvester gently, as he set a foot on the step, reached in and bodily picked up a little old lady, starting up the walk with her in his arms.

"Careful there, sir!" roared a voice after him.

The Harvester could feel the quake of the laughing woman, so he smiled broadly as he entered the cabin, placing her in a large chair before the fire. Then he wheeled and ran back to the car, reaching it as the man was making an effort to descend. It could be seen that he had been tall, before time and sorrow had bent him, while keen eyes gleamed below shaggy white brows from under his hat brim. He had a white moustache, and his hair was snowy.

"Allow me," said the Harvester, reaching a hand.

"If you touch me I will cane you," said Mr. Alexander Herron.

There was nothing to do but step back. The cane, wheel, and a long coat skirt interfering, the old man fell headlong; only quick hands saved him a severe jolt and bruises. He stood glaring in the moonlight while his hat was restored.

"If you run your car to the curve you can back toward the south and turn easily," said the Harvester to the driver. As the automobile passed them he offered his arm. "May I show you to the fire? These spring nights are chilly."

"'Chilly!' Demnition cold is what they are! I'm frozen to the bone! This will be the end of us both! Dragging people of our age around at this hour of night. Of all the accursed stubbornness!"

"There are three low steps," said the Harvester, "now a straight stretch of walk, now two steps; there you are on the level. Here is an easy chair. It would be better to leave on your coat, until I light the fire."

He knelt to scratch a match, so instantly a flame sprang from the heap of dry kindling, and began to wrap around the big logs.

"How pretty!" exclaimed a soft voice.

"Kind of a hunting lodge in the wilds, is it?" growled a rough one. "Marcella, you will take your death here!"

"I'm sure I feel no exposure. Really, Alexander, if I had passed away every time you have prophesied that I would in the past twenty years you'd have the largest private cemetery in existence. If you would not be so pessimistic I could quite enjoy the trip. It's so long since I've ridden in the cars."

"Of all the abandoned places! And for you to be here, after your years in bed!"

"But I'm not nearly so tired as I am at home, Alexander, truly."

"Let me help you, grandfather," offered the Girl.

She went to him, taking his hat and stick.

"Leave me my cane," he cried. "Any instant that beast may attack some of us."

The Girl laughed merrily.

"Why grandfather!" she chided, "Bel is the finest dog you ever knew, he is my best friend here. By the hour he has protected me; he is gentle as a kitten. He's crazy over my coming home."

She knelt on the floor, putting her arms around the dog's neck, while the delighted brute quivered with the joy of her caress and the sound of her loved voice.

"Ruthie!" cautioned the gentle lady.

"Put that cur out of doors, where animals belong," roared the old man, lifting his stick.

"Careful!" warned the grave voice of the Harvester.

"I thought you said he was gentle as a kitten!"

"Grandfather, I said that," cried the Girl.

"Well wasn't it the truth?"

"You can see how he loves me. Didn't I ever tell you that Bel made the first friendly overture I ever received in this part of the country? He's watched me by the day, even while I slept."

"Then what's all this infernal fuss about?"

"Try striking him, if you want to find out," explained the Harvester. "You see, Belshazzar and I are accustomed to living here alone and very quietly. He is excited over the Girl's return, because she is his friend, and he has not forgotten her. Then this is the first time in his life he ever heard an irritable voice from a visitor or saw a cane, so it angers him. He is perfectly safe to guard a baby, if he is gently treated, but he is a sure throat hold to a stranger who bespeaks him roughly or attempts to strike. He would be of no use as a guard to valuable property while I sleep if he were otherwise. Bel, come here! Lie still."

The dog sank to the floor beside the Harvester, but his sharp eyes followed the Girl, while the hair arose on his neck at every rasping note of the old man's voice.

"I wouldn't give such a creature house room for a minute," insisted the guest.

"Wait until you see him work and become acquainted with him, and you will change that verdict," prophesied the Harvester.

"I never was known to change an opinion. Never, sir! Never!" cried the testy voice.

"How unfortunate!" remarked the Harvester suavely.

"Explain yourself! Explain yourself, sir!"

"There never has been, there never will be, a man on this earth," said the Harvester, "wholly free from mistakes. Are you warm now?" He turned to the little lady, cutting off a reply with his question.

"Nice and warm and very sleepy," she said.

"What may I bring you for a light lunch before you go to bed?"

"Oh, could I have a bite of something?"

"If only I am fortunate enough to have anything you will care for. What about a bowl of hot milk and a slice of toast?"

"Why I think that would be just the thing!"

"Excuse me," said the Harvester, rising. He went to the kitchen, where they could hear him moving around.

"I wish the big brute would take his beast along," growled Mr. Alexander Herron.

"Come, Bel," ordered the Girl.   "Let's go to the kitchen."

The dog instantly arose and followed her.

"What can I do to help?" she asked as they reached the door.

"Remain where you won't dazzle my eyes," said the Harvester, "until I help the gentle lady and the gentle man to bed."

Presently he came with a white cloth, two spoons, and a plate of bread. He spread the cloth on the table, laid the spoons on it, then opening the little cupboard, took out a long toasting fork, and sticking it into a slice of bread, he held it over the coals. When it grew golden brown he lifted the table beside the chair, and brought a bowl of scalded milk.

"Marcella, that stuff will be too smoky for you! Your stomach will rebel at it."

"Grandfather, there will not be a suspicion of odour," said the Girl.   "I have had it that way often."

"Then no wonder you came from this place looking like a picked crane, if that is a sample of what you were fed on!"

The face of the Harvester grew redder than the heat of the fire necessitated, but at the ringing laugh of the Girl he set his teeth and went on toasting bread. Grand-mother crumbled some in the milk and picking up the spoon tested the combination. She was very hungry, while it was good. She began eating with relish.

"Alexander, you will be the loser if you don't have some of this," she said. "It's just delicious!"

"Maybe smoked spoon victuals are proper for invalid women," he retorted, "but they are mighty thin diet for a hardy man."

"What about a couple of eggs and some beef extract?"

"Sounds more sensible by a long shot."

"Ruth, you make this toast," said the Harvester as he disappeared.

Presently he placed before his guest a couple of eggs poached in milk, a steaming bowl of beef juice, and a plate of toast. For one instant the Harvester thought this was going into the fire, the next a slice was picked up and smelled testily. The Girl sat on her grandfather's chair arm, and breaking a morsel of toast dipped it into the broth and tasted it.

"Oh but that is good!" she cried. "Why haven't I some also? Am I supposed to have no 'tummy?'"

"Your turn next," said the Harvester, as he again gave her the fork and went to the kitchen.

When he returned to serve the Girl he found her grand-father eating heartily.

"Why I think this is fun," said the gentle lady. "I haven't had such a fine time in ages. I love the heat of the flame on my body while things taste so good. I could go to sleep without any narcotic, right now."

At her knee the Harvester knelt on the hearth with his toasting fork. She leaned forward, running her fingers

"'You're a braw laddie,' she said. 'Now I see why Ruthie *would* come'"

through his hair. "You're a braw laddie," she said. "Now I see why Ruthie *would* come."

The Harvester took the frail hand, kissing it. "Thank you!" he returned.

"Mush!" exploded the grizzled man in the rear.

When no one wanted more food the Harvester stacked and carried away the dishes, swept the hearth, and replaced the toaster.

"Ruth and I often lunched this way last fall," he said. "We liked it for a change."

"Alexander, have you noticed?" asked the little woman as she lifted wet eyes to a beautiful portrait of her daughter beside the chimney.

"D'ye think I'm blind? Saw it as I entered the door. Poor taste! Very! Brown may match the rug and woodwork, but it's a wretched colour for a young girl. Should be pink and white with a gold frame."

"That would be beautiful," agreed the Harvester. "We must have one that way. This is only an enlargement from an old photograph."

"We have a number of very handsome likenesses. Which one can you spare Ruth, Marcella?"

"The one she likes best," said the lady promptly.

"And the other is your mother, no doubt. What a girlish, beautiful face!"

"Wonderfully fine!" growled a gruff old voice tinctured with tears; then the Harvester began to see light.

The old man arose. "Ruthie, help your grandmother to bed," he said. "And you, sir, have the goodness to walk a few steps with me."

The Harvester sprang up, brought Mr. Herron his coat, then hat, and held the door. The Girl brushed past him.

"To the oak," she whispered.

They went into the night; without a word the Harvester took his guest's arm, guiding him up the hill. When they reached the two mounds the moon shining between the branches touched the lily faces with holy whiteness.

"She sleeps there," said the Harvester, indicating the place. Then he turned, going down the path a short distance and waiting until he feared the night air would chill the broken old man. "You can see better to-morrow," he said as he touched the shaking figure, assisting it to arise.

"Your work?" Mr. Alexander Herron touched the lilies with his walking stick.

The Harvester assented.

"Do you mind if I carry one to Marcella?"

The Harvester trembled as he stooped to select the largest and whitest; with sudden illumination, he fully understood. He helped the tottering old man to the cabin, where he sat silently before the fireplace softly touching the lily face with his lips.

"I have put grandmother in my bed, tucked her in warmly, and she says it is soft and fine," laughed the Girl, coming to them. "Now you go before she falls asleep, and I hope you will rest well."

She bent, kissing him. The Harvester held the door.

"Can I be of any service?" he inquired.

"No, I'm no helpless child."

"Then to my best wishes for sound sleep the remainder

of the night, I will add this," said the Harvester——
"You may rest in peace concerning your dear girl. I
sympathize with your anxiety. Good night!"

Alexander Herron threw out his hands in protest.

"I wouldn't mind admitting that you are a gentleman in a month or two," he said, "but it's a demnation humiliation to have it literally wrung from me
to-night!"

He banged the door in the face of the amazed Harvester, who turned to the Girl as she leaned against the
mantel. He stood absorbing the glowing picture of
beauty and health that she made. She had removed her
travelling dress and shoes, she was draped in a fleecy
white wool kimono and wearing night slippers. Her hair
hung in two big braids as it had during her illness. She
was his sick girl again in costume, but radiant health
glowed on her lovely face. The Harvester touched a
match to a few candles, then turned out the acetylene
lights. He stood before her.

"Now, bluebird," he said gently. "Ruth, you always
know where to find me, if you will look at your feet. I
thought I loved you all in my power when you went, but
absence has taught its lessons. One is that I can grow
to love you more every day I live, and the other that I
probably trifled with the highest gift you had to offer,
when I sent you away. I may have been right; Granny
and Doc think I was wrong. You know the answer.
You said there was another kiss for me. Ruth, is it the
same or a different one?"

"It is different. Quite, quite different!"

"And when?" The Harvester stretched out longing arms. The Girl stepped back.

"I don't know," she said. "I had it when I started, but I lost it on the way."

The Harvester staggered under the disappointment.

"Ruth, this has gone far enough that you wouldn't play with me, merely for the sake of seeing me suffer, would you?"

"No!" cried the Girl. "No! I mean it! I knew just what I wanted to say when I started; but we had to take grandmother out of bed. She wouldn't allow me to leave her, and I wouldn't stay away from you any longer. She fainted when we put her on the car and grandfather went wild. He almost killed the porters, while he raved at me. He said my mother had ruined their lives; now I would be their death. I got so frightened I had a nervous chill and I'm so afraid she will grow worse——"

"You poor child!" shuddered the Harvester. "I see! I understand! What you need is quiet and a good rest."

He placed her in a big easy chair, then sitting on the hearth rug he leaned against her knee and said: "Now tell me, unless you are so tired that you should go to bed."

"I couldn't possibly sleep until I have told you," said the Girl.

"If you're merciful, cut it short!" implored the Harvester.

"I think it begins," she said slowly, "when I went because you sent me and I didn't want to go. Of course, as soon as I saw grandfather and grandmother, heard them talk, and understood what their lives had been, and what might have been, why there was only one thing to do, as I could see it, and that was to compensate their agony the best I could.   I think I have, David.   I really think I have made them almost happy.   But I told them all any one could tell about you in the start, and from the first grandmother would have been on your side; but you see how grandfather is, and he was absolutely determined that I should live with them, in their home, all their lives.   He thought the best way to accomplish that would be to separate me from you and marry me to the son of his partner.

"There are rooms packed with the lovely things they bought me, David, and everything was as I wrote you. Some of the people who came were wonderful, so gracious and beautiful, I loved them.   They took me places where there were pictures, plays, and lovely parties, so I studied hard to learn some music, to dance, ride and other things they wanted me to do, and to read good books, and to learn to meet people with graciousness to equal theirs, and all of it.   Every day I grew stronger and met more people, while there were different places to go, and always, when anything was to be done, up popped Mr. Herbert Kennedy saying and doing exactly the right thing, and he could be extremely nice, David."

"I haven't a doubt!" said the Harvester, laying hold of her kimono.

"And he popped up so much that at last I saw he was either pretending or else he really was growing very fond of me, so one day when we were alone I told him about

you, to make him see that he must not. He laughed at
me, and said exactly what you did, that I didn't love you
at all, that it was gratitude, that it was the affection of a
child. He talked for hours about how grandfather and
grandmother had suffered, how it was my duty to live
with them and give you up, even if I cared greatly for
you; but he said what I felt was not love. Then he tried
to tell me what he thought love was, and I could see very
clearly that if it was like that, I didn't love you, but I
came a whole world closer it than loving him, and I told
him so. He laughed again and said I was mistaken, that
he was going to teach me what real love was, then I could
not be driven back to you. After that, everybody and
everything just pushed me toward him with both hands,
except one person. She was a young married woman. I
met her at the very first. She was the only real friend
I ever had, and at last, the latter part of February, when
things were the very worst, I told her. I told her every
single thing. She was on your side. She said you were
twice the man Herbert Kennedy was, and as soon as I
found I could talk to her about you, I began going there
and staying as long as I could, just to talk and to play
with her baby.

"Her husband was a splendid young fellow, and I
grew very fond of him. I knew she had told him, because
he suddenly began talking to me in the kindest way, and
everything he said seemed to be what I most wanted to
hear. I got along fairly well until hints of spring began
to come; then I would wonder about my hedge, my gold
garden, if the ice were off the lake, about my boat and

horse, and I wanted my room, and oh, David, most of all I wanted you! Just you! Not because you could give me anything to compare in richness with what they could, not because this home was the best I'd ever known except theirs, not for any reason at all only just that I wanted to see your face, hear your voice, and have you pick me up and take me in your arms when I was tired. That was when I almost quit writing. I couldn't say what I wanted to, and I wouldn't write trivial things, so I went on day after day just groping."

"And you killed me alive," said the Harvester.

"I was afraid of that, but I couldn't write. I just couldn't! It was ten days ago that I thought of the bluebird's coming this year and what it would mean to you, and *that* killed me, Man! It just hurt my heart until it ached, to know that you were out here alone. That night I couldn't sleep, because I was thinking of you, and it came to me that if I had your lips then I could give you a much, much better kiss than the last, so when it was light I wrote that line.

"Nearly a week later I got your answer early in the morning, and it almost drove me wild. I took it and went for the day with May, and I told her. She took me upstairs, and we talked it over. Before I left she made me promise that I would write you and explain how I felt, and ask you what you thought. She wanted you to come there and see if you couldn't make them at least respect you. I know I was crying, and she was bathing the baby. She went to bring something she had forgotten, so she gave him to me to hold, just his little naked body. He stood on my lap and mauled my face, pulled my hair, hugged me with his stout arms and kissed me big, soft, wet kisses; then something sprang to life in my heart that never before had been there. I just cried all over him and held him fast, and I couldn't give him up when she came back. I saw why I'd wanted a big doll all my life, right then; and oh, dear! the doll you sent was beautiful, but, David, did you ever hold a little, living child in your arms like that?"

"I never did," said the Harvester huskily.

He looked at her face and saw the tears rolling, but he could say no more, so he leaned his head against her knee, and finding one of her hands he drew it to his lips.

"It is wonderful," said the Girl softly. "It awakens something in your heart that makes it all soft and tender, and you feel an awful responsibility, too. Grandmother had them telephone at last, so May helped me bathe my face and fix my hat. When we went to the carriage Mr. Kennedy was there to take me home. We went past grandmother's florist to get her some violets—— David, she is sleeping under yours, with just a few touching her lips. Oh it was lovely of you to get them; your fairies must have told you! She has them every day, and one of the objections she made to coming here was that she couldn't do without them in winter, and she found some on her pillow the very first thing. David, you are wonderful! And grandfather with his lily! I know where he found that! I knew instantly. Ah, there are fairies who tell you, because you deserve to know."

The Girl bent and slipping her arm around his neck

hugged him tight an instant; then she continued unsteadily: "While he was in the shop——Harvester, this is like your wildest dream, but it's truest truth——a boy came down the walk crying papers, and as I live, he called your name. I knew it had to be you because he said: 'First drug farm in America! Wonderful medicine contributed to the cause of science! David Langston honoured by National Medical Association!' I stood in the carriage and screamed: 'Boy! Boy!' until the coachman thought I had lost my senses. He whistled and got me the paper. I was shaking so I asked him how to find anything you wanted quickly, so he pointed the column where events are listed; when I found the third page there was your face so splendidly reproduced, you seemed so fine and noble to me I forgot about the dress suit and the badge in your buttonhole, or to wonder when or how or why it could have happened. I just sat there shouting in my soul, 'David! David! Medicine Man! Harvester Man!' again and again.

"I don't know what I said to Mr. Kennedy or how I got to my room. I scanned it by the column, at last I got to paragraphs, and finally I read all the sentences. David, I kissed that newspaper face a hundred times, and if you could have had those, Man, I think you would have said they were right. David, there is nothing to cry over!"

"I'm not!" said the Harvester, wiping the splashes from her hand. "But Ruth, forget what I said about being brief. I didn't realize what was coming. I should have said, if you've any mercy at all, go slowly! This is the greatest thing that ever happened or ever will happen to me. See that you don't leave out one word of it."

"I told you I had to tell you first," said the Girl.

"I understand now," said the Harvester, his head against her knee while he pressed her hand to his lips. "I see! Your coming couldn't be perfect without knowing this first. Go on, dear heart, and slowly! You owe me every word."

"When I had it all absorbed, I carried the paper to the library and said: 'Grandfather, such a wonderful thing has happened. A man has had a new idea; he has done a unique work that the whole world is going to recognize. He has stood before men and made a speech that few, oh so few, could make honestly, and he has advocated right living, oh so nobly, while he has given a wonderful gift to science without price, because through it he first saved the life he loved best. Isn't that marvellous, grandfather?' And he said, 'Very marvellous, Ruth. Won't you sit down and read to me about it?' And I said, 'I can't, dear grandfather, because I have been away from grandmother all day, so she is fretting for me, and to-night is a great ball. She has spent millions on my dress, I think, and there is an especial reason why I must go, so I have to see her now; but I want to show you the man's face; then you can read the story.'

"You see, I knew if I started to read it he would stop me; but if I left him alone with it he would be so curious he would finish. So I turned your name under and held the paper and said, 'What do you think of that face, grandfather? Study it carefully,' and, Man, only

guess what he said! He said, 'I think it is the face of
one of nature's noblemen.' I just kissed him time and
again and then I said: 'So it is grandfather, so it is; for it
is the face of the man who twice saved my life, and lifted
my mother from almost a pauper grave and laid her to
rest in state, and the man who found you, and sent me
to you when I was determined not to come.' Then I
just stood and kissed that paper before him and cried,
again and again: 'He is one of nature's noblemen, and he
is my husband, my dear, dear husband and to-morrow I
am going home to him.' Then I laid the paper on his
lap and ran away. I went to grandmother and did everything she wanted, then I dressed for the ball. I went
to say good-bye to her and show my dress and grandfather was there, and he followed me out and said: 'Ruth,
you didn't mean it?' I said: 'Did you read the paper,
grandfather?' and he said: 'Yes'; and I said: 'Then I
should think you would know I mean it, and glory in
my wonderful luck. Think of a man like that, grandfather!'

"I went to the ball, and I danced and had a lovely
time with every one, because I knew it was going to be
the very last, and to-morrow I must start to you.

"On the way home I told Mr. Kennedy what paper
to get and to read it. I said good-bye to him, and I
really think he cared, but I was too happy to be very
sorry. When I reached my room there was a packet for
me, and Man, like David of old, you are a wonderful
poet! Oh Harvester! why didn't you send them to me
instead of the cold, hard things you wrote?"

"What do you mean, Ruth?"

"Those letters! Those wonderful outpourings of love and passion and poetry and song and broken-heartedness. Oh Man, how could you write such things and throw them in the fire? Granny Moreland found them when she came to bring you a pie, so she carried them to Doctor Carey, and he sent them to me, and David, they finished me. Everything came in a heap. I would have come without them, but never, never with quite the understanding, for as I read them the deeps opened up, and the flood broke, and there did a warm tide go through all my being, like you said it would; and now, David, I know what you mean by love. I called the maids and they packed my trunk and grandmother's, and I had grandfather's valet pack his, and go and secure berths and tickets, and learn about trains, and I got everything ready, even to the ambulance and doctor; but I waited until morning to tell them. I knew they would not let me come alone, so I brought them along. David, what in the world are we going to do with them?"

The Harvester drew a deep breath while looking at the flushed face of the Girl.

"With no time to mature a plan, I would say that we are going to love them, care for them, gradually teach them our work, and interest them in our plans here; and as soon as they become reconciled we will build them such a house as they want on the hill facing us, just across Singing Water, and there they may have every luxury they can provide for themselves, or we can offer, and the pleasure of your presence, and both of them can grow strong and happy. I'll have grandmother on her feet in ten days, and the edge off grandfather's tongue in three. That bluster of his is to drown tears, Ruth; I saw it to-night. And when they pass over we will carry them up and lay them beside her under the oak, and we can take the house we build for them, if you like it better, and use this for a storeroom."

"Never!" said the Girl. "Never! My sunshine room and gold garden so long as I live. Never again will I leave them. If this cabin grows too small, we will build all over the hillside; but my room and garden and this and the dining-room and your den there must remain as they are now."

The Harvester arose and drew the davenport before the fireplace, and heaped pillows. "You are so tired you are trembling, while your voice is quivering," he said. He lifted the Girl, laid her down and arranged the coverlet.

"Go to sleep!" he ordered gently. "You have made me so wildly happy that I could run and shout like a madman. Try to rest, and maybe the fairies who aid me will put my kiss back on your lips. I am going to the hill top to tell mother and my God."

He knelt, gathering her in his arms a second, then called Belshazzar to guard, and went into the sweet spring night, to jubilate with that wild surge of passion that sweeps the heart of a strong man when he is most nearly primal. He climbed the hill at a rush, and stand-ing beneath the oak on the summit, he faced the lake, and stretching his arms widely, he waved them, merely to satisfy the demand for action. When urgency for expression came upon him, he laughed a deep rumble of exultation.

The night wind swept the lake and lifted his hair, the odour of spring was intoxicating in his nostrils, small creatures of earth stirred around him, here and there a bird, restless in the delirium of mating fever, lifted its head and piped a few notes on the moon-whitened air. The frogs sang uninterruptedly at the water's edge. The Harvester stood rejoicing. Beating on his brain came a rush of love words uttered in the Girl's dear voice. "I wanted you! Just you! He is my husband! My dear, dear husband! To-morrow I am going home! Now, David, I know what you mean by love!" The Harvester laughed again and sounds around him ceased for a second, then swelled in fuller volume than before. He added his voice. "Thank God! Oh, thank God!" he cried. "And may the Author of the Universe, the spirits of the little mothers who loved us, and all the good fairies who guide us, unite to bring unbounded joy to my Dream Girl and to guard her safely."

The cocks of Medicine Woods began their second salute to dawn. At this sound and with the mention of her name the Harvester turned down the hill, and striding forcefully approached the cabin. As he passed the Girl's room he stepped softly, smiling as he wondered if its unexpected occupants were resting. He followed Singing Water, and stood looking at the hillside, studying the exact location most suitable for a home for the old people he was so delighted to welcome. That they would remain he never doubted. His faith in the call of the wild had been verified in the Girl; it would reach them also. The hill top would bind them. Their love for the Girl would compel them. They would be company for her and a new interest in life.

"Couldn't be better, not possibly!" commented the delighted Harvester.

He followed the path down Singing Water until he reached the bridge where it turned into the marsh. There he paused, looking straight ahead.

"Wonder if I would frighten her?" he mused. "I believe I'll risk it."

He walked on rapidly, vaulted the fence enclosing his land, crossed the road, and unlatched the gate. As he did so, the door opened, and Granny Moreland stood on the sill, waiting with keen eyes.

"Well I don't need neither specs nor noonday sun to see that you're steppin' like the blue ribbon colt at the County Fair, and lookin' like you owned Kingdom Come," she said. "What's up, David?"

"You are right, dear," said the Harvester. "I have entered my kingdom. The Girl has come and crowned me with her love. She had decided to return, but the letters you sent made her happier about it. I wanted you to know."

Granny leaned against the casing, and began to sob.

The Harvester supported her tenderly.

"Why don't do that, dear. Don't cry," he begged. "The Girl is home for always, Granny, and I'm so happy I am out to-night trying to keep from losing my mind with joy. She will come to you to-morrow, I know."

Granny tremulously dried her eyes.

"What an old sap-head I am!" she commented. "I stole your letters from your fireplace, pitched a willer plate into the lake——you got to fish that out, come day, David——fooled you into that trip to Doc Carey to get him to mail them to Ruth, and never turned a hair. But after I got home I commenced thinkin' 'twas a pretty ticklish job to stick your nose into other people's business, an' every hour it got worse, until I ain't had a fairly decent sleep since. If you hadn't come soon, boy, I'd 'a' been sick a-bed. Oh, David! Are you sure she's over there, and loves you to suit you now?"

"Yes dear, I am absolutely certain," said the Harvester. "She was so determined to come that she brought the invalid grandmother she couldn't leave and her grandfather. They arrived at midnight. We are all going to live together now."

"Well bless my stars! Fetched you a family! David, I do hope to all that's peaceful I hain't put my foot in it. The moon is the deceivingist thing on earth I know, but does her family 'pear to be an a-gre-able family, by its light?"

The Harvester's laugh boomed down the road.

"Finest people on earth, next to you, dear. I'm mighty glad to have them. I'm going to build them a house on my best location, and we are all going to be happy from now on. Go to bed! This night air may chill you. I can't sleep. I wanted you to know first—— so I came over. In mother's stead, will you kiss me, and wish me happiness, dear friend?"

Granny Moreland laid an eager, withered hand on each shoulder, and bent to the radiant young face.

"God bless you, lad, and grant you as great happiness as life ort to fetch every clean, honest man," she prayed fervently, with closed eyes and her lined old face turned skyward. "And, O God, bless Ruth, and help her as You never helped mortal woman before to know her own mind without 'variableness, neither shadow of turnin'.'"

The Harvester was on Singing Water bridge before he gave way. There he laughed as never before in his life. Finally he controlled himself and started toward the cabin; but he was chuckling as he passed the driveway, and walked down the broad cement floor leading to his bathing pool, where the moonlight bridged the lake, falling as a benediction all around him.

He stood a long time, when he recognized the familiar crash of a breaking backlog falling together, and heard the customary leap of the frightened dog. He walked to his door and listened intently, but there was no sound; so he decided the Girl had not been awakened. In the midst of a whitening sheet of gold the Harvester dropped to his stoop, leaning his head against the broad casing. He broke a twig from a hawthorn bush beside him, then sat twisting it in his fingers as he stared down the line of the gold bridge. Never had it seemed so material, so like a path that might be trodden by mortal feet and lead them straight to Heaven. As on the hill top, night again surrounded him while the Harvester's soul drank deep wild draughts of a new joy. Sleep was out of the question. He was too intensely alive to know that he ever again could be weary. He sat there in the moonlight, with unbridled heart glorying in the joy that had come to him.

He turned his face from the bridge as he heard the click of Belshazzar's nails on the floor of the bathing pool. Then his heart and breath stopped an instant. Beside the dog walked the Girl, one hand on his head the other holding the flowing white robe around her and grasping one of the Harvester's lilies. His first thought was sheer amazement that she was not afraid, for it was evident now that the backlog had awakened her, and she had taken the dog and gone to her mother. Then she had followed the path leading down the hill, around the cabin, and into the sheet of moonlight gilding the shore. She stood there gazing over the lake, oblivious to all things save the entrancing allurement of a perfect spring night beside undulant water. Screened from her with bushes and trees the Harvester scarcely breathed lest he startle her. Then his head swam, and his still heart leaped wildly. She was coming toward him. On her left lay the path to the hill top. A few steps farther she could turn to the right and follow the driveway to the front of the cabin. He leaned forward watching in an agony of suspense. Her beautiful face was transfigured with joy, aflame with love, radiant with smiles, and her tall figure fleecy white, rimmed in gold. Up the shining path of light she steadily advanced toward his door. Then the Harvester understood, and from his exultant heart burst the wordless petition:

"*Lord God Almighty, help me to be a man!*"

With outstretched arms he arose to meet her.

"My Dream Girl!" he cried hoarsely. "My Dream Girl!"

"Coming, Harvester!" she answered in tones of joy, as she dropped the white flower and lifted her hands to draw his face toward her.

"Is that the kiss you wanted?" she questioned.

"Yes, Ruth," breathed the Harvester.

"Then I am ready to be your wife," she said. "May I share all the remainder of life's joys and sorrows with you?"

The Harvester gathered her in his arms and carried her to the bench on the lake shore. He wrapped the white robe around her and clasped her tenderly as behooved a lover, yet with arms that she knew could have crushed her had they willed. The minutes slipped away; still he held her to his heart, the reality far surpassing his dream; for he knew that he was awake, and he realized this as the supreme hour that comes to the strong man who knows his love requited.

When the first banner of red light arose above Medicine Woods and Singing Water the cocks on the hillside announced the dawn. As the gold faded to gray, a burst of bubbling notes swelled from a branch almost over their heads where stood a bark-enclosed little house.

"Ruth, do you hear that?" asked the Harvester softly.

"Yes," she answered, "and I see it. A wonderful bird, with Heaven's deepest blue on its back and a breast like a russet autumn leaf, came straight up the lake from the south, and before it touched the limb that song seemed to gush from its throat."

"And for that reason, the greatest nature lover who ever lived says that it 'deserves preëminence.' It always settles from its long voyage through the air in an ecstasy of melody. Do you know what it is, Ruth?"

The Girl laid a hand on his cheek and turned his eyes from the bird to her face as she answered: "Yes, Harvester-man, I know. It is your first bluebird——but it is far too late, and Belshazzar has lost his high office. I have usurped both their positions. You remain in the woods and reap their harvest, you enter the laboratory and make wonderful, life-giving medicines, you face the world and tell men of the high and holy life they may live if they will, and then——always and forever, you come back to Medicine Woods and to me, Harvester."

THE END